The 100 Most Important People in Musical Theatre

The 100 Most Important People in Musical Theatre

Andy Propst

ROWMAN & LITTLEFIELD
Lanham • Boulder • New York • London

Published by Rowman & Littlefield
An imprint of The Rowman & Littlefield Publishing Group, Inc.
4501 Forbes Boulevard, Suite 200, Lanham, Maryland 20706
www.rowman.com

6 Tinworth Street, London, SE11 5AL, United Kingdom

British Library Cataloguing in Publication Information Available

Library of Congress Cataloging-in-Publication Data

Names: Propst, Andy, author.
Title: The 100 most important people in musical theatre / Andy Propst.
Description: Lanham : Rowman & Littlefield, [2019] | Includes bibliographical references and index.
Identifiers: LCCN 2019003564 (print) | LCCN 2019014683 (ebook) | ISBN 9781538116197 (electronic) | ISBN 9781538116180 (cloth : alk. paper)
Subjects: LCSH: Musical theater—Encyclopedias. | Musicals—Encyclopedias. | Composers—Biography. | Lyricists—Biography. | Singers—Biography. | Musical theater producers and directors—Biography.
Classification: LCC ML102.M875 (ebook) | LCC ML102.M875 P76 2019 (print) | DDC 792.6092/2 [B] —dc23
LC record available at https://lccn.loc.gov/2019003564

∞™ The paper used in this publication meets the minimum requirements of American National Standard for Information Sciences—Permanence of Paper for Printed Library Materials, ANSI/NISO Z39.48-1992.

For Ken and Caesar

Contents

Preface

All good theatre artists know that establishing ground rules and sticking to them are crucial to the success of any play or musical. If you establish at the outset what sort of reality you are inviting your audience into, they'll follow you and your production anywhere you want. I had to follow this sort of mandate as I considered the word *important* for this book. What were the various meanings of it in relation to musical theatre? For each of the entries in this book, I believe that I have adhered to the answers to my question. The individuals included here have had a significant impact on the form because of their innovations or the perceptions they helped to create about what musicals are.

With these two criteria I set about looking at roughly 150 years of theatrical history and developed a list of luminaries. Then the tough part began: putting together a final list that conveyed the breadth of musical theatre, from the stories it tells to the music it employs to the technologies that allow creators to flourish. Beyond this—and because theatre requires an audience—who inspired ticket buyers to line up at the box office (in days gone by) or run to their computers (or cell phones) to purchase their seats?

With these questions in mind, I set one limit on the book: I chose 1870 as a start date. What this means is that John Gay, who wrote *The Beggar's Opera* in 1728 and brought popular sounds of the period to the stage, is not included. Similarly, William Wheatley, a producer who stumbled on putting drama, dance, and music together to create *The Black Crook* in 1866, doesn't have an entry.

There were many other tough calls in finalizing the list, and as I made my decisions, I relied on many years of experience sitting on award committees in New York. In any given year, there might have been several dozen best performances by a leading actor or actress in a musical, but one can only nominate five or six. The shadings become grueling, and as a theatre artist who sat on one committee remarked during deliberations one year, "This is unbearable work."

That person was right, and yet, the privilege of seeing so many incredible performances in the course of a year cannot be underestimated. In the case of what's contained on the following pages, the exciting and joyful part has been revisiting beloved classics, exploring little-known works, and looking at reactions to artists' work from the time in which it was created. Victor Herbert's music may sound, at best, quaint to contemporary ears, but in his time he was pushing some boundaries. I've attempted to convey some of my own sense of discovery (or rediscovery) within each entry.

Ultimately, I hope that what you find on the following pages provides you with a starting point for thinking about the incredible array of people who have shaped this genuinely unique American art form. Also, be aware, as I am, that this is an incredibly fluid list. There is an entirely new generation of artists creating exciting musical theatre in New York and beyond. I look forward to the day in which some of these names take their place on the list of *The 100 Most Important People in Musical Theatre*.

A

GEORGE ABBOTT

(June 25, 1887–January 31, 1995)

Director / Producer / Actor / Book Writer

As a director-writer, Abbott was responsible for both a vast number of shows that are considered landmarks in musical theatre history and in establishing the careers of two generations of musical theatre artists.

"Mr. Abbott is the recognized panjandrum of the Broadway carnival," Brooks Atkinson wrote in the May 26, 1957, edition of the *New York Times*, adding that, as a director, Abbott had the ability to translate material "into comedy, dancing, uproar, sentiment and revelry and exuberate the audience." In the same story, Atkinson also lauded Abbott as a writer, labeling him a "celebrated technician."

The praise came as Abbott was almost exactly at the midpoint of his seven-decade career on Broadway, one in which he penned superlative books for musicals, shepherded classics to the stage, and introduced audiences to several generations of exceptional new talent.

Abbott came to the theatre from an unlikely background. Hailing from Forest-ville, New York, a small town near Buffalo on Lake Erie, his interest in theatrics started while he was still a child with a tendency toward creating fantasies. Eventually he came to know the professional theatre by attending touring productions in Buffalo.

His Broadway bow came in 1913 when he appeared in *The Misleading Lady*. The farce, now long forgotten, attracted both critical and audience praise and began what became a twelve-year period of near continual work for Abbott as an actor. During this time, he appeared in not only Broadway productions but also in vaudeville.

In 1925, Abbott added the credit of playwright to his growing résumé, coau-thoring with actor James Gleason *The Fall Guy*. In his March 11 review, the *New York Herald Tribune*'s Percy Hammond labeled it as being in the "first class of good American shows." After Abbott appeared in the second play he had penned, *A Holy Terror*, he stopped performing, concentrating instead on his work as writer, director, and producer.

His first foray into the world of musical comedy came in 1935 when he directed the book scenes for Richard Rodgers and Lorenz Hart's *Jumbo*, the spectacular produced by Billy Rose and featuring overall direction by John Murray Anderson. It was just the beginning of a long-term association with Rodgers and Hart. Abbott would go on to stage *On Your Toes* (1936), *The Boys from Syracuse* (1938), and *Pal Joey* (1940), among others. The latter show, based on John O'Hara's short stories and having a cad nightclub singer as its antihero, was something of a risky venture, and after it opened, Richard Watts Jr. noted in a January 5, 1941, *Herald Tribune* column that it was controversial, leaving some theatregoers feeling that it "cannot—despite its incontestable virtues of vivid writing and enchanting music—be palatable as a musical show." Nevertheless, Abbott saw its merits and produced it.

By this point Abbott's reputation meant that his projects could (and frequently did) attract established talent, and yet he continued to look for young and unknown artists for his productions, both performers and writers. Immediately following *Pal Joey*, Abbott produced and directed *Best Foot Forward* and turned to a pair of untested songwriters, Hugh Martin and Ralph Blane, for its score. He also asked book writer John Cecil Holm to create a part for a young woman who auditioned: Nancy Walker. Abbott's decision to include Walker resulted in reviews such as this from "Abel." in the October 8, 1941, edition of *Variety*: "She is a surprise comedienne, mugging her way to a solid click."

Three years later, neophyte producers Oliver Smith and Paul Feigay approached Abbott about a new musical they wanted to get on the boards, one created by Leonard Bernstein, Betty Comden, Adolph Green, and Jerome Robbins, a quartet of artists who had never created a Broadway musical. Abbott read the book and immediately saw its potential. He took the assignment, and in a January 7, 1945, story in the *Times*, Lewis Nichols indicated that some of the success *On the Town* enjoyed was due to Abbott's savvy: "[The director] is at his best when keeping youthful spirits bubbling in the right direction."

By this juncture Abbott was nearly thirty years into his career and continued working for another forty. Along the way he gave such future stars as Shirley MacLaine and Carol Burnett early breaks and worked with such songwriting teams as Jerry Ross and Richard Adler, Jerry Bock and Sheldon Harnick, and John Kander and Fred Ebb as they were just beginning their careers. In these instances, the results were the musicals *The Pajama Game* (1954); *Damn Yankees* (1955); *Fiorello!* (1959); *Tenderloin* (1960); and *Flora, the Red Menace* (1965), three of which boasted books that Abbott coauthored with librettists making their Broadway debuts. Abbott also played a crucial role in the early professional life of another director-producer, Harold Prince, and was responsible for giving Bob Fosse his first choreographic credit on the Main Stem.

As Abbott entered his eighties, he remained an active member of the Broadway community, but the successes he had enjoyed for the previous forty years were never to be matched. Although he continued to seek out interesting work, such as the Wall Street–set *How Now, Dow Jones* (1967); the experimental *The Fig Leaves Are Falling* (1969); and even a semi-mod version of Shakespeare's *Twelfth Night* called *Music Is* (1976), musicals were changing, and so were the artists who were creating them. As Richard Hummler noted in a December 18, 1968, *Variety* story,

"The hierarchy of top musical stagers is changing. Fresh talent is moving into a field that has traditionally been slow to accept newcomers."

Abbott's last two credits on the Great White Way came in the 1980s when he directed revivals of two of his early successes, *On Your Toes* (1983) and *Broadway* (1987). The former outran the original 1936 production by nearly two hundred performances. In conjunction with the latter (which opened on his one hundredth birthday), Abbott received a special Tony Award. It was his ninth. That year he also directed a revival of *Damn Yankees* at New Jersey's Paper Mill Playhouse. During a talkback, someone asked him what the most important development in theatre had been during his lifetime. Abbott thought for a moment and then replied "Electric Light."

After Abbott passed away in 1995, a *New York Times* obituary by Marilyn Berger opined, "Probably no one in this century brought more verve and excitement to the American stage than the versatile man who was known to the theater world as Mr. Abbott."

JOHN MURRAY ANDERSON

(September 20, 1886–January 30, 1954)
Director / Designer / Writer

Anderson innovated the revue in the 1920s, directly influencing the form for the next decade, and then continued to keep the form alive for another thirty years, often helping to spur the careers of young artists.

A politician's son born in Newfoundland before the dawn of the twentieth century, the European-educated Anderson arrived in New York in his early twenties, intent on becoming an antiques dealer. He plied this trade for a brief period but eventually turned toward working in the arts, where his earliest jobs included stints as both a dance instructor at the Hotel Astor and as a dancer and lyricist at one of the city's first nightclubs, the opulent Palais Royale, located in what is now the center of Manhattan's theatre district.

He eventually came to direct the offerings at the venue, and his success there paved the way for his first theatrical outing: *Greenwich Village Nights*. This downtown revue, retitled *Greenwich Village Follies* during a troubled rehearsal period, sparked with critics and audiences when it opened in July 1919. Its popularity spurred, less than two months later, a transfer uptown to the Nora Bayes Theatre in the heart of Times Square.

Anderson's *Follies* boasted both a decidedly bohemian tone (among the songs were "I Do Not Care for Women Who Wear Stays" and "I Want a Daddy Who Will Rock Me to Sleep") and an intrinsic beauty and elegance. These latter two qualities would be Anderson's hallmarks as he brought to Broadway another five editions of the *Greenwich Village Follies* from 1920 to 1924. They were also on ample display with his follow-up to the first incarnation of the series: the innovative revue *What's in a Name?* in March 1920.

The praise Anderson's first *Follies* garnered paled in comparison to the accolades he earned for *Name*. Alexander Woollcott called it the "most beautiful staging of a musical comedy New York has known" in a March 20 *New York Times* review, and a *Variety* review from critic "Fred." on March 26 announced that it "is the acme of anything that the theatre in America has seen to date," noting that Anderson "had combined the ideas of Gordon Craig and the famous German producer [Max] Reinhardt" in the staging.

Anderson explained the philosophy in a March 28 *New York Tribune* feature: "I am trying to put ideas of the new theater into the form which has very wide and popular appeal—the musical comedy." One year later, for the 1921 edition of the *Greenwich Village Follies*, Anderson continued to push the boundaries of how revues were staged by engaging Russian artist Nicolas de Lipsky to design portions of the production. Thanks to de Lipsky's unique sense of how color and light interact, certain sets and costumes, which were painted in multiple levels, could transform because of mere shifts in the color of the lighting.

Three years later, Anderson helmed an edition of Irving Berlin's *Music Box Revue*, and then in 1925, he staged one of Richard Rodgers and Lorenz Hart's earliest book musicals, *Dearest Enemy*. An uncredited September 18 review in the *Times* lauded how the show was "glowing with color in costume and stage setting," adding that "if the settings please the eye, the music pleases the ear no less."

From this point until his death in 1954, Anderson's creativity and vision could be found both on Broadway and beyond. Among his nontheatrical efforts were the groundbreaking movie musical *King of Jazz* in 1930. He also supervised the visuals for seven incarnations of the Ringling Bros. and Barnum & Bailey Circus and four editions of Billy Rose's aquacades.

Between 1930 and 1950, he was also responsible for more than a dozen Broadway offerings, both book musicals and revues. In the latter category, he staged editions of the *Ziegfeld Follies*, as well as 1934's *Life Begins at 8:40*, which boasted a score by Harold Arlen, E. Y. "Yip" Harburg, and Ira Gershwin and featured two men who would become immortalized in the movie *The Wizard of Oz* (which had songs by Arlen and Harburg) five years later, Ray Bolger and Bert Lahr.

Beyond these revues, Anderson helmed another Rodgers and Hart tuner, *Jumbo* (1935); Sigmund Romberg and Oscar Hammerstein II's *Sunny River* (1941); and Kurt Weill, Ira Gershwin, and Edwin Justice Mayer's *The Firebrand of Florence* (1945), among others.

By the early 1950s, the appearance of television in American households was beginning to have an impact on theatre and Anderson's signature form there, the revue. And yet, during the first half of the decade, he managed to deliver three productions that gave the new electronic medium a run for its money. First came Leonard Sillman's *New Faces of 1952*, which introduced audiences to such performers as Alice Ghostley, Eartha Kitt, Carol Lawrence, and Paul Lynde. The show also marked the Broadway debut of lyricist Sheldon Harnick, who was one of many who contributed to the score and would go on to write such landmark shows as *Fiorello!* and *Fiddler on the Roof*.

Anderson's penultimate Broadway production, *Two's Company*, opened seven months after *New Faces*. The show, headlined by film star Bette Davis in her musical theatre debut, overall got mixed notices, but Anderson was still at the top of his game. Brooks Atkinson in his December 16, 1952, *Times* review wrote, "John Murray Anderson, the genius of the revue, has made 'Two's Company' look keen and elegant."

One year later, Anderson brought his eponymous *Almanac* revue to Broadway, which gave an acclaimed British performer, Hermione Gingold, her Broadway debut. Next to this veteran were such fresh (at least to the Main Stem) faces as singer Harry Belafonte and comedian Orson Bean. Musical numbers came from Richard Adler and Jerry Ross (just months before their *Pajama Game* debuted) and composer Cy Coleman in his Broadway bow. After the show's December 10 opening, John Chapman in the *Daily News* stated simply that Anderson was the "best revue director in the business."

After Anderson's death, a January 31, 1954, *New York Herald Tribune* obituary proclaimed, "It is said that his name attached to a show was as good as 'sterling' stamped on silver."

BORIS ARONSON

(October 15, 1898–November 16, 1980)
Scenic Designer

Abstract and edgy, Aronson's artistry helped to create the environments in which several unconventional musicals of the 1940s could unfold, which then became an integral part of the "concept musical" twenty years later, informing such landmark works as Company *and* Follies.

A December 22, 1929, *New York Herald Tribune* feature story about this Russian-born designer proclaimed, "'Too Modern' in '19, Boris Aronson Has Found Himself." Interestingly, Aronson would remain a bit too experimental across another three decades—at least as far as musical theatre was concerned. The form itself needed to catch up with his aesthetic.

The theatre entered Aronson's life while he was still a child and studying painting. When he decided he wanted his work to have a more three-dimensional sensibility, he began to create plays that he would direct and act in. He eventually returned to painting and studied art in Kiev and later Moscow but found that instructors disliked his work because it broke with tradition. In frustration he began to socialize and work with Alexandra Exter, a leading figure among Russia's avant-garde designers. It rekindled his interest in theatre, but his work was still too experimental for the theatrical establishment in his homeland. After a period in Europe, where he met with a modicum of success, he immigrated to America in 1923, still filled with ideas about stage design inspired by Exter, as well as director-designer Vsevolod Meyerhold.

Aronson's earliest designs in the States were for two Yiddish theatre companies and Eva Le Gallienne's Civic Repertory Theatre. He got his first Broadway assignment in 1932: the revue *Walk a Little Faster,* featuring songs by Vernon Duke and E. Y. Harburg and starring Beatrice Lillie. The show received generally tepid reviews, and critics for the most part opted not to mention Aronson's contributions. One exception was John Mason Brown in the *Evening Post* on December 8. He called the design, which included a curtain that unzipped from top to bottom, "striking," saying it was "in a vigorous modern idiom" and that "more distinguished scenery New York has not seen this season."

It was the beginning of Aronson's five-decade career on the Great White Way, which for the balance of the 1930s consisted of plays. Some of these were the most highly regarded works of the period, including Clifford Odets's *Awake and Sing* and Thornton Wilder's *The Merchant of Yonkers* (later *The Matchmaker*).

Aronson returned to the realm of musical theatre in 1940, providing scenic and costume designs for another show that Duke composed, *Cabin in the Sky*. Aronson's aesthetic was perfectly suited to this musical, labeled "A Negro Fantasy," about a woman whose belief in her wastrel husband convinces God that, though the rascal has died, he deserves a second chance at life to escape the Devil. In his October 26 *New York Times* review, Brooks Atkinson opined, "Aronson has done his finest work, giving to pure imagination many vivid shapes and flaring colors."

As the 1940s continued, Aronson, sometimes designing as many as three shows a season, was principally hired for plays. There were occasional forays into the realm of musicals, but such shows as *What's Up* (1943), Alan Jay Lerner and Frederick Loewe's Broadway debut, and *The Desert Song* (1946), an operetta with music by Sigmund Romberg, still didn't perfectly fit Aronson's style.

A more apt fit was another 1946 show, *Sweet Bye and Bye*. It was set in 2076, but the production shuttered on the road. Kurt Weill and Lerner's *Love Life* (1948) was also a musical created for Aronson's gifts. Dubbed a "vaudeville" by its creators and deemed by many as the first "concept musical," the piece traced the history of a marriage over the course of 150 years. As with *Cabin,* it provided Aronson a unique opportunity to display his sometimes-representative approach to design, particularly as the musical used various "acts," such as a magician and high-wire performers, in its telling.

Aronson's scenic work on Broadway in the 1950s included designs for modern classics ranging from Arthur Miller's *A View from the Bridge* to Archibald MacLeish's *J. B.* but no musicals. The 1960s, though, changed both musicals themselves and Aronson's relationship with them.

His breakthrough came in 1965 with *Fiddler on the Roof,* for which he created, at the request of director-choreographer Jerome Robbins, the realm of the small Russian village of Anatevka as it might have been conceived by Marc Chagall, an artist whose work Aronson had chronicled while still a young man living in Berlin. In his September 24 review for *Women's Wear Daily,* Martin Gottfried enthused about how the designer's "great watercolored washes" gave Robbins's staging a "brilliant background in bright, imaginative colors."

Harold Prince produced *Fiddler*, and it was the first time the men had worked together. Prince remarks in his memoir *Sense of Occasion*, "I consider the day I met Boris second only to the day I met [George] Abbott." Aronson joined with Prince for *Cabaret* the year after *Fiddler* premiered, and for this the designer placed a trapezoid mirror above the action, facing the audience. Its inclusion surprised Prince, and he comments in his book, "It cast an additional uneasy metaphor over the evening." The design won Aronson his fourth Tony—his first for a musical.

After this, Prince relied on the designer, and in the 1970s, Aronson designed a quartet of shows with songs by Stephen Sondheim, starting with *Company* (with a book by George Furth) in 1970. For this very modern New York–set musical, Aronson provided, as John Chapman described it in an April 27, 1970, *Daily News* review, a "setting of aluminum-and-plastic rectangles, including a few working elevators, that enclose us inescapably in this city of ours."

With *Follies* the following year, Aronson's design took audiences into a once-grand theatre that was about to be demolished. As former chorus girls reunited amid the debris of the former showplace, Aronson eventually brought it back to opulent life, re-creating the splendor that was part of their youth.

Aronson's other two musicals with Prince were *A Little Night Music* (1973) and *Pacific Overtures* (1976), his last show on the Main Stem. For the latter, about the collision of East and West in the nineteenth century, Aronson won some of the highest praise of his career. In a January 16, 1976, *Christian Science Monitor* review, John Beaufort wrote, "Of all of Boris Aronson's great scenic contributions to the American theater, 'Pacific Overtures' could at this point be rated the masterpiece of a master artist."

Aronson earned his eighth Tony for *Overtures*. He passed away four years later, leaving a legacy of designs for some one hundred shows.

B

GEORGE BALANCHINE

(January 22, 1904–April 30, 1983)
Choreographer

Balanchine was the first choreographer to integrate dance into the story line of the musical and with this set the stage for the innovations of such artists as Agnes de Mille and Jerome Robbins.

Balanchine, labeled by Anna Kisselgoff in a May 1, 1983, *New York Times* obituary as "one of the greatest choreographers in the history of ballet," intriguingly straddled the worlds of modern and classical dance from the outset of his career. He combined training in the four-hundred-year-old academic movement in ballet with a sense of humor and modern techniques. Once he brought this sensibility to musicals, he fundamentally changed the way in which dance was used on Broadway.

He was born Georgi Melitonovich Balanchivadze in St. Petersburg, Russia, and his composer father and bank employee mother enrolled him in the Maryinsky's ballet school there when he was just ten. After graduation, he created both avant-garde dances and ones in the classical mode while also continuing as a performer. During the early 1920s, he worked with both the experimental Maly Theater and the State Academic Theater.

In 1924, he was part of a group known as the Soviet State Dancers that was allowed to leave Russia to perform in Germany. Although they were ordered home, the company remained in the West. In short order Sergei Diaghilev brought them into his Ballet Russes, where Balanchine (as he had been rechristened by Diaghilev) became choreographer.

Balanchine's work with this company propelled him to other countries and assignments. For instance, in 1930, he contributed to one of British impresario Charles Cochran's West End revues, and in 1931, he devised a ballet that became a centerpiece of the shows at London's Alhambra Music Hall. He moved to the United States in 1933 and formed the School of American Ballet with Lincoln Kirstein. They presented their first season of dances at Broadway's Adelphi Theatre in March 1935.

Balanchine's dances for this series put him on the radar of New York's theatrical community, and his first musical theatre assignment came with *The Ziegfeld Follies of 1936*. One of the show's segments that featured Balanchine's work was "5 A.M.," and it revolved around Josephine Baker. It was the number in which "she looks her best," according to critic "Ibee." in a February 2 *Variety* review, adding, "[She] sings and dances with four shadowy black men. It is a Balanchine ballet."

Two months later, Balanchine lent his artistry to a book musical, Richard Rodgers and Lorenz Hart's *On Your Toes*. For this satire about ballet companies, he demanded a credit of "choreography by" rather than the then-standard "dances by," and his principal creations for the show were a parody of a Scheherazade ballet and "Slaughter on 10th Avenue," a climactic extended dance in the show's second act.

Balanchine's work on these two sequences moved ballet away from being tangential to a musical's plot or merely a decorative interlude. It also demonstrated that this "highbrow" form could be funny. Balanchine described to Lucius Beebe for an April 19 *New York Herald Tribune* feature how the Scheherazade piece, devised as satire, came to be: "It is presented precisely as the foremost European corps used to present it only a few years ago; especially companies with but one or two stars, who would allow nothing but incompetence and mediocrity around them."

After this, Balanchine worked steadily on Broadway and provided dances for three more Rodgers and Hart shows, starting with *Babes in Arms* in 1937. In this musical one of his dances was "Peter's Journey," and with it he integrated dance into musical theatre in yet another way. It is widely considered to be the first dream ballet, setting the stage for work that Agnes de Mille would create in *Oklahoma!* six years later.

Balanchine's dances in *I Married an Angel*, also by Rodgers and Hart, prompted John Martin to dub him, in July 17, 1938, *Times* review, the "first choreographer of Broadway," adding "to be able to do the job of light and fanciful choreography as beautifully as Balanchine is an art." Martin was particularly impressed with Balanchine's substitution of dancer Charles Laskey for leading man Dennis King in one number (a conceit that de Mille would also come to use). The dance critic was also taken with the surreal sensibility Balanchine brought to a dance set at the Roxy Music Hall. It included "all the various types of entertainment dispensed in the stage shows of the great cinema palaces fused into one horrendous whole."

In 1940, Balanchine assumed the role of director-choreographer for *Cabin in the Sky*. The scenic designer for this production was Boris Aronson, and the work of these two Russian-born artists resulted in a show about African Americans in the South that Brooks Atkinson, in his October 26 *Times* review, described as being "original and joyous in an imaginative vein that suits the theater's special genius." Further, the critic applauded the way in which Balanchine deployed the show's all-black cast: "He has released them from the bondage of hack dancing and ugliness." Unfortunately, African American dancer-choreographer Katherine Dunham, who was in the production and collaborated with Balanchine on the dances, received no official credit for her part in this achievement.

Over the course of the next fourteen years, during which Balanchine would help found New York City Ballet, he created dances for such operettas as *The*

Merry Widow (1943) and *Song of Norway* (1944) and musicals that included Frank Loesser's *Where's Charley?* (1948). He also served in the dual capacity of director-choreographer for Alan Jay Lerner and Frederick Loewe's *What's Up* in 1943.

Balanchine's final outing with original Broadway choreography came in 1951 with *Courtin' Time*. Sadly, this musical set in Maine during the Spanish–American War failed to show him or any of the other artists involved in their best light, and it closed after a mere thirty-seven performances.

This master artist did return three years later for a revival of *On Your Toes*, and in 1974 his work was seen in the special engagement *Nureyev and Friends*. But on many levels, his absence was hardly felt because his work had had such a deep impact on everything that followed. New Yorkers could still experience his choreography through the dances he created for New York City Ballet, where some of his theatrical work, such as "Slaughter," also entered the company's repertory.

MICHAEL BENNETT

(April 8, 1943–July 2, 1987)
Director / Choreographer / Performer

Building on traditions of Robbins and Champion, Bennett took the musical into new realms, both visually and in terms of dance, creating stunning individual numbers as well as remarkable musical-dance narratives.

Michael Bennett DiFiglia's mother wanted to ensure culture played a role in his life as he grew up in Buffalo, New York, and so when he was just three, she enrolled him in dance classes. From that moment on, dance played a central role in his life, and before he was a teenager, he was studying in New York during the summer.

He had dropped his surname and become simply Michael Bennett by 1961, when he joined his first Broadway show, *Subways Are for Sleeping*, directed and choreographed by Michael Kidd. The tuner turned into an exceptional opportunity for the young performer, who got a chance to shine alongside the production's leading lady, Carol Lawrence, in a specialty number set on a subway platform. Critic Howard Taubman singled out the moment in his December 28 *New York Times* review: "Two teen-age boys wander in, lay aside their books and join the sorrowing girl [Lawrence] in a brief dance that has a bittersweet grace." After *Subways*, Bennett assisted Ron Field on *Nowhere to Go but Up* (1962) and then moved into the ensembles of *Here's Love* (1963) and *Bajour* (1964).

In 1966, Bennett choreographed his first Broadway show, the short-lived *A Joyful Noise*. Although it only played twelve performances, Bennett earned a Tony Award nomination for his work. He received a similar honor in 1968 for his dances for *Henry, Sweet Henry*, which Clive Barnes, in an October 24, 1967, *Times* review, described as being the "most original aspect of the show."

Bennett's next gig, Neil Simon, Burt Bacharach, and Hal David's *Promises, Promises*, had more longevity and showcased how seamlessly his dances could fit into everyday situations. In fact, a review from "Hobe." in the December 4, 1969, edition of *Variety* proclaimed, "Bennett's choreography, with engaging energetic routines developed from situations, is superb."

For his next show, Alan Jay Lerner and André Previn's *Coco* (1969), Bennett worked—as credited choreographer and uncredited director—with Katharine Hepburn, who was making her musical theatre debut as legendary dress designer Gabrielle "Coco" Chanel. Barnes was once again enthused about Bennett's contribution and noted in a December 19 *Times* review that a number celebrating the designer's success in America was "quite definitely one of the best staged musical numbers I have ever seen."

In the early 1970s, Bennett joined Harold Prince on two musicals with scores by Stephen Sondheim. The first was *Company*, where Bennett was working with an ensemble of primarily nondancers. In his memoir *Sense of Occasion*, Prince applauded his collaborator, writing, "Michael's singular achievement was taking thirteen actors with little dance experience and making capital of it." Bennett's second show with Prince was *Follies*, and for this Bennett served as both choreographer and codirector. Martin Gottfried, in the April 25, 1971, edition of the *Times*, described Bennett's work as "dazzling" and also noted, "This team [Prince and Bennett] has integrated itself so thoroughly as to create a whole indivisible into its parts."

Bennett became a two-time Tony winner with *Follies*, sharing the award for direction with Prince and receiving the award for best choreography as well. Among Bennett's contributions to this landmark production was his choreography for "Who's That Woman?," in which past and present collided as the women reunited to remember their days as members of the fictional *Weissman Follies* and were joined by young incarnations of themselves dressed in glittering black-and-white costumes. In the May 5, 1971, edition of *Newsday*, George Oppenheimer told readers, "It provides the sort of moment that causes a catch in your throat."

Bennett shifted to a nonmusical for his next Broadway outing, the comedy *Twigs* by George Furth (*Company*'s book writer), and then served as a doctor on the troubled Cy Coleman–Dorothy Fields–Michael Stewart musical *Seesaw* (1973), taking a show that had received mixed notices in Detroit and turning it into a Tony-nominated best musical.

This director-choreographer's artistry was receiving such universal acclaim that it prompted New York Shakespeare Festival producer Joseph Papp to invite him to stage a classical production, but Bennett demurred. He did, however, request that Papp consider allowing him to develop a musical under the festival's auspices. It would be a show about the men and women—known as "gypsies"—who move from musical to musical on Broadway. Papp agreed, and the result was *A Chorus Line*, which debuted at the festival's downtown home, the Public Theater, on May 21, 1975. The following morning, Barnes announced in the *Times*, "We have for years been hearing about innovating musicals; now Mr. Bennett has finally innovated one."

Barnes was referring primarily to how Bennett fused dance, song, and spoken word in new ways. This happened most notably in a montage in which the dancers revisit their teenage years, which in Bennett's staging became a vivid theatrical collage that floated back and forth in time. The show quickly moved to Broadway and within a year had earned the Pulitzer Prize along with nine Tonys.

Bennett expanded on the cinematic sweep he infused in *A Chorus Line* with his next two shows. In 1979's *Ballroom*, he created what might be described as a half-flashback for his middle-aged characters as they entered the hall where they spent their evenings. Walter Kerr in a February 22 *Times* story lauded the show as the "most undervalued musical of the season" and then described Bennett's wizardry with his performers' transformation in physicality but not appearance: "[They] became the animated, carefree, syncopated souls they remembered themselves being." Despite such high regard, the show only ran 116 performances.

With *Dreamgirls* in 1981, Bennett, working with designer Robin Wagner, created a production that appeared to never stop dancing and also seemed to whisk theatregoers through the story of an African American girl trio's rise to fame as if it were a movie on stage. In his December 21 *Times* review, Frank Rich proclaimed that it was a "show that strikes with the speed and the heat of lightning."

Bennett's following show was to have been the London production of *Chess*, but he had to withdraw for health reasons. He contracted AIDS and died in 1987 from lymphoma brought on by the disease. In a July 4 *Los Angeles Times* appreciation of Bennett's work, Dan Sullivan summed up his contribution to the musical: "His genius was the way in which he got the whole show to move in one inexorable line from the first image to the last."

ROBERT RUSSELL BENNETT

(June 15, 1894–August 18, 1981)
Orchestrator / Conductor / Composer

During the first half of the twentieth century, this artist's work was pivotal in creating what audiences came to think of as the "Broadway sound," providing lyrical, lush, buoyant orchestrations for many landmark musicals.

A native Missourian, Bennett arrived in New York in 1916 with a substantial musical background, thanks to both his parents' and his own passion, and a drive to put it to use. He found a variety of jobs, ranging from one as a copyist at the music publisher G. Schirmer to a Broadway gig. In 1917, he played piano in the pit for *Peter Ibbetson*, a play that starred John and Lionel Barrymore. At one point in the production, Bennett also shifted backstage to play piano so that it looked as if Lionel Barrymore's character was actually playing onstage.

During World War I, Bennett served as a bandmaster in the army in Kansas, and after the armistice he returned to Manhattan, securing a job with another music publisher, T. B. Harms. One assignment at the firm proved particularly important: Bennett arranged the song "An Old-Fashioned Garden," by emerging composer-lyricist Cole Porter, for dance bands. It was, as Bennett writes in his memoir *The Broadway Sound*, "my entrance music for orchestration for Broadway."

Bennett's work for Harms included other such arrangements for songs, ranging from George Gershwin and Irving Caesar's "Swanee," written for *The Demi-Tasse Revue*, to Jerome Kern and B. G. "Buddy" DeSylva's "Look for the Silver Lining," composed for *Zip Goes a Million* and later used in the phenomenally successful tuner *Sally*. At the same time, he continued composing, providing incidental music for productions of *Macbeth* in 1921 and *Hamlet* in 1922 that starred, respectively, Lionel Barrymore and John Barrymore in the title roles.

One month after the opening of the latter production, Bennett had his first Broadway credit as an orchestrator, for the musical *The Clinging Vine*. It set in motion forty years of working with some of America's greatest theatrical composers. In 1923, he worked with Herbert Stothart and Vincent Youmans, as well as Jerome Kern, on the musical *Stepping Stones*. Bennett's relationship with Kern soon encompassed *Sitting Pretty* (1924), *Sunny* (1925), and *Show Boat* (1927), among others. Starting in 1924, Bennett began working on shows with George Gershwin's music as well, providing orchestrations for *Lady, Be Good!* before moving onto such works as *Girl Crazy* (1930) and *Of Thee I Sing* (1931).

Thanks to a series of 1990s recordings of the first two of these Gershwin shows that used Bennett's original charts, it is possible for listeners today to experience exactly what he brought to Gershwin's exceptional musicality. In "I Got Rhythm," for instance, Bennett's orchestrations, particularly the use of cymbals, electrify an already-driving number as these instruments pop underneath the singer's vocals like small firecrackers.

Bennett maintained his heavy workload on Broadway during the 1930s, sometimes contributing his talents to as many as six shows a season. Among the new musicals in that decade that benefitted from his musical acumen were Porter's *Anything Goes* (1934); Sigmund Romberg's *May Wine*; and Kern's final original score for Broadway, *Very Warm for May*.

It was during the 1940s that Bennett began his association with Richard Rodgers, starting with *Oklahoma!*, and it was during this decade, too, that critics began singling out Bennett's contributions. With this show, for instance, Lewis Nichols, in his April 1, 1943, *New York Times* review, noted, "[Bennett] knows his humor and has on this occasion let himself go with all the laughter he can command." What Nichols couldn't have known was the extent to which Bennett had contributed to the show. Making a hasty revision during the musical's out-of-town tryout, he embellished the title song, originally "Oklahoma, O K," so that, as the ensemble came to the end, they spelled out the entirety of the state's name.

By the middle of the 1940s, Bennett was so well regarded that Irving Berlin and Rodgers, as producer, called Bennett in to create last-minute changes to the orchestrations for *Annie Get Your Gun*. Beyond this musical, some of Bennett's varied assignments during this decade were the college-set musical *Best Foot Forward* (1941); *Carmen Jones* (1943), the Americanization of Bizet's opera *Carmen*; the fantastical *Finian's Rainbow* (1947); and the classic backstage musical romance *Kiss Me, Kate* (1948).

Bennett was not always the sole orchestrator on a musical. The demands of creating full charts for a multitude of musicians when changes happened during tryouts meant that he would often work with others who sometimes received credit and sometimes didn't. One instance in which credit was shared came in

1956 with *My Fair Lady*. And for this Walter F. Kerr praised both Bennett and his co-orchestrator in a March 25, 1956, *New York Herald Tribune* review: "The Robert Russell Bennett–Phil Lang musical arrangements are rich enough to create one dramatic climax—the exit to the ball—without so much as a word of help from dialogue or lyrics." The following year (before the Tony Awards had an official category for orchestrations), Bennett received a special Tony honor for his contributions to the theatre.

Two years later, when Bennett orchestrated *The Sound of Music* (his sixth Rodgers and Hammerstein stage show), Brooks Atkinson described the orchestrations as being "dainty," writing that they "uphold the traditions of musical production on a high level." After this, Bennett's Broadway work continued with two more Lerner scores, *Camelot* (1960) and *On a Clear Day You Can See Forever* (1965), and one by Noël Coward, *The Girl Who Came to Supper* (1963), among others.

Beyond his prodigious output on Broadway as an orchestrator, Bennett was an accomplished composer in his own right, and even as he plied his exceptional craft in theatre work he wrote symphonies, an opera, and other classically based work. He helped to popularize Broadway in concert halls with his symphonic treatments of great scores, notably his *Porgy and Bess: A Symphonic Picture*. He also had a presence on the big screen sporadically throughout his career, earning an Oscar for his work on the film version of *Oklahoma!*, and for television he scored *Victory at Sea* (1952–1953), using and augmenting Richard Rodgers's melodies for all thirteen hours of the epic World War II documentary.

In Bennett's August 20, 1981, *Los Angeles Times* obituary, he was toasted with a statement Rodgers had once made: "[Bennett] wouldn't know how to put down a vulgar bar of music."

IRVING BERLIN

(May 11, 1888–September 22, 1989)
Songwriter / Producer

Berlin gave the world countless hits that endure, some after more than one hundred years, and brought a genuine pop song mentality to the Broadway musical that informed America's perception of itself for the first half of the twentieth century.

Composer Jerome Kern is often reported to have said, "Irving Berlin has no place in American music.—He *is* American music," and this peer's tribute stands as proof of Berlin's achieving what he himself once said was his goal in songwriting: "My ambition is to reach the heart of the average American."

Berlin, born Israel Balin in Russia near the Siberian border, immigrated to the United States with his parents when he was five years old. His father died when Izzy, as he was familiarly called, was just eight, and after only two years of formal schooling the boy had to find work to help support his mother and siblings. For a while he was a newspaper boy, and then he began to help a local blind man who earned his living singing in Lower East Side saloons. Young Izzy would take the man into bars, look after the money he earned, and sometimes sing himself. Eventually Izzy was on his own singing in bars and later plugged songs at Tony Pastor's music hall. There, after hours, he would sit at the piano and improvise with his own melodies. He published his first song in early 1907, "Marie from Sunny Italy." Vaudevillians, such as Leah Russell, adopted the song for their acts, and thus Berlin's life as a professional songwriter began.

By the end of 1909, his publisher and sometimes-collaborator Ted Snyder could boast that Berlin had written some half-dozen hits, mostly catchy, syncopated melodies with direct, colloquial lyrics that suited both stage artists and nonprofessionals who would play Berlin's songs on their home pianos.

In 1910, Berlin got his first Broadway credit, contributing "Stop Dat Rag" to the revue *The Jolly Bachelors*. The tune stood out for many reviewers, and six months after this he penned the opening number for the fourth edition of Florenz Ziegfeld Jr.'s annual *Follies*.

Over the course of the next three years, Berlin's music became part of the aural fabric of the country. His biggest hit was a nontheatre song, "Alexander's Ragtime Band," published in 1911. This tune was so pervasive that cadets at the US Naval Academy in Annapolis were banned from whistling it. Berlin's songs were featured in some twelve Broadway productions between 1911 and 1913, and then, in 1914, producer Charles Dillingham engaged Berlin to write his first complete Broadway score. Some arts journalists were skeptical about whether this pop songwriter, known for his ragtime rhythms, would live up to musical theatre expectations, but when the musical *Watch Your Step* opened, any doubts were erased. The morning after the production's December 8 opening, an unidentified *New York Times* critic wrote, "More than to anyone else, 'Watch Your Step' belongs to Irving Berlin," adding that the songs were "born to be caught up and whistled at every street corner." Berlin had brought a new and then "pop" sound to Broadway.

Berlin had both highs and lows in the years that followed. One of his most successful shows, *Yip Yip Yaphank*, was created for the army as America entered World War I. In it, Berlin himself performed, originating what became one of his signature tunes, "Oh, How I Hate to Get Up in the Morning." According to Berlin's September 23, 1989, *New York Times* obituary, the revue raised some $150,000 for the camp service center on Long Island where he was stationed.

Equally successful during the first half of the 1920s were his *Music Box Revues* (named after a theatre he built), which fused Ziegfeld's extravagance with the artistic minimalism of others, such as John Murray Anderson. But as the 1920s drew to a close, Berlin's ability to repeatedly succeed waned. It wasn't until he partnered (nervously) with a younger writer, Moss Hart, that the songwriter regained his confidence and found a new kind of success.

Hart and Berlin's first venture together was *Face the Music*, which giddily and pointedly skewered politicians, showbiz folk, and the Depression itself. Berlin told the *New York Tribune*'s Perry N. Stone for a February 24 feature that he worried, "What if I can't write any more good ones?" as the show was being prepared. His fears were for naught. He supplied, as Brooks Atkinson described it in his February 18 *Times* review, a "bountiful merry-go-round" of tunes. Two years later, Hart and Berlin brought *As Thousands Cheer* to Broadway and with it set a new standard for the topical revue. Songs Berlin wrote for this production include "Easter Parade" and "Supper Time."

The former number, of course, became the title song for an MGM film, and throughout his career, Berlin's work from the theatre found a home in movies for which he would also pen new material. A terrific example is *White Christmas*, where "Heat Wave" from *As Thousands Cheer* is included alongside the title song (written as pop song) and new material. Among the hits that came from his screen work are such songs as "Cheek to Cheek" and "Top Hat, White Tie and Tails" from *Top Hat* (1935).

As the period of the revue on Broadway gave way to integrated book musicals, Berlin, despite his antipathy for them, demonstrated that he could fit his tunes into a story and have them live comfortably outside of it. Such hits as "There's No Business like Show Business," "Anything You Can Do," and "It's a Lovely Day Today" emerged from *Annie Get Your Gun* (1946) and *Call Me Madam* (1950).

Subsequent to *Madam*, Berlin wrote only one more Broadway musical, *Mr. President* (1962). The show, about a first family that bore striking similarities to the Kennedys, was deemed old-fashioned by critics out of town and in New York, but as Berlin reportedly quipped, "After 'White Christmas,' 'Blue Skies,' 'God Bless America,' I know my songs are corny. But so is 'My Old Kentucky Home.'"

His final new song to reach Broadway came in 1966. Berlin wrote it for the twentieth-anniversary revival of *Annie Get Your Gun*, when he was one year shy of hitting his sixtieth year as a songwriter. *Variety* critic "Hobe." described the number "An Old-Fashioned Wedding" as a "rousingly amusing counterpoint song" in a June 8 review.

For the balance of the 1960s, Berlin concentrated on songwriting for a film, *Say It with Music*, but it went unproduced. After this, specialty material and musical noodling were his primary artistic outlet.

LEONARD BERNSTEIN

(August 25, 1918–October 14, 1990)
Composer

Bernstein brought symphonic richness to Broadway musicals and fused it with popular sounds—from boogie-woogie to jazz—from a variety of eras, enriching the form and also creating four enduring cornerstones of the musical theatre.

When *On the Town* opened on Broadway on December 28, 1944, it was the culmination of an extraordinary thirteen months for composer Leonard Bernstein, who took the nation by storm on November 11, 1943, when, as assistant conductor for the New York Philharmonic, he substituted (with no rehearsal) for an ailing Bruno Walter. The year also included the premiere of Bernstein's complete orchestral work *Jeremiah Symphony* in January 1944 and the debut of his ballet *Fancy Free*, which had opened to rapturous reviews in April. Bernstein's accomplishments were emblematic of his varied career and of the serious and symphonic musical traditions he brought to the Broadway musical.

Boston-born and raised, Bernstein first discovered his talents after an aunt, in the middle of a divorce, left a piano with his parents. Lessons ensued, and as he moved from high school to Harvard, his natural abilities and interest in a wide array of musical forms resulted in credits that included conducting Marc Blitzstein's *The Cradle Will Rock* at the university, staging and performing in a production of the opera *Carmen* when he was sixteen, and serving as music counselor at a summer camp, where his responsibilities included directing a production of Gilbert and Sullivan's *The Pirates of Penzance*.

After graduating from Harvard, Bernstein trained in Philadelphia at the prestigious Curtis Institute of Music and later moved to New York. Through it all, he established connections within a variety of artistic circles. His intimates included composers Aaron Copland, Roy Harris, and William Schuman; writer-performers Betty Comden and Adolph Green; and dancer-choreographer Jerome Robbins.

It was with the last three that Bernstein created the musical *On the Town*, which drew its inspiration from Robbins's scenario for *Fancy Free*. Telling the story of three sailors on a twenty-four-hour leave in New York, *Town* opened to some glowing notices, including one in the *Brooklyn Eagle* on December 31, 1944. In it, Arthur Pollock announced that the musical contained "songs by the country's liveliest composer of really good music, Leonard Bernstein." In the *New York Times* on December 29, Lewis Nichols commended Bernstein on writing a score that meant "this morning he will start up the ladder at ASCAP." This critic was particularly impressed with the diversity of sounds in the show: "'Lonely Town' is strict Broadway, 'Lucky to Be Me' is strict torch. For a scene in Times Square, [Bernstein] has provided the roar of that crossroads of the world."

Comden and Green had hoped to collaborate with Bernstein on their second musical outing, but under pressure from his mentor, Serge Koussevitzky, he turned toward conducting and writing more classically oriented music. It wasn't until 1950 that new Bernstein music echoed in a Broadway theatre when he provided songs and underscoring for a production of *Peter Pan* that starred Jean Arthur. It was "excellent musical accompaniment for the action," according to Howard Barnes's April 25, 1950, *New York Herald Tribune* review. The critic added, "The music heightens the fantastical mood of the drama at every turn."

Bernstein was back on Broadway three years later with *Wonderful Town*, which had lyrics by Comden and Green. For this show set in Greenwich Village in the 1930s, Bernstein wrote, for the first time, music that was meant specifically to recall styles of a bygone period. Bernstein evokes Cab Calloway's music in "Swing!" and "Ohio" brings to mind gently rolling western songs that were popular in the 1930s. In a February 26, 1953, *Times* review, Brooks Atkinson called Bernstein's work a "bright and witty score in a variety of modern styles," adding, "[It] carries forward the crack-brained comedy of the book with gaiety and excitement."

Trouble in Tahiti, which had its Broadway premiere in 1955, was more serious, both in content and style. The one-act opera played as part of a varied evening of theatre, *All in One*, which also featured a dance piece by Paul Draper and a play by Tennessee Williams. *Tahiti* explores the emptiness of a suburban couple's life and indicts the capitalist influences that have caused it. Bernstein dedicated the work to his colleague and friend Marc Blitzstein, and like many of that composer's works, *Tahiti* has gone on to enjoy a place in opera repertoires around the world.

Candide, a zinging stage version of Voltaire's satirical novel that had a book by Lillian Hellman and lyrics by a variety of writers, arrived in 1956 with a Bernstein score that merged musical theatre and opéra bouffe sounds to innovative ends. Atkinson commended Bernstein in his December 3 *Times* review: "None of his previous theatre music has had the joyous variety, humor and richness of this score. . . . Bernstein is obviously having a good time." Despite such critical plaudits, the piece failed to capture audiences' hearts, and it wasn't until Harold Prince opened a dramatically reconceived production that featured some new lyrics by Stephen Sondheim that the work was recognized as a masterwork of musical theatre.

Bernstein's music was both more serious and jazzier for his next show, *West Side Story*, the groundbreaking retelling of Shakespeare's *Romeo and Juliet* set among warring teenage gangs in then-contemporary New York. As with *On the Town* and *Wonderful Town*, Bernstein's score captures a sense of urban life, even as it musicalizes its teenage characters' edgy, angry energy. John Chapman in his September 27, 1957, *Daily News* review enthused, "It takes up the American musical idiom where it was left when George Gershwin died."

Conducting and classic composing consumed most of Bernstein's career for the remainder of his life, although there were sporadic returns to theatrical work. In the 1960s, he started on two musicals that went unproduced, and in 1971, he and lyricist Stephen Schwartz created *Mass*, a theatrical interpretation of the traditional religious service that also examined notions of faith. Then, in 1976, he and Alan Jay Lerner created *1600 Pennsylvania Avenue*, a metaphorical and satirical excursion through American history that explored specifically racial inequality. In a year of bicentennial celebration, the work proved to be too bitter for critics during tryouts, and before the production reached Broadway both its director and choreographer were replaced and Bernstein's score edited and condensed without his approval. *1600* only ran seven performances in New York. After it, he wrote only one more theatrical work, an opera, *A Quiet Place* (1983).

MARC BLITZSTEIN

(March 2, 1905–January 22, 1964)
Composer / Lyricist / Librettist

Blitzstein set the stage for serious, dramatic stories and themes with his original works, and with his translation of Threepenny Opera, *he helped to make one of the audacious, socially conscious pieces that had inspired him accessible to American audiences.*

Classically trained in both the United States and Germany, Blitzstein wrote works that challenged theatregoers' and listeners' perceptions about the difference between classical and popular music, a distinction at which he bristled. In a December 7, 1941, letter to the *New York Times*, he railed against a "generalization based upon the old Puritan notion that if a piece is serious, it ought not to give too much pleasure; and per contra, if it does give pleasure, or even fun, it cannot be much good."

Blitzstein, who was born in Philadelphia, had been immersed in music for more than three decades by the time he wrote the letter. He began playing classical works by ear while he was still an infant and at the age of six gave his first public performance. After his high school graduation and before settling in New York, he attended the University of Pennsylvania, the Curtis Institute in Philadelphia, and finally the Akademie der Künste in Berlin.

His initial work in Manhattan consisted of composing, performing, and occasional lecturing. He became prominent among a new breed of composer in the city, and his Broadway debut came in 1930 with an edition of the Theatre Guild's revue *Garrick Gaieties*. For it, he wrote a fifteen-minute parody of opera, *Triple-Sec*, establishing his theatrical voice as one that was both challenging and entertaining.

In 1935, Blitzstein contributed such songs as "Life Could Be So Beautiful" and "Send for the Militia" to the Theatre Guild's politically charged satirical revue *Parade*. Comedienne Eve Arden scored with audiences and critics as she delivered the latter, which is set to a giddily loopy melody and tells of a society matron's discovery of socialism. Blitzstein's work is more somber with the former number, a bluesy lament about life during the Depression.

German playwright Bertolt Brecht suggested Blitzstein write a politically charged theatre piece, and the result was the seminal *The Cradle Will Rock*, which centers on workers attempting to unionize in "Steeltown USA" and the efforts of politicians and businessmen to stop them. *Cradle* attracted the attention of director-producer Orson Welles and his partner producer John Houseman, who slated it for production through the Federal Theatre Project (FTP). After federal officials learned of the show's content, however, a freeze on all new FTP productions was issued disguised as a cost-cutting move. *Cradle* was the only affected show.

Scrambling during the afternoon and early evening on the day that *Cradle* had been scheduled to play its first performance resulted in one of the most historic theatrical events of the twentieth century. The cast performed the work in a hastily secured alternate venue, performing not from the stage (Actors' Equity banned the cast's many nonunion performers from appearing on a commercial stage) but rather from various spots throughout the auditorium, accompanied by Blitzstein at the piano onstage. Further, they did it to a capacity crowd. The *New York Herald Tribune* reported the next morning, June 17, 1937: "The audience en route evidently had telephoned to friends, because when the production was underway the house was packed and there were more than 100 standees."

A second offering of the show the following night was scuttled by authorities, but by the end of the year, Welles and Houseman's Mercury Theatre produced it. On December 6, New York's critical community finally weighed in on *Cradle*, and in the *Herald Tribune* the next day, Richard Watts Jr. described it as an "exciting and savagely humorous cartoon, with music that hits hard and sardonically." One year later, the Musicraft label issued a recording of the score, and *Cradle* finally had a Broadway production with full orchestra in 1947 with a cast that included Alfred Drake.

Even as *Cradle* was making headlines, Blitzstein was at work on *No for an Answer*. He described the piece, about a group of hotel workers stranded by their employers at the end of a summer season, as an "opera," but as Brooks Atkinson pointed out in his January 6, 1941, *Times* review, "It might just as well be put down as a musical drama." The critic wasn't being disparaging. He was attempting to lure audiences to the show that contained music that was "joyous and dramatic by turns" and gave the characters "flesh, blood, humor, love, loyalty, indignation [and] courage."

Blitzstein served in the army starting in 1941, and after his discharge in 1946 he completed the orchestral work he began while stationed overseas, *Airborne Symphony*. His next major stage work, *Regina*, came in 1949. An adaptation of Lillian Hellman's dark drama about a decaying Southern clan, *Regina* blurred lines between musical theatre and opera, so much so that the *Herald Tribune* sent both its theatre critic, Howard Barnes, and its music critic, Virgil Thomson. Unfortunately, reviewers felt that Blitzstein's audacious, wide-ranging score didn't exactly succeed as either theatre or opera, but in the years that followed, *Regina* developed a reputation for being a work ahead of its time and has moved into productions in opera houses around the world.

Blitzstein brought *Let's Make an Opera*, an interactive piece of theatre, to Broadway the following year, and then, in 1952, his translation of Brecht and Kurt Weill's *The Threepenny Opera* premiered as a concert conducted by Leonard Bernstein. A full production of Blitzstein's version, which allowed audiences to appreciate both its comedy and social agenda, opened off-Broadway in 1954, and in a March 21 review, the *Herald Tribune*'s Thomson wrote, "Marc Blitzstein's translation of the Brecht text is, to my mind, the finest thing of its kind in existence. He has got the spirit of the play and rendered it powerfully, colloquially, compactly." The production, after a brief hiatus, eventually ran for six years.

Threepenny's return to the stage came just four months after Blitzstein saw *Reuben, Reuben*, a musical about a war veteran teetering on the verge of a nervous breakdown, close out of town. And then, in 1959, *Juno*, an adaptation of Sean O'Casey's *Juno and the Paycock* about an Irish family enduring their country's civil war in the 1920s, brought Blitzstein back to Broadway. This musical drama, with a book by Joseph Stein, was highly regarded by some critics but unfortunately became Blitzstein's last produced musical. Five years later, and after writing two songs performed in Hellman's *Toys in the Attic*, Blitzstein died in a gay bashing on the Caribbean island of Martinique, leaving his final work, an opera about Sacco and Vanzetti, unfinished.

JERRY BOCK AND SHELDON HARNICK

(November 23, 1928–November 3, 2010) / (April 30, 1924–)
Songwriters

Bock and Harnick wrote the score for one of the touchstone hits of the American musical theatre, earned a Pulitzer for another, and repeatedly demonstrated a unique gift for crafting scores that gracefully molded themselves to a wide range of stories.

This team—who celebrated the life of New York City mayor Fiorello La Guardia in song and captured the voices and plight of Russians enduring anti-Semitism in Tsarist Russia—started their lives far from the lights of Broadway. Bock hailed from Connecticut and was raised in Queens, while Harnick grew up in Chicago.

Both men had an interest in music and theatre from an early age. For Bock it began with the songs he heard his grandmother singing and the music playing on the radio. There were even minor attempts at writing melody in his early teens, and later he wrote a full musical that was presented at his high school. He enrolled at the University of Wisconsin not entirely certain of a major, but he eventually settled on music. Between his second and third years there, Bock started on a second musical, *Big as Life*, which he entered in a competition sponsored by the songwriter service group Broadcast Music, Inc. (BMI). It won first prize, and the show, based on the legend of Paul Bunyan, toured Wisconsin and even played Chicago's Blackstone Theater.

For Harnick, poetry and music intertwined while he was still a preteen, and as he grew older his interest in the former blossomed, even as he continued to study the latter. After his high school graduation, Harnick entered the army, and once discharged he enrolled at Northwestern University. There he continued his music studies and also his songwriting, contributing to the school's student-created WAA-MU revues.

In the early 1950s, Harnick moved to New York and began making a name for himself with the material he contributed to a number of Broadway revues, starting with *New Faces of 1952*. Alice Ghostley, who would go on to a substantial career in television, made her Broadway bow singing Harnick's "Boston Beguine," an extravagant retelling of a bookish woman's night out with a Harvard man. Walter F. Kerr, in the May 17 edition of the *New York Herald Tribune*, called it the "evening's happiest inspiration." Harnick contributed to another three revues on Broadway, as well as several off, and wrote specialty material for cabaret during the next four years.

For the first half of the 1950s, Bock contributed to a variety of projects. He wrote for television's *Your Show of Shows*; provided specialty material for the Mello-Tones; and in the theatrical realm, along with his then-partner Larry Holofcener, contributed songs for the 1955 revue *Catch a Star!* Their Broadway break came the following year when Jule Styne hired the team, joined by George Weiss, to write the songs for *Mr. Wonderful*. The musical showcased star Sammy Davis Jr.'s varied talents, and while critics were impressed by him, the score and book were largely dismissed. One of the most supportive notices for the music came from Kerr, who wrote in his April 1, 1956, *Herald Tribune* review that there were "two or three marketable ballads" in the production.

The first time Bock's and Harnick's names were linked came in January 1957 when Bert McCord informed his *Herald Tribune* readers that they had been signed to write the songs for *The Body Beautiful*, about a Dartmouth grad who tries to make a go of it as a boxer. *Body* opened a year later to tepid reviews, although Brooks Atkinson in his *New York Times* review applauded Bock's flair in a blues number as well as a "sort of rock 'n' roll tune" called "Uh-Huh, Oh Yeah!"

Body Beautiful folded after sixty performances, but Bock and Harnick's work in it did attract the attention of producer Harold Prince. In Prince's book *Sense of Occasion*, he recalls thinking that it had an "interesting score," and this prompted him to invite Bock and Harnick to join a project that he was assembling about the life of New York's colorful Mayor La Guardia. The result was *Fiorello!* and for it Bock wrote a richly varied score that the *Herald Tribune*'s Kerr, in a November 24, 1959, review, described as having persistently "sassy rhythms." As for Harnick's shrewd lyrics, the *Times*' Atkinson that day remarked that they came from a man in an "unfailingly humorous frame of mind." The show snagged both a Tony for Bock and Harnick as well as the Pulitzer Prize.

Bock and Harnick's next show, *Tenderloin*, also revisited a New York of another era and centered on a social reformer intent on sanitizing the city's red-light district. For this Bock and Harnick contributed what Bob Rolontz, in an October 24, 1960, *Billboard* review, called a "bright and breezy score," but it wasn't enough to assuage his (or other critics') concerns about the book, which he wrote suffered from a "lethargic plot."

In the musicals that followed, the team moved beyond shows set in the Big Apple of the past, starting with *Man in the Moon* (1963), a tuner that took a child to outer space, featured Bil Baird's puppets, and enjoyed a brief Broadway outing. *She Loves Me*, which opened alongside this children's offering, allowed Bock and Harnick to channel their European sides, as it told the story of a pair of squabbling coworkers in a small boutique who are unaware that, as pen pals, they have fallen in love. The show, which marked Prince's debut as a director, was an intimate, vest-pocket affair, and it eschewed big ensemble or choral numbers. Howard Taubman in his April 24 *Times* review called *She Loves Me* a "bonbon of a musical" and remarked that the team's songs "capture not only the gay, light spirit of the story but also add an extra dimension of magic to it."

Bock and Harnick shifted from 1930s Hungary to Tsarist Russia in 1905 for *Fiddler on the Roof* (1964), and for this adaptation of Sholem Aleichem's short stories, the team wrote their most enduring score. From "Tradition," the number that introduces the denizens of the village of Anatevka; to "If I Were a Rich Man," milkman Tevye's gently comic number about dreams of wealth; to "Sunrise, Sunset," the show's songs have become classics in and out of the theatre, and for their work, Bock and Harnick won their second Tony Award.

The team turned to a project of a very different nature for their next Broadway outing, *The Apple Tree*. This trio of one-act musicals—one based on Mark Twain's vision of Adam and Eve in the Garden of Eden; one based on a story by Frank R.

Stockton about a princess who must choose between her position and her lover; and one based on *Passionella*, Jules Feiffer's modern-day *Cinderella* set in Tinseltown—allowed Bock and Harnick to step away from the European modes that informed their last two pieces, and as *Billboard* critic Mike Gross described them in his November 5, 1966, review, the songs were "simple but artful."

Bock and Harnick shifted back to European and historical themes after this and began work on a musical about British Royal Navy officer Lord Nelson. When the show foundered, they started work with book writer Sherman Yellen on *The Rothschilds*, a musical portrait of the noted German banking family in the late eighteenth and early nineteenth centuries. Respectful notices of the piece, such as Clive Barnes's "It has geniality rather than incandescence" in the October 20, 1970, *Times* and warmer reviews for the cast, helped propel the show to a year's run. Sadly, it was the last Bock and Harnick musical.

For several years after *The Rothschilds*, Bock and Harnick would often say that they were continuing to work together, but nothing materialized. In later years, Harnick explained what happened. They clashed during *Rothschilds*, specifically about a decision to replace its original director, Derek Goldby, with director-choreographer Michael Kidd. The rancor from the dispute lasted for nearly thirty years. Eventually the two men would meet to discuss revivals but never wrote a new show together. They did, however, write one more song, "Topsy-Turvy," for the 2004 revival of *Fiddler*.

In those intervening years, Harnick never ceased writing. Always ambitious, his works for the past forty years have ranged from *Rex*, a musical about Henry VIII with music by Richard Rodgers that played Broadway in 1976; to an English-language version of Michel Legrand's *The Umbrellas of Cherbourg*, which ran off-Broadway at the New York Shakespeare Festival in 1979; to a musical version of the film classic *It's a Wonderful Life* with a score by Joe Raposo that premiered at Arena Stage in Washington, DC, in 1991. More recently, Harnick began work in 2003 on a musical version of Moliere's *The Doctor in Spite of Himself* that has yet to be produced, and in 2015, he and Yellen revised *The Rothschilds* as a one-act musical produced by the York Theatre Company off-Broadway.

Bock, as Robert Berkvist wrote in his November 4, 2010, *Times* obituary for the composer, "stepped away from the spotlight more or less for good," although he would occasionally compose. In 2010, he shared, with Billy Aronson and Larry Hochman, a Daytime Emmy award for the children's song "A Fiddler Crab I Am," written for the series *Wonder Pets!*

GUY BOLTON AND P. G. WODEHOUSE

(November 23, 1884–September 5, 1979) / (October 15, 1881–February 14, 1975)
Book Writers / Lyricists

This team laid the groundwork for what is considered integrated, book-driven musicals, departing from the overblown operettas and musical revues of their time and thus pulling the form from rarified to the realm of the relatable.

A September 2, 1917, *New York Tribune* article about these two writers began, "For the past four or five months no edition of any news paper has been considered genuine unless it contained somewhere an announcement [that] . . . the book and lyrics . . . of the new piece will be written by Guy Bolton and P. G. Wodehouse." Indeed, for much of the 1910s and early 1920s, these men were the hottest writers on Broadway; they were also helping to shape what audiences came to expect of musical theatre.

Wodehouse, the older of the two and whose initials stood for Pelham Grenville, was born in Guildford, England, and educated at Dulwich College in anticipation of a career in the Royal Navy. When his family's finances declined, he went into banking rather than the military after his graduation, but in short order, the gift for writing that he had demonstrated in his boyhood took him in a new direction. He began penning a column for London's *Globe* newspaper and augmented his income from the paper by writing stories for British magazines. In 1909, two American magazines printed Wodehouse fiction, and in response, he settled in New York to carve out a niche for himself as a writer.

Bolton was also born in England, and in 1893 his family moved to America. He trained to be an architect at both the Pratt Institute in Brooklyn and the Atelier Masqueray in France. Like Wodehouse, Bolton had shown a flair for writing in his youth, and while he was still a student his stories were published. He eventually focused on his literary pursuits, and by 1914 his play *The Rule of Three* was on Broadway.

In January 1915, Bolton had both a play and a musical open, yet neither had any longevity. But his next Broadway outing, *Nobody Home*, a play with music (some by Jerome Kern), caught critics' and theatregoers' attention and fancy. Presented at the intimate Princess Theatre, the loosely constructed show enjoyed a healthy (for the period) five-month run. It also spurred the theatre to begin a policy of producing new musicals that would break with the opulent and exotic pieces being presented in other Broadway houses.

Bolton was co–book writer on the next Princess show, *Very Good Eddie*, about romantic entanglements between three couples, first on a boat headed toward Poughkeepsie and later in Manhattan. A musicalization of the farce *Over Night* by Philip Bartholomae (who worked with Bolton on the adaptation), it boasted music by Kern and lyrics by Schuyler Greene, and the morning after its December 23, 1915, opening, the *New York Herald*'s critic noted, "It is jolly and tuneful and will probably make its producers wish the little Princess Theatre could be expanded." The theatre couldn't be enlarged, so *Eddie* moved to accommodate ticket buyers' demands, and the production ultimately ran for nearly a year.

In their joint autobiography, *Bring on the Girls!*, Bolton and Wodehouse relate that it was on *Eddie*'s opening night that Bolton suggested to Wodehouse that they collaborate. The team was formed, and in under a year they had adapted a Viennese operetta into *Miss Springtime*. Bolton provided the book, Wodehouse the lyrics, and Emmerich Kálmán the music. Kern also supplied some of the show's melodies. It was after this that the Bolton–Wodehouse–Kern collaboration began in earnest, and during 1917 they had three pieces bow, which combined set new standards for American musical comedy.

Their first outing was *Have a Heart*, and for this show, about a couple eloping on the eve of their divorce, the uncredited critic in the January 12 edition of the *New York Times* praised the book specifically, writing, "[The show's] authors seem to have read the newspapers and magazines for material instead of old libretti, and as a result, topical words, names, and subjects bob up quite frequently."

The triumvirate's next offering, *Oh, Boy*, was even more highly regarded when it debuted at the Princess Theatre a month later. Again, the team created an original story for the show, this one about a separated married couple, and as the critic for the *Herald* proclaimed on February 20, "It is a marked stride forward in the renaissance of that popular form. . . . Even the lyrics are funny." The production ultimately ran for more than a year after it transferred to the larger Casino Theatre.

Leave It to Jane was the third musical the three men premiered during 1917, and with it they turned in an adaptation of George Ade's popular comedy *The College Widow*, about the son of a millionaire Baptist who finds himself playing for football at a college of a different religious denomination. Again, the Bolton–Wodehouse book was praised, but in several reviews, it was a Wodehouse rhyme that caught critics' attention. In "Cleopatterer," Wodehouse had paired "ginks" and "sphinx." Ironically, in the August 29 *Brooklyn Eagle* review, the writer wondered, "Who in the world but an American would ever have thought of such a combination?"

Following the successes of these three shows, producers were vying for the writers, who found themselves penning shows for some of Broadway's largest theatres. Grandeur and opulence, however, did not translate to similar accolades for Bolton and Wodehouse. And neither *The Riviera Girl*, seen at the New Amsterdam Theatre, nor *Miss 1917*, which bowed at the Century, caught on as their other shows had.

These two shows opened in late 1917, and at the same time Bolton, Wodehouse, and Kern were at work on their next show for the Princess, *Oh, Lady! Lady!* For this, Bolton and Wodehouse concocted a story about a bridegroom who's surprised to see his former fiancée reappear on the eve of his nuptials to another woman. Complicating matters is the man's valet, who is a former con and about to be married himself. The *Times* critic on February 1, 1918, wrote that the show was "virtually flawless." As for the book, it has a "measurably novel plot that actually sustains interest for itself alone." One song that the critics never heard in the production because it was cut before opening was the classic "Bill," which Kern would use in *Show Boat*, with its Wodehouse lyric, nine years later.

As 1918 continued, Bolton and Wodehouse provided book and lyrics for *The Girl behind the Gun*, an adaptation of a French operetta, and then returned to the Princess with *Oh, My Dear!*, which had a score by Louis A. Hirsch.

They collaborated only once in 1919, on *The Rose of China*, and after it they began working independently. Bolton had several plays and musicals for which he wrote books produced in New York, including the hit *Sally*. Wodehouse's stage work during the early 1920s was produced in London. In 1921, he provided, with Fred Thompson, book and lyrics for Ivor Novello's *The Golden Moth*. Two collaborations with Kern followed: *The Cabaret Girl* (1922) and *The Beauty Prize* (1923).

Wodehouse returned to America that same year to assist with interpolations for a revival of Bolton and Kern's *Sally*, and his presence in New York set in motion a renewed collaboration for the trio. In 1924, they saw their musical *Sitting Pretty* bow. Having the team back together may have cheered critics. Percy Hammond, in the April 9 edition of the *Herald Tribune*, lauded Bolton and Wodehouse as the "nimblest of librettists," for instance. But most reviewers also found the piece wanting. For example, the *Times'* critic that day said the "story is weak and wandering."

A happier reaction lay in store for them as they joined forces with George and Ira Gershwin in 1926, writing *Oh, Kay!*, a musical about bootleggers on Long Island. The show, which marked Gertrude Lawrence's first appearance in a book musical in the United States, received some rapturous notices when it opened. The *Times'* J. Brooks Atkinson began his review with "Musical comedy seldom proves more intensely delightful than 'Oh, Kay!'"

Bolton and Wodehouse's collaboration continued the following year with two more musicals. They worked with both the Gershwins and Sigmund Romberg on *Rosalie* and Rudolf Friml on *The Three Musketeers*. After this, they returned to working individually.

The writers did reunite for one more show, however. They wrote the original book, later revised by Howard Lindsay and Russel Crouse, for *Anything Goes* in 1934. After this, Wodehouse concentrated primarily on his fiction (notably his "Jeeves" stories and books), while Bolton wrote plays, worked in Hollywood, and scripted musicals. None of the latter, which included *Follow the Girls* (1944), *Ankles Aweigh* (1955), and *Anya* (1965), had the impact of his collaborations with Wodehouse and Kern.

Ward Morehouse lamented the men's not working together in the December 14, 1931, edition of the *Herald Tribune*: "That irresistible firm of Bolton, Wodehouse & Kern no longer operates. Without warning, and against the shrieking protests of American theatergoers, the firm dissolved and its members scattered."

C

GOWER CHAMPION

(June 22, 1919–August 25, 1980)
Director / Choreographer / Performer

Champion shifted dance on Broadway away from ballet and helped to create what is known today as musical choreography, a hybrid of dance forms from classical to tap to popular.

Born in a suburb of Chicago and raised primarily in California, Champion began his life as a dancer casually when he was twelve years old. His mother enrolled him in dance school, not because she believed that he would have a career on stage or in films, but rather because she believed societal dancing was essential to a young man's good upbringing. Five years later, he put his lessons to use when he and a classmate, Jeanne Tyler, entered a dance competition at the Cocoanut Grove supper club in Los Angeles. To their delight, they won both a cash prize of $150 and a week's engagement there.

After they concluded their extended run at the Grove, they appeared in other spots in California and later New York. Their act consisted of dances that Champion devised and regularly altered to keep them fresh. It was the beginning of his life as a director-choreographer.

The team's success led to appearances in three Broadway shows between 1939 and 1942, and during the last of these, *Count Me In*, Champion enlisted in the coast guard, where he served until the war's end. Immediately after his discharge, Bert McCord reported in his December 13, 1945, *New York Herald Tribune* theatre column that Champion was already "considering several offers to appear in musical shows."

Nothing materialized for him in the theatre, but offstage he married and with his new bride, Marge (born Marjorie Bell), returned to performing in clubs. In an October 15, 1947, review of their work at New York's Persian Room, McCord extolled the team, labeling them "even more proficient than the old" and taking particular delight in their "appreciation of satire," which he found in one of Champion's routines, a fantasy that imagined a classical ballet devised by both Agnes de Mille and Ray Bolger.

A year later, Champion had two back-to-back assignments as a Broadway choreographer for the revues *Small Wonder* and *Lend an Ear*. For his work on these shows, he attempted to create a new style of dancing. An August 28, 1948, *Billboard* story explained his philosophy: "Champion says the ballet trend has been exploited to great length until the public is tired and looking for something new." As for his work, the reporter labeled it "stylized musical comedy dancing."

Champion, who had made two film appearances after the war, returned to Hollywood after working on the revues, and for the next decade, he and his wife-partner moved fluidly between the big screen, television, nightclubs, and Broadway. Among their notable film appearances are *Show Boat* (1951), *Lovely to Look At* (the 1952 modified movie version of *Roberta*), and *Everything I Have Is Yours* (1952), where the Champions were the stars. On Broadway, Champion created the dances for *Make a Wish* (1951) and then in 1955 served as both director and choreographer for *3 for Tonight*, a revue in which he and his wife were also featured. In his April 7 review of the production for the *New York Times*, Brooks Atkinson wrote, "Mr. and Mrs. Champion are effortless dancers. But they are also people of intelligence who hate the hackneyed and despise the pretentious. '3 for Tonight' is ideal for them and vice versa."

The Champions continued to lend their talents to television shows and perform in clubs for the balance of the 1950s, and as the decade was drawing to a close, Marge opted to withdraw from performing, preferring instead to stay at home. Concurrently, Champion received an offer to direct and choreograph a new musical that had been written by a trio of relative unknowns, book writer Michael Stewart, lyricist Lee Adams, and composer Charles Strouse. The show was *Bye Bye Birdie*, and after it opened on April 14, 1960, Walter Kerr enthused about the way in which Champion had brought adolescent energy to the stage. Kerr described the show's opening number as featuring teenagers "undulating like enchanted earthworms all over the jungle-gym setting, every rhythmically wiggling ear glued to a telephone." Champion received a pair of Tony Awards for his work on the show, for best direction and best choreography.

He followed this high-octane production with *Carnival!*, a musical version of the movie *Lili*, in which a young man and woman conduct their romance speaking through his puppets. The delicate tale required something quite different than *Birdie*, and Champion created a production and dances that felt both European and intimate, particularly after he extended the stage into the house, helping to lay foundations for what is generally considered today to be an "environmental staging."

In 1964, Champion took on yet another sort of musical with *Hello, Dolly!*, and his eye for elegance, acrobatics, and wit combined perfectly for this musical set in the nineteenth century. Champion delivered high-leaping waiters for the show's title song; an elegant promenade that became a spectacle—replete with steam train—in "Put on Your Sunday Clothes"; and even a gently humorous lesson for two young men looking for love in "Dancing." The musical, of course, became a triumph for star Carol Channing. It also was a new high point for Champion. "[He] has even stopped this show no less than four or five times with his choreographic pyrotechnics," reported George Oppenheimer in his January 17, 1964, *Newsday* review.

Champion continued to bring his unique sense of style to Broadway musicals for another sixteen years, shifting easily from the two-character *I Do! I Do!* (1966) to the rousingly nostalgic *Irene* (1973) and the comically charged *Mack & Mabel* (1974). And then, after a pair of disappointing outings, *Rockabye Hamlet* (1976) and *A Broadway Musical* (1978), Champion reached another height in his stagecraft with *42nd Street*, an opulent theatrical reimagining of the classic Busby Berkeley movie. From an electrifying tap dance opening to a glamorous costume parade awash in color to his whimsical homage to the filmmaker's style in "Shuffle Off to Buffalo," Champion created what Frank Rich described in his August 26, 1980, *Times* review as a "perfect monument to his glorious career." Rich's eulogistic tone was intentional; Champion had passed away the previous morning, leaving behind the production that, as Rich noted, "features his best choreography."

CAROL CHANNING

(January 31, 1921–January 15, 2019)
Performer

Channing created not one but two iconic roles in musical theatre, and for many, the image of her in a beaded scarlet dress in Hello, Dolly! *is the very symbol of the form.*

This Seattle native and future star of the stage demonstrated her ability to win audiences' hearts while she was still in grade school. When she was campaigning to be fourth-grade class secretary, her campaign speech consisted of impressions of her teachers and principal. Channing used other similar sorts of theatrics in high school, and when it came time to attend college, she chose Bennington in Vermont for its theatre and dance programs.

Channing began making inroads in the New York scene while she was still studying. In 1941, she was cast for a three-performance presentation of Marc Blitzstein's *No for an Answer*. In it she delivered "Fraught," a sort of parody of Cole Porter's "I've Got You under My Skin," in which she delicately cooed of having someone "under my nails, between my teeth." At the end of the year, Channing got her first Broadway credit, serving as Eve Arden's understudy in Porter's *Let's Face It*.

Even as she was engaged for the musical comedy, she began appearing at Barney Josephson's renowned Café Society downtown, where she satirized other singers, ranging from Ethel Merman to Ethel Waters. In reviewing her for the *New York Herald Tribune* on July 11, 1942, Robert W. Dana recognized the limitations of her act and also lauded her: "Her talent could be worked into something great with the right attention."

Other nightclub engagements (and a role in a short-lived Broadway play) came her way during the next few years, and then in 1948, she was cast in the revue *Lend an Ear*, one of Gower Champion's early successes on the Great White Way. Channing appeared in a variety of roles in the show, and the *Herald Tribune*'s Howard

Barnes called her work "triumphant" in his December 17 review. Barnes's peers agreed, and as *Variety* conducted its annual poll of critics about the bests of the year, Channing's performance placed second in the category of Best Performance by an Actress in a Supporting Part. (The winner was Mildred Dunnock for her turn as Linda Loman in Arthur Miller's classic *Death of a Salesman*.)

Channing's breakout performance in *Lend an Ear* led to her first role in a book musical on Broadway: the 1920s flapper with an eye for diamonds, Lorelei Lee, in *Gentlemen Prefer Blondes*. In this show by composer Jule Styne, lyricist Leo Robin, and book writers Joseph Fields and Anita Loos, she delivered a star-making turn. On December 9, 1949, the day after the production opened, Brooks Atkinson wrote in the *New York Times*, "Let's call her portrait of the aureate Lee the most fabulous comic creation of this dreary period in history." The *Herald Tribune*'s Barnes was equally effusive, noting, "She is hilarious, even when she is only walking stiltedly across the stage." Bert McCord, theatre columnist for the paper, reminded readers of her initial success in the role as he reported on the show's closing nearly two years later. In the September 9, 1951, edition of the paper, he recalled that she was "hailed as the first authentic new star to hit Broadway in more than a decade."

Both the character—and one of her songs, "Diamonds Are a Girl's Best Friend"—became signatures for Channing for the balance of her career, and after the show played its last Broadway performance, she toured the country with it. In the process she also developed an enduring affinity for playing for audiences well outside of New York.

Channing's next Broadway gig came in 1954 when she stepped into the role of Ruth Sherwood, replacing Rosalind Russell, in the musical *Wonderful Town*. Critics and audiences were once again delighted by her work, and after the production shuttered on Broadway, she was back on the road.

The tuners that came her way for the next five years, including *The Vamp* (1955) and *Show Girl* (1961), were not successes, but regardless of the way in which the pieces themselves were reviewed, critics and audiences found themselves cheering for Channing. During this same period, Channing's national profile grew, thanks to frequent television appearances and engagements at high-profile nightclubs, including the Tropicana in Las Vegas.

Two years after the brief *Show Girl* run, Channing was working once again with Champion, who cast her as Dolly Gallagher Levi in Jerry Herman and Michael Stewart's musicalization of Thornton Wilder's *The Matchmaker*. History repeated itself with *Hello, Dolly!* as Channing wowed critics and originated a role that would be associated with her for the rest of her life.

The morning after *Dolly!* opened on January 16, 1964, Howard Taubman extolled her "shrewdly mischievous performance" and described her appearance in the show's title number—which has since become an iconic image—as being that of a "gorgeous animated kewpie doll." In the January 22 edition of *Variety*, reviewer "Hobe." told readers of how the show benefited from the "spectacular Channing presence." She played the role on Broadway for more than two years and then on the West Coast. She returned to Broadway as Dolly two more times, in 1978 and again in 1996.

Subsequent to the original *Dolly!* run, Channing appeared opposite Julie Andrews in the movie *Thoroughly Modern Millie* (1967) and returned to Broadway twice, in Abe Burrows's play *Four on a Garden* (1970) and in *Lorelei* (1974), a revised version of *Blondes*. Among her other theatrical credits is a revue of Herman's songs, *Jerry's Girls*, which toured in 1984.

During the 1980s, 1990s, and beyond, Channing lent her unique voice to a variety of animated television series and features and also played a recurring role on the television series *The Love Boat*. Another notable appearance for the star came in 2004, when she performed a rap with LL Cool J on the national broadcast of the Tony Awards.

GEORGE M. COHAN

(July 3, 1878–November 5, 1942)
Songwriter / Director / Producer / Performer

Cohan put the American *in musical comedy, and his often flag-waving work also began to shape audiences' expectations for musicals having cohesive plotlines.*

George Michael Cohan, a multitalented man of the theatre, liked to claim that he had been born on the Fourth of July, making him a de facto "Yankee Doodle Boy." In fact, he was born to entertainer parents in Providence, Rhode Island, just one day shy of the national holiday. His slight deception regarding his birth seems, at this juncture, unnecessary, because his life, career, and works—embedded in the country's cultural consciousness thanks to the Hollywood biopic starring James Cagney, *Yankee Doodle Dandy*—all bear hallmarks of natural, exuberant patriotism.

Cohan's early life, as well as that of his older sister, Josephine, was spent touring the country with his vaudevillian parents. Before he was a teenager, he was performing alongside them and writing material, including some songs, for the act. By the time he was in his midteens, the group came to be known as the Four Cohans, and the song-and-dance family delighted and charmed audiences around the country. A review of the group in the *Cincinnati Enquirer* on March 24, 1895, described them as the "best high class comedy and sketch artists on the road," and advertisements in Boston for the group a year later promised that audiences would be treated to "Georgie Cohan's great Comedy Dancing."

In 1901, the vaudevillian family made its Broadway bow in *The Governor's Son*, a musical farce for which the youngest Cohan had provided the book, music, and lyrics. The show, with a plot about the entanglements of a pair of married couples and featuring several unrelated acts, such as an imitator of German comedians, was deemed "not worth considering" by an uncredited reviewer in the *New York Times* on February 26, 1901, but even so, the writer admitted that several of the numbers Cohan had penned, including "Oh, Mr. Moon" and "The Story of the Wedding March," had landed well with theatregoers.

Two years later, Cohan and his family, after touring with *Son*, were back in New York with *Running for Office*, a show that prompted the *New York Times*' critic to wonder in an April 28, 1903, review why it had taken the Four Cohans "so long to arrive." Cohan added direction to his triple-threat writing credits for this show about a widow and widower in Vermont who have married and not admitted to having adult children, unaware that their offspring have met and themselves gotten married. Cohan spiced his main plot with topical subplots galore, including one about a political campaign and one about a young man bent on selling a beer bottle patent. He also starred ("[He] makes the most of the fun," said the *Times'* reviewer), and while Cohan's far-flung story line might be ungainly by today's standards, it was laying the groundwork for what has become known as the book musical.

His success with *Office* led to other opportunities in short order. Notably, producer Sam H. Harris engaged him to write a musical that would play at the just-opened Liberty Theater on Forty-Second Street. The result was *Little Johnny Jones*, a tuner about an American jockey in England who overcomes a multitude of romantic hurdles to reach his happy ending. With action that spanned both sides of the Atlantic and both coasts of North America, the musical confounded some critics, but it clicked with audiences because of its populist nature; Cohan's portrayal of its spunky hero; and its score, which contained numbers that would become two of the performer-writer's signature songs: "Give My Regards to Broadway" and "Yankee Doodle Boy."

Once again Cohan strove to entertain and hone his craft, and his efforts in the latter regard were recognized in the December 3, 1904, edition of *Billboard*, where the show was extolled as being an "innovation in musical production. It is almost melodramatic, interspersed with the quickest action."

Little Johnny Jones returned to Broadway twice in 1905, and Cohan followed it with *Forty-Five Minutes from Broadway* in January 1906, a play with yet two more songs destined to become standards: the title number and "Mary Is a Grand Old Name." One month later, Cohan had a new musical bow, *George Washington Jr.*, and for this show, where he once again set an American hero against British adversaries, Cohan provided a novel beginning: It started with a patriotic display rather with the usual bevy of chorus girls. Cohan was continuing to innovate even as he entertained, and his efforts to create cohesive musical comedy spurred the reviewer in the February 13, 1906, edition of the *New York Tribune* to remark, "The story is strictly adhered to (this is meant for a merit)."

For the next twenty years or so, the arrival of a new Cohan play or musical or revue (including one penned with Irving Berlin) became not just an annual occurrence on Broadway but sometimes a biannual one. Some were hits, some were misses, but throughout it all, Cohan's combination of patriotism and optimism remained a staple. The qualities may be best exemplified in one song that he penned, not for the stage, but for the country at large, "Over There," which he wrote as America entered the fray of World War I.

Eventually, as Cohan hit his fifties in the 1930s, his output as a writer waned, but he remained a staple on Broadway and even appeared in shows from other writers. Two of his most notable performances in this regard came in *Ah, Wilderness!*, Eugene O'Neill's sepia-toned revisitation to his summers as a young man, and *I'd Rather Be Right*, in which he played an unnamed US president not unlike Franklin Delano Roosevelt, who would ultimately award Cohan with Congressional Medal of Honor for the patriotism of his work.

Cohan received this tribute just one year before he died. In a November 6, 1942, *New York Times* obituary, he was hailed, as he might have wanted, as the "Yankee Doodle Dandy of the American stage." In 1959, spurred by admiration from such colleagues as Oscar Hammerstein II, a statue of Cohan was erected in Times Square as a tribute to his work and legacy.

CY COLEMAN
(June 14, 1929–November 18, 2004)
Composer

Always mercurial, Coleman continually surprised audiences with scores musically tailored to their stories while simultaneously bringing a pop music sensibility both to his writing and the promotion of his work.

Coleman, born Seymour Kaufman in the Bronx, showed a talent for piano before he was old enough to attend grade school. Soon he was taking part in and winning New York City competitions, resulting in appearances at such places as Town Hall. During his youth he was groomed to be a classical pianist and conductor by such artists as Adele Marcus, Constance Tallarico, and Arved Kurtz.

He rebelled against his classical training as a teenager and turned to jazz, forming a trio, and, with his newly adopted name of Cy Coleman, proved to be a phenomenal success with audiences both in Manhattan and nationwide, thanks to radio broadcasts of his nightclub performances and regular appearances on such early television programs as *Date in Manhattan* and *The Kate Smith Show*.

Music publisher Jack Robbins recognized Coleman's gifts at the keyboard and for composing and believed the young man was a natural successor to George Gershwin. After commissioning a set of preludes to be written in the style of Gershwin, Robbins paired Coleman with lyricist Joseph A. McCarthy Jr. The Coleman–McCarthy partnership resulted in such pop hits as "Why Try to Change Me Now?" and "I'm Gonna Laugh You Right out of My Life." With this lyricist, Coleman also got his first Broadway credit as a composer, contributing "Tin Pan Alley" to the 1953 revue *John Murray Anderson's Almanac*.

In the mid-1950s, Coleman joined forces with another lyricist, Carolyn Leigh, then riding high on the success of the songs she and Mark "Moose" Charlap penned for the musical *Peter Pan*, which starred Mary Martin. Coleman and Leigh quickly found success in the pop music world with such tunes as "Witchcraft" and "The Best Is Yet to Come."

At the same time, they had an eye on Broadway, and after several false starts, they were engaged to write the score for the 1960 musical *Wildcat*, which brought television star Lucille Ball to the Main Stem. The score boasted one breakout hit, "Hey! Look Me Over," an anthemic march that demonstrated Coleman's instinct for melody and Leigh's gift for sly wordplay. In short order they were at work on their next musical, *Little Me* (1962). Once again this team—who had started off at the Brill Building writing for the pop world—penned two tunes that stood on their own outside of the show: "Real Live Girl" and "I've Got Your Number."

The Coleman–Leigh collaboration was, almost from the outset, tumultuous, and the composer opted to shift to working with another lyricist—Dorothy Fields—for his next musical, *Sweet Charity* (1965). For this show about a dance hall hostess, Coleman wrote a distinctly modern score that Fields ably outfitted with tart, witty lyrics. Fields (Coleman's senior by more than twenty years) passed away in 1974, just after their second musical together, *Seesaw*, had opened.

From this point forward, Coleman worked with a variety of lyricists, and with each project he used his classical training to adapt his musical style to fit it. As a result, with Michael Stewart as lyricist, he penned the pop-infused 1976 musical *I Love My Wife*, which included everything from a country-western number to a soft pop ballad, and *Barnum* (1980), where songs drew from musical Americana.

With both of these shows, Coleman also continued to promote his work as having popular appeal in an era when Broadway music was becoming marginalized on turntables and on the air. Both the title song for *Wife* and "The Colors of My Life" from *Barnum* were released as singles, performed by artists Frank Sinatra and Perry Como, respectively.

Between these two shows was *On the Twentieth Century*, written with Betty Comden and Adolph Green. For this tuner Coleman borrowed from operetta traditions to underscore the oversized personalities of the central characters. It was the show that won Coleman his first Tony Award. Another collaboration with Comden and Green, along with book writer Peter Stone, *The Will Rogers Follies* (1991), also earned each of the songwriters a Tony. In this latter musical, Coleman evoked the sounds of the *Ziegfeld Follies* era in his score.

Coleman also won a Tony in 1990 for the score he and lyricist David Zippel wrote for *City of Angels*. This noir musical, with a book by Larry Gelbart, showed Coleman as a composer in yet another light. It's a dark and distinctly jazz score.

Coleman's final outing on Broadway came in 1997; it was *The Life*, which examines the gritty side of sex workers in Times Square in the 1970s and early 1980s. For this Coleman worked in a rhythm-and-blues-infused vein, and though his contribution was widely praised, *The Life* had just a brief run.

After this Coleman continued to develop new musicals, among them *Grace*, a bio-tuner about film star Grace Kelly that boasted a largely symphonic-sounding score (with Dutch lyrics) and debuted in Amsterdam in 2002. Other projects during the late 1990s and early 2000s were *Exactly like You*—a reworking of his 1989 Broadway flop *Welcome to the Club*—that played off-Broadway and regionally, and *Like Jazz*, which, featuring lyrics by Marilyn and Alan Bergman, had begun as a song cycle about the history of jazz. This latter piece, tailored for the theatre with a book by Gelbart, premiered at the Mark Taper Forum in Los Angeles in 2003.

Coleman passed away in 2004. At the time of his death, he was at work on several projects, including an English-language version of *Grace*, which was to have lyrics by the Bergmans and a book by A. R. Gurney; *Napoleon*, an examination of the love affair between Bonaparte and Josephine that reunited Coleman with Zippel and Gelbart; and *Pamela's First Musical*, with lyrics by Zippel and a book by Wendy Wasserstein. This last title afforded Coleman a posthumous premiere in 2018 when it was produced by Two River Theatre in Red Bank, New Jersey. Reviewing the production (which featured new material from Christopher Durang) on September 28, NJArts.com's Jay Lustig remarked that there was "a lot of talent behind" *Pamela's*, adding, "If I had to pick an MVP, it would be the late Coleman." The melodies, Lustig wrote, were "totally appropriate for a musical that's so enamored with Broadway's past, while still hinting . . . that the Great White Way has a bright future."

BETTY COMDEN AND ADOLPH GREEN

(May 3, 1917–November 23, 2006) / (December 2, 1914–October 23, 2002)
Lyricists / Book Writers / Performers

Comden and Green injected a healthy dose of satire and delirious wit into musical comedy while never allowing it to overwhelm genuine emotion and also revealed ways that sketch comedy could inform the book musical.

The theatre's longest-running team (neither worked with another collaborator), Comden and Green started their lives in two different boroughs of New York City, but as they grew up, they each discovered a passion for the theatre and a love of wordplay.

Green was born in the Bronx and started performing in plays while still in grade school. For Comden, who was born Basya Cohen in Brooklyn, play-acting began at home and then continued once she was attending school. The pair's similarities in childhood extended beyond this to their avid theatre- and moviegoing, and in adulthood both drew on their extensive knowledge of those forms to fuel their writing.

Comden and Green took different paths toward lives in the theatre after their high school graduations. She attended New York University, studying drama, and he toiled at a variety of day jobs while simultaneously attempting to get a foothold in the profession. The two casually met during this period, but it would take some time before they began to collaborate.

The Comden and Green partnership actually came about thanks to another aspiring theatre artist, Judy Tuvim (who, after a name change, would become the award-winning actress Judy Holliday). Green and Tuvim met in 1938 at an adult summer camp where she was a vacationer and he was appearing as a performer. Later that year she learned that Max Gordon, who had established the downtown nightspot the Village Vanguard, was looking for entertainers. She thought of Green and suggested they might put together some sort of act. He, in turn, called another performer he knew, Alvin Hammer, as well as Comden, who recruited one of her NYU classmates, John Frank. Together, these five formed a sketch-comedy group called the Revuers and almost immediately enjoyed success with both the press and New York's cognoscenti.

Their work with the Revuers satisfied Comden's and Green's urges to perform, and at the same time, it required them to use their love of language and wordplay in a way they had never anticipated, writing scenes and lyrics with their fellow performers.

From 1939 to 1943, the Revuers were fixtures in New York's nightclub world. At some performances they were accompanied by none other than Leonard Bernstein, whom Green had met at a Massachusetts summer camp the year before he met Tuvim. It was Bernstein who helped propel Comden and Green to their Broadway bows when he suggested in 1944 that they join him and Jerome Robbins in creating a musical that was inspired by Robbins and Bernstein's hit ballet *Fancy Free*. The project became the musical *On the Town*, and as they worked, they wanted to create a piece in which music, book, lyrics, and dance were seamlessly integrated.

They met their goal and at the same time brought their unique voices to the musical theatre. *On the Town* viewed its characters and setting through rose-colored glasses while also satirically winking at them. It was a new sort of musical comedy that critics found to be groundbreaking. In his December 29, 1944, *New York Times* review, Lewis Nichols proclaimed this musical about three sailors with just twenty-four hours shore leave in New York to be the "freshest and most engaging show since the golden day of 'Oklahoma!' Everything about it is right."

Because Comden and Green still had their sights set on performing, they wrote two roles for themselves into *On the Town*, and while their work as actors was greeted enthusiastically, it was their writing that propelled their careers. Almost exactly one year after *On the Town* opened, their second musical, *Billion Dollar Baby*, debuted on Broadway. With this darkly sardonic show about a gold digger clawing her way to a wealthy husband during the heyday of the 1920s, Comden and Green demonstrated even more fully than they had in their first tuner their ability to craft wry musical comedy. Their heroine laid the groundwork for two now-classic musicals about the period: *Gentlemen Prefer Blondes* and *Chicago*.

Hollywood beckoned shortly after the debut of *Baby*, and for the balance of the 1940s and most of the 1950s, Comden and Green split their time between the two coasts. For the screen they penned the scripts for such movies as *Singin' in the Rain*, *The Band Wagon*, and the screen version of *On the Town*, all of which are part of the Library of Congress's National Film Registry.

During this period their writing for the stage included a variety of projects. They provided sketches and lyrics (for songs by Jule Styne) for the revue *Two on the Aisle* in 1951. In it they poked fun at modern parenting woes and science-fiction serials, and the result was, according to the *Times'* Brooks Atkinson on July 20, the "pithiest material any revue has had in these parts in a long time."

Comden and Green reunited with composer Bernstein for their next show, *Wonderful Town* (1953). For this musical about two midwestern sisters' adventures in Greenwich Village in the 1930s, their linguistic playfulness was complemented by heartfelt sentiment. Walter Kerr, in his *New York Herald Tribune* review on February 26, praised their "eminently suitable lyrics" and made sure to mention their other contribution: "They have further added to the hilarity with a group of short sketches parodying the literary style [of one of the sisters]." The show earned them their first Tony Award.

They took their whimsicality to new heights when Mary Martin soared through *Peter Pan* in 1954. Among their and composer Styne's last-minute contributions to this classic are "Neverland," "Mysterious Lady," and the Gilbert and Sullivan–inspired "Hook's Waltz."

In 1956, Comden and Green returned to writing both the book and lyrics for an original musical, working once again with composer Styne. The show was *Bells Are Ringing*, penned for their old friend Judy Holliday. In this new musical, as they had with *On the Town*, they portrayed New York as a sort of fairy-tale place where strangers' lives coincidentally intersect as romance blossoms between an answering-phone operator and a down-on-his-luck playwright. Their ability to craft deeply felt lyrics was evident in the show's hit songs "Just in Time" and "The Party's Over," while their deftness with loopy, satiric comedy shone in "Drop That Name."

After crafting lyrics for songs in *Say, Darling*, a play with music, they returned to performing in 1958 with *A Party with Betty Comden and Adolph Green*. This retrospective of their revue, theatre, and film material prompted the *Daily Mirror's* Robert Coleman to write on January 7, 1959, "They know what to do with smart material, and they are lucky enough to have themselves as their own scripters."

As the 1960s dawned, they brought a trio of shows to the stage, and each brimmed with their signature humor and wry worldview. The first, *Do Re Mi* (1961), featured their lyrics and clicked with critics as it told a tale of a second-rate con who dreams up a get-rich-quick scheme involving the jukebox business. The other two, *Subways Are for Sleeping* (1962) and *Fade Out–Fade In* (1964), were troubled by offstage issues, as well as ones involving the material itself.

As the 1960s turned into the 1970s, Comden and Green provided lyrics for *Hallelujah, Baby!*, an ambitious original musical by Arthur Laurents about a woman's experiences with racial inequality over the course of six decades. Sly humor ran through all of their contributions to this show, which earned Tonys in the best musical and best composer and lyricist categories. As book writers they started the new decade with *Applause*, a musical version of *All about Eve*. Starring Lauren Bacall as a middle-aged actress who is duped by a young woman, the show gave the team some of their best notices in years, as well as another Tony. "It has a welcome lovely cynicism about show business," wrote Clive Barnes in his March 31 *Times* review. He added that the team had written a "musical play that is bright, witty, direct and nicely punchy."

They served as lyricists, and later directors, for *Lorelei* in 1973, a revision to *Gentlemen Prefer Blondes*, and then they joined forces with composer Cy Coleman. After writing individual songs with him for an off-Broadway revue, they penned book and lyrics for *On the Twentieth Century* (1978). They matched Coleman's grandiose melodies with witty, barbed lyrics, and the musical farce about events on a luxury train in the 1930s earned them all Tony Awards. Less happy was their foray—along with composer Larry Grossman—into more serious fare with *A Doll's Life* in 1982, which imagined the events that unfolded after the end of Henrik Ibsen's drama *A Doll's House*.

When they reunited with Coleman in 1991 for *The Will Rogers Follies*, they discovered they had a popular hit on their hands. Directed and choreographed by Tommy Tune, the show unfolded as if Florenz Ziegfeld Jr. were presenting a spectacular about the famed humorist. John Beaufort, in his May 16 *Christian Science Monitor* review, called their contributions to the extravaganza as "amusingly attuned to the now and the then." The songwriting team earned both a Tony and Grammy for their efforts.

For the balance of their careers, Comden and Green continued to look for one more show to write, but it never materialized. Luckily they had always wanted to be performers, and they continued their appearances in New York and beyond into the twenty-first century.

D

AGNES DE MILLE

(September 18, 1905–October 7, 1993)
Choreographer / Director

This choreographer built on terpsichorean strides made by George Balanchine in the 1930s, using dance as a way of both furthering narrative and revealing the psychology of the characters within specific musicals.

This creator of landmark dances for musicals ranging from the plains-set *Oklahoma!* to Scotland-environed *Brigadoon* grew up in a world steeped in the arts. Her father, William C. deMille, was a playwright and screenwriter, and her uncle was film director Cecil B. DeMille. Further, she had her own world of fantasy. She often created dances for herself in the woods outside the upstate New York summer colony where her family vacationed.

As a girl de Mille was also a frequent attendee of dance and took some dance classes, but when it came time for her to attend college, she majored in English at the University of California, Los Angeles. Subsequent to her graduation, she moved to New York, and in 1928, she made her choreographic debut.

As she was carving out a niche for herself in New York dance circles, she also got her first major theatrical choreographic assignment. She created the dances for a major revival of *The Black Crook* presented at the Lyric Theater in Hoboken, New Jersey, in 1929. The *New York Times'* theatre critic Brooks Atkinson, in an April 7 column, widely trounced the production and the rowdy audiences who attended it. But he couldn't dismiss de Mille's work on this sixty-year-old relic, writing, "The dancing as a whole is no quaint conceit. It is lovely." The paper's dance critic, John Martin, had even more profuse praise in a March 17 story: "[She] has done a superb job with the 'grand' ballets," he wrote, adding that they contained both the "finish of an old hand and the spontaneity of a novice."

For the next few years, her choreography and dancing garnered increasingly generous encomiums, and then in 1932, she received her first Broadway assignment, devising the dances for the Howard Dietz and Arthur Schwartz revue *Flying Colors*. Poor notices during the production's tryout in Philadelphia, however, resulted in her being replaced. But a year later, de Mille was in London and choreographing Cole Porter's *Nymph Errant*, starring Gertrude Lawrence.

After she returned to the United States and for the remainder of the decade, she divided her time between New York and Hollywood. On the West Coast, she was to have appeared as a dancer in her uncle's movie *Cleopatra*, but creative differences resulted in her leaving the project, and the scenes that she had filmed were deleted from the film's final cut. Her work as a choreographer did, however, make it into the 1935 movie version of Shakespeare's *Romeo and Juliet*, starring Leslie Howard and Norma Shearer.

A Broadway musical beckoned again in 1939 with the short-lived *Swingin' the Dream*, an all-black, jazz-infused rendering of another of the Bard's plays, *A Midsummer Night's Dream*, which featured, among others, Louis Armstrong and Maxine Sullivan. De Mille applied herself, as the 1940s began, primarily to choreographing for various groups, including Ballet Theater (later American Ballet Theatre); the modern dance ensemble Ballets Jooss; and American Actors' Company, where she created and danced in *American Legend*, a combination of text, song, and dance based on American folklore that premiered in 1941.

De Mille's penchant for using the iconography of the American West in her work led to her creation of her first popular breakthrough the following year: *Rodeo* for the Ballet Russes. This piece, described by the *Times'* Martin as being a "heartwarming piece, full of flavor" in an October 17, 1942, review, led to an invitation from the Theatre Guild asking her to devise dances for a new Rodgers and Hammerstein musical, a show that would ultimately be known as *Oklahoma!*

It was a turning point for both de Mille and the American musical. With her work on the production, she took the advances that George Balanchine had made in integrating dance into the fabric of a show to a new level, particularly with "Laurey Makes Up Her Mind." This ballet took theatregoers into the heroine's subconscious, revealing her hidden desires and fears. Howard Barnes described her overall work in his April 1, 1943, *New York Herald Tribune* review: "[She] has worked small miracles in devising original dances to fit the story and the tunes." Ten days later in the *Times*, Lewis Nichols labeled the ballet "completely perfect."

She would remain an almost-continual presence on Broadway until 1969, and during these decades, her work ranged from *One Touch of Venus* (also 1943), where she imagined a collision of suburbia and mythic splendor for her heroine; to *The Girl in Pink Tights* (1954), in which she revisited *The Black Crook* for a show that investigated its origins; to *Juno* (1959), in which the *Times'* Brooks Atkinson, in a March 10 review, found that her "festive ballets admirably capture the decorum of Irish folk dancing."

During this time, too, de Mille collaborated on the movie version of *Oklahoma!* Released in 1955, the movie brought her work vividly to life on the big screen, thanks to what was billed as the "Todd AO, Eastman Color and Orthosonic Sound" process, and in an August 21, 1955, *Los Angeles Times* review, Philip K. Scheuer wrote, "The film really galvanizes in the first half (there is an intermission) with Miss de Mille's 'Out of My Dreams.'" The critic particularly enthused about how the dance and the cinematography combined to create the "most sensational use of the new medium."

De Mille never ceased creating pieces in the dance world and eventually established her own company, the Heritage Dance Theater, which performed from 1973 to 1975. During this time, too, she finished a series of acclaimed memoirs that she had started writing during the 1950s. The books, such as *Dance to the Piper* (1952) and *Where the Wings Grow* (1978), are erudite explorations of both her life and work.

Her last Broadway outing came in 1980 when she oversaw the re-creation of her work in a revival of *Brigadoon*. Two months after that production's opening, she received a Kennedy Center Honor, alongside, among others, composer-conductor Leonard Bernstein. In 1986, de Mille received the highest honor that can be bestowed on an artist when she was awarded the National Medal of Arts.

De Mille died in 1993, and Anna Kisselgoff's October 17 *New York Times* appreciation of the choreographer recalled one of her credos about dance and theatre. They were, de Mille had said, a "statement that has to be witnessed and shared."

ALFRED DRAKE

(October 7, 1914–July 25, 1992)
Performer

Drake's combination of vibrant singing and heartfelt acting in the original productions of Oklahoma!; Kiss Me, Kate; *and* Kismet *set standards for performance in musical theatre.*

This charismatic baritone who brought humor and sex appeal to two of the biggest hits of the 1940s was born Alfred Capurro to Italian immigrant parents. He grew up primarily in Brooklyn, and from his youngest days, Drake was singing, thanks to his mother. She sang at her church and encouraged both him and his brother (who would perform professionally in adulthood as Arthur Kent) to be part of the choir there.

After Drake enrolled at Brooklyn College, he joined the school's glee club and also began auditioning for work. One of his earliest jobs was for a radio program that debuted in January 1935 and was sponsored by Lifesavers candy. The biweekly serial centered on a wealthy heiress rescued by a mysterious stranger. Drake was on hand to sing this lifesaver's part. A few months later, Drake was cast in the chorus for repertory productions of four Gilbert and Sullivan operettas being produced by the Civic Light Opera Company at Broadway's Adelphi Theatre. More classical work followed in the summer of 1936 when he joined the Steel Pier Opera Company in Atlantic City, performing featured roles in both Beethoven's *Fidelio* and Bach's *Phoebus and Pan*.

That fall, Drake was back on Broadway (and once again in the ensemble) in *White Horse Inn*, an operetta spectacle that concerns the romantic doings of the headwaiter at the titular establishment, its proprietress, an American attorney, and the heiress of a bathing suit mogul. Shortly after the production opened, Drake assumed duties as understudy to the show's male star, William Gaxton, and when a severe flu outbreak hit New York in early 1937, Drake had the opportunity to go on as the male lead. His subbing for the *White Horse Inn* star led directly to his next show, Richard Rodgers and Lorenz Hart's musical *Babes in Arms*. While Drake played only two small roles in the show, it established a relationship with composer Rodgers, whose work would become central to Drake's career.

Before returning to Rodgers's work, Drake amassed a variety of Broadway credits, including two John Murray Anderson revues; *The Two Bouquets* (1938), a "Victorian operetta" that had a score comprising songs by Gounod and Offenbach, among others, and also featured Patricia Morison; and *The Straw Hat Revue*. In reviewing this last show, Eugene Burr, in the October 14, 1939, edition of *Billboard*, described Drake as a "singer who once again proves he is one of the pleasantest performers in town."

Drake then took roles in several nonmusicals, including Shakespeare's *As You Like It*. Then, in 1942, Rodgers approached him about singing for backers' auditions for a new show. It was then titled *Away We Go!* and Rodgers had written it with Oscar Hammerstein II. Drake's work at these presentations prompted Rodgers to offer Drake the lead role, Curly, in the musical that became *Oklahoma!* On April 1, 1943, Lewis Nichols described Drake and his costar, Joan Roberts, playing Laurey: "[They] are fresh and engaging; they have clear voices and the thought that audiences might also like to hear Mr. Hammerstein's poetry." Not only had the book musical arrived, but so, too, had the sort of performer who would be necessary to both sing and act in it.

Following his success in *Oklahoma!* Drake made a single film in Hollywood and then was back in New York. His affinity for experimental work, which had included the Rodgers and Hammerstein show, became more pronounced with his appearances in a compendium of American songwriting, *Sing Out, Sweet Land!* (1944); *Beggar's Holiday* (1946), an interracial reimagining of *The Beggar's Opera*; and the first Broadway production of Marc Blitzstein's historic *The Cradle Will Rock* (1947).

Drake's flair with Shakespearean verse and his rich voice were perfectly suited for Cole Porter's *Kiss Me, Kate*. In this 1949 tuner, Drake played Fred Graham, an actor-director working to bring a production of Shakespeare's *The Taming of the Shrew* to the stage. The musical also required Drake to play the Bard's leading role, Petruchio. In reviewing the show for the *Times* on December 31, 1948, Brooks Atkinson wrote, "Mr. Drake's pleasant style of acting and unaffected singing are the heart of the show." The critic added, "[He] has become about the most valuable man in his field."

Even with this second major success as a performer, Drake was eager to stretch, and he turned to directing while also looking for a play to star in, even though offers were plentiful for musical work. One finally materialized in 1952 in the form of Ugo Betti's morality drama *The Gambler*. Drake, working with Edward Eager, adapted the Italian play, and though Drake's performance received some warm notices, critics dismissed the work, which ran only twenty-four performances.

The following year Drake was once again appearing in musicals. He stepped into *The King and I*, substituting while the show's original star, Yul Brynner, made a film. After this Drake took on the leading role in *Kismet*. This musical, which uses melodies by Russian composer Alexander Borodin and is set in Baghdad, gave Drake another dashing, witty role to play, and, as in *Oklahoma!* and *Kate*, he garnered raves. He also won a Tony Award for a performance that the *Times'* Atkinson, in a December 1, 1953, review, called "superb." The critic labeled Drake an "immensely resourceful actor" and said he delivered the music "like a thoroughbred with one of the best voices in the theater."

From this point forward, Drake continued to perform on Broadway and nationally, but he never attained the sort of success he had during the 1940s and early 1950s. Even so there were minor triumphs for him, such as *Kean* (1961), a musical about nineteenth-century Shakespearean actor Edmund Kean, and *Hamlet* (1964), in which he played Claudius opposite Richard Burton in the title role.

Drake appeared in one last musical on Broadway, *Gigi*, in 1973, and after starring in a revival of Thornton Wilder's *The Skin of Our Teeth* two years later, he concentrated on teaching, directing, and appearances outside of New York. In 1990, two years before his death, he received the special Tony honor for excellence in theatre award.

E

WILLIAM AND JEAN ECKART

(October 21, 1920–January 24, 2000) / (August 18, 1921–September 6, 1993)
Scenic, Costume, Lighting Designers

The Eckarts brought a deft sense of the whimsical to musicals during Broadway's Golden Age and, with their innovations for automating scene changes, revolutionized the way musicals moved.

On March 28, 1954, in his weekly Sunday column for the *New York Herald Tribune*, Walter Kerr expanded on his review of the recently opened musical *The Golden Apple*. The off-Broadway tuner by Jerome Moross (music) and John Latouche (book and lyrics) had charmed critics. So, too, had the show's scenery, and in his assessment, Kerr wrote, "The Eckarts have made it perfectly clear . . . that an elaborate musical can be mounted inexpensively without the slightest loss in style, color or visual excitement." In particular he was taken with how "extraordinarily simple but extraordinarily captivating" their design was; crepe-paper streamers attached to a cutout lowered onto the stage made it seem, Kerr thought, that "something light and fanciful has floated in from above." This sort of inventiveness and whimsy was the hallmark of the team, who, from the 1950s to the 1960s, brought playfulness and innovation to the musical theatre.

The couple hailed from two distinctly different environments. She was born and raised in Chicago, while he came from New Iberia, a small town in Louisiana roughly 150 miles due west of New Orleans. Growing up, however, they had had one common interest—theatre—and this brought them together while they were students at Tulane University. They both enlisted in the military and also married during World War II following their graduation, and after their discharge, they each enrolled at the Yale School of Drama. With new degrees they soon began careers as scenic designers in New York.

The couple's designs for *Apple* came three years into their lives in Manhattan. It wasn't that they had been wanting for work; they had credits both on Broadway and off. It's just that the musical perfectly showcased their aesthetic, and thanks to it, they found new opportunities, beginning with the chance to create the sets, as well as their first Broadway costumes, for *Damn Yankees*.

Directed by George Abbott, the musical was a Faustian tale set in a baseball milieu, and to help set the mood for it they used multicolored baseballs on strings to create the show curtain that hung from the proscenium as audience members entered the theatre. Not only did their choice indicate the great American pastime, but it also helped to create a seductive effect as it resembled a beaded drape, one that might dangle from an entry into some exotic, sensuous locale.

Although the Eckarts witnessed their next musical project, Marc Blitzstein's *Reuben, Reuben* (1955), fold out of town, they were able to see a show that boasted their scenic, costume, and lighting designs open on Broadway in March 1956. Norman Rosten's play *Mister Johnson* not only had an overall design by the couple, but it also used one of their greatest innovations in scenic design: a raised deck built on top of the entirety of the stage floor. Under this were cables and winches that could pull set pieces into position through grooved tracks. Thanks to their concept, scenic elements could glide onstage from the wings without the assistance of stagehands or performers physically guiding them.

They went to the realm of the funny pages in their next show, a musical version of Al Capp's beloved comic strip *Li'l Abner*. For this they faced having to make their visuals match the expectations of theatregoers, who, most likely, read Capp's work on a daily basis, and whether it was a bucolic fishing hole or cramped cabin home, they succeeded. Their deftness in bringing Capp's fictional Southern town to the stage prompted John Chapman to muse in his November 17, 1956, *Daily News* review, "[They] must have been born and bred in Dogpatch."

The couple remained in a Southern vein for their next show, *Livin' the Life*, which was drawn from Mark Twain's tales. The musical underwhelmed critics, such as the *New York Herald Tribune*'s Walter Kerr, who in his April 29, 1957, review reported that "with the exception of designers William and Jean Eckart," no one involved had "come close" to capturing Twain's work. Before his review ended, he returned to the design, saying, "The shiny autumn trees and bright red-and-white churches of the Eckarts are stunning."

It was the first in a trio of short-lived stage musicals they worked on in less than twelve months, but 1957 also was the year in which the Eckarts' brand of visual magic came to television, as they designed the sets and costumes for Rodgers and Hammerstein's *Cinderella*.

In 1959, they returned to working with director Abbott, starting with a show off-Broadway that the couple both designed and coproduced, a musical version of "The Princess and the Pea" fairy tale. Written by Dean Fuller, Marshall Barer, and Jay Thompson and featuring music by Mary Rodgers and lyrics by Barer, *Once upon a Mattress* bowed at the Phoenix Theatre on May 11 and received rapturous reviews, catapulting it to Broadway. The critics' raves off-Broadway also turned Carol Burnett into a star overnight, but in his *New York Herald Tribune* review, Kerr pointed out, "Our heroine is getting some handsome help from [the] designers and co-producers." Their work, which included "beautifully cartooned battlements" and "stunningly silhouetted tournament tents," all added to the production that was, he said, "simple, sly, and full of light-hearted malice."

In the fall, the Eckarts designed another Abbott show, *Fiorello!*, the musical about New York's Mayor La Guardia that ultimately earned the Pulitzer. For this they strove to bring early-twentieth-century Manhattan back to life in both their

sets and costumes. Kerr was the most vocal in championing their contribution to
the show in a Sunday November 29 assessment. He applauded how, in rendering
La Guardia's Lower East Side office, they "have not tried to glamorize this minor
mecca to which the insolvent and the indicted come." Kerr was equally taken with
a sequence in the second act when things were dire for most of the characters.
Thanks to the Eckarts' scenic and lighting design, he said, "The sun and air that
seem to pour through a second-story window somehow wash the premises with
glory. . . . The skyline is bleak with spidery black chimneys, and still you believe
it's a beautiful day."

The husband-and-wife design team alternated between plays and musicals that
enjoyed varying degrees of success between 1960 and 1962, and then in 1963, Harold Prince, who had produced *Fiorello!*, engaged them to design scenery and lights
for *She Loves Me*, an intimate musical about pen-pal lovers in Budapest before
World War II. It marked the first time that Prince directed a Broadway show from
scratch. In reviews, the word *confection* appeared repeatedly, both when describing the show overall and with regard to the Eckarts' contributions, which were
inspired by the Art Nouveau movement. Their sets moved gracefully, thanks both
to their stage-tracking system and a trio of turntables that were sometimes reminiscent of a revolving door of a small boutique, such as the perfumery in which
the characters worked.

Following this, the Eckarts were off-Broadway designing the sets for Arthur
Kopit's *Oh Dad, Poor Dad, Mamma's Hung You in the Closet and I'm Feelin' So Sad*,
and then they returned to Broadway for a pair of big tuners, *Here's Love*, the
musicalized version of *Miracle on 34th Street*, and Stephen Sondheim and Arthur
Laurents's *Anyone Can Whistle*, an experimental tuner that had, as Howard Taubman put in his April 4, 1964, *Times* review, "beds, balconies and rocks pirouetting
across the stage."

After this and through the end of the decade, the couple provided designs for
seven more musicals, each of which required the Eckarts' unique brand of stage
magic. In the 1964 musical *Fade Out–Fade In* (which also starred Burnett), they
brought the glamour of 1930s Hollywood to life with sets that the *Daily News*'
Chapman lauded for having "ingenious, amusing tricks" in his May 27 review.
He might have been referring to the way in which the Eckarts deployed stage me-
chanics. Turntables moving in opposite directions with different scenic elements
created the effect of a cinematic dissolve without the use of projections.

For *Mame* two years later, they created sets that evoked a wide variety of locales
over the course of the 1920s to the 1940s, and nowhere were their efforts to integrate a visual style that mirrored their material more evident—so much so that
Kerr's May 25 *New York Herald Tribune* review devoted two paragraphs to their
achievements and specifically the action of one number, "Open a New Window."
He said they had "turned the process into music, letting their isolated uprights
glide away like forever-held whole notes and scooping their black silk opera-
draping upwards like an arpeggio aimed at the moon."

Their last musical on Broadway came in 1969 when they created the sets for
The Fig Leaves Are Falling, a musical by Albert Hague and Allan Sherman that attempted to put a hip spin on a suburban man's consideration of his marriage and
a potential infidelity. After nearly twenty years of superlatives, the Eckarts, along

with director Abbott, received some of the most damning notices of their careers. Clive Barnes in his January 3 *New York Times* review called the settings "nasty and so movable that it almost made me restless."

After this they designed another three Broadway plays, but they also moved on from New York, settling in Texas. For the balance of their lives, he taught design at Southern Methodist University, and she segued into a new career in the field of social work, founding the Dallas-based nonprofit the Community Psychotherapy Center.

LEHMAN ENGEL

(September 14, 1910–August 29, 1982)
Conductor / Musical Director / Composer / Educator

Engel's keen instincts about musical theatre helped to shape many of Broadway's best shows in the 1950s, and he developed the curriculum for the influential BMI Workshop that has helped to hone the writing skills of several generations of songwriters.

In the introduction to Engel's 1967 book *The American Musical Theater: A Consideration*, the *New York Times*' chief theatre critic Brooks Atkinson pays tribute to the author: "Mr. Engel knows more about the American musical theater than anyone else." Atkinson's praise of Engel is not mere hyperbole. As the book was being published, Engel was approaching his fortieth year in New York. In that time his career encompassed everything from conducting choral work to composing for modern dance to helping shepherd some of the greatest musicals of the Golden Age to Broadway.

Engel's earliest music memories were of the small orchestra that accompanied silent movies in his hometown of Jackson, Mississippi, and the piano lessons he took starting at the age of ten. After his high school graduation, he enrolled at the Cincinnati Conservatory but later transferred to the Cincinnati College of Music. With his degree from this latter school, he moved to New York in 1929 and received a scholarship to study composition at Juilliard.

During his time there, he met dancer-choreographer Martha Graham and in 1932 wrote music for her dance *Ceremonials*. His association with Graham extended well into the decade, and in 1936, he accompanied her to the White House when she performed for President and Mrs. Franklin D. Roosevelt.

Not long after Engel started working with Graham, Margarete Dessoff, founder of the noted choir that still bears her name, premiered one of his works, and the following year, Engel undertook one of his first major theatrical endeavors, conducting the American premiere of Kurt Weill and Bertolt Brecht's *Der Jasager* (*He Who Says "Yes"*), directed by Sanford Meisner. "Engel conducted with vivacity and assurance," wrote critic "H. H." in the *New York Times* on April 26, 1933.

Engel's Broadway bow came in 1934, when he wrote the incidental music for Melvyn Douglas's production of Sean O'Casey's allegorical drama *Within the*

Gates. It was the first in what became a series of similar undertakings for Engel as a composer for the next seven years. Among the other productions that featured Engel's original music were Maurice Evans's *Hamlet*; the Elizabethan comedy *The Shoemaker's Holiday*, produced by Orson Welles's Mercury Theatre; and the American premiere of T. S. Eliot's *Murder in the Cathedral*. Atkinson, in his March 29, 1936, *Times* review of this last show, said that Engel had written a "sternly prescient score that cries a swiftly phrased warning." The result, Atkinson wrote, was that Engel gave the piece an "audible architecture."

Eliot's drama was presented by one arm of the Federal Theatre Project of the Works Progress Administration (WPA), and it didn't represent the only work Engel got in the 1930s through this government-sponsored agency. He also conducted an acclaimed madrigal singers' group, which made numerous recordings, and composed music for a children's theatre piece based on the fairy tale *The Emperor's New Clothes* that played at Broadway's Adelphi Theatre.

Engel's boundless energy in the 1930s allowed him to gain two additional Broadway credits. In 1936, he served as musical director for Weill's first American-penned show, *Johnny Johnson*, and in early 1937, Engel was represented on Broadway with his own musical, another project for the WPA, *A Hero Is Born*.

Musical direction, as well as conducting and sometimes providing vocal arrangements for Broadway shows, became a primary occupation for Engel in the 1940s and 1950s. The shows he worked on ranged from Harold Rome's revue *Call Me Mister* to Gian Carlo Menotti's opera *The Consul* to *Wonderful Town*, the frothy musical comedy with an impressive score by Leonard Bernstein, Betty Comden, and Adolph Green. Sometimes collaborators, such as these three, found sage advice from Engel, who recalls in his memoir *This Bright Day* recommending cuts and changes for the score. At other times his work in the pit would even cause a critic to comment, such as John Chapman reviewing *Destry Rides Again* in the *Daily News* on April 24, 1959, who wrote, "Engel puts his spurs to rough-riding orchestra in the pit."

Engel continued working on Broadway in this capacity into the 1960s, and as he did he also began an association with Broadcast Music, Inc. (BMI), a service organization for songwriters. For BMI, via a series of workshops, he served as an educator-mentor to songwriters interested in theatre careers. Educational work had been part of Engel's career since it began, and he taught singing in the 1930s and worked at the Manhattan School of Theatre in the early 1940s.

As he began working with BMI, he drew on three decades of experience, and in the Musical Theatre Workshop, as it was called, artists met regularly to discuss the unique ways in which musicals are created. They also completed assignments developed by Engel, such as musicalizing scenes from novels or plays, and then shared their work in session for feedback. Eventually, Engel would request full musicals from the workshop members.

The workshop, which to this day carries Engel's name, became such a success that for a brief period in the 1970s, BMI expanded the initiative to Los Angeles. In the East Coast sessions, some of the songwriters who honed their craft with Engel's help included Alan Menken and Maury Yeston, and in the workshop this latter writer began work on the Tony Award–winning musical *Nine*. Another participant was lyricist Ed Kleban, who went on to pen the lyrics for *A Chorus Line*. Songwriters who came to the workshop after Engel's death in 1982 range from Jeff Marx and Robert Lopez (writer of *The Book of Mormon* and *Frozen*), who wrote *Avenue Q* together, to Michael John LaChiusa and Jeanine Tesori.

F

Fields, as both lyricist and book writer, broke barriers in two male-dominated fields. More importantly, in her lyrics, she brought a wry, protofeminist bent to the musical theatre.

This daughter of Lew Fields, the theatrical producer-performer who first achieved success as one-half of the vaudeville duo Weber and Fields, was warned off a life in the theatre by him. In fact, by some accounts, he forbade it. Nevertheless, it was a profession to which she aspired, and her knack with words and poetry eventually led to a nearly five-decade career as one of the industry's foremost lyricists and book writers.

She attended the Benjamin Franklin School for Girls, and while she was in school—and after her graduation—her poetry was both praised and published. Her first entrance into the world of songwriting came when she was in her early twenties and met composer Jimmy McHugh, who had enjoyed some success with writing partners Al Dubin and Ted Koehler. McHugh invited Fields to work with him, and soon their work was being performed at Harlem's famed Cotton Club. This led to an invitation from Lew Leslie to contribute material for a show he planned for his newly acquired nightclub. Among the tunes they penned for him was the classic "I Can't Give You Anything but Love," in which Fields first demonstrated her gift for writing a colloquial lyric accessible to the average American. The show—and their tunes—was a success, and in short order, Leslie revised the floor show as a revue for Broadway: *Blackbirds of 1928*.

After the premiere of *Blackbirds*, Fields and McHugh wrote the songs for *Hello, Daddy*. The production was a Fields family affair, starring her father and featuring a book by her brother Herbert. One of the most written-about tunes in the production was "Let's Sit and Talk about You," where Fields's knack for interweaving rhymes in both amusing and gently moving ways shines.

The Fields–McHugh team found themselves writing numbers on short notice for the 1929 edition of Florenz Ziegfeld Jr.'s *Midnight Frolic*, after which they contributed material to another Leslie revue. Immediately following these two shows, they moved to Hollywood, having signed a lucrative contract with MGM.

Film work, for the most part, consumed Fields's professional life for nearly six years, and during this period she split with McHugh because of a dispute over publishing rights, leading to collaborations with other composers, notably Jerome Kern. She and Kern first worked together on the 1935 movie version of his musical *Roberta*, and then they provided songs for *Swing Time* (1936), which included the enduring "Never Gonna Dance" and "A Fine Romance," as well as the Academy Award–winning "The Way You Look Tonight."

Fields and Kern continued their film work until 1938, and then, from 1939 to 1946, a new Broadway musical with material she had written premiered nearly once a year. In 1941, Fields started cowriting libretti with her brother Herbert. Their first joint venture *Let's Face It*, which focuses on three married women who hire soldiers to take them dancing, has songs by Cole Porter. The siblings and Porter would go on to write two more shows together: *Something for the Boys* (1943), which starred Ethel Merman, and *Mexican Hayride* (1944).

In 1946, Fields and her brother penned the book for another Merman show, *Annie Get Your Gun*. Their work was lauded for its ability to showcase both the star and the show's songwriter, Irving Berlin. At the same time, many found the book had its own virtues. Howard Barnes, in his May 17 *New York Herald Tribune* review, wrote, "The libretto is both lively and funny."

Fields's work as a lyricist resumed the following year. She joined forces with Sigmund Romberg for *Up in Central Park*, a sepia-toned look back at romance in nineteenth-century New York. Their songs included the future standard "Close as Pages in a Book," as well as "Currier and Ives," where Fields's lyric makes merry with a woman lamenting a pickup line men used.

Fields worked with composer Morton Gould on *Arms and the Girl* in 1950, and then she rejoined forces with composer Arthur Schwartz. They had written the songs for Merman in *Stars in Your Eyes* in 1939, and as the 1950s dawned, they penned tunes for another inimitable leading lady, Shirley Booth. For this actress they wrote the songs for both *A Tree Grows in Brooklyn* (1951) and *By the Beautiful Sea* (1954). In these shows, both set at the dawn of the twentieth century, Fields's unique feminist perspective shimmers; her lyrics deftly help to define each musical's heroine, both women who disregard many of the conventions of their time.

Fields had only one more Broadway production during the decade, *Redhead* (1959), but that didn't mean she was resting on her laurels. She and Burton Lane wrote several songs for the television musical *Junior Miss* (1957), and she began work on several projects that never reached fruition.

In the mid-1960s, a newcomer to Broadway, composer Cy Coleman, helped reinvigorate Fields's three-decade-long career. Together they wrote the songs for *Sweet Charity*, and in it Fields demonstrated that she could speak to a new generation of theatregoers and give voice to a then-contemporary woman desperately seeking love. Her lyrics for *Charity* range from slyly racy ("Big Spender") to satirically beatnik ("Rhythm of Life") to plaintive ("Where Am I Going?") to cleverly sardonic ("Baby, Dream Your Dream"). For some critics, such as *Newsday*'s George Oppenheimer, Fields outshone her younger collaborator. In his January 31, 1966, review, he wrote, "Maybe subsequent hearings will make me feel that the music is up to the high quality of Miss Fields' lyrics." He confirmed his instinct in a review of the show's cast album two months later, and just after that Fields received her first Tony Award nomination, specifically for her word craft in song.

Coleman and Fields collaborated on four more musicals, only one of which reached the stage: *Seesaw* (1973). Again, Fields, who had given voice to so many unconventional female characters, was the ideal fit for this show about an un-conventional woman's up-and-down romance with a recently divorced man. She and Coleman were once again Tony-nominated for their work, and it ultimately came to feature her last song, "The Party's on Me," which has a marvelously 1970s hedonistic tone. It was incorporated into the show as it prepared to tour just days before her death in 1974.

HARVEY FIERSTEIN

(June 6, 1954–)
Performer / Book Writer

*Fierstein's writing and performances have bridged a pre- and post-*Hair *sensibility in the musical theatre, and he has been a pioneer in bringing an openly gay perspective to the form.*

Before he was twenty, this artist, who has earned four Tony Awards, each in a separate category, was honing his craft as both writer and performer far from the world of Broadway. In fact, he was on Manhattan's Lower East Side, working with the legendary Andy Warhol and performing in that artist's *Pork*, presented at La MaMa ETC (Experimental Theatre Club). Fierstein's downtown work con-tinued through the rest of the 1970s, first working with the Theater of the Lost Continent, performing in an all-male production of *The Trojan Women* and writing such plays as *Cannibals Just Don't Know Better*. By 1978, he was back at La MaMa, which produced *The International Stud*, the first play in what would become his acclaimed *Torch Song Trilogy*.

Fierstein's performing had actually begun when he was just a child; this Brooklyn-born son of Eastern European immigrants sang as a soprano with a professional boys' choir. In a 1982 *Newsday* interview with Jerry Parker, Fierstein discussed his upbringing: "My father was an orphan, and we were brought up with the feeling that the family unit was everything. Something as miniscule as my being gay was not going to disrupt that." It's this sense of family that has informed all of the writer-performer's musical theatre work, which has, in turn, broken ground for how gay men are portrayed in tuners.

It was the success of *Torch Song* in 1982 that paved the way for Fierstein's first musical, an adaptation of the French film *La Cage aux Folles* (1983). The tale of a gay couple coping with the premarital woes of the young man they've raised (he's the biological son of one of the two) was called a "golden-hearted gay love story" by W. J. Weatherby in a *Guardian* feature on August 22. He also pointed out that the show's arrival on Broadway was unique at the time: "Once upon a time [it] would have run off Broadway to specialized audiences." In a *Newsday* review that day, Allan Wallach said it was a "musical celebrating a loving homosexual couple" and added that the "true heart" of the show was "located in Harvey Fierstein's book." When the Tonys were handed out, Fierstein picked up his third prize, complementing the two that he had won for *Torch Song* the previous season.

A play and film work kept him busy for a few years, but by 1988, Fierstein was back on Broadway with *Legs Diamond*, a troubled bio-tuner that had a score by Peter Allen, about the infamous 1920s gangster. The show folded in relatively short order after damning reviews, and it would take nearly fifteen years for Fierstein to return to the Main Stem. When he did, it was not as a writer but as a performer (once again in drag) and once again in a show about family: *Hairspray*.

Based on the 1988 John Waters film, the show whisked audiences back to Baltimore in the early days of the civil rights movement, and Fierstein played Edna Turnblad, the mother of a young girl whose desperation for a spot on a teen dance show awakens her awareness of racial inequality. Fierstein, labeled the "new belle of Broadway" in a preopening feature in the August 11 edition of the *Hartford Courant*, garnered some glowing reviews. Ben Brantley in his August 16, 2002, *Times* review wrote that he made Edna "not just a cross-dressing sight gag." In Fierstein's portrayal, she became, Brantley wrote, "every forgotten housewife, recreated in monumental proportion and waiting for something to tap her hidden magnificence." Fierstein also picked up his fourth Tony Award for his turn.

Moving from mother to father, Fierstein stepped into a revival of *Fiddler on the Roof* in 2005, and in a January 24 *Variety* review, David Rooney praised Fierstein as "one of the most droll, expansive and Jewish performers in the Broadway pantheon," adding that the actor's performance "dusts vitality off the role and rediscovers the humor with a crinkled mischievous smile and a teasing raised-eyebrow irreverence."

Fierstein returned as a book writer a few years later, when *A Catered Affair*, based on the 1956 movie, bowed. An intimate tale of a Brooklyn family as its daughter marries, the show has a score by John Bucchino, and on many levels, it is the vest-pocket version of *La Cage*. For the musical, Fierstein penned a role for himself, the bride-to-be's outspoken gay uncle, and though there were admiring notices, it was an unusual piece that ended up having just a brief run.

A Disney show, a stage version of the movie *Newsies*, followed, and for this Fierstein drastically reworked the story about a group of newsboys going on strike in the early twentieth century. The musical premiered at the Paper Mill Playhouse in Milburn, New Jersey, in September 2011, and though there had been no plans of it moving to Broadway, a rave review from the *New York Times* changed that. "[Fierstein] has chiseled a sweet, funny, emotionally satisfying book" was only part of the praise Rooney, writing for the *Times*, gave on September 28, 2011. By March, the show had opened at the Nederlander Theatre and went on to earn eight Tony nominations, including one for Fierstein.

His most recent musical outing came in 2013 when he penned the book for *Kinky Boots*, which featured a score by pop singer-songwriter Cyndi Lauper. Fierstein recruited the Grammy winner for this musical about a drag queen who helps resuscitate a failing shoe company in England. Once they began work, he helped mentor her as she composed her first Broadway score, and the result was a Tony for best musical and one for Lauper's music and lyrics.

Since *Kinky Boots*, Fierstein has seen his drama *Casa Valentina* premiere on Broadway and enjoyed a successful off-Broadway revival of *Torch Song* that transferred to Broadway in October 2018. He is currently at work on a play about maverick politician Bella Abzug.

WILLIAM FINN

(February 28, 1952–)
Composer / Lyricist / Librettist

This songwriter has brought a distinctly gay, urban perspective to the musical theatre and has also established a new sound for tuners, one that reflects the edginess of modern existence.

In an April 10, 1981, *New York Times* review of Finn's *March of the Falsettos*, Frank Rich wrote, "The songs are so fresh that the show is only a few bars old before one feels the unmistakable, revivifying charge of pure talent." The show wasn't the first that Finn had had produced in New York, but with this tuner, the man whose previous work had inspired another *Times* critic to carp about Finn's work being "precious" had made his mark.

Finn, born in Boston and raised in northeastern Massachusetts, developed an interest in theatre at an early age, so much so that he wrote a play for his class at Hebrew school. While attending Williams College, where he majored in English literature and American studies, he wrote and directed school musicals. This theatrical work led to a prize for directing and a fellowship that allowed him to study composition after graduation.

He settled in New York and began work on what would become his first produced musical, *In Trousers*, which Playwrights Horizons offered as part of a developmental series in late 1978. With book, music, and lyrics by Finn, *In Trousers* tells the story of Marvin, a Jewish man who is living in a heterosexual relationship with a wife and child and can't reconcile that with his growing awareness of being gay. Just over two years later, Second Stage Theatre gave *In Trousers* a full production, but most critics were unconvinced by the material. "[It] is original enough to make you wish that the gap between what is, and what might have been, wasn't so large," was John Corry's assessment in his March 4, 1981, *Times* review.

Between the first and second offerings of this musical, Finn worked on another about the hero, *March of the Falsettos*, imagining what transpires once Marvin decides to leave his wife and son for a man. Playwrights Horizons once again stepped forward to produce the show, and *March*, which marked Finn's first time working with director James Lapine, opened in April 1981 to some rapturous reviews. One came from the *Times'* Walter Kerr, who extolled the score, writing, "Finn's crossfire of melodies—now agitated, now serene—perfectly mirror a thoroughly confused world." As for Finn's lyrics, Kerr cited the "straightforward lament 'My father's a homo/My mother's not thrilled at all,'" noting that it reminded audiences "that half the secret of comedy lies in its utter solemnity."

After its engagement at the nonprofit, the musical transferred for a brief commercial run at the Westside Arts Theatre, and Finn began work on his next musical, one that examined life during the Depression. Originally titled *America Kicks Up Its Heels*, the show, with a book by Charles Rubin, had a troubled production at Playwrights in 1983 that starred Patti LuPone and never officially opened. A second production, under the title *Romance in Hard Times* and featuring a revised book by Finn, opened in 1989 courtesy of Joseph Papp and the New York Shakespeare Festival. It received tepid critical praise and played out its originally scheduled limited engagement.

Finn worked on another musical during this period, a follow-up to *March* that took Marvin; his family; and his on-again, off-again lover Whizzer squarely into the AIDS crisis, and the result, *Falsettoland*, premiered in 1990. In his June 29 *Times* review, Rich described the piece as an "achingly articulate musical," adding that it was a "musical of jubilance and courage, not defeat." Eventually, this musical and *March* (both one-act pieces) were combined into a full evening under the title *Falsettos*, which gave Finn his Broadway debut in 1992 and earned him a Tony Award.

Finn's interest in pursuing unconventional stories in his work continued with *A New Brain* (1998), which draws on his experiences after being misdiagnosed with an inoperable brain tumor, and then with *The 25th Annual Putnam County Spelling Bee*, which imagines a group of school children grappling with very adult issues as they compete in the titular contest. With a book by Rachel Sheinkin, the musical, after a developmental workshop at Barrington Stage Company in Massachusetts, had its New York premiere in 2005 at Second Stage Theatre. In her February 8 *Newsday* review, Linda Winer called the show an "endearingly deranged spelling-bee spoof," adding, "[Finn's] smartly innocent lyrics celebrate and mutilate a tiny world 'Where they treat you well, all because we love to spell.'"

Three days later in the *Wall Street Journal*, Terry Teachout called *Spelling Bee* "that rarity of rarities, a super-smart show that is also a bona fide crowd-pleaser," and indeed it was. The production transferred to Broadway the following May and ultimately ran for 1,136 performances. It received Tony nominations for best musical and best score, among others.

A musical adaptation of the 2006 indie movie *Little Miss Sunshine* occupied Finn for nearly seven years after *Spelling Bee*'s debut. The show, about a quirky family pushing a little girl into the spotlight of a beauty pageant, premiered at La Jolla Playhouse in 2011 and then bowed off-Broadway in 2013, with book and direction by Finn's longtime collaborator Lapine. Critics were admiring but not convinced by the work, and *Sunshine* simply played its limited nonprofit engagement.

Throughout this period and after, Finn has maintained a relationship with Barrington Stage, serving as producer for the company's Musical Theatre Lab, helping to shepherd nearly a dozen musicals to their world premieres. Among them are Joe Iconis's *The Black Suits*, about a group of Long Island teenagers' garage band; *The Memory Show*, about a daughter coping with her mother's Alzheimer's;

and *Southern Comfort*, a musical about a small community of transgendered individuals.

In 2018, Finn saw a new show reach the stage and also provided the score for a small-screen offering. The former was a musical adaptation of *The Royal Family*, George S. Kaufman and Edna Ferber's comedic look at a Broadway acting clan not unlike the Barrymores. Retitled *The Royal Family of Broadway* and featuring a book by Sheinkin, the tuner opened at Barrington Stage in June. Many critics had reservations about the piece's merits, but the *Wall Street Journal*'s Teachout raved, "it looks like a winner in the making," in a June 14 review. The critic went on to praise "[Finn's] score, in which Great American Songbook–style pastiche is freshened with his own spiky harmonic language." Finn's excursion to the small screen came a few weeks later when he provided the songs for *The Emperor Needs New Clothes*, a giddy revisitation to the Hans Christian Andersen fairy tale that aired on HBO in the fall of 2018.

JULES FISHER

(November 12, 1937–)
Lighting Designer / Projection Designer

This designer's work has set standards for electric visuals in musical theatre during the last half of the twentieth and the beginning of the twenty-first centuries, and he has also helped bring a new generation of designers into the field.

Leah D. Frank, in a November 12, 1978, *New York Times* feature on this Tony Award–winning artist, proclaimed, "Mr. Fisher became a lighting designer by magic." Frank went on to explain that, while Fisher was in grade school, he performed magic shows semiprofessionally, and after his high school graduation, he was working at the Valley Forge Music Fair in Pennsylvania, where he began to pay attention to the lighting design. He told Frank, "Hey, I think I can do that."

For college Fisher attended Carnegie Mellon University in Pittsburgh, Pennsylvania, and during his school time, he also began working in New York, designing for three off-Broadway shows during his senior year. Fisher's presence continued in Manhattan after his graduation, and as would be the case for the entirety of his career, he moved between plays and musicals with ease. Between 1961 and mid-1963, his lighting graced more than two dozen productions, including the revival of *Best Foot Forward* that featured a young Liza Minnelli and opened in April 1963.

Five months later, Fisher celebrated his Broadway bow with *Spoon River Anthology*, which translated to the stage Edgar Lee Masters's collection of poems paying tribute to the residents of a small Illinois town. The scenery for the production consisted of only a few low benches and a lectern, meaning Fisher's design had to help carry audiences through the show and its moods. The Associated Press's William Glover extolled the designer's work in an October 1963 review, calling it "disciplined [and] potent."

Fisher has been a consistent presence on the Main Stem ever since, lighting some of the most important works of their time. For instance, it was Fisher who lit both *Hair* (1968) and *Jesus Christ Superstar* (1971). With the former, the Associated Press's Jack Gaver noted in a May 1968 review that Fisher's work and that of the other designers "combine for a total psychedelic effect," and in his November 7, 1971, *Boston Globe* review of *Superstar*, Kevin Kelly commended how Fisher's lighting "adds full dimension to [Robin] Wagner's scenic design." Fisher received his first Tony nomination for the production.

Before and well after these, Fisher would also design less flashy musicals. One of them was Richard Rodgers, Stephen Sondheim, and Arthur Laurents's *Do I Hear a Waltz?* (1965), which Fisher thought was some of "his best work," according to Frank in her 1978 *Times* feature. Another intimate musical with lighting design by Fisher, Al Carmines and Maria Irene Fornes's absurdist *Promenade*, opened off-Broadway while *Hair* was on Broadway. In a June 5, 1969, *Women's Wear Daily* review, Martin Gottfried called Fisher's contribution "delightful."

Two years after *Superstar*, Fisher again worked with scenic designer Wagner, on the musical *Seesaw*, and in this production the men conspired to take projection designs to a new level. Beyond the credit for lighting, there was one for "Projection system devised by Jules Fisher Associates," and indeed Fisher created new ways of integrating still images into the show, projecting them onto Wagner's moving scrims. In Edwin Wilson's March 20, 1973, *Wall Street Journal* review, he commented on the trend toward using projections, saying that the work in this musical was "one of the best" he had seen.

In the 1970s, Fisher worked with Bob Fosse on three shows: *Pippin* (1972), *Chicago* (1975), and *Dancin'* (1978). Fisher's ingenuity in the first allowed Fosse to achieve a remarkable opening in which lighting illuminated only the performers' hands as they intoned the opening notes of "Magic to Do." Fisher earned his first Tony Award for it. His second came for *Dancin'*.

During the 1980s, his work was seen in such shows as *La Cage aux Folles* (1983), *The Rink* (1984), *Song and Dance* (1985), and *Grand Hotel* (1989). This last musical, directed and choreographed by Tommy Tune, set in motion an extraordinary three years for Fisher as he won a trio of Tonys back to back, the others being for *The Will Rogers Follies* (1991) and *Jelly's Last Jam* (1992). David Richards, in a May 3, 1992, *New York Times* review of this last musical, complimented the work that Fisher had done (once again for Wagner's sets): "Robin Wagner's sets, as lighted by Jules Fisher, are oases in [the musical's] cosmic gloom."

George C. Wolfe directed *Jelly's*, and their collaboration has continued to this day, including such musicals as *Bring in 'da Noise, Bring in 'da Funk* (1996); *The Wild Party* (2000); and *Caroline, or Change* (2004). Fisher, along with his new professional partner, Peggy Eisenhauer, received the Tony for the first and a nomination for the second.

As the millennium dawned, Fisher, working with Eisenhauer, once again contributed projections, as well as lighting, to a musical in the case of *Jane Eyre* (2000). In a December 18, 2000, *Variety* review, Charles Isherwood remarked on the design, writing that the production "conjures Jane's journey through projections and eloquently dappled lighting effects, which are wondrously engineered."

Fisher and Eisenhauer have continued their collaboration for the past eighteen years, illuminating new musicals ranging from *9 to 5* (2009) and *Shuffle Along, or, The Making of the Musical Sensation of 1921 and All That Followed* (2016) to revivals of *Assassins* (2004) and *Once on This Island* (2017).

Fisher has also helped to train a new generation of lighting designers, mentoring them as he works on his assignments. One of them, Eisenhauer, became his professional partner in the early 1990s after six years of apprenticeship with him. In a January 2006 *American Theatre* magazine interview, she commented about his work in this regard, saying a number of his assistants "have gone on to be notable lighting designers, and I think that is a testament to the kind of mentor he is."

BOB FOSSE

(June 23, 1927–September 23, 1987)
Director / Choreographer

Fosse took dance in the Broadway musical in entirely new directions, imbuing it with bite and sexiness unlike any who preceded him or followed.

This director-choreographer started his life as a teenage entertainer in vaudeville and burlesque houses. He and a pal developed an act and entertained in cities in and around his native Chicago. Later, Fosse struck out on his own, and as he related to Robert Rosenberg for an April 22, 1973, *Chicago Daily News* feature, "I remember the first place, the Silver Cloud. They had the stripteasers, the comic and me."

Fosse enlisted in the navy after graduating from high school and following his discharge settled in New York. He started taking acting and dance classes, courtesy of the GI Bill, and then joined a touring company of Harold Rome's *Call Me Mister*. After it ended, he and his wife, Mary Ann Niles, began performing at nightclubs throughout the country, à la Marge and Gower Champion.

As a performer, Fosse had his Broadway debut with the revue *Dance Me a Song* (1950), for which he, along with Niles, got consistently positive notices. Understudying Harold Lang in a revival of *Pal Joey* (1952) followed, and then Fosse picked up a trio of Hollywood credits in 1953, most notably the film version of *Kiss Me, Kate*, for which he devised a dazzling sextet dance that he performed with Jeanne Coyne, Carol Haney, Tommy Rall, Bobby Van, and Ann Miller.

Fosse returned to New York in 1954 to choreograph *The Pajama Game*. He introduced some of what audiences came to know as his signature style—bowler hats, intriguingly angled limbs, and implicit sexiness—in the number "Steam Heat." Walter F. Kerr in his *New York Herald Tribune* review on May 14, 1954, specifically mentioned this number, writing that, thanks to Fosse's work and dancer Carol Haney, it was "hotter than even its doting composers could have hoped."

Walter Terry, the paper's dance critic, weighed in on Fosse's work in a June 6 piece, writing, "[Fosse] has designed production numbers that accelerate, rather than slow up, the pace of the show." Terry added that Fosse's dances "contribute richly to the color, humor and characterization of a play in musical form."

Fosse earned a Tony Award for this musical, as well as the one that followed, *Damn Yankees*. In it he created several sizzling numbers for his soon-to-be third wife, Gwen Verdon, including the über-sexy "Whatever Lola Wants," as well as a baseball player ballet in which on-the-field moves (catching, sliding, batting) were put through his unique dance prism.

Fosse and Verdon were a team for his next two shows. The first was *New Girl in Town*, in which he created the "Red Light Ballet." The sexually charged dance shocked some people out of town; "Bone.," in the April 10, 1957, edition of *Variety*, described it as "artistic or blue depending on individual interpretation." A reimagined number was inserted for the show's New York opening, but Fosse continued to refine and reassert his vision for it during the musical's run. The result, the *Herald Tribune*'s Terry noted on July 21, was a "happy medium between shocking and mild."

After his Tony win for *New Girl*, Fosse both directed and choreographed Verdon in *Redhead* (1959) and then assumed the same dual role for *The Conquering Hero* (1961). For this show, however, he was replaced on the road. Four years later, another musical he completely staged, *Pleasures and Palaces*, folded before reaching New York.

Fosse's career, however, hardly faltered. Between *Hero* and *Pleasures*, he created the dances for *How to Succeed in Business without Really Trying* (1961), applying his witty terpsichorean vision to life in corporate America. For *Little Me* (1962), Fosse both choreographed and codirected, and in this tuner, he created a striptease for a male dancer. In "I've Got Your Number," Swen Swenson's "furiously volatile propositioning" (Howard Taubman's description in the November 18 edition of the *Times*) of the show's heroine stopped the show nightly.

Three years later, Fosse directed and choreographed *Sweet Charity*, creating a musical to showcase Verdon, who played a taxi dancer with a heart of gold. Not only did she have the opportunity to shine in numbers ranging from the quirkily ecstatic solo "If They Could See Me Now" to the exuberant parade-march "I'm a Brass Band," but so, too, did the entire cast, as Fosse parodied current dance styles and took on street religions.

Fosse directed the movie version of *Charity* a few years later, and following it he lent his singular cinematic style—fast cuts, unusual camera angles that prefigured the style of MTV—to the film *Cabaret* (1972). He shifted to the small screen, directing and choreographing the TV special *Liza with a "Z."* And even as he was working on these, he brought Stephen Schwartz's *Pippin* to Broadway in 1972. The result of all of this activity was Oscar, Tony, and Emmy Award wins in 1973, and Fosse is the only artist to have been so honored in a single year.

With *Pippin*, as well as *Chicago* (1975), Fosse's wry, sardonic worldview came into its sharpest focus. With his spare, tautly conceived dances in these shows, Fosse commented on the brutality of war and the emptiness of free love in *Pippin*, and in *Chicago*, which he coauthored, the justice system became a curious form of sexy show business. Kerr summed up Fosse's style for *Chicago* in the *Times* on June 8, "[He] is a man without peer when it comes to making navels undulate, hips quiver, toes stutter, [and] white spats and white gloves create succulent patterns against the night sky."

Fosse demonstrated his virtuoso skill with a variety of forms with *Dancin'* (1978), a show, as the title suggests, consisting entirely of choreographed numbers. After this, his work was back on the screen with the autobiographical *All That Jazz* (1979), in which open-heart surgery became an exhilarating production number. His last original Broadway musical was *Big Deal* (1986), set in Depression-era Chicago, which he knew from childhood. For this he penned the book and used period songs for the score, and while critics applauded the dancing, they were unenthusiastic about the show as a whole. It shuttered after a mere sixty-nine performances.

Fosse's final Broadway outing was an award-winning revival of *Sweet Charity*. He oversaw the national tour that followed, and as it was launching in Washington, DC, Fosse unexpectedly died of a heart attack in 1987. His style, however, lives on. The 2011 music video for Beyoncé's "Get Me Bodied," for instance, references Fosse's "Rich Man's Frug" from *Charity*.

G

GEORGE GERSHWIN

(September 26, 1898–July 11, 1937)
Composer

George Gershwin brought both genuine jazz sensibility and classical sounds to his work, creating a unique body of musical comedy work and, ultimately, an enduring folk opera that is equally at home in legitimate theatres and opera houses.

One week after this composer's premature death from a brain tumor, Charles Collins in the *Chicago Tribune* paid tribute to Gershwin's music, focusing not, as many had in the previous days, on *Rhapsody in Blue* and other "serious pieces" of music but rather on Gershwin's theatrical work. It was for Broadway, Collins wrote, that "his happiest and, in my opinion his best work was done. . . . He was the troubadour of the era of 'sophistication'; he enriched the blatant frenzies of pre-war jaz [*sic*] with light satire and gay mockery." And indeed, from 1918 forward, Gershwin brought an invigorating new sound to the Broadway musical.

Gershwin's musical talent revealed itself when he was twelve, and he showed a remarkable ability at the piano at home. In short order, Charles Hambitzer, one of New York's most prominent music teachers, was educating the boy. Gershwin left high school before graduating, having decided to become a professional musician, and his first job was serving as a song plugger for J. H. Remick and Sons. Each day, Gershwin played the company's newest songs for performers looking for new material for their acts. During this period, too, Gershwin continued his studies and also began considering new musical forms.

Gershwin's introduction to Broadway came after his work took him into cafés, where he would play Remick-owned songs to help familiarize the general public with them. Producer Charles Dillingham, impressed with the young man's skills, hired him as rehearsal pianist for *Miss 1917*. Gershwin's official Broadway bow came a year later, when he and his brother, Ira, who wrote lyrics, contributed "The Real American Folk Song (Is a Rag)" to the musical *Ladies First*.

Gershwin melodies were heard in a trio of shows during 1919, including his first big hit, "Swanee," with lyrics by Irving Caesar. The gentle parody of Stephen

Foster's "Old Folks at Home" caught on thanks to Al Jolson, who recorded it and put it into his show *Sinbad*.

Gershwin's first complete score for a Broadway musical came with *La La Lucille* in 1920, and after this he was a fixture in the theatre, penning songs for five editions of George White's *Scandals* series, as well as other revues and the score for the musical *Sweet Little Devil*, which opened in January 1924. The following month, Gershwin's *Rhapsody in Blue* premiered as part of a concert called *An Experiment in Modern Music*, an event put together by bandleader Paul Whiteman. With this work for piano and orchestra, Gershwin demonstrated his classical music acumen and unique gift for fusing it with jazz sounds. *Billboard* critic "L. M. M." hailed the work, saying it was a "piano concerto containing a beauty of rhythm and of a style which may later on be found to form the basis of the long looked for and much talked of American school."

At the end of the year, *Lady, Be Good!* opened on Broadway, and with it, Gershwin shattered the traditional sound of musicals. The morning after it opened, critics were unsurprisingly rapturous about the show's stars, Fred and Adele Astaire, and their dancing. They were equally taken with two distinctly different songs Gershwin had written: the gentle "So Am I" and the beautifully edgy and now-classic "Fascinating Rhythm," a theatrical extension, on many levels, of *Rhapsody*.

Another three musicals came in quick succession in 1925, and then in 1926, *Oh, Kay!* premiered. This show contained a bevy of stand-alone hits, including "Clap Yo' Hands," "Do Do Do," and "Someone to Watch over Me." This last song in particular was singled out in a November 9 *Herald Tribune* review. Percy Hammond wrote that with it "[Gershwin] wrung the withers of even the most hard-hearted present."

Oh, Kay!, with a book by Guy Bolton and P. G. Wodehouse centering on a group of bootleggers who appear unexpectedly in the middle of Long Island high society, felt and sounded like the perfect tuner for the Jazz Age. Four years later, Gershwin moved into a different realm with the musical satire *Strike Up the Band*, which struck the right note for America as it entered the Depression. The show's exuberant title song, outfitted with Ira Gershwin's punchy lyrics, has become a national standard, and the work itself set the stage for the Pulitzer-winning *Of Thee I Sing*, which opened December 26, 1931. In this one, George S. Kaufman and Morrie Ryskind skewer the American political system, and Gershwin deploys similar patriotic melodies, as well as ones that sound as if they might be a new American form of operetta and more traditional popular music strains.

Between these two politically themed pieces, Gershwin offered up more rustic sounds for *Girl Crazy* in late 1930, in which a Manhattan playboy finds himself on a dude ranch in Arizona. The score boasts such romantic classics as "Embraceable You" and "But Not for Me," as well as a pair of numbers, also standards, that Ethel Merman delivered on opening night to galvanizing effect: "I Got Rhythm" and "Sam and Delilah." The *Herald Tribune*'s Hammond, writing about the production on November 11, described the score as "now tough, then tender, here surprising, there expected, and always blessed by the composer's irresistible originality."

Porgy and Bess, which came four years and three shows later, showcases Gershwin at his most versatile and daring. This "American folk opera" about the lives of a group of African Americans in rural South Carolina reveals Gershwin's mastery of a variety of musical forms and his keen instinct on how to combine them theatrically.

In the *New York Times* on October 11, 1935, the paper's drama critic, Brooks Atkinson, and its music critic, Olin Downes, reviewed the show's premiere. Atkinson lauded Gershwin's contribution to the play on which the piece was based. Thanks to the score, Atkinson wrote, "Fear and pain go deeper in 'Porgy and Bess' than they did in penny plain 'Porgy.'" Downes, examining it as an opera, was appreciative of Gershwin's work and yet was not convinced that the composer had "completely formed his style as an opera composer." Hindsight, however, has proven Downes's conservatism incorrect, and *Porgy* has been adopted into opera repertoires, with scholars generally agreeing that it shows Gershwin at the height of his career. Sadly, any further growth as a composer or developments he might have made in musical theatre were forestalled by his early death two years later.

IRA GERSHWIN

(December 6, 1896–August 17, 1983)
Lyricist

Craftsmanship meets casualness in Ira Gershwin's lyrics, leading to both a host of classic American songs and giving a new language to the Broadway musical.

Although this lyricist is generally associated with his younger brother, George, Ira Gershwin also provided words for melodies by composers ranging from Harold Arlen to Arthur Schwartz to Kurt Weill to Victor Youmans. Ira Gershwin's word craft brought a new sort of playfulness to lyric writing, helping to establish a certain sort of casualness and accessibility in musical theatre.

From an early age, the older Gershwin demonstrated both an ease with and a love for writing. John S. Wilson's August 18, 1983, *New York Times* obituary described how both of the Gershwin boys began piano lessons concurrently, but Ira Gershwin "preferred nickel novels and soon let his brother monopolize the piano." The future lyricist contributed toward school publications while in high school, as well as during his brief time at City College. He left this school after two years and continued his writing while also taking a variety of jobs to earn a living. One of his earliest successes was an essay published in the *New York Mail* in 1917.

During this time, too, Gershwin began to attend theatre and found himself particularly drawn to the shows penned by P. G. Wodehouse and Guy Bolton, and then his brother asked him to collaborate on songs that he was writing for the music publisher for whom he worked. By 1918, a song with an Ira Gershwin lyric and a George Gershwin melody, "The Real American Folk Song (Is a Rag)," made it to Broadway in *Ladies First*, and in it Ira Gershwin brought a new sort of argot to musical theatre: slang. In describing ragtime, the lyric proclaims, "It's a riot!"

The brothers continued to work together and separately, and between 1921 and 1923, Ira adopted the pseudonym "Arthur Francis," not wanting to appear to capitalize on his younger brother's growing success. Among the "Arthur Francis" lyrics from this era that have endured are "Boy Wanted," written for *A Dangerous Maid* (1921), a show that never reached Broadway, and "I'll Build a Stairway to Paradise," which served as the first-act finale for the 1922 edition of *George White's Scandals* and had a lyric that the older Gershwin cowrote with B. G. "Buddy" DeSylva.

Beyond their durability, these two songs demonstrate Ira Gershwin's ability to write with emotional directness and to also match words to the sometimes-tricky rhythms that his brother composed. In "Boy" the lyric simply and effectively communicates four women's criteria for a boyfriend and even employs the word *oodles*. In "Stairway" Gershwin and DeSylva beautifully match the phrase "to always be sitting around" to a trio of rapid musical triplets.

The brothers' genuine breakthrough on Broadway came in 1924, as the Francis nom de plume was dropped and *Lady, Be Good!* premiered. The music was perfect for the Jazz Age, and the lyrics for songs raging from "Fascinating Rhythm" to "So Am I" to "You Don't Know the Half of It Dearie Blues" sparkle with colloquial ease and gentle wit. "Simple in its treatment, its effectiveness was all the stronger because of its simpleness" was the way that "Fred." characterized "So Am I" in a December 3 *Variety* review.

Even more quintessential for the era of Prohibition was *Oh, Kay!* (1926), which centers on a female bootlegger chased by detectives to Long Island, where she finds love with a local scion. The show boasted a trio of numbers that have become classics: "Do Do Do," "Clap Yo' Hands," and "Someone to Watch over Me." Lesser known today but beautifully illustrating Gershwin's penchant for slang (and his disinclination for standard-issue love songs) is "Ain't It Romantic?"

Among the exceptional songs that followed were "'S Wonderful" and "He Loves and She Loves" from *Funny Face* (1927), "Feeling I'm Falling" and "I've Got a Crush on You" from *Treasure Girl* (1928), and "How Long Has This Been Going On?" from *Rosalie* (1928). In these enduring songs, Gershwin demonstrates repeatedly a theory about lyric writing that he shared in an April 26, 1925, *New York Herald Tribune* feature: "Good lyrics are just like rhymed conversation."

Strike Up the Band arrived on Broadway in 1930, and with it Gershwin demonstrated that his style could be used to satirical purpose. One year later, he provided the lyrics for the Pulitzer Prize–winning comic examination of presidential races *Of Thee I Sing*. Gershwin's lyrics in this musical flow in and out of the action and are reminiscent of Gilbert and Sullivan's work. In one sequence, five distinct pieces of music comprise a scene, and Gershwin outfits one of them with words written in what could be described as "pigeon French."

Gershwin tackled a different, more traditional musical in between, *Girl Crazy*, and for it he deploys, in "I Got Rhythm," the ungrammatical to create a hit. The brothers' last show together was *Porgy and Bess* (1935), and for this folk opera, Gershwin's colloquialism and simplicity resulted in the lasting lyrics, written with DuBose Heyward, for such songs as "I Got Plenty o' Nuthin'" and "It Ain't Necessarily So."

George Gershwin died in 1937, and it took four years for a distraught Ira Gershwin to return to Broadway. When he did, he worked with Kurt Weill on *Lady in the Dark* (1941), about a magazine editor's experiences with psychotherapy. Gershwin's cunning lyrics fit ably with both the show's fantasy sequences as well as with the heroine's introspective songs such as "My Ship," and the *Times'* Brooks Atkinson called them "uproariously witty" in a January 24 review, noting also that they were "written in impeccable taste for the meditative sequences." Gershwin only wrote two more Broadway shows: *The Firebrand of Florence* (1945), also with music by Weill, and *Park Avenue* (1946), with melodies by Arthur Schwartz. He finished his career in Hollywood.

He and his brother had occasionally worked on films, most notably writing the Oscar-nominated "They Can't Take That Away from Me" just before the composer's death. But during the late 1940s and 1950s and before retiring from the business, Ira Gershwin wrote lyrics for a host of films, including *Cover Girl* (1941), with music by Jerome Kern; *The Shocking Miss Pilgrim* (1947), which used previously unheard melodies by his brother; *Give a Girl a Break* (1953), his only collaboration with Burton Lane; and *A Star Is Born* (1954), for which he and Harold Arlen wrote the classic, Oscar-nominated "The Man That Got Away," where Gershwin purposefully used *that* in relation to "man" because he wanted the song to call to mind fisherman's tales about the "one *that* got away."

W. S. GILBERT AND SIR ARTHUR SULLIVAN

(November 18, 1836–May 29, 1911) / (May 13, 1842–November 22, 1900)
Composers / Librettists

This famed team's work influenced several generations of musical theatre creators, setting standards for intricate wordplay and social awareness for decades to come.

In his January 18, 1976, *New York Times* review of Stephen Sondheim and John Weidman's *Pacific Overtures*, Walter Kerr described the number "Please, Hello," writing, "The musical effect here is strictly Gilbert-and-Sullivan-meet-Kabuki." This critic's ability to use the nineteenth-century operetta writers' names as a shorthand for his readers attests to their enduring popularity. The fact that another reviewer that day, Douglas Watt in the *Daily News*, recognized how one portion of the song caricatured "G&S patter" attests to their exceptional influence on musical theatre songwriting.

Gilbert, whose initials stood for William Schwenck, was born in London and educated on the Continent and in England, showing from an early age a facility for word craft. After his graduation from Kings College, London, he served as a military civil servant and pursued (unsuccessfully) a career as a barrister. Gilbert supplemented his income during this period by writing stories, poems, and theatre reviews.

Sullivan was also born in London, the son of a military bandmaster. His gift for composition was seen when he was just eight years old, and six years later, he was studying at the Royal Academy of Music and later at Leipzig Conservatory in Germany. Subsequent to his graduation, he wrote a variety of classical pieces, including a ballet, symphony, and cello concerto. More lucrative for young Sullivan were hymns and parlor ballads, popular songs that were meant to be played by amateurs in their homes. In 1866, he had a stage success with the one-act opera *Cox and Box*, which had a libretto by F. C. Burnand.

Five years later, the first work by the team of Gilbert and Sullivan, the lost opera *Thespis*, premiered at London's Gaiety Theatre. Gilbert's libretto imagines that the ancient Greek gods take over the bodies of a group of actors in order to mingle among humans, with disastrous results. A December 31, 1871, review of the piece in London's *Observer* extolled how Sullivan had "entered with heart into the spirit of Mr. Gilbert's fun" and how he had "brightened it with the most fanciful and delightful music." The critic also noted that Sullivan's melodies could accommodate Gilbert's triple and double rhymes.

Gilbert and Sullivan sporadically collaborated during the ensuing years on nontheatrical work, and then in 1875, Richard D'Oyly Carte needed a short musical piece to round out a bill he was producing that was to feature Offenbach's *La Périchole*. D'Oyly Carte asked Sullivan to create something to serve the purpose, and the result, after Gilbert came onboard as librettist, was *Trial by Jury*. The one-act comedy about a breach of promise with regard to a marriage proposal was an unexpected hit. Audiences and critics savored both the jaunty score and Gilbert's wry wit and barbs.

This success led to another twelve collaborations between the two men, and in them Sullivan unleashed his melodic merriment as Gilbert satirized Victorian society. With *H.M.S. Pinafore* (1878), the British class system is tweaked as a common sailor attempts to marry the daughter of the lord high admiral of the British navy, and with *Ruddigore* (1887), the writers spoof bloody melodramas of the era. Even when Gilbert's librettos took to foreign lands, such as in *The Mikado* (1885), or centered on more-flamboyant characters, as is the case with *The Pirates of Penzance* (1879), it is impossible to miss the fact that he is mocking topics and trends of the day. The team, who eventually disbanded because of the fractious nature of their partnership, did take one excursion into more emotional realms with *Yeoman of the Guard* (1888).

The effect that Gilbert and Sullivan's work had on musical comedy in the twentieth century and beyond is twofold. To begin, both American composers and lyricists were inspired by their work. For instance, Yip Harburg would come to recall how he and Ira Gershwin listened to recordings of Gilbert and Sullivan's operettas for hours when they were in school together, savoring the construction of the pieces and marveling at how the team had married plots, lyrics, and melodies. Gershwin also had the opportunity to see many of the operettas in performance when he was young, and as Penelope Hobhouse reports in the book *Fascinating Rhythm*, "For the rest of his life, he knew most of Gilbert and Sullivan's songs by heart."

For the next generation of lyricists, Gilbert and Sullivan were equally influential. Adolph Green was introduced to their work when he played the lord high executioner in *The Mikado* in grade school. He was so taken with the show that he memorized all of the team's musicals, and later their *Pirates* provided him with a lifelong friend. In 1937, Green played the pirate king at an adult summer camp, and Leonard Bernstein was the production's musical director. Once Green began writing sketches and scenes with Betty Comden, the operettas provided them with inspiration. "We absorbed all we could," she told Al Kasha and Joel Hirschhorn, adding, "We learned a lot from them."

Sullivan's musical influence reached to composers, as well. Jerome Kern admired his predecessor's work and paraphrased him in "Oh You Beautiful Spring" in *The Red Petticoat* (1912), using some of "The Flowers That Bloom in the Spring" from *The Mikado*. George Gershwin was also inspired by Sullivan, whose work echoes in such Gershwin scores as *Primrose*, which premiered in the West End in 1924, and especially in *Of Thee I Sing*, where the music brings to mind Sullivan's work; book writers George S. Kaufman and Morrie Ryskind's and lyricist Ira Gershwin's merrymaking with presidential politics echoes the best of Gilbert's tart Victorian satires.

Beyond this sort of inspiration, Gilbert and Sullivan's canon informed a host of writers and directors who adapted the nineteenth-century works. In the middle of the twentieth century, Broadway audiences were treated to *The Hot Mikado* (1939) and *Hollywood Pinafore* (1945). More recently, Gilbert and Sullivan's *H.M.S. Pinafore* was adapted to take on the policy of "Don't Ask, Don't Tell" with *Pinafore!* which premiered at Los Angeles's Celebration Theater in 2003.

Gilbert and Sullivan's works have also proven their durability without such adaptations both on Broadway and beyond in the past century and a half. Their operettas are performed by light opera companies throughout the United States, and in 1981, one, *The Pirates of Penzance*, enjoyed a Tony Award–winning revival thanks to Joseph Papp, the New York Shakespeare Festival (NYSF), and director Wilford Leach. The production opened in Central Park in 1980 as part of the NYSF's Free Shakespeare in Central Park summer season. Starring Linda Ronstadt, Rex Smith, Kevin Kline, and Estelle Parsons, the show garnered raves and transferred to the Uris Theater, and in his January 9 *New York Times* review, Frank Rich lauded Leach and his company, along with the writers, extolling the "literate humor of Gilbert's libretto and the enchanting melodies of Arthur Sullivan's score."

As recently as 2013, Steven Lutvak and Robert L. Freedman drew on the Gilbert and Sullivan style, integrating it, with contemporary embellishments, into their Tony Award–winning musical *A Gentlemen's Guide to Love and Murder*.

H

OSCAR HAMMERSTEIN II

(July 12, 1895–August 23, 1960)
Lyricist / Book Writer / Producer

Hammerstein, the father of what is known as the "book musical," pushed the musical theatre forward into the realm of cohesion during two distinct eras and also set standards for poeticism and humanity in lyric writing.

In a four-decade career, Hammerstein, as book writer and lyricist, penned not one but two shows that are considered landmarks in the evolution of musical theatre, *Show Boat* and *Oklahoma!* Between these two (and afterward), he was lyricist of some of the country's most beloved songs and writer of some of history's most enduring shows.

Hammerstein was born into a family with a rich theatrical legacy. The grandfather for whom he was named had been an important opera impresario; his father, William, ran the Victoria Theatre, a vaudeville house owned by the family; and his Uncle Arthur was a respected Broadway producer. Given this pedigree it would have seemed that the younger Hammerstein's career in theatre would have been a given, but his parents wanted him to become an attorney. While attending Columbia University, however, Hammerstein gravitated toward the school's Varsity shows and, in short order, was performing in—and writing material for—them.

Hammerstein's Broadway debut came in 1917 with *Furs and Frills*, which boasted one song with a lyric he had written. Three years later, *Always You*, a variation on the *Madame Butterfly* story set in France, boasted book and lyrics by Hammerstein, with music by Herbert Stothart. An unnamed *New York Times* critic labeled Hammerstein's lyrics "more clever than those of average musical comedy" in an October 10 review.

Three more musicals with Stothart followed, and with two of these, Hammerstein partnered with Otto Harbach on lyric-writing duties. Harbach became the younger writer's mentor, passing on his theories of how songs should integrate into a musical's plot. It was with Harbach, along with Stothart and composer Vincent Youmans, that Hammerstein enjoyed his first major success on Broadway:

Wildflower (1923). The show, about an Italian heiress who must curb her temper for a year if she is to receive her fortune, enjoyed a 477-performance run, and as noted by *Billboard*'s Gordon Whyte on February 17, the story was "better than most, as musical comedy books go."

In 1924, Hammerstein, Harbach, Stothart, and Rudolf Friml brought *Rose-Marie* to Broadway, and with this musical set in the Canadian Rockies, Hammerstein saw songs with his lyrics—"Indian Love Call" and "Song of the Mounties"—become popular hits. More importantly, the book made strides in bringing seriousness into the musical. *Rose-Marie* features a murder as part of its plot.

Lighter fare followed with *Sunny* in 1925, but it began Hammerstein's collaboration with composer Jerome Kern, and after Hammerstein had had four other musicals bow, including the enduring *The Desert Song* (1926), he and Kern adapted Edna Ferber's sweeping novel *Show Boat* as a musical. Combining lighthearted elements with more-serious ones regarding racism and miscegenation, Hammerstein's book was touted for having "not patronized the past nor enshrined the present." His lyrics ranged from the pungent ("Old Man River") to the comedic ("Life upon the Wicked Stage") to the gently poetic ("You Are Love").

Hammerstein and Sigmund Romberg conspired to create a great operetta the following year with *The New Moon*, and after this, in such shows as *Music in the Air* (1932), Hammerstein, with Kern, continued to integrate innovations into the libretti he wrote, and though this musical and others may not be remembered today, individual songs from his projects during the late 1920s and through the 1930s, such as "I've Told Every Little Star," endure.

His book-writing art reached a new level in 1943 with the landmark *Oklahoma!* With this musical about life among the settlers in the future titular state, Hammerstein, in his first collaboration with composer Richard Rodgers, fused narrative, song, and dance in new and unexpected (for the time) ways.

From this point until his death, Hammerstein's shows, all written with Rodgers, continued to build on the new standard of cohesiveness in book musicals that *Oklahoma!* established. Just two years later, he created a landmark fusion of book and song in what came to be known as the "Bench Scene" in *Carousel*, where dialogue and song ("If I Loved You") are carefully spliced together to create a moving portrait of two young people falling in love. At the same time, the works that Hammerstein dramatized resulted in musicals that concurrently entertained and contained serious thematic issues, from James A. Michener's World War II stories that became *South Pacific* (1949), where themes of prejudice are addressed squarely; to *Flower Drum Song* (1958), based on C. Y. Lee's novel about Asian assimilation in San Francisco; to the story of Maria von Trapp, resulting in *The Sound of Music* (1959), where romance blossoms against a backdrop of the Nazi party's rise to power.

Hammerstein also wrote original musicals, such as *Allegro* (1947), which chronicles how success derails a young doctor's intention of doing good and healing people. Hammerstein's writing for this can be occasionally abstract (a chorus chants advice at the hero sporadically throughout it) and has a decided allegorical tone, making it very unlike the musicals he and Rodgers had previously brought to the stage. In the mind of *Herald Tribune* reviewer Howard Barnes, it was a "show to be remembered with 'Show Boat' and 'Oklahoma!'" Yet despite such critical success, the musical never made it to its one-year anniversary.

This musical, as well as Hammerstein's others from 1942 to 1959, also contain a host of songs that are known the world over—numbers that are filled with simplicity and lyricism wedded to Rodgers's superlative melodies, from "People Will Say We're in Love" (*Oklahoma!*) to "You'll Never Walk Alone" (*Carousel*) to "Getting to Know You" (*The King and I*) to "Do Re Mi" (*Sound of Music*). The same can be said of *Carmen Jones*, where he set English lyrics to Bizet's score for the opera *Carmen*. "The libretto has been brilliantly translated," the *Herald Tribune*'s Barnes wrote on December 3, 1943, "into a contemporary negro fable."

Since his death, the depth of Hammerstein's classics has been discovered time and again. In 2018, off-Broadway revivals of *Carmen Jones* and *Oklahoma!* thrilled critics and theatregoers. Director Daniel Fish's revival of the latter prompted the *Times*' Ben Brantley to comment, in an October 7 review, how Hammerstein's writing contained a "sense of untapped hormonal energy in a land where there's a dangerous, heady sense of making up your own rules as you go along." This new interpretation transferred to Broadway in March 2019.

Beyond his shows Hammerstein left an additional legacy. He was both friend and mentor to Stephen Sondheim as a young adult. In his foreword to Hugh Fordin's biography of Hammerstein, *Getting to Know Him*, Sondheim writes, "If he had been a geologist, I would have become a geologist."

E. Y. "YIP" HARBURG

(April 8, 1896–March 5, 1981)
Lyricist / Book Writer / Composer

Although Harburg will always be the man who wrote "Over the Rainbow," his contribution to musical theatre cannot be underestimated because through his work audiences learned that political and societal satire could have concurrent bite and whimsy.

Even as a preteen, this lyricist, known for his shrewd whimsy, could make people laugh with his words. For Max Wilk's book *They're Playing Our Song*, Harburg recalled having an English teacher in grade school who would call him in front of the class after reading something funny that the boy had written: "I'd read, and there would be twenty-odd kids laughing out loud, and my God, that was really something."

Harburg continued writing for his classes—and for school newspapers—while in high school and learned the joys of theatre from plays that were put on in school and the local settlement house (a place that would now be called a community center). He eventually enrolled at City College, earned a bachelor's of science degree, and used it to start a successful electrical supply company that collapsed when the stock market crashed in 1929. "I was left with a pencil, and finally had to write for a living. As I told Studs Terkel once, what was the Depression for most people was for me a life-saver!" Harburg told Wilk for his book.

Just before this, Harburg met composer Jay Gorney through one of his City College classmates, Ira Gershwin, and by June 1929, Harburg and Gorney provided songs for *Earl Carroll's Sketch Book*. Harburg joined forces with Vernon Duke (as well as Gershwin) the following year for the *Garrick Gaieties*, and in July 1930, four Harburg–Gorney numbers were featured in that year's edition of *Earl Carroll's Vanities*.

Harburg's lyrics continued to be heard in revues in 1931, and then he and composer Lewis Gensler provided the songs for *The Ballyhoo of 1932*, which took its name from a recently launched and phenomenally popular humor magazine that, on some levels, presaged *Mad* magazine. Harburg's wry sense of humor, which had been a key part of his writing from the outset, perfectly matched the *Ballyhoo's* irreverence, particularly in a song such as "How Do You Do It?," which gently mocks Cole Porter's "You Do Something to Me."

Less than a month after *Ballyhoo* opened, another revue, *Americana*, debuted, and for it Harburg, once again working with Gorney, penned his first major hit, "Brother, Can You Spare a Dime?" The song, described as a "ballad of the Depression" by *Variety* critic "Bige." on October 11, 1932, showcased Harburg's gift for creating poetry out of even the most serious subjects, and it was singled out not just in this review but also in many others. Within two weeks both Bing Crosby and Rudy Vallee recorded the song.

More hit songs emerged from Harburg as he worked with Duke in the ensuing years. Among the songs they contributed to the American songbook are "April in Paris," from *Walk a Little Faster* (1932), and "I Like the Likes of You," which they penned for the *Ziegfeld Follies of 1934*. In 1937, Harburg came to Broadway with Harold Arlen, with whom he had partnered for two 1936 movies: the Al Jolson vehicle *The Singing Kid* and Busby Berkeley's *Stage Struck*. Their Broadway bow was *Hooray for What!*, a musical about an inventor of gases who is sought by diplomats hoping to exploit his creations in warfare. Harburg conceived the satirical show (which had a book by Howard Lindsay and Russel Crouse), and among the future standards, the score includes "Down with Love."

It wasn't long after this that Arlen and Harburg got what became an all-important Hollywood assignment, *The Wizard of Oz*, and when it premiered in 1939, the movie brought the world the song "Over the Rainbow," among others. During the early 1940s, Harburg continued to pen lyrics for various film projects, notably *Panama Hattie* (1942) and *Cabin in the Sky* (1943).

His West Coast work did not mean Harburg was absent from Broadway. In 1941, he, working with composer Burton Lane, wrote the songs for *Hold on to Your Hats*, another Jolson vehicle, and then in 1944, he and Arlen returned to Broadway with *Bloomer Girl*. Harburg was both lyricist and director for this musical, with a book by Sig Herzig and Fred Saidy, about a woman who defies convention just before the Civil War by refusing to wear hoopskirts, even though her father is a prominent manufacturer of them. The result was what Ward Morehouse called a "warm, melodious and beautiful song-and-dance show" in an October 6 *New York Sun* review, and John Chapman to proclaimed in the *Daily News* on the same day, "There isn't a bad or dull song in the Arlen–Harburg collection."

Harburg's most enduring stage work, *Finian's Rainbow*, came in 1947. With music by Lane and a book penned by the lyricist and Saidy, it centers on an Irish man and his daughter who move to Missitucky to bury a pot of gold, followed by the leprechaun to whom it belongs. Fantasy elements blend with social commentary (the racism of the South is both humorously and bitingly portrayed) in both the book and lyrics. Chapman in his January 11, 1947, *Daily News* review remarked that the former was a "nice combination of nonsense and standard boy–girl romance which packs a good wallop at the Bilbos of the South." As for the lyrics, Chapman wrote, "they are top-grade—witty or pretty, funny or satirical as needs dictate." The show, featuring such standards as "How Are Things in Glocca Morra?" and "Old Devil Moon," ran 725 performances, has returned to Broadway in several revivals, and was adapted as a movie musical in 1965.

Harburg would never achieve the same sort of theatrical success, and his ability to work in Hollywood was curtailed by his blacklisting. Nevertheless, his desire to comically explore serious issues never waned. Between 1951 and 1968, he brought another four musicals to Broadway, ranging from a toy factory satire, *Flahooley* (1951), to an adaptation of Aristophanes's antiwar *Lysistrata, The Happiest Girl in the World* (1961). His last Broadway outing was *Darling of the Day*, an exploration of fame and class set in Edwardian England. The piece misfired for critics and audiences, but even in it, Dan Sullivan, writing for the *Times* on January 1, 1968, noted how "typically skillful" Harburg's writing could be.

EDWARD "NED" HARRIGAN AND DAVID BRAHAM

(October 26, 1844–June 6, 1911) / (c. 1834–April 11, 1905)
Book Writers / Lyricists / Composers

With their tuneful depictions of life on Manhattan's Lower East Side, Harrigan and Braham took an early but crucial step forward toward the book musical.

When people think of Ned Harrigan, they naturally extend their thoughts to Tony Hart, the man with whom Harrigan performed for most of his career, and indeed, it was the team of Harrigan and Hart that captured audiences' affection in the United States in the years just following the Civil War. More important, however, was the collaboration of Harrigan with composer David Braham. Their work elevated the material that Harrigan and Hart performed and in doing so helped set the stage for what audiences would come to expect in their musical comedy entertainment.

Harrigan was born in New York in 1844 to Irish parents. His father, a ship's carpenter, assumed that the boy would also take up the trade, but while still a teenager, the younger Harrigan ran away from home with some friends and headed west. It was there, his June 7, 1911, *New York Times* obituary related, that "he found his mission in life—that of making others laugh." Harrigan made his stage debut in 1867 in San Francisco and for a brief time enjoyed a partnership with comic Sam Rickey. Harrigan also performed in works by himself. In 1870, he was impersonating journalist Horace Greeley in a "ripped from the headlines" melodrama about a high-profile New York murder case.

Several years later, Harrigan joined forces with a young performer he met in Chicago, Tony Hart, who was born Anthony Cannon in Worcester, Massachusetts. The younger man had been working since he was in his teens and had developed a successful career performing in blackface.

The men shared an instant chemistry onstage, and thus the team of Harrigan and Hart was born. Harrigan penned their sketches and songs, and within short order they became a highly popular act in variety shows, particularly at New York's Theatre Comique, which was located on Broadway between Prince and Broome Streets and which also sent them on tour. A review from the June 15, 1873, edition of the *Chicago Tribune* noted that their various sketches were "invariably clever and amusing."

Not long after this, they were joined by a third—off-stage—collaborator, composer David Braham, who was also affiliated with the Comique. Braham, who had been performing as a musician since he was a child, had come to the United States when he was a teenager and found work as a violinist with groups ranging from pit orchestras to variety hall bands. While he did this, he was also composing music, and in 1869, his musical *Pluto* premiered at the Comique.

Once the writing partnership of Harrigan and Braham was established, the stage partnership of Harrigan and Hart soared, particularly after the premiere of the first song Harrigan and Braham wrote, "The Mulligan Guard." A lilting military march for a fictional makeshift militia, the number sparks, both musically and lyrically, with the lightheartedness of Harrigan's sketches, which center on life among the denizens of the Lower East Side, particularly the Irish and African Americans.

Less than a year after the song premiered, the May 29, 1874, *Pittsburgh Daily Post* touted the Comique's touring bill: "Edward Harrigan and Tony Hart, who appear conjointly in the famous sketch of the 'Mulligan Guard,' are known all over the country as the best eccentric and comedian actors in America." Similarly, when the team appeared at Ford's Opera House in Washington, DC, in 1875, the readers of the *National Republican* on September 22 learned that "pure fun, and plenty of it, is the reward of going to see Harrigan and Hart."

Another reward for theatregoers in taking in a Harrigan and Hart show at this juncture was seeing an entertainment that offered something more than just a series of unrelated acts. Harrigan, working with Braham, started giving a story line to their shows. For instance, in *The Donovans* in 1875, they wrote about the titular Irish immigrants who, as reported in the June 3 edition of the *Buffalo Commercial*, "rescue all sorts and kinds of people from all sorts and kinds of places." The writers inserted a modicum of spectacle into the show (a working steam engine for a fire scene), and in order to accommodate just about any act imaginable (and the show contained jugglers and acrobats), there was a scene set inside a variety theatre.

Later that year, a new show debuted, *The Doyle Brothers*. This one took the sensibility of the previous piece a step further, attempting to shoehorn varied offerings into a melodrama about a woman with two lovers, one of whom murders her father and then tries to prove his rival guilty of the crime. Harrigan and Hart's routines, including "Slavery Days" and "St. Patrick's Day Parade," were integrated in segments in which two Irishmen attempt to prove the one man's innocence.

The writing bore little resemblance to what audiences have come to expect from a book musical, but it was a step closer. Just as important, Harrigan's plotlines featured the "common man" in America of the day, instead of royalty or the privileged in foreign lands, which was the purview of opera and operetta. Further, Braham wrote not in a classical vein but rather a popular one. The songs Harrigan and Hart performed could be whistled while walking down the street, and a great indication of how popular Braham's songs became comes from period advertisements for sheet music that ran not only in the United States but also abroad.

Harrigan took over the management of the Comique a year after the premiere of *Doyle*, and as the years progressed, his and Braham's work continued to evolve. Eventually, their shows began to revolve around the Lower East Side community featured in their first hit song and specifically a saloon owner—Dan Mulligan (generally played by Harrigan). The plots of the *Mulligan Guard* musicals involved topics of the day: racial tensions (Hart would sometimes play a black washerwoman), political corruption, and even gang violence, and while the bill at the Comique continued to contain a variety of acts, they were offered on either side of the principal *Mulligan* musical.

One of the earlier offerings in the series was *The Mulligan Guard Picnic* (1878), which was followed by *The Mulligan Guard Ball* (1879). As the latter premiered, the *Times* on January 14, 1879, told readers that Harrigan "has again been digging into the peculiar social stratum of the metropolis which he had previously explored with such marked success." Further, the *Times* reported, Harrigan had found a "great deal of humorous ore" that was on display in the show. The paper also pointed out three song hits: "Babies on Our Block," "Hallway Door," and "Skidmore Fancy Ball." Before the year was out, *The Mulligan Guards Chowder* and *The Mulligan Guards Christmas* premiered, and as the *Times* reported on December 21, "They have so far succeeded that the traditional 'variety' performance is almost banished from [the Comique's] stage."

The *Mulligan* shows became popular around the country as Harrigan and Hart toured with them. So, too, did the songs. A story about sheet music in the *Williamsport Sun-Gazette* in Pennsylvania on December 17, 1880, reported that the songs from the *Mulligan* series were "being printed in unending editions."

The Comique shuttered a year later for financial reasons, and soon after, they opened the New Theatre Comique. When fire destroyed the latter building in 1884, the Harrigan and Hart partnership crumbled. Hart retired and died in 1891.

Harrigan and Braham, however, continued together. In 1888, a musical that focused on the foibles and tribulations of a hack driver named Waddy Googan approximated the success of the *Mulligan* series. Harrigan and Braham continued to collaborate into the 1890s, and for five years, their work was seen at Harrigan's eponymous theatre in Herald Square (it became the Garrick Theatre when actor-manager Richard Mansfield took ownership in 1895).

Harrigan continued to perform in the *Mulligan* musicals and others that had songs by Braham until his death in 1911. In addition, Harrigan performed in a handful of plays by others during the last ten years of his life. Braham predeceased his writing partner in 1905.

The day after Harrigan died, an editorial in the June 7, 1911, edition of the *Times* sniped that he "had long outlived the vogue of his crude but wholesome and original comic plays" and that "no flower of enduring charm ever blossomed on the shrubs that Harrigan planted." What the writer failed to recognize or admit was that George M. Cohan's musicals (then the vogue on Broadway) had grown from the sort of work Harrigan had written, and what he or she couldn't have known was that other writers, principally Guy Bolton, P. G. Wodehouse, and Jerome Kern, would soon begin to merrily expound on New Yorkers' lives, expanding on the tradition Harrigan and Braham had begun.

LORENZ HART

(May 2, 1895–November 22, 1943)
Lyricist

The mercurial nature of Lorenz Hart's lyrics makes him difficult to categorize, but there's little question about his having had a profound impact on Broadway's lyric writing; he demonstrated time and again that lyrics could be dichotomous: colloquial and poetic, brittle and deeply felt, funny and bittersweet.

Puckish was the word ascribed to Hart's lyrics in a *New York Times* editorial-appreciation that ran on November 25, 1943. In many ways the adjective feels as if it is one of the few that aptly fits Hart's body of work, created with Richard Rodgers over the course of two decades. Words for songs, when they came from Hart's pen, could have elements of Cole Porter's sophistication, Irving Berlin's straightforwardness, Ira Gershwin's colloquialism, and Oscar Hammerstein II's poetry.

Hart, a native New Yorker, demonstrated literary promise early on, writing poems by the time he was six, and ten years later he wrote a song—in both rhyming English and German—for his parents' twenty-fifth wedding anniversary. He enrolled at Columbia University to study journalism and then moved on to work for the Shubert Brothers, translating German plays. At the same time, he was introduced to a Columbia freshman, Rodgers. The two shared both a love of theatre and similar thoughts on it and decided to collaborate.

Their first published song, "Any Old Place with You," came in 1919. It was interpolated into *A Lonely Romeo*, and in it, Hart rhymes *Portugal* with *court you, gal* and *go to Hell for ya* with *Philadelphia*. It was Broadway's first taste of Hart's cunning use of words and knack for creating the unexpected rhyme.

Rodgers and Hart contributed half the score of another show the following year, *Poor Little Ritz Girl*, and then turned to penning numbers for Varsity shows at Columbia. Their next Broadway outing came in 1925 when they provided songs for the Theatre Guild's satirical *Garrick Gaieties*, and in this, Hart's love of the theatre and his ability to lovingly tease it were evident in such songs as "Soliciting Subscriptions" and "Ladies of the Box Office." But the song that stood out, and has continued to live for more than ninety years, was "Manhattan," a love song that also takes the listener on a sightseeing trip through New York City. Hart's lyrics for the revue were so exceptional that a writer in the July 25, 1925, edition of *Billboard* reported, "There isn't a publisher on song row that hasn't buzzed Hart to do some lyrics."

He very well might have been able to write with others, but for nearly two decades, Hart worked exclusively with Rodgers, and in the space of eighteen months after the premiere of the *Gaieties*, they had written three musicals, contributed a song for another, and provided a variety of numbers for the 1926 edition of the Theatre Guild's annual revue. In anticipation of this production and just after the opening of the team's *The Girl Friend*, Hart explained some of his thoughts on lyric writing to a reporter for a story in the March 21, 1926, edition of the *New York Herald Tribune*. He said one important quality was "'Spontaneity.' And spell it with a capital 'S.'" More crucial, Hart continued, "Find something living, a word everyone uses. . . . I try to make [lyrics] as fresh and as natural as ever, close to earth as may be."

From Rodgers and Hart's mid-1920s shows, such popular songs as "Mountain Greenery," "What's the Use of Talking?," "The Blue Room," and the title song for *The Girl Friend* emerged. Not long after the 1926 *Gaieties* opened and just in advance of their musical *Peggy-Ann*, an October 26 report in the *New York Sun* estimated that Rodgers and Hart had surpassed the one-million mark in sheet-music sales, "considerably in excess of other writers."

Hart's rapid rise to being among Broadway's hottest lyricists was also marked by his knack for topping himself. For instance, in *A Connecticut Yankee* (1927), he incorporated a vaguely medieval argot into "Thou Swell." This classic opens with the deliciously dichotomous "Babe, we are well met," that combines slang with a Shakespearean construction. At the other end of the spectrum, and from another standard, "You Took Advantage of Me" from *Present Arms* (1928), the refrain begins with the exceptionally direct "I'm a sentimental sap, that's all."

Hart's (and Rodgers's) output for the stage continued unabated as the 1920s came to an end, and then, at the beginning of the 1930s, they had a brief period in which they wrote songs for movies. By the middle of the decade, though, they were back on Broadway.

They returned with the spectacle *Jumbo*, which included Hart's exceptional lyric for the intimate "My Romance," where he cleverly itemizes the clichés that love does not need. Later in 1935 came *On Your Toes* with the remarkably simple "There's a Small Hotel." The Hart lyrics that endure from the 1937 musical *Babes in Arms* are for such songs as "Where or When," "I Wish I Were in Love Again," "My Funny Valentine," and "The Lady Is a Tramp," and in these latter two songs, Hart's skill at irony in lyric writing shines. A similar number of standards, including "This Can't Be Love," emerged from *The Boys from Syracuse* the next year, and in this specific number, Hart beautifully combines emotion and paradox. It can't be love because "I feel so well." In this musical, based on Shakespeare's *The Comedy of Errors*, Hart, as he had with *Connecticut Yankee*, crafts lyrics that have a modern feel while also evoking a sense of a time gone by.

"I Could Write a Book," "You Mustn't Kick It Around," and "Bewitched, Bothered and Bewildered" from *Pal Joey* (1941) are three songs that display Hart at his most versatile, and in Richard Watts Jr.'s January 5 *New York Herald Tribune* review, the critic wrote, "Mr. Hart's lyrics are sly and witty and decidedly frank, particularly in the song with what I can only think of as the height of euphemism, 'Bewitched, Bothered and Bewildered.'"

By this point the relationship between Hart and Rodgers was fraying because of Hart's frequent disappearances due to alcoholism, fueled by being gay in a time in which it was entirely taboo. Hart did, however, provide lyrics for one more musical, *By Jupiter*, in 1942, as well as the words for new songs in a revival of *A Connecticut Yankee* that opened November 17, 1943. Hart passed away five days later. He was only forty-seven years old.

MOSS HART

(October 24, 1904–December 20, 1961)
Book Writer / Director

Moss Hart took the topical revue to new heights during the 1930s and then in the 1940s and beyond helped shape the concept of a "musical play" with such shows as Lady in the Dark *and* My Fair Lady.

Moss Hart begins his autobiography *Act One* by describing how he yearned for a few moments alone at the music store job that he had when he was just twelve years old. At these times he could daydream, and the "fantasies and speculations, I indulged in after I reluctantly turned the last page of *Theatre Magazine*, were always of Broadway." Hart eventually rose from the poverty in which he was raised and also realized his goal of having a life in the theatre, as both a writer and director of classic plays and musicals. He was, as Brooks Atkinson opined in the *New York Times* on December 21, 1961, a "virtuoso theatre man, he knew as much about staging as he did playwriting."

It's through his plays, frequently cowritten with George S. Kaufman, that Hart secured his earliest—and some of his most famed—successes. Among their collaborations are such works as *Once in a Lifetime* (1930) and *The Man Who Came to Dinner* (1939), along with the Pulitzer Prize–winning *You Can't Take It with You* (1936). But before Hart teamed with Kaufman, he had already penned the book for a now-forgotten musical, *Jonica*, which had a brief run early in 1930.

Hart's next foray into musical theatre came in 1932 when he wrote the book for *Face the Music*, which features a score by Irving Berlin. At the time, Hart was cresting on his first success with Kaufman (who was directing *Face the Music*). But Berlin, already twenty years into his career, was worried that his days of writing hits might have come to an end. Hart's freshness, however, helped to reinvigorate Berlin, and the result was a satiric production that some critics favored over Kaufman's then-current collaboration with the Gershwins, *Of Thee I Sing*.

Hart and Berlin teamed in 1933 for another show, the topical revue *As Thousands Cheer*. For this piece they imagined that the numbers all corresponded to sections of a newspaper. The result was a show that was "ripped from the headlines" as it lampoons such targets as Britain's royal family and defeated President Hoover and his wife leaving the White House. It also addressed more-serious issues of the day (a lynching was at the center of Ethel Waters's number "Supper Time"). Atkinson, writing about the revue in the *Times* on October 15, remarked that their concept was "ingenious," calling it "lucid and simple and feverishly up to date."

Hart put current events behind him for *The Great Waltz* (1934), an extravaganza that pulled together music by the Strausses (both the older and younger Johann) and boasted a cast of 136. After crafting the book for this operetta (he based it on the rivalry between the father and son composers), he returned to contemporary satire with a new Cole Porter musical, *Jubilee*, about a royal family looking to enjoy pleasures that nobles might not otherwise savor (a sexy star from jungle movies is the apple of the queen's eye). It bowed on October 12, 1935, and the next day, Percy Hammond, in the *New York Herald Tribune*, described it as "first-class fun" and Hart's book as being "jolly and amiable."

For his next musical, Hart joined forces with Kaufman (their first outing as a book-writing team), composer Richard Rodgers, and lyricist Lorenz Hart. In *I'd Rather Be Right*, the much-lauded writing team took aim at American politics and life inside the Beltway, specifically Franklin D. Roosevelt and the New Deal. There was something audacious about a Broadway musical satirizing the sitting president, but even as critics and audiences savored George M. Cohan's performance as the commander-in-chief, Kaufman and Hart's book, for some, was too tame.

The same could not be said of Hart's next venture in musical theatre. For many years he had been undergoing psychoanalysis because of his ongoing struggle with being gay, and he began to contemplate a musical about the practice of delving into a person's psyche. The result, written with composer Kurt Weill and lyricist Ira Gershwin, was *Lady in the Dark*, which opened January 23, 1941. Starring Gertrude Lawrence as a fashion editor exploring her troubled dreams, the show was hailed for the way in which its score and book intertwined. Further, critics were wowed by the production itself.

Hart made his debut as a director for the show's book scenes, while Hassard Short, who had masterminded bringing a newspaper to life for Hart and Berlin's *As Thousands Cheer*, was responsible for *Dark*'s dream sequences. Some critics struggled with the production's mixture of fantasy and reality and drama and music, but most recognized *Dark* to be something special. Burns Mantle's February 2, 1941, *Daily News* review praised the musical for having spectacle as well as a "serious and seriously interesting plot."

It took eight years for Hart to work on another musical, and when he did, he reunited with Berlin, staging the composer's *Miss Liberty* (1949). With a book by Robert E. Sherwood, the show imagined the creation of the Statue of Liberty, and despite the pedigree of the creative team (which also included choreographer Jerome Robbins), the tuner was deemed to be almost as old-fashioned as its nineteenth-century setting.

Between this and his final two Broadway musicals, Hart continued to have a robust career directing plays. He also enjoyed one of his sporadic periods working in film, providing the screenplays for *Hans Christian Andersen* (1952) and *A Star Is Born* (1954).

With Hart's stagings of Alan Jay Lerner and Frederick Loewe's *My Fair Lady* (1956) and then *Camelot* (1960), he appears to have synthesized his experiences as book writer and the lessons he learned from Short's staging of musical spectacle. Atkinson, in the March 25, 1956, edition of the *Times*, heralded Hart's work in bringing the musical version of *Pygmalion* to the stage, writing, "Hart has been one of the most valuable particles on Broadway for years. . . . This is his most impeccable job."

Sadly, with *Camelot*, health issues sidelined Hart while the show was having its out-of-town tryout. Further, the musical was invariably compared to *My Fair Lady* and fell short of its predecessor in many critics' eyes, but this didn't stop it from becoming a major hit.

Hart died just a year later. The December 21, 1961, *New York Times* obituary for him quoted from a letter he had written just three days before his death: "I am still charmed and fascinated by the amusement racket."

VICTOR HERBERT

(February 1, 1859–May 26, 1924)
Composer / Lyricist / Conductor

Herbert's ability to combine his knowledge of classical with a sense of popular music resulted in some of the earliest hits of twentieth-century musical theatre and also began to shape the public's sense of Broadway as being the source for American music.

In 1895, Herbert saw his second major piece of theatrical writing, *The Wizard of the Nile*, produced. The show, a hit with audiences in New York and well beyond, was something of a landmark in musical theatre writing. An unnamed writer for the *N.Y. Dramatic Mirror* pointed out in a November 16 review: "In reality it is something on the boundary line between comic opera and burlesque." One reason *Nile* straddled both forms stemmed from Harry B. Smith's libretto for the Egypt-set show that also contained American humor. Another factor was Herbert's score; it fused the sounds audiences associated with operetta with popular music of the day.

That Herbert, with this work and many others, had a hand in shaping American musical theatre isn't surprising. He was born in Dublin; spent some of his earliest years in England; and starting at nine was classically trained as a musician, primarily on the cello, in Germany. He had an upbringing that echoed the cultures of the United States' melting pot.

He came to America in 1886 when his wife had an engagement at the Metropolitan Opera. Herbert was hired to play with the company's orchestra and moved on to serve as soloist and conductor for other groups.

Within days of the opening of *Nile*, Herbert was back at work as a conductor. In anticipation of a concert he was to give with Gilmore's Band in Syracuse, New York, a reporter in the November 10 edition of the city's *Sunday Herald* touted the success of *Nile* and added, "Mr. Herbert is in every sense a fine musician, and one of whom greater things are expected than any other composer in America."

For the next six years, Herbert's reputation continued to flourish. Often his concerts would include both classical music and his own compositions. At the same time, Herbert continued to write for Broadway. Between 1897 and 1900, he had six new shows premiere, and then in 1903, working with librettist Glen Mac-Donough, he wrote *Babes in Toyland*. A mash-up of fairy tales, the show captivated critics and audiences. In the October 18 edition of New York's *The Sun*, the critic went so far as to observe, "[Herbert] has written a toy symphony for the second act that outvies Haydn in simplicity."

Herbert's music was never far from a Broadway theatre after this. In 1904, he penned the music for *It Happened in Nordland*, a boisterous production that starred comedian Lew Fields, and in 1905, Herbert had four shows featuring his music open. This string of productions culminated with *Mlle. Modiste*, a musical with a book by Henry Blossom, who would become a longtime Herbert collaborator, that focuses on a female worker in a hat shop who dreams of becoming an opera singer. The show boasted the future standard "Kiss Me Again."

Not only was Herbert's productivity and accessibility having an impact on Broadway, but it was also translating into enormous sales of sheet music. An April 7, 1906, story from *Billboard* reported that the demand for Herbert's music "from the public is unequaled by any other living artist in his line." The piece went on, "His compositions have the faculty of pleasing those who wish to scale classic heights for their music, as well as others who prefer it in a lighter vein."

Herbert followed *Modiste* with yet another critical and popular hit, *The Red Mill*. The show was a vehicle for David C. Montgomery and Fred Stone, who were at that time the men identified with being the Tin Man and Scarecrow in *The Wizard of Oz*. In the September 26, 1906, edition of the *New York Evening World*, the paper's critic reported that the music was "original and refreshing. [Herbert's] well of melody never runs dry."

Over the next four years, Herbert had another ten shows open, and his next major hit came in late 1910, when *Naughty Marietta* debuted. Set in the 1780s, the musical centers on a ship's captain abetted in his search for a French pirate by the titular heroine, a high-spirited countess. Reviewers lavished superlatives on the score. According to the *Times* critic on November 8, it was "one of his very most tuneful scores," and *Marietta* is now part of what is considered the canon of American operetta.

As the 1910s progressed, musical theatre writing began to change, as such other songwriters as Irving Berlin, Jerome Kern, George Gershwin, and Richard Rodgers came onto the scene. It was as if a thought Herbert had shared in May 21, 1906, *New York Evening Standard* feature had come true: "Recently, the managerial point of view has changed and the composer is now given so much opportunity that we may expect more good writers lured into this field of composition."

Herbert kept pace with the changes and simultaneously remained true to his own musical voice. In 1916 (and nine shows after *Marietta*), he and Berlin even collaborated on the score for *The Century Girl*. One year later, Herbert's *Eileen* premiered. This operatic-sounding musical about an Irish revolutionary arrested by the British was one of Herbert's most ambitious pieces and also a very personal one, allowing him to musically pay tribute to his homeland of Ireland. As the *Times* critic pointed out, the show came from the "dean of American light opera composers" and was "fairly bursting with rich melodies of the kind for which the composer is famous."

Shortly after the opening of *Eileen*, Herbert made his first contribution to an edition of Ziegfeld's *Follies*: "Can't You Hear Your Country Calling?" The patriotic number coincided with America's entry into World War I, and with it Herbert began a relationship with the producer that lasted for another six years. At the same time, Herbert continued writing full shows as well.

Herbert died suddenly in May 1924, and just a month after his death, Ziegfeld lavishly paid tribute to him in an extended sequence in the *Follies*. And before 1924 had ended, Broadway heard one last Herbert score premiere when *The Dream Girl*, on which he was working at the time of his death, opened.

JERRY HERMAN

(July 10, 1931–)
Songwriter

Herman wrote the score for two of the theatre's most iconic musicals, took the art of the title song to new heights, and as late as 1983 was able to write melodies that had the ability to become minor standards.

Herman's childhood was steeped in music. Before he was five, he demonstrated the ability to play piano by ear. Further, he and his parents (both musically adept) would often play together after dinner, family theatregoing was a habit, and during the summers Herman eventually served as the drama counselor at the camp his parents ran.

Herman's father wanted him to go into the family business, but Herman had his sights set on the theatre. After graduating from the University of Miami, he struck out on his own and made a living working as a pianist in night spots around Manhattan. During this period, too, a revue he penned at school—*I Feel Wonderful*—played off-Broadway in 1954, and he contributed material to a revue starring Tallulah Bankhead that played the Westport Country Playhouse in Connecticut in 1956.

Reviews for the former show were disappointing, and his material for the latter one garnered scant notice, and so Herman returned to his work as a pianist. Two years later, he got his big break when *Nightcap*, another revue composed of his material, played at a club in Greenwich Village. The *New York Post*'s Richard Watts Jr. praised the show in a May 22, 1958, column, calling it "charming" and saying that "it brought to back memories of the historic Rodgers and Hart

'Garrick Gaieties.'" Capacity audiences and more critical attention followed, and the show eventually transferred to the Players Theatre and, with the new title *Parade*, played for six months.

It was during this time that Gerald Ostreicher approached Herman about a project that he hoped to assemble for Broadway: a musical about Israel. Ostreicher wanted Herman to write the score for it; bankrolled a trip to the Middle East for him; and the result was the musical *Milk and Honey*, which arrived on Broadway three years later.

The show wasn't Herman's Main Stem debut; that had come the year before when he contributed a number to a short-lived revue starring Hermione Gingold. However, *Milk and Honey* was his bow as a writer of a score for a full book musical, and for his efforts, he received encouraging reviews. Howard Taubman, in the October 11, 1961, edition of the *New York Times*, reported, "[Herman] has provided songs that range from functional to exultant."

While Herman was at work on *Milk and Honey*, he was also readying another show, *Madame Aphrodite*, which centers on a woman peddling a phony beauty cream and bowed off-Broadway in December 1964. Tad Mosel's book underwhelmed reviewers, but Herman's score contained gems and prompted the *Times'* Lewis Funke to write, "[It] is further evidence that Mr. Herman will be heard from again."

Such critical and popular acclaim attracted the attention of producer David Merrick who invited Herman to submit sample songs for a new project he was developing, a musical based on Thornton Wilder's *The Matchmaker*. Herman penned a quartet of numbers for his audition and impressed Merrick, earning him the gig of writing the score for the show that would become *Hello, Dolly!* In the process Herman created some tunes that have become part of a national, if not global, consciousness, and as George Oppenheimer remarked in his January 17, 1964, *Newsday* review, "[Herman] keeps the promise that he made in 'Milk and Honey' with a series of rousing and one or two restful numbers." When the original cast recording was released, Herman's score could be considered more carefully, and the *Times'* John S. Wilson pointed out in his February 16 review that, divorced from Gower Champion's galvanizing direction and Carol Channing's vibrant performance, "it seems more impressive on disc than it does in the theater."

Herman's title song for *Dolly* stopped the show nightly and went on to have a life of its own. Many popular artists recorded it, including Petula Clark, Ella Fitzgerald, and Louis Armstrong. The last version became a hit that ranked alongside two songs by the Beatles for the entirety of 1964.

Herman had a second Broadway hit just two years later when he provided the songs for the musical adaptation of the play *Auntie Mame*. As with *Dolly*, he filled the tuner, *Mame*, with immensely catchy melodies and wrote a title song that stopped the show. The production made a musical theatre star of Angela Lansbury, but critics felt that Herman's score wasn't entirely as good as what he wrote for *Dolly*. Still, there was praise. Richard P. Cooke, in his May 26, 1966, *Wall Street Journal* review, called the music "light and cheerful, although not at all saccharine."

After these two shows, both of which became major motion pictures, Herman struggled to write another one that would replicate their success. But his next three musicals—*Dear World* (1969), *Mack & Mabel* (1974), and *The Grand Tour* (1979)—struggled with critical response and at the box office. His contributions could always find supporters. His most daring departure from his previous upbeat shows was *Dear World*, which centers on a woman going head to head with a group of industrialists intent on demolishing a section of Paris. Herman's music is darker and more European in this musical, and Alan N. Bunce in the February 15 edition the *Christian Science Monitor* called Herman's work "pleasantly wistful" and the "show's most successful effect—a fond reverie about fine old values and glories."

Herman was finally able to savor another hit in the early 1980s with *La Cage aux Folles*, based on the 1978 French film about two gay men and the problems they face when the young man they raised announces his plans to marry the daughter of a right-wing politician. The musical opened on August 21, 1983, and the next morning, Frank Rich wrote in the *Times* that the score provided a charge of "passion" to "every genuine sentiment in the show." With *La Cage*, Herman consciously retired from the Broadway theatre.

Since that time Herman has written the popular television musical *Mrs. Santa Claus* (1996) that reunited him with Lansbury and one other unproduced musical, *Miss Spectacular*, planned for Las Vegas. And his music has endured and captured new generations. Two songs from *Dolly* were used in the 2008 hit film *Wall-E*. On Broadway, theatregoers have savored revues featuring Herman's songs, two Broadway revivals of *La Cage*, and most recently a 2017 revival of *Hello, Dolly!* that starred Bette Midler.

J

The Jones–Schmidt partnership resulted in not only one of the longest-running and most beloved musicals of the twentieth century, but it also showed audiences (and producers) the importance of small-scale musicals.

Ironically, the two men who created the longest-running musical in the world never intended to be musical theatre writers. Instead, Jones and Schmidt, as they are collectively known, had their sights set on other things, and yet they are the writers who gave the globe *The Fantasticks* and also set standards for small-scale musicals, often boldly experimenting with the form.

Jones grew up in Littlefield, Texas, and his earliest brushes with live performance came from the tent shows that came to his small town every summer. Movies eventually figured prominently in his life, and after discovering a knack for comedy and impersonation, Jones decided that he wanted to be an actor. He enrolled at the University of Texas at Austin (UTA) to study the craft, later switching to directing.

Also a Texas native, Schmidt plunked out tunes on the family piano as well as ones in the churches where his father, a Methodist minister, served. His mother might have been a piano teacher, but until he was in college, Schmidt would only play the white keys. In fact, whenever she pushed him toward using the black keys, he hurried off to indulge in his passion for drawing. Eventually, he also enrolled at UTA to study art.

It was his artwork that brought him into Jones's sphere. Schmidt started designing sets and posters for the student theatre group the Curtain Club, and Jones was the organization's president. When Jones began looking through the student submissions for a musical he was scheduled to direct, he found they were all "terrible," as he recalls in the liner notes for Harbinger Records' CD *Jones and Schmidt: Hidden Treasures, 1951–2001*. He decided to write the show himself and turned to Schmidt to serve as composer. The result was a revue called *Time Staggers On,* and it, as well as a second one, was a popular success on campus, so much so that Helen Sheehy in the August 2014 edition of *Opera News* reported, "Schmidt jokes that their careers have been downhill ever since."

Military service for both men followed their graduations, and after their discharges they settled in New York. To make ends meet, Schmidt found work as a painter and graphic artist. As for Jones, he was able to earn money writing, notably penning material for comedian Tom Poston.

During this time they were also contributing material to various revues in New York, including the ones Julius Monk presented at his club Upstairs at the Downstairs and Ben Bagley's *Shoestring '57*. They also continued to work on a project that had been on their minds for some time, a musical version of Edmond Rostand's *Les Romanesques*. They had envisioned it as a full-scale Broadway musical set in the Southwest. But when another classmate of theirs, Word Baker, invited them to submit it as a one-act for a series he was directing at Barnard College, they rethought their adaptation entirely, resulting in *The Fantasticks*.

After the piece, which centers on a young man and young woman whose love has blossomed because they believe their fathers disapprove of their romance, played at the school in August 1959, the team continued to rework it. By December, it was slated for an off-Broadway premiere at the Sullivan Street Playhouse in the new year. In *The Fantasticks*, the writers melded a narrator reminiscent of the stage manager from Thornton Wilder's *Our Town* with archetypes from commedia dell'arte into a tiny musical accompanied by just piano and harp, and when it opened on May 3, 1960, the show charmed critics and audiences.

In his *New York Times* review the following day, Brooks Atkinson described the musical as being a "masque," adding, "Harvey Schmidt's simple melodies with uncomplicated orchestrations are captivating." And in a May 9 *Daily News* review, Charles McHarry wrote, "Tom Jones, author of the book, has supplied lyrics of wit and tenderness." It was the beginning of an off-Broadway institution; *The Fantasticks* continued its run on Sullivan Street until 2002.

The writers' success attracted the attention of playwright N. Richard Nash, who approached them about musicalizing his most acclaimed play, *The Rainmaker*, about a con man who comes to a drought-stricken southwestern town and promises to make it rain. It was a natural fit for Jones and Schmidt, and they and Nash began working on the piece that became *110 in the Shade*. Critics were sharply divided about the show and its score when it opened on Broadway in October 1963; nevertheless, the production ran for a nearly a year. Jones and Schmidt received a Tony nod for their work, and while *Shade* was running, they enjoyed the unique distinction of having productions playing both off-Broadway and on.

Jones and Schmidt followed this with the two-character *I Do! I Do!* based on Jan de Hartog's play *The Fourposter*, which follows a couple through fifty years of highs and lows in their marriage. With this piece Jones and Schmidt found an ideal match for their folksy, gently sentimental style. It led *Variety* critic "Hobe." to pronounce the score "by far their best work so far" in a December 7, 1966, review.

Stripping a Broadway musical to just two characters was an audacious step in the mid-1960s, and as the decade wound down, Jones and Schmidt became even more experimental with *Celebration*, a musical fable centering on Orphan (the writers eschewed character names) and his journeys through an uncaring world. Orphan's travels and encounters with an angel, a rich man, and a cynic explore the issues of youth and aging, wealth and poverty, innocence and jaded corruption. The production, directed by Jones himself, drew some admiring notices, particularly from *Time* magazine's T. E. Kalem. In his January 31, 1969, review, the critic noted how the creators were using Brechtian techniques in the show, simultaneously distancing theatregoers and drawing them in. The result, Kalem wrote, was a "charmer for sophisticates who have never quite forsaken the magic realm of childhood." Such praise did not, however, translate into ticket sales, and *Celebration* closed after 109 performances.

The year after this, Jones and Schmidt were working off-off-Broadway at La MaMa in the East Village, providing incidental songs for Elinor Jones's play *Colette*. The show about the French novelist earned raves for its star, Zoe Caldwell, and the songs were also frequently applauded. In a May 13 *Variety* review, critic "Sege." singled out "Earthly Paradise": "[It] is lovely and should be recorded."

For the remainder of their careers, Jones and Schmidt continued to explore their work on musicalizing the flamboyant woman's life. In 1982, their full musical, also titled *Colette*, starred Diana Rigg and aimed for (but never reached) Broadway. Nine years later, they offered *Colette Collage* off-Broadway for a brief run.

From 1971 to 1974, Jones and Schmidt gave themselves an artistic incubator, Portfolio Productions, in which to create. "We were interested in experimenting," Schmidt told Lee Alan Morrow for a May 4, 1984, *Back Stage* feature. Schmidt added, "We did a lot of work in the areas of myth and theatre mixed with vulgar street and clown theatre." The composer noted, "[We were] experimenting with some lofty things that sometimes led us far astray."

In late 1974, Jones and Schmidt revealed what they had been working on in a four-production season. It included a revue of their songs, a revised version of *Celebration*, and two new musicals: *Philemon*, about a street clown in ancient Rome who's asked to impersonate a revered priest who has died in prison, and *The Bone Room*, about a worker at the Museum of Natural History suffering from a midlife crisis.

One of New York's daily critics, the *Daily News'* Douglas Watt, took in all four of the pieces, and he continually found reasons to admire the Portfolio offerings; although he had reservations, he concluded his March 16, 1975, review of *Bone Room* with "I'm inclined to admire the team, not alone for their skill but for at least attempting to find new designs while working proudly within the mainstream of theater music." After the short runs of the four-title season, Jones and Schmidt offered *Philemon* in a longer run, and eventually the musical was filmed for TV.

From this point forward (beyond their two *Colette* musicals), Jones and Schmidt brought only a handful of shows to the stage. Their most notable effort came in 1987, when *Grover's Corners*, their adaptation of Wilder's *Our Town*, premiered in Chicago. Sid Smith's July 30 *Chicago Tribune* review praised the piece for containing "rivery sweet melodies" and Jones and Schmidt for delivering a musical that was "serenely in sync with the rich feelings embedded [in the original]." After its premiere, Mary Martin expressed interest in appearing in a New York production of the musical, but her cancer diagnosis precluded her involvement. Rights for the piece eventually reverted to the Wilder estate.

Jones and Schmidt's subsequent work included a biographical revue about their career, *The Show Goes On* (1998), and the Western-set musical *Roadside* (2001), which used a traveling tent show, like the ones Jones enjoyed as a child, as a framing device. In addition, the team worked periodically on *Mirette*, a fanciful piece based on a children's book, from 1994 to 2000, seeing it through a variety of workshop incarnations, productions, and concert presentations.

K

JOHN KANDER AND FRED EBB

(March 18, 1927–) / (April 8, 1928–September 11, 2004)
Songwriters

For nearly four decades, this songwriting team provided scores for musicals that challenged and entertained, along the way creating some songs that have become cornerstones of the American songbook.

These songwriting partners literally gave Broadway "Razzle Dazzle" in their 1975 musical *Chicago*, but long before that show—and well after—they were offering up witty, glitzy, and slightly naughty numbers to the delight of critics and audiences alike. Their scores, written over the course of nearly four decades, are considered among the most tuneful—and adult—of the late twentieth century.

Kander and Ebb, as they are familiarly referred to, both grew up far away from the glamour that would so often surface in their work. Kander, the team's composer, was raised in Kansas, and his love for music was evident at an early age, so much so that when his teacher asked him why he wasn't paying attention to a math lesson in second grade, he answered that he was writing a Christmas carol, and indeed, on his desk was a paper containing his notations for the song. Not long after, Kander took in his first live performance when an opera company toured to his native Kansas City.

After high school, there was some military service for the young man, who ultimately received his bachelor's degree in music from Oberlin College in 1951 and a master's degree from Columbia University in 1953.

The lyricist of the team, Ebb, grew up on New York's Lower East Side. "As a boy, I had very little exposure to the arts," he recalls in the book *Colored Lights*, which he and Kander wrote in 2003. Ebb goes on to joke, "I wouldn't have known what a Philharmonic was." By his teens, though, Ebb discovered theatre, and though his parents wanted him to become a doctor or lawyer, he enrolled as an English major at New York University. There a teacher encouraged him to pursue writing as a profession. Ebb earned his bachelor's degree and went on to graduate studies at Columbia University.

In the 1950s, both Kander and Ebb were able to earn a living working in the arts. Kander, who had begun to think of a career in musical theatre, coached singers, played piano at auditions, and worked in summer stock. His acceptance of a job substituting for the pianist for the original production of *West Side Story* was a crucial move and led to his first job writing music for Broadway; it was because of this show that he met Jerome Robbins, who later invited him to pen the dance arrangements for *Gypsy*.

Ebb's work as a lyric writer began in both the pop and theatre worlds. His earliest successes were in the former, working with composer Phil Springer. Among their songs were "I Never Loved Him Any Less," recorded by Carmen McRae, and "Heartbreaker," which Judy Garland recorded. Ebb also gained several theatrical credits during this time, including the off-Broadway revue *Baker's Dozen* (1951) and *Isn't America Fun?* (1959), a revue presented at the Blue Angel nightclub. His Broadway bow came with another revue, *From A to Z*, which had Hermione Gingold as its headliner.

After Kander had written, with William Goldman and James Goldman, the lighthearted *A Family Affair* for Broadway in early 1962, his music publisher, Tommy Valando, introduced him to Ebb, and the men began collaborating. One of the first songs they wrote together was "My Coloring Book," which Sandy Stewart debuted to acclaim on *The Perry Como Show* late that year. Other jointly written songs followed, and even as they were working together, a musical set during the Civil War that Ebb wrote with Paul Klein, *Morning Sun*, opened off-Broadway in October 1963.

The songwriting team of Kander and Ebb arrived on Broadway two years later thanks to producer Harold Prince who engaged them for *Flora, the Red Menace*, a breezy musical about a young woman inadvertently swept into the Communist Party at the height of the Depression. The musical also marked Liza Minnelli's Main Stem bow. She garnered most of the acclaim in the dailies' reviews when the show opened, but when the original cast recording was released, critics began to pay more attention to Kander and Ebb's contributions. In a May 23, 1965, *New York Times* review of the LP, John S. Wilson praised them for writing songs that "have provocatively comic or tuneful qualities that provides the bases for [Minnelli's] distinctive performance."

Just a year later, Kander and Ebb were working with Prince again, having written the score for the landmark musical *Cabaret*. For this show, with a book by Joe Masteroff, that unfolds during the Nazis' rise to power in Germany, Kander wrote melodies that tunefully (and sometimes eerily) echo songs of the era, while Ebb's lyrics playfully (and pungently) delineate character, comment on the action, and underscore the troubling political climate in which the characters live. Walter Kerr, in his November 21, 1966, *Times* review, wrote that the songs "snatch up the melodic desperation of the era and make new, sprightly, high voltage energy of it." Kander and Ebb earned their first Tony Award.

The Kander–Ebb partnership continued to display a flair for giving musical voice to a diverse range of stories, starting with *The Happy Time* (1968), an amiable tuner about an impressionable boy and his world-traveling uncle. That same year, *Zorba*, a heartfelt examination of friendship, romance, and cultural differences, opened, and then the team brought *70, Girls, 70* (1971), about a group of older people who scheme and steal to buy their retirement home, to Broadway.

Film and television work began to occupy the team in the early 1970s. First, the movie version of *Cabaret*, featuring two new numbers, opened in early 1972, and at the end of the year, Minnelli's television special *Liza with a "Z"* aired. For the latter they received a pair of Emmys, sharing one with director Bob Fosse. In 1975, they also provided songs for the movie *Funny Lady* and were Academy Award–nominated for their tune "How Lucky Can You Get?" Interestingly, their "Theme for 'New York, New York'" for director Martin Scorsese's 1978 movie musical was not similarly honored, and yet it has become one of their most iconic songs.

As they worked on these projects, they also joined Fosse for a new stage musical, *Chicago*. The show, based on a 1920s play about a woman accused of murder who sees her trial as a bid for stage stardom, featured another Kander and Ebb classic, "All That Jazz." The musical, which in revival has become one of the longest-running shows in Broadway history, was not nearly as big a hit when it premiered, though it ran a healthy 936 performances and eventually was turned into the 2003 Oscar-winning film.

During the second half of the 1970s and throughout the 1980s, the songwriters were never far from Broadway. Their musicals from the period—*The Act* (1977), *Woman of the Year* (1981), and *The Rink* (1984)—showcased such powerhouse performers as Minnelli, Lauren Bacall, and Chita Rivera while serving as ongoing reminders of how a Kander–Ebb number could be simultaneously catchy, sly, and sometimes raucously funny. For one, *Woman of the Year*, they also won their second Tony.

After *The Rink*, it took them twelve years to return with a new musical, but they had been working on it with their longtime collaborator, director-producer Prince, since the late 1980s: *Kiss of the Spider Woman*. Based on Manuel Puig's novel of the same name, the musical centers on a pair of prisoners in a Latin American jail, one of whom fantasizes about a screen goddess. The collision of grit and glamour in the story, combined with the South American locale, took the team to new levels. In his May 4, 1993, *Daily News* review, Howard Kissel wrote, "[They] have written one of their most pungent and intelligent scores." The critic praised their ability to compose a number, such as "Morphine Tango," which he labeled "satiric," as well as the numbers of "deep tenderness" and "great delicacy" for the two inmates. *Spider Woman* netted them their third Tony Award.

Their last new musical in the twentieth century was *Steel Pier* (1997), a portrait of marathon dancers in Atlantic City at the height of the Depression. The show was something of a departure for the team, more sentimental than their previous works. Ben Brantley, in his April 25 *Times* review, mentioned this and then opined, "[They] are simply more engaging when they're in a more cynical mood." Ultimately, *Steel Pier* ran only seventy-six performances.

Ebb passed away on September 11, 2004, but his death did not signal an end to the premieres of new Kander and Ebb musicals on Broadway because the men had so many projects in process. For the next eleven years, Kander carefully shepherded three to New York, starting with the murder mystery *Curtains* in 2007. Three years later, *The Scottsboro Boys*, a bold look at the trial of a group of African Americans in Alabama in the 1930s, had a brief and critically acclaimed run, and in 2015, the team's musicalization of *The Visit*, which centers on a woman demanding that a bankrupt town's citizens take revenge on the man who jilted her when she was younger, opened. This trio of musicals demonstrated how a partnership begun in the 1960s still had the knack to both amuse and stimulate theatregoers.

GEORGE S. KAUFMAN

(November 16, 1889–June 2, 1961)
Book Writer / Director

Kaufman's shrewd judgment and urbane comic sensibility elevated what made Broadway musicals funny from the 1920s to the 1930s, both in terms of content and execution, and helped to create two of the theatre's most enduring musical comedies.

In 1932, George S. Kaufman, along with Morrie Ryskind and Ira Gershwin, shared the first Pulitzer Prize for drama awarded to a musical. (Composer George Gershwin was not included in the prize, as he had supplied "only" music.) The honor, for *Of Thee I Sing*, came just fourteen years into Kaufman's impressive four-decade tenure on Broadway, one in which his innate comic sensibility bolstered, time and again, the humorous side of "musical comedy."

Kaufman was born in Pittsburgh, Pennsylvania, and later raised in Paterson, New Jersey, and demonstrated his gift for language and comedy while he was still a teenager. He studied law for a brief period after high school, but the profession and he were unsuited to one another. To earn a living, he took a series of unrelated jobs, at the same time contributing humor pieces to Franklin P. Adams's popular *The Conning Tower* column in the *New York Mail*. The two men became friends, and it was Adams who helped Kaufman secure a position at the *Washington Times*, which eventually led to Kaufman becoming a drama reporter for the *New York Tribune* in 1915. He became drama editor for the *New York Times* two years later, holding that position until 1930.

It was while Kaufman served in this position that he began his career as a playwright. His first effort, *Someone in the House* (1918), ran for less than two months on Broadway, but his second one, *Dulcy* (1921), was a hit. Written with Marc Connelly, the play centers on a woman who speaks only in clichés and her disastrous attempts at entertaining a group of weekend guests. Alexander Woollcott, in an August 21 *Times* review, called it "witty and dexterous" and remarked that it is "that rarity in our theatre—an urbane satirical comedy of American authorship."

Kaufman entered the world of Broadway musicals with the revue *The 49ers* in 1922. Percy Hammond in his November 11 *New York Herald Tribune* review singled out one of Kaufman's sketches, "Life on the Back Page," as one of the evening's highlights, writing that it was "too funny to be blue-penciled, wounding as it will, the feelings of all the monstrous [advertisers]" found at the end of newspapers.

Kaufman and Connelly reunited after this, first for *Merton of the Movies* (1922), a nonmusical satire about Hollywood, and then a book musical, *Helen of Troy, New York* (1923), that jeered the clothing business and advertising. "Its only handicap is that it is considerably beyond the intelligence of the average musical-comedy audience" was Hammond's response to the writing in his June 20 *Herald Tribune* review.

For the balance of the 1920s, Kaufman, working with a variety of partners, established himself as one of Broadway's premiere comic writers with such plays as *Beggar on Horseback, The Royal Family,* and *June Moon.* He also turned to directing, most notably with the classic newspaper comedy *The Front Page.* The show immediately established Kaufman's reputation for being a master of technique. Malcolm Goldstein reports in the biography *George S. Kaufman* that actors from the show told colleagues that "his sense of timing was uncanny—that he knew not only where the laughs would appear, but how long each would last to the second."

Kaufman hadn't abandoned musicals during this period. With Ryskind he penned the books for two highly successful ones that starred the Marx Brothers: *The Cocoanuts* (1925) and *Animal Crackers* (1928). Of course, we can still experience some of the exuberance of Kaufman's writing today, thanks to the movies based on these shows, but Kaufman's considerable impact on musical theatre began with two shows that followed during the first years of the 1930s. The first was 1931's *The Band Wagon,* which featured songs by Arthur Schwartz and Howard Dietz and sketches by Kaufman and Dietz. Kaufman's writing—crisp, fast-paced, and intelligently biting—set a benchmark for sophistication in revues for the decade.

Six months after this opening, Kaufman, once again working with Ryskind, celebrated the premiere of the political satire *Of Thee I Sing,* which imagines a presidential nominee whose slate is based on a theme of love. Kaufman garnered critical and popular cheers, not just for the writing, but also for his staging of it, and just three months later, there were more accolades for his direction of another revue, *Face the Music.* J. Brooks Atkinson remarked in his February 18 *Times* review, "[The director's] brisk finger is in nearly every satiric pie these days," adding, "[He] has staged the piece at an ebullient pace."

Kaufman's knack for direction meant that he was often turned to for assistance when shows were having their out-of-town tryouts. Shortly after these last two shows premiered, he served as "play doctor" to another Dietz and Schwartz venture, *Flying Colors* (1932), and to *Pardon My English* (1933), which had a score by the Gershwins.

Another series of hit plays ensued, including *You Can't Take It with You,* for which Kaufman, along with Moss Hart, won a Pulitzer, making Kaufman the only writer to win this award for both a straight play and a musical. Among Kaufman's less successful forays into book writing during the 1930s were *Let 'Em Eat Cake* (1933), a sequel to *Of Thee I Sing,* and *I'd Rather Be Right* (1937).

Kaufman's comic sensibility did not prove a match for that of audiences and critics during the 1940s, when more-serious book musicals came to the stage, but in 1950, he returned to musical theatre with a major success, *Guys and Dolls* (1950), for which he served as a director. In his memoir *I Got the Show Right Here,* producer Cy Feuer recalls how it was Kaufman who suggested the plotline involving Nathan Detroit, the gambler perpetually engaged to nightclub performer Miss Adelaide. Feuer writes, "With that single stroke, George Kaufman expanded the story of *Guys & Dolls* to its proper proportions. It was magnificent." For his direction, Kaufman earned a Tony Award.

Kaufman's last foray into the Broadway musical, *Silk Stockings* (1954), was an unhappy experience. He cowrote the book and directed this barbed examination of Western relations with Russia, but when the show ran into trouble out of town, producer Feuer took over staging, and Abe Burrows heavily revised the script. Kaufman's career on Broadway concluded in 1957 as it had begun, with a nonmusical: Peter Ustinov's *Romanoff and Juliet*.

JEROME KERN

(January 27, 1885–November 11, 1945)
Composer

Kern, during the first two decades of the twentieth century, set standards for how songs could be integrated into musical theatre, created a new and distinctly American style of songwriting for the stage, and composed one of the first genuine book musicals that combined comedy and serious themes.

In 1919, Jerome Kern told the *New York Tribune*'s Rebecca Drucker, "Who cares about the composer anyway? He's the least spectacular part of a show." The May 25 interview came on the heels of Kern's most recent opening, *She's a Good Fellow*. What's ironic about the composer's modest, vaguely self-deprecating comment is that, while most of the musicals for which he provided songs during the teens have now been forgotten, his songs from them have lingered.

New York City native Kern came to music thanks to his mother who taught him to play the piano. Eventually, his family sent him to study composition in Germany and England, and upon his return Kern began staking out a claim for himself in the music industry. His first jobs were as a pianist and song plugger, eventually landing at T. B. Harms and Company, which provided him his entree to the theatrical world. When singer Marie Dressler called the company looking for an accompanist, Kern was the only one available. She took an instant liking to the young man and began introducing him to others in the business.

His first Broadway credit was for two songs placed in *An English Daisy*, a show for Joe Weber and Lew Fields (two of Dressler's peers) in 1904. It set in motion what would become the composer's bread and butter: For the next eight years, he contributed songs to nearly thirty shows on Broadway.

Kern's second Main Stem outing, *Mr. Wix of Wickham*, opened in September 1904, and although one critic wrote a notice for the show in the form of an obituary, Alan Dale, in his September 20 *New York Evening Journal* review, profusely lauded the composer: "Who is this man Jerome Kern whose music towers in an

Eiffel way above the primitive hurdy-gurdy accompaniment of our present-day musical comedy?" A new sort of composer had arrived on Broadway, one with a distinct taste for the sort of melody found in Victor Herbert's work but with a modern flair.

In addition to individual songs, Kern provided revised scores for foreign operettas during this time. One of the most notable was *The Opera Ball* (1912), an adaptation for American audiences of the German *Der Opernball*, and shortly after it opened, Kern's first full Broadway score premiered. It was for *The Red Petticoat*, a musicalization of a semisuccessful melodrama that had premiered the year before. Critics were charmed by Kern's music. The *New York Herald*'s critic noted on November 14 that the composer had "embroidered or appliquéd" the piece with melody.

It would be another three years before Kern supplied a complete score for a musical, but he continued to have multiple "additional music" or "featuring songs" credits. One of them, the long-forgotten *The Girl from Utah* (1914), featured a Kern number that endures to this day, "They Didn't Believe Me."

A turning point for Kern came the following year with *Nobody's Home*. The musical instituted a policy of presenting musicals at the intimate Princess Theatre and began Kern's relationship with the venue's manager-producers. Before the year ended, he provided the preponderance of music for *Very Good Eddie*, which also premiered at the Princess and set a new standard for a sort of intimate, modern storytelling in musical comedy. *Eddie* also contained the classic "Babes in the Wood."

Englishman Guy Bolton worked on the books for both of these musicals, and he and Kern, joined by another Englishman, P. G. Wodehouse, began to collaborate. Their first show together, *Miss Springtime*, was not in the same style as *Eddie*, but after they premiered this revision to a Hungarian operetta in September 1916, they opened *Have a Heart* in early 1917. Like *Eddie*, *Heart* was set squarely in America (Blueport, Rhode Island, to be precise) and told an entirely original story. The morning after its January 11 opening, the *New York Times'* critic announced that the piece was a "refutation of the belief of some managers that musical comedy must rattle along the same old ruts." As for Kern's music, the reviewer wrote, "It would be idle to single out individual numbers, for all are pleasing."

The Kern–Bolton–Wodehouse partnership continued to pen similar shows at a remarkable pace. They premiered *Oh, Boy* at the Princess a month later and *Leave It to Jane*, which contained the hit "Cleopatterer," at the Longacre the following August. Between these openings, the *Dramatic Mirror*'s Louis R. Reid profiled Kern, noting that at thirty-two he had contributed to eighty-six musicals. In the same June 2 article, Kern told the writer some of his thoughts about writing for the stage: "Songs must be suited to the action and mood of the play." He added, "Good taste, refinement, daintiness and charm—these should be the keynotes of all musical plays."

Over the next ten years, another twenty shows in New York featured Kern's work, and then in 1927, his and Oscar Hammerstein II's *Show Boat* premiered. It was a landmark event for the musical theatre, and as the *Times'* J. Brooks Atkinson pointed out on January 8, 1928, "For such musical drama no tin-pan clatter of eclectic melodies suffices," and then he proceeded to enumerate how such disparate songs as "Old Man River" and "Life upon the Wicked Stage" fit perfectly into the book while also sounding as if they came from one piece of musical cloth.

After *Show Boat* Kern wrote scores for such shows as *Sweet Adeline* (1929), *The Cat and the Fiddle* (1931), *Music in the Air* (1932), *Roberta* (1933), and *Very Warm for May* (1939), all but the last a hit and each producing at least one timeless standard: "Why Was I Born?," "She Didn't Say 'Yes,'" "The Song Is You," "Smoke Gets in Your Eyes," and "All the Things You Are." During the 1930s and early 1940s, too, he penned an extraordinary array of songs for Hollywood, including "A Fine Romance" and "The Way You Look Tonight." He was also the subject of MGM's star-studded biopic *Till the Clouds Roll By* (1946).

Sadly, Kern died suddenly and unexpectedly from a cerebral hemorrhage before this last film's release. At the time he was in planning stages for a new musical and had just completed work on a new song for a revival of *Show Boat*.

MICHAEL KIDD

(August 12, 1915–December 23, 2007)
Choreographer / Director

Like de Mille and Robbins, Kidd used classical dance as a basis for his Broadway numbers, but unlike his predecessors, he added athleticism and naturalism to create his own style, whose influence is felt today.

This artist began his dance studies as a teenager after attending a modern dance performance. When it came time for him enter college, however, Kidd, born Milton Greenwald in Brooklyn, enrolled as a chemistry major to please his immigrant parents. The following year, he received a scholarship to the School of American Ballet, and all thoughts of the sciences disappeared. It was the beginning of a career that would earn him five Tony Awards and an honorary Oscar for his work on such films as *The Band Wagon* and *Seven Brides for Seven Brothers*.

Kidd's Broadway bow came in 1939 when the American Lyric Theatre presented a short season of dances at the Martin Beck Theatre. He performed in such works as *Filling Station* (music by Virgil Thomson) and *Billy the Kid* (with a score by Aaron Copland). The latter piece was choreographed by Eugene Loring, and Kidd went on to work as both the assistant director and a soloist for Loring's company, Dance Players.

In 1942, Kidd joined the Ballet Theater (later American Ballet Theater), and of his performances in the company's spring 1942 season, Walter Terry in the April 25 edition of the *New York Herald Tribune* wrote, "[He] has been outstanding in every role, major and minor, that he has touched this season." Three years later, Kidd was back on Broadway in *Interplay*, devised by and also featuring Jerome Robbins, who had just had *On the Town* open.

Kidd's choreographic debut with the company came in October 1945 with *On Stage*. Margaret Lloyd, in her October 5 *Christian Science Monitor* review, called the work a "happy, young American ballet." This dance work included dialogue and, on some levels, prefigured *A Chorus Line*, as it depicted life among a group of dancers as some rehearse and others audition. And though the *Herald Tribune*'s Walter Terry was less than enchanted by it, he did observe in an October 14 piece about the dance, "[It] should take him to Broadway before the winter is out."

Kidd's reality didn't quite match this timeline. He spent another year with Ballet Theater, and then in 1947 he choreographed *Finian's Rainbow*. This light-hearted fantasy gave him the opportunity to create a wide range of dances, and in a January 10 *New York Times* review, Brooks Atkinson rhapsodized about Kidd's opening number, "Kidd and his dancers have interpreted the theme of 'Finian's Rainbow' like thoroughbreds and artists." Eight days later, Howard Barnes in the *Herald Tribune* wrote simply, "The dancing finds 'Finian's Rainbow' at its most joyous."

A trio of musicals that managed only minor runs followed, and then in 1950, Kidd was hired to create the dances for *Guys and Dolls*. For this fable of Times Square based on Damon Runyon's stories, Kidd had the chance to create showy diegetic numbers for scenes set in a nightclub, intimate dances for its leads, and several larger ensemble pieces. One of these was for a crap game featuring the song "Luck Be a Lady," and in a January 21, 1951, *Herald Tribune* column, Terry wrote, "[It] represents the finest example of welding of dance with dramatic action that I have ever seen. . . . One never notices who is dancing and who is acting for both groups are as one." Terry's impressions are borne out by one of the dancer's memories. In 1985, Peter Gennaro, who, after his days in Broadway choruses enjoyed a career of his own as a choreographer, told the *Hartford Courant*'s Malcolm Johnson for a July 6 feature, "For the first time, I was made to act, to sing, and to dance. We had to do everything."

Kidd went on to choreograph the film version of the show in 1955, but it wasn't his first Hollywood credit. He also created the dances for *The Band Wagon* (1953), including the acclaimed private-eye "The Girl Hunt" ballet danced by Fred Astaire and Cyd Charisse, and costarred with Gene Kelly in *It's Always Fair Weather* (1955). Kelly and Kidd reunited fourteen years later when Kidd devised dances for the film version of *Hello, Dolly!*

This work for the big screen did not keep Kidd away from New York. He choreographed *Can-Can* in 1953, and in it his dances helped catapult Gwen Verdon to stardom. The *Times'* Atkinson once again had high praise for Kidd: "He makes real theatre out of the revelry in the dance halls," adding, "With Gwen Verdon leading the ballets with impudence, recklessness and humor, the dancing is spectacular."

Kidd's life as a director-choreographer began in 1956 with *Li'l Abner*, based on Al Capp's popular comic strip. The show divided critics, but most agreed that Kidd's work had flair, or, as John Chapman put it in his November 16, 1956, *Daily News* review, "incredible skill and joyfulness." The show earned Kidd his fourth Tony Award for best choreography.

A similar fate lay in store for Kidd for the balance of his stage career. He was acclaimed for his work on flawed properties, and generally critics would point to one or two moments in which Kidd, as director or choreographer, enlivened the material and the story. Additionally, he won one more Tony and received an additional four nominations.

Examples of the disparate dances Kidd created include a vigorous whip dance in *Destry Rides Again* (1959), the deployment of his ensemble to erect a seemingly functioning oil rig in *Wildcat* (1960), and a dance for a group of sidewalk Santas in *Subways Are for Sleeping* (1961). This last show also included a brief dance sequence for Carol Lawrence, John Sharpe, and future choreographic great Michael Bennett that had critics and audiences talking. After Bennett's phenomenal successes some fifteen years later, he pointed to Robbins, Bob Fosse, and Kidd as the men who had inspired his work.

One reason for the success Kidd had with such disparate numbers stemmed from the philosophy that informed their creation. He described it to Anna Kisselgoff for a March 13, 1994, *Times* feature, "I always use real-life gestures and most of my dancing is based on real life." His work was, he said, "human behavior and people's manners, stylized into musical rhythmic forms." He said this after his final outing on Broadway, a short-lived musical version of the movie *The Goodbye Girl*, where he had stepped in as a last-minute replacement director.

L

With a distinct musical voice and an interest in exploring unconventional narratives, La-Chiusa has been at the forefront of creating cutting-edge musicals for nearly three decades.

In the space of two months in late 1993 and early 1994, LaChiusa had two musicals premiere at two of off-Broadway's most prominent institutions. *First Lady Suite* bowed at the Public Theater in December 1993, and *Hello Again* opened at Lincoln Center Theater (LCT) the following month. One year later, master director Harold Prince staged LaChiusa's *The Petrified Prince* at the Public. It was a period that signaled the arrival of an artist whom Stephen Holden, in a December 12, 1993, *New York Times* feature, described as a "Broadway modernist, whose style can range from early Schoenberg to Richard Rodgers." For LaChiusa it was the culmination of thirteen years of determined work in Manhattan after his arrival from Chautauqua, New York, where he had grown up.

LaChiusa began making a name for himself four years earlier when the WPA Theatre (the organization that originally produced *Little Shop of Horrors*) presented *Buzzsaw Berkeley*. LaChiusa penned the songs for this cross-pollination of glitzy Hollywood movie musicals and horror films, and in an August 21, 1989, *Newsday* review, Drew Fetherston noted that LaChiusa's lyrics are "filled with witty glints and funny rhymes." LaChiusa followed this production with the score for a one-man show by comedian Jeffrey Essmann and two pieces that premiered at Ensemble Studio Theater's annual One-Act Play Marathon. LaChiusa also provided librettos for a trio of operas that premiered across the country, most notably Anthony Davis's *Tania*, a surreal exploration of Patty Hearst's kidnapping by the Symbionese Liberation Army.

With *First Lady Suite*, a quartet of short musicals, LaChiusa brought a similar sensibility to the White House and the wives of four presidents. He imagined, for instance, Eleanor Roosevelt on a delirious midnight flight with her secretary Lorena Hickok and aviator Amelia Earhart, and Mamie Eisenhower traveling to Africa with Marian Anderson. The musical fantasia, which boasted a score that veered from abstractly operatic to more traditional musical theatre sounds, received both some raves and some cautiously appreciative words about its ambitions.

First Lady Suite also created a sense of anticipation for *Hello Again*, a time-bending retelling of Arthur Schnitzler's interlocking romances, *La Ronde*. Again, LaChiusa's daring and interest in experimenting with form wasn't always successful, and yet it inspired David Patrick Stearns in the January 31, 1994, edition of *USA Today* to deem it an "excellent new musical." In Vincent Canby's *Times* review the same day, the critic favorably compared LaChiusa to Sondheim.

As the 1990s progressed, LaChiusa had two nonprofit theatres to call home, and between the Public and LCT, he had another three pieces produced, starting with *The Petrified Prince* at the former. After this he provided music for *Chronicle of a Death Foretold* (1995), a theatre-dance piece created by Graciela Daniele, which LCT mounted at Broadway's Plymouth Theatre, and *Marie Christine* (1999), which featured book, music, and lyrics by LaChiusa. The show, set in New Orleans at the end of the nineteenth century, is an adaptation of the Medea myth, and LaChiusa wrote it expressly for its star, Audra McDonald. The piece displays his work as a composer at its most dramatic, and in a December 3, 1999, *Times* review, Ben Brantley lauded the "swirling, complex music" and the way in which LaChiusa "taps into [McDonald's] oceanic potential [as a performer]." It led to a Tony nomination for LaChiusa for best score.

Thanks to the Public, LaChiusa had a second Broadway musical four months later: *The Wild Party*. Based on Joseph Moncure March's narrative poem about a raucous Prohibition-era fete during which the host and hostess's turbulent relationship devolves, LaChiusa, working with director George C. Wolfe as co–book writer, structured the show as a vaudeville with sketches outfitted with intricately jazzy and sometimes pungently mordant songs. In an April 14, 2000, *Daily News* review, Fintan O'Toole described the music as having a "blazing energy" and wrote, "LaChiusa writes jazz as if it's just been invented," adding, "The score creates a dizzy, delirious musical world." Ultimately, though, the musical proved too dark for audiences (and many critics) and only ran sixty-nine performances.

Since then LaChiusa has refused to compromise his artistic vision to achieve commercial success, choosing to create musicals exclusively off-Broadway and at regional theatres and making occasional forays into concert halls and opera houses. He has been remarkably productive, and in New York alone, six LaChiusa musicals have premiered, many of them having unusual subjects. In *Little Fish* (2003), he explored how quitting smoking affected a woman's life. In *See What I Wanna See* (2005), he told a trio of stories that unfolded in three different time periods and allowed audiences to witness events from a variety of characters' perspectives. The musical *Queen of the Mist* (2011) centered on the life of Annie Edson Taylor, the first woman to attempt going over Niagara Falls in a barrel.

All three of these projects featured LaChiusa as book writer, composer, and lyricist. With others, such as *Bernarda Alba* (2006), he reunited with Daniele, and for this adaptation of Federico García Lorca's classic tragedy about a widow and her daughters, LaChiusa stretched musically, delivering a score filled with Latin influences. His most expansive score came with the premiere of *Giant*, which features a book by Sybille Pearson based on Edna Ferber's novel of the same name.

It's a musical that unfolds over the course of thirty years and features dozens of characters, and for it LaChiusa wrote what Brantley called "his most tuneful and accessible score" in a November 16, 2012, *Times* review. The critic also noted that audiences familiar with the artist's work could be assured that he still could "set notes to swooping and fluttering like wind-borne leaves in a storm."

The Public gave *Giant* its New York premiere, and three years later, the theatre was home to *First Daughter Suite*, a companion piece to LaChiusa's *First Lady Suite*, which had premiered some twenty-two years before. Since that time, LaChiusa has seen a musical adaptation of W. Somerset Maugham's *Rain* open at the Old Globe in California in 2016, a revival of *The Wild Party* in London that starred Frances Ruffelle in early 2017, and the film version of *Hello Again* that hit screens in early 2018. He is currently at work on musicalizing Martyna Majok's Pulitzer Prize–winning play *The Cost of Living*, which tells the story of four different people attempting to make ends meet.

NATHAN LANE

(February 3, 1956–)
Performer

Although Lane may have bid farewell to musical theatre, his work has helped to ensure that a legacy of comic bravado begun in the form's heyday has continued into the twenty-first century.

With credits that range from plays by Eugene O'Neill and Tony Kushner and to such Golden Age musicals as *Guys and Dolls* and *A Funny Thing Happened on the Way to the Forum*, three-time Tony Award–winner Nathan Lane has repeatedly demonstrated that he is the artistic heir to such Broadway legends as Bert Lahr and Zero Mostel. Lane is a performer who, like these men, can inspire roars of laughter and also delve into dramatic roles with aplomb.

He was born Joseph Lane and raised in Jersey City. As a child he discovered that his love of theatre and a good joke in class were escapes from an unhappy home life and his outsider status at school: "I was the classic fat kid who avoided trouble by always being ready with a quip," he told the *New York Times'* Glenn Collins for an April 22, 1992, feature. For college Lane received a scholarship to Saint Joseph's University in Philadelphia, but when he discovered it wouldn't cover all of his expenses, he decided to move to New York and look for work.

Stints in summer stock, dinner theatre, and off-off-Broadway ensued. In 1977, he appeared as Nathan Detroit in a production of *Guys and Dolls* at the Meadowbrook Summer Theatre in New Jersey. Reviewing the revival in the June 17, 1977, edition of *Back Stage*, David Levy wrote that Lane and costar Candy Calnan "effortlessly steal the show." Not long after, Lane discovered that, because a Joe Lane was already registered with Actors' Equity (the stage performers' union), he would need to use a different name, and he opted for Nathan.

The actor's Broadway breakthrough came in 1982 when he was cast in a production of Noël Coward's *Present Laughter* starring George C. Scott. Playing a young aspiring playwright, Lane attracted some terrific notices and garnered a Drama Desk Award nomination.

Before the show closed, Lane moved on to his first Broadway musical, *Merlin*, which featured magician Doug Henning and Broadway powerhouse Chita Rivera. After the troubled tuner disappeared from Broadway, his next Main Stem musical outing came when he landed a lead role in *The Wind in the Willows*. This production shuttered after four performances in December 1985, and his work in both it and *Merlin* led him to quip to Collins for a June 14, 1989, *Times* feature, "I've done some of the most unsuccessful musicals in the American Theater."

Lane's association with these shows didn't tarnish his reputation, however, and for the next seven years he regularly appeared on and off Broadway, originating roles in plays by Terrence McNally, Jon Robin Baitz, and Richard Nelson.

His return to musicals came in 1992 when once again he assumed the role of Nathan Detroit, this time in director Jerry Zaks's highly acclaimed revival of Frank Loesser's classic. Linda Winer described Lane's performance as "winsome" and "extravagantly endearing" in her April 15 *Los Angeles Times* review, and after more than fifteen years in the business, Lane's reputation as an always-dependable talent for comic roles was firmly established. Further, *Guys and Dolls* earned Lane his first Tony Award nomination.

Three years and two plays later, Lane was once again headlining a classic musical: *A Funny Thing Happened on the Way to the Forum*. In it he played Pseudolus, the Roman slave desperate for his freedom, a role originated by actor-comedian Zero Mostel. In his April 19, 1996, *New York Times* review, Vincent Canby proclaimed that in the production "he's as priceless in uncharacteristic repose as when he's cavorting about the stage." Beyond such praise, Lane's performance won him a Tony.

The actor concentrated on a television career for several years after his success and then returned to Broadway in 2000 to play Sheridan Whiteside in a revival of Moss Hart and George S. Kaufman's *The Man Who Came to Dinner*. A year later, he was once again headlining a musical, the stage version of Mel Brooks's *The Producers*. In it he played Max Bialystock, the conniving producer desperate for a flop, a role Mostel originated in the 1967 movie. Once again, Lane made the character his own, and as Charles Isherwood put it in his April 23 *Variety* review, it was a "career-topping turn. . . . [His] sad-sack eyes and air of desperate disgust are perfect for the frenzied, hapless Max." Lane scored his second Tony.

Lane served as both star and adaptor for his next musical outing, Stephen Sondheim and Burt Shevelove's *The Frogs*, which had premiered at Yale in 1974 and was belatedly making a Broadway bow in 2004. After this production's limited run at Lincoln Center Theater, Lane tackled a quartet of plays between 2005 and 2009, including Samuel Beckett's *Waiting for Godot*, in which Lane took the role that Bert Lahr had originated.

In 2010, Lane returned to musical comedy with *The Addams Family*, playing Gomez Addams, the patriarch of the creepy, kooky family made famous on television in the 1960s. Lane's status as both a comedic powerhouse and box-office draw were confirmed with the show. "Lane, sporting a thick comic accent, brings his ever-reliable comic genius to the role," said Frank Scheck in an April 9 *Hollywood Reporter* review, and when the star took a vacation four months later, Sam Thielman and Gordon Cox reported in the August 23 edition of *Variety*, "Anyone who doubted how valuable topliner Nathan Lane is to 'The Addams Family' got a wakeup call during week 14." Lane's absence had resulted in a 32 percent drop in box-office revenue.

Family had endured a difficult tryout period, and during its run, Lane told Kevin Sessums of the *Daily Beast*, "We've done the best we could. . . . I think this might be my farewell to the musical theater." And since that time, Lane has only appeared in plays, most recently assuming the role of Roy Cohn in Tony Kushner's *Angels in America*, for which he earned a third Tony Award.

JONATHAN LARSON
(February 4, 1960–January 25, 1996)
Composer / Lyricist / Librettist

With Rent, *Larson successfully married rock 'n' roll with a narrative story line, and with this one work, he inspired a new generation of musical theatre artists.*

Just after Larson's untimely death in 1996 and just days before the official opening of his musical *Rent* at New York Theatre Workshop, Stephen Sondheim told the *New York Times*' Anthony Tommasini that "[Larson] was on his way to finding a real synthesis" of contemporary pop and theatre music. Sondheim added, "Jonathan knew instinctively" how "you use music to tell a story, as opposed to writing a song."

Pop music, and rock in particular, had arrived on Broadway almost thirty years before *Rent* in the form of *Hair*, but while that show was, as Clive Barnes called it in his October 30, 1967, *Times* review, a "mood picture of a generation," Larson, with his transformation of *La Bohème*, used the popular music vernacular to tell the story—or, more precisely, a set of stories—about the generation that followed.

Music had always been a part of Larson's life, and though for pleasure he listened to pop music, he was also becoming familiar with other genres. In high school he played the tuba in the marching band at his White Plains, New York, high school and performed with its choir. When he attended Adelphi University, where he studied acting, he was involved in many of the school's musicals.

After graduation he settled in Manhattan and, while working a day job as a waiter, began to carve out a niche for himself in theatre. His music background got him a job as a pianist in summer stock, which allowed him to become a member of Actors' Equity, the union for stage performers. He also began composing and writing.

Theatregoers had the opportunity to hear Larson's work in Manhattan as early as 1983, when *Saved*, a satire about the Moral Majority that he and David Armstrong wrote, played a short engagement at an off-off-Broadway venue in Times

Square, Storefront Blitz. After this show closed, Larson continued to develop musical projects, including *Superbia*, a rock adaptation of George Orwell's novel *1984*, and one autobiographical piece, *tick . . . tick . . . BOOM!* For the first piece, Larson won a Stephen Sondheim Award from the American Musical Theater Festival, and Playwrights Horizons gave the musical a workshop production. The latter piece brought Larson's music back to the New York stage. In 1991, he performed it as a "rock monologue" at the famed Village Gate in Greenwich Village. Not long after, Larson, along with writer Hal Hackady, received a commission from Broadway Arts to write a children's musical called *Let's Be Friends*.

During this time Larson was also at work on an adaptation of *La Bohème*. He was drawn to the opera about artists struggling in France for an obvious reason: It contained direct parallels to his own existence in Manhattan. Larson, who initially worked on the adaptation with Billy Aronson, developed the musical that would become *Rent* over the course of more than five years, during which time he garnered several commissions from New York's nonprofit theatres to help him continue his writing. In 1994, he won the Richard Rodgers Production Award from the American Academy of Arts and Letters, which allowed New York Theatre Workshop to give the show a developmental presentation.

Two years later, *Rent*, with its fusion of rock, Latin, soft pop, and musical theatre sounds, premiered at the off-Broadway institution, but when it did, Larson was not in attendance. He had died unexpectedly of an aortic dissection after attending the show's final dress rehearsal. The morning after the musical's official February 13 opening, *Newsday*'s Linda Winer mourned the theatre's loss with Larson's premature death. He was, she wrote, "on his way to becoming precisely what the American musical theater has needed so desperately: a cultural synthesizer and popularizer, a missing link to connect new sensibilities and the old commercial forms for the next generation."

As for the musical itself, Ben Brantley's February 14 *Times* review lauded its "glittering, inventive score," adding that Larson had given a "pulsing, unexpectedly catchy voice to one generation's confusion, anger and anarchic, pleasure-seeking vitality." Michael Feingold's *Village Voice* review on February 20 proclaimed, "*Rent* is the only important event in the rock musical since *Hair*. And thanks to its Sondheimian formal sense, it's a work of consistently higher quality than *Hair*."

Rent transferred to Broadway the following April and eventually came to win Tony Awards for best musical, best book, and best score, as well as the Pulitzer Prize for drama. The show also developed an ardent fan base who saw the show repeatedly. Among *Rent*'s young admirers were future pop music star Lady Gaga and musical theatre sensation Lin-Manuel Miranda, who told *Playbill* in December 2018 that the show was what inspired him to become a composer.

Rent closed on Broadway in September 2008 after playing 5,123 performances. In that time Larson's *tick . . . tick . . . BOOM!* returned to the stage. Director Scott Schwartz and playwright David Auburn fused Larson's musical monologue with a related unproduced work, *30/90*, to create a multicharacter show, that, as Charles Isherwood wrote in a June 1, 2001, *Variety* review, "illustrates how rich were the gifts just about to reach fruition. As in 'Rent,' the songs are melodic and instantly appealing, blending pop-rock orchestrations with classic musical theater structures."

Since then both this show and *Rent* have been revived off-Broadway, and the latter musical has enjoyed myriad international productions, been transformed into a major motion picture, and offered as a live television presentation. Beyond these two shows, a revue featuring unheard material from both musicals, as well as from Larson's unproduced projects and specialty material he penned over the years, premiered in October 2018 at the supper club Feinstein's/54 Below in Manhattan. The production afforded audiences the opportunity to appreciate the depth and breadth of Larson's talent and has been preserved with a cast recording.

ARTHUR LAURENTS

(July 14, 1917–May 5, 2011)
Book Writer / Director

Laurents was responsible for writing the books to two of the theatre's most enduring musicals and experimented with the form, helping to broaden the range of stories that could be told with song and dance.

In a May 7, 2011, *New York Times* appreciation of Laurents's work, Charles Isherwood wrote, "He practically stands alone as a writer who owes his lasting fame to his authorship of two great musical books." Isherwood was referring to *West Side Story* and *Gypsy*, of course, but while these two shows stand apart in Laurents's six-decade career, they are just a part of his exceptional body of musical theatre work that often strove to break with tradition.

His interest in theatre started when he was growing up in Brooklyn and his lawyer father and schoolteacher mother would take him to see shows. His interest in writing for the theatre came later, and after he graduated from Cornell University he began taking writing classes at New York University. Among his earliest writing credits were a radio drama for CBS and sketches that he cowrote and performed in clubs with a group called the Nite-Wits. When he was drafted during World War II, he wrote scripts for training films and service radio shows.

Laurents's first Broadway credit came in 1945 with the play *Home of the Brave*. After this he enjoyed a successful career as both playwright and screenwriter, penning *The Time of the Cuckoo* (1952) for Broadway and the screenplays for such movies as *Rope* (1948), *The Snake Pit* (1948), *Anna Lucasta* (1949), and *Anastasia* (1956). Laurents returned to Hollywood to write the screenplays for *The Way We Were* (1973) and *The Turning Point* (1977), earning an Academy Award nomination for the latter.

While working on the earlier screenplays, Laurents, Jerome Robbins, and Leonard Bernstein began discussing an idea for a new musical, a modern take on Shakespeare's *Romeo and Juliet*. Originally conceived in 1949 as a musical that would be set on the Lower East Side and portray antagonism between Catholic and Jewish families, the musical later transformed into one that centered on the violence erupting in midtown Manhattan between gangs of Caucasian and Puerto Rican teenagers. Nearly ten years in the making, *West Side Story* opened on September 26, 1957, and the following morning, the creators, who had been joined by lyricist Stephen Sondheim in his Broadway debut, were hailed for their breakthrough achievement in integrating music, book, and dance. It was, as John Chapman put it in the *Daily News*, a "venturesome forward step" for American theatre. In a piece in the *New York Herald Tribune* eight days later, Walter Kerr praised Laurents's writing for capturing the young characters' voices: "[He] has given us busy and accurate language of the streets . . . spare and direct."

Laurents's next Broadway project was also musical and reunited him with Sondheim and Robbins, along with a new collaborator, composer Jule Styne. Together they transformed stripper Gypsy Rose Lee's memoir into *Gypsy*. In distilling her portrait of her childhood in vaudeville and eventual ascent to being the queen of ecdysiasts, Laurents opted to center his book on Lee's domineering mother, creating a searing role originated by Ethel Merman. As with *West Side Story*, the reviews for *Gypsy* were rapturous, and Laurents's craft eventually came to be seen as a landmark in musical theatre writing. When reviewing a 1974 revival starring Angela Lansbury that Laurents directed, Kerr recalled his initial impressions of the writing in a September 29 *Times* feature: "[It] had overnight joined the theater's program of Great Books."

Laurents had begun directing projects long before. He started with his play *Invitation to March* (1960) and then continued with the musical *I Can Get It for You Wholesale* (1962). He reteamed with Sondheim in 1964, writing the book for and directing *Anyone Can Whistle*. In this unconventional, absurdist piece, they imagined a bankrupt town run by a corrupt mayoress, where the inmates from a local asylum appear to be the sanest of the citizenry. The musical presaged the antiestablishment mood that would grip the country by the end of the decade, but it confounded critics, shuttering quickly.

After this, Laurents, working with Sondheim and composer Richard Rodgers, transformed his play *The Time of the Cuckoo* into *Do I Hear a Waltz?* The bittersweet story of a repressed American woman discovering love during a European vacation was an unlikely one for musicalization at the time, and many critics, while expressing reservations about the musical's merits, admired what the team had attempted to accomplish. Howard Taubman, in his March 19, 1965, *Times* review, applauded how "it has the courage to abjure garishness and stridency," adding, "It speaks and sings in a low key."

Laurents penned a third piece of adventuresome musical theatre in 1967: *Hallelujah, Baby!* which had music by Styne and lyrics by Betty Comden and Adolph Green. This show explored the African American experience throughout the twentieth century, following a heroine who never aged from decade to decade while examining how the prejudices and hurdles she faced evolved over time. With this show Laurents's efforts to examine issues of racism and the civil rights movement were applauded, but his approach was deemed too timid. Interestingly, it was for this musical that he won his first Tony Award for book writing.

After this Laurents returned primarily to playwriting, but there were still musicals in his life. In 1983, he directed *La Cage aux Folles*, the first Broadway musical that put a gay couple center stage, and for his work, he earned his second Tony.

Laurents also scripted and directed *Nick & Nora*, a musical based on the *Thin Man* mysteries, in 1991. The musical marked his last outing as a book writer, but it was not his last production on the Main Stem. Before he passed away in 2011, he was responsible for revivals of his two landmark works. The first came in 2008 when he staged *Gypsy* starring Patti LuPone. It marked the third New York production of the show that he had directed, and even fifty years after the show's premiere, he was refining the book and finding new ways to approach the classic he penned. A year later, he staged a bilingual production of *West Side Story*, which used translations by future Pulitzer Prize–winner Lin-Manuel Miranda.

GERTRUDE LAWRENCE

(July 4, 1898–September 6, 1952)
Performer

A consummate actress, Lawrence could play high and low comedy as well as drama, making her one of a handful of performers able to score repeatedly both in the giddy entertainments of the 1920s and 1930s and the more substantial book musicals that came later.

Lawrence's stage career began while she was still a young girl in England, and until her untimely death in 1952, she entranced audiences on both sides of the Atlantic. This actress-singer segued seamlessly between plays and musicals, in the process putting an indelible stamp on several touchstone roles of twentieth-century musical theatre.

During her childhood, Lawrence, who was born Gertrude Alexandria Dagmar Lawrence-Klasen, shuttled not only between her divorced parents but also from show to show, touring England. When she looked back on this period of her life in her autobiography *A Star Danced*, she observed, "I was determined to make good, and deep inside myself was the unshaken conviction that I would be a success someday."

It was through her work in tours that she came to the attention of impresario Andre Charlot who cast her in the 1916 edition of his wartime revues. She continued performing in these productions through the war years and after, and then in 1922, Charlot cast her in the musical *Dede*. It was the beginning of breakout success for an actress whom critic J. E. described in an October 22 *London Observer* review as possessing "beauty and grace and personality." The writer added, "She can act, she can sing, she can dance—in other words she is very nearly unique in the musical comedy world."

A year later, Charlot announced that he would be bringing one of his revues to Broadway for the first time, and in a June 14, 1923, *Variety* announcement of his plans, readers were informed that New Yorkers would be getting their first glimpse of this triple-threat actress-dancer-singer with the "reputation of being the peer of any single artist in the English musical comedy." Neither critics nor audiences were disappointed when she, Beatrice Lillie, and Jack Buchanan opened in *Andre Charlot's Revue of 1924*. Even the critic for the *New York Times* noted in the paper's January 10, 1924, review that "no amount of advance word" about Lawrence could "take the edge off" enjoying her work in both the show's songs and sketches.

Another edition of the revue followed (first in London and then in New York), and after that Lawrence debuted in her first book musical in the States: *Oh, Kay!* In it she played the titular female bootlegger and introduced the Gershwin classic "Someone to Watch over Me." The musical, with its star, transferred to London, and then she was back on the Main Stem in a second show with a Gershwin score, *Treasure Girl*. Lawrence played the title character, a spoiled, spendthrift woman hunting for a hidden lode of riches that will allow her to pay off sizable debts. Critics were unforgiving of the book because, as Brooks Atkinson put it in his November 9, 1928, *Times* review, "It takes the unforgiveable liberty of presenting the accomplished Miss Lawrence in a disagreeable light."

Despite such critical concerns, *Treasure Girl* did no damage to audiences' regard for her, and less than a year later, she was back on Broadway in the play *Candle Light*, after which she appeared in *The International Revue*, which had songs by Dorothy Fields and Jimmy McHugh.

It was a two-year period that set, for the most part, the arc of Lawrence's career for the remainder of her life. She would move with ease from musicals to plays and would also perform on both sides of the Atlantic.

The 1930s began for Lawrence with a show written by Noël Coward. He and Lawrence had toured together as children and enjoyed a friendship ever since. Coward tailored *Private Lives* to both of their talents, imagining a divorced couple who meet by chance on their respective second honeymoons and, to their new spouses' chagrin, reunite. The opportunity to see Lawrence's combination of refined elegance, musicality, and rambunctiousness in the comedy proved irresistible to audiences, first in London and then in New York.

Lawrence followed *Private Lives* with a period of moviemaking and the London production of Cole Porter's *Nymph Errant*. She then reunited with Coward for *Tonight at 8:30*, nine one-act plays that were performed in groups of three over the course of three evenings. Again, he wrote each specifically for himself and Lawrence, and the pieces ranged from rollicking to subdued comedy. The works themselves prompted divergent responses, but the leads' performances drew consistent praise. Howard Barnes, in a November 28, 1936, *New York Herald Tribune* review, went so far as to say that one piece, *Shadow Play*, found the "incomparable Miss Lawrence in her most dazzling mood."

She received similar accolades for the two plays that ensued (*Susan and God* in 1937 and *Skylark* in 1939), and then in 1941, she took on her most ambitious musical theatre role to date, playing a fashion magazine editor allowing her dreams to be psychoanalyzed in *Lady in the Dark*. With it she gave, according to the *Times'* Atkinson on February 7, "one of the most brilliant performances of her incendiary career."

The critic's hyperbole was, however, premature because Lawrence had one more musical to headline, Rodgers and Hammerstein's *The King and I*. It came one decade later after she played her first classic role (Eliza in *Pygmalion*) and then toured Europe entertaining troops during World War II. *The King and I* afforded her the chance to work with the most successful team then writing Broadway musicals. Playing the iconic role of schoolteacher Anna Leonowens opposite Yul Brynner's imposing King of Siam, Lawrence demonstrated once again her superb acting skills and introduced some of the songwriters' loveliest tunes, including "Getting to Know You" and "Hello, Young Lovers."

Lawrence passed away suddenly while she was still performing in *The King and I*, and on September 8, 1952, the *New York Herald Tribune* published an editorial that proclaimed, "To many people, on both sides of the footlights, she personified the theater itself, its unique glamour and magic."

CAROLYN LEIGH

(August 21, 1926–November 19, 1983)
Lyricist

Although she only had three Broadway musicals produced, Leigh, through the concurrent intricacy and directness of her words, shifted a sense of how lyrics could be crafted for the theatre.

In his book *Look I Made a Hat*, Stephen Sondheim describes this lyricist as the "greatest technician of them all with the possible exception of Cole Porter," and Carolyn Leigh's gift with words was evident at an early age. One story goes that in grade school she wrote an essay for a boy on whom she had a crush. When the teacher handed back the papers, she chided the boy—not for having someone else write his work but because she thought that, because it was so good, he must have copied it directly from a book.

Leigh's higher education included studying at both Queen's College and New York University. After graduating she took a job as a copywriter for an ad agency, and when a short verse she wrote found its way to the Armo Music Corporation (which was a subsidiary of the Memphis-based King Records), Leigh was offered a one-year contract as a lyric writer. While with the label, she was paired with a variety of composers, most notably Nacio Porter Brown, son of the "Singin' in the Rain" songwriter, Nacio Herb Brown.

Leigh and the younger Brown collaborated on a number of songs, and two of theirs made inroads with some of the most popular singers of the day, including Jo Stafford. From her period at Armo, Leigh also saw "I'm Waiting Just for You" (with music by Henry Bernard Glover) become one of the top R&B songs of 1951. Leigh's most important early writing partnership came two years later when she and Johnny Richards wrote "Young at Heart." Frank Sinatra recorded it, resulting in one of his big hits from the period.

In these songs and others, Leigh's ability to craft a lyric that was concurrently colloquial and meticulously honed can be heard. Her rhyme schemes don't always conform to standard patterns, and yet she always satisfies a listener by resolving anticipated rhymes.

"Young at Heart," which also inspired a Sinatra film of the same name, led to Leigh's first outing on Broadway. The song caught Mary Martin's attention as she was preparing for a new production of J. M. Barrie's *Peter Pan*. She suggested that producer Leland Hayward and director Jerome Robbins consider using Leigh as lyricist for the show. The two men agreed and invited Leigh to join the project. She, in turn, brought onboard Mark "Moose" Charlap, another composer with whom she had been working.

While Leigh and Charlap's full score was ultimately not used and instead was augmented with songs from Jule Styne, Betty Comden, and Adolph Green, the Charlap–Leigh contributions were substantial and include many of its most famous numbers: "I've Gotta' Crow," "I'm Flying," and "I Won't Grow Up." Critics were generally underwhelmed by both teams' contributions, but in his October 21, 1954, review for the *New York Herald Tribune*, Walter Kerr did acknowledge the "impish swing" that Leigh and Charlap's work contributed to the production.

Not long after *Peter Pan*, Leigh began working with composer Cy Coleman. The combination of her linguistic slyness and his musical acumen resulted in a number of pop hits, including "Witchcraft" and "The Best Is Yet to Come."

During the first years of their collaboration, they also began to cast an eye on writing the score for a musical, and they arrived on Broadway in 1960 with *Wildcat*. The show brought television star Lucille Ball to the Main Stem, and while she earned raves, the Coleman–Leigh score, which included the future standard "Hey! Look Me Over," failed to excite most critics. There was, however, one who disagreed. *Billboard*'s June Bundy informed readers in a December 26, 1960, review that the songs were the "best thing about the show."

Leigh and Coleman returned to Broadway two years later with *Little Me*, and for this lighthearted musical about a woman's many marriages as she strives to improve her place in the world, the team wrote such songs as "I've Got Your Number," "Real Live Girl," and "The Other Side of the Tracks." Leigh's versatility shines throughout but is particularly noticeable when the first two of these are placed side by side. In the former, staged as a male striptease, there is a decidedly driving directness to her words. In the second, sung by a World War I doughboy, the lyrics cascade onto one another, even as they boast marvelous internal rhymes. At one point, the character sings about how the heroine's presence "fogs up my goggles."

The Leigh–Coleman relationship was widely known to be a stormy one, and while they sporadically reunited as a team, notably with "Pass Me By" for the movie *Father Goose* (1964), they never wrote another musical together.

Leigh wrote only one more produced musical, *How Now, Dow Jones*, in 1967. For this fanciful show with music by Elmer Bernstein and set on Wall Street, she wrote some of her tartest lyrics, from "A. B. C.," the show's opening number about the stock market and investors that includes a reference to analysts taking LSD, to "Rich Is Better," where a woman sings about waking up in her Neiman Marcus push-button bed. Even in his negative December 6 *Times* review, Clive Barnes had to applaud her lyrics. They were, he wrote, a "high cut above the music they are droned to."

For the balance of her life, Leigh initiated projects, but none ever came to fruition. Most notable were two collaborations with composer Lee Pockriss, an adaptation of F. Scott Fitzgerald's *The Great Gatsby* and *Caesar's Wife*, a musical about Julius Caesar's spouse who reportedly prophesized his murder.

Her last new material to be heard on Broadway came in 1982 when she and Coleman wrote two new songs for a revival of *Little Me*. In his January 22 *Times* review, Frank Rich wrote, "It seems tragic that these songwriters haven't teamed up on another Broadway musical in 20 years." He even praised the new numbers as being "so good" that he could forgive the excision of four others from the original score.

Leigh, at the time of her death, was working with composer Marvin Hamlisch on the musical *Smile*, which centered on the beauty pageant circuit. When it finally opened on Broadway, Howard Ashman had written a completely new set of lyrics for the show.

ALAN JAY LERNER

(August 31, 1918–June 14, 1986)
Book Writer / Lyricist

Throughout his career Lerner delivered sparkling lyrics brimming with wit and immacu-lately conceived wordplay, worked to find new ways to tell stories within the framework of musical theatre, and with Frederick Loewe created four classic musicals.

Lerner, working with composer Frederick Loewe, wrote such acclaimed musicals as *Brigadoon*; *Camelot*; and, perhaps most famously, *My Fair Lady*. Beyond these, Lerner also penned a number of other tuners, collaborating with composers rang-ing from Leonard Bernstein to Burton Lane to Kurt Weill, among others. Regard-less of his writing partner, Lerner's lyrics always sparkled and set standards for craft, and his books frequently pushed boundaries in terms of both form and content.

Born in New York and educated in England and Connecticut, Lerner attended Harvard University and, during his first two summers there, studied at Juilliard. His interest in writing flourished at Harvard, and he wrote several of the school's Hasty Pudding Club shows. In one, *So Proudly We Hail* (1938), he also performed, and an April 6 review from *Variety*'s "Fox." related that there was "some very good tapping by Alan Jay Lerner."

After graduating, Lerner found work creating advertising copy and penning radio scripts. He also wrote sketches and lyrics for an annual Lamb's Club show, and it was through this work that he met the Viennese-born Loewe. They began collaborating, and in November 1943, their first Broadway show, *What's Up*, opened, helmed by George Balanchine. Critics found the musical, which was cowritten by Lerner and Arthur Pierson and centers on an airplane crew and In-dian potentate who are all quarantined at an all-girls school because of measles, amateurish, and it quickly folded.

Lerner strove for something more cerebral with his next Broadway outing with Loewe. *The Day before Spring* was about a woman who, while attending a college reunion, becomes torn between her marriage and the romantic feelings she still has for a man with whom she almost eloped years before. A song for Voltaire, Plato, and Freud as they offer advice to the heroine was only one of the unusual touches to the musical; it also featured a trio of narrative ballets that commented on her dilemma. For a musical arriving just two years after *Oklahoma!*, Lerner was pushing musical theatre boundaries. The *Wall Street Journal*'s Richard P. Cooke called the show "welcomely intelligent" in a November 24 review, but even Cooke noted that Lerner had not calibrated the show's varying tones properly.

Lerner continued with fanciful storytelling in *Brigadoon*, and in this 1947 musical about romance flourishing between an American man and a Scottish girl from a town that only materializes for one day every century, his and Loewe's work genuinely clicked. The musical captured critics' and theatregoers' imaginations, and MGM purchased the film rights. *Brigadoon* also contained "There but for You Go I" and "Almost like Being in Love," two of the first enduring Lerner and Loewe songs in which sumptuous melody and perfectly crafted lyrics blend seamlessly.

A temporary rift with Loewe led Lerner to a collaboration with Kurt Weill on *Love Life* (1948), and once again Lerner penned a book that broke with the norm. The musical explores a couple's marriage over the course of more than 150 years through both standard narrative and vaudeville sketches. It was an audacious conceit and the theatre's first concept musical. It set the stage for such works as *Cabaret* and *Company*, as well as *Chicago*, which also employs, to a lesser degree, the vaudeville structure.

Lerner's time in Hollywood began after this, and while working for MGM, he provided the screenplay and lyrics (for melodies by composer Burton Lane) for *Royal Wedding* and devised the scenario and Academy Award–winning script for the studio's compendium of Gershwin songs, *An American in Paris*. Before the 1950s ended, he also adapted *Brigadoon* for the screen, and he and Loewe, with whom he reunited in 1951, wrote one musical specifically for film, *Gigi*.

Their fourth Broadway musical was the ambitiously adult *Paint Your Wagon*, which, set in the mid-nineteenth century, centers on a miner, a single father who has raised his daughter to adulthood, and the racial issues that arise for them both when she falls in love with a Mexican. Walter F. Kerr, in a November 13, 1951, *New York Herald Tribune* review, remarked on how Lerner's book "eschewed the caricature of routine musical comedy," but even with such songs as "I Talk to the Trees" and "They Call the Wind Maria," *Wagon* failed to attract audiences in the way that *Brigadoon* had.

Lerner and Loewe told a similarly serious-minded tale with their next musical, *My Fair Lady*, in which Lerner pares George Bernard Shaw's *Pygmalion* to its essential core, both in terms of the relationship between its leading male and female characters and its social commentary about women's status in Edwardian England. Filled with sublime melody matched with crisp, witty lyrics, it became a thundering hit. On March 25, 1956, the *New York Times*' Brooks Atkinson remarked, "It takes rank with the best musical comedies of the century."

Lerner never managed to achieve the same sort of success in a career that continued for nearly twenty-five more years. His last stage collaboration with Loewe, *Camelot*, inevitably suffered in comparison to *My Fair Lady* but was still a considerable hit. Indeed, in *Camelot* Lerner's lyrics have a sparkle that on some levels surpass its predecessor. In "Take Me to the Fair," for instance, he rhymes "this Gallic bag of noise and nerve" with "plate of French hors d'oeuvres."

Lerner, with Loewe, went on to write the screenplay and lyrics for a movie version of *The Little Prince* (1974). For the stage he continued to explore serious themes and outré stories. *On a Clear Day You Can See Forever*, a 1965 show with music by Lane, explores ESP and reincarnation; *Lolita, My Love*, written in 1971 with John Barry, musicalized Vladimir Nabokov's controversial novel about a man's sexual obsession with a teenage girl; and *1600 Pennsylvania Avenue*, with a score by Leonard Bernstein, celebrated America's bicentennial by putting a mirror to the country's long history of racism against African Americans and political corruption in Washington. These latter two shows failed with critics and audiences (*Lolita*, in fact, closed out of town), but Lerner's daring as he neared the thirty-year anniversary of his Broadway bow impresses.

As a lyricist he might have enjoyed one more hit. He agreed to collaborate on Andrew Lloyd Webber's *The Phantom of the Opera*, but he withdrew after being diagnosed with lung cancer. He died in 1986, four months before the musical's premiere.

GODDARD LIEBERSON

(April 5, 1911–May 29, 1977)
Recording Industry Executive / Producer

Lieberson's work at Columbia Records set new standards for original cast recordings and ensured that Broadway shows—both hits and ambitious, important misses—were preserved for future generations.

Born in England and raised in the United States, Lieberson began what might be considered a career as "renaissance man" of the recording industry studying at the Eastman School of Music. In class he concentrated on classical piano and composition, but outside of it, he was, among other things, playing piano in a nightclub to earn a living. After graduation, he served as director of dramatics for the Harley School in Rochester and continued his composing in his off hours. Eventually, his works made it to the concert hall courtesy of the Works Progress Administration in Manhattan. In a March 28, 1935, *New York Herald Tribune* review of one program, a critic using the initials "F. D. P." applauded the young composer's talent, writing, "It would be interesting to hear more of his music, which employs modern harmonics with ability and discretion." The reviewer's hopes were answered; Lieberson's work was sporadically represented in similar concerts for the next few years.

In 1939, Lieberson shifted to the business side of music, joining Columbia Records as "masterworks recording director." The title belied the job's responsibilities, which ranged from turning musicians' pages during sessions and to serving as assistant to the company's director of classical recording. Three years later, Lieberson assumed that directorship position.

By the mid-1940s, his duties at Columbia extended to heading up a division intended to capitalize on the growing market of child listeners. Among the talents he recruited for the initiative were performer Gene Kelly and composer Lehman Engel. Lieberson also brokered a deal with radio personality Nila Mack, who was cresting with her hit show *Let's Pretend*, to bring her unique musicianship to disc. In a May 25, 1946, *Billboard* feature about the plans, Joe Csida noted, "[He] will use Miss Mack's original material (words and music) as well as the original *Pretend* cast."

Lieberson was primed for what would happen next at the company: Columbia brass decided to begin releasing original cast recordings. Since 1943, Decca had dominated the field following its release of the album featuring the Broadway cast and orchestra of *Oklahoma!* Other labels had followed suit, but Columbia had not, even though in early 1946 one of its contracted stars, Pearl Bailey, was set to wax *St. Louis Woman*. Rather than bid on the cast recording, Columbia "loaned" her to rival Capitol Records.

Columbia's first deals for such albums were for *Finian's Rainbow*, with a score by Burton Lane and E. Y. "Yip" Harburg, and *Street Scene*, with music by Kurt Weill and lyrics by poet Langston Hughes. Lieberson produced the former recording, and over the course of the next three years, he fulfilled the same duties for another five musicals, including Rodgers and Hammerstein's *South Pacific*.

Within a year of this release, Lieberson spearheaded a new initiative at Columbia: preserving scores of shows that predated the advent of the cast album. Under his guidance, and often with Engel as conductor, recordings of, among others, Rodgers and Hart's *Pal Joey* and *Babes in Arms*; Cole Porter's *Anything Goes*; and Sigmund Romberg, Oscar Hammerstein II, and Otto Harbach's *The Desert Song* hit stores.

As he was doing this, Lieberson wrote eloquently—in the November 1950 edition of *Theatre Arts* magazine—about the creation of a show album and the need for preservation of the country's musical theatre heritage. He also described how successful cast recording needed to re-create "aural values of excitement, tension, and dramatic process" that audiences experienced in the theatre. This meant, Lieberson went on to explain, not simply "putting microphones in front of an orchestra and singers." A year later, he demonstrated how a cast recording could replicate the theatrical experience with the first almost-complete recording of *Porgy and Bess*. In the September 13, 1951, edition of the *Herald Tribune*, Bert McCord reported that the album "includes such sounds as a crap game, a fight, footsteps, the clink of penny burial contributions falling into a saucer."

The Columbia studio cast recordings were greeted with both critical and popular acclaim, and when the Lieberson-produced recording of George and Ira Gershwin's *Girl Crazy* was released, it prompted Howard Taubman in a March 16, 1952, *New York Times* story, to muse, "You wonder if there isn't room for a repertory theatre devoted to the best musicals of the past generation or two."

Lieberson wasn't just looking to musical theatre's past in his work with Columbia. He was also preserving many of the decade's new shows and wasn't always interested in big hits. For instance, it was Lieberson who produced the original cast recording of *Candide*, featuring Leonard Bernstein's now-iconic score, even though it ran a mere seventy-three performances. Another piece of daring on the producer's part was releasing Frank Loesser's *The Most Happy Fella* on a three-LP set that retailed for $14.98 (about $140.00 in 2018).

About the same time, Lieberson convinced Columbia's parent company to make an investment in a new Broadway production: a musicalization of George Bernard Shaw's *Pygmalion*. The show became, of course, the phenomenal hit *My Fair Lady*. Not long after it opened, he assumed the title of president at the label, and the June 6, 1956, *Variety* story announcing his new position specifically mentioned the role he had played: "He was instrumental in getting CBS, Col's parent company, interested in the smash Broadway legi-tuner."

For the next twenty-one years, Lieberson would be a record executive (he had a brief hiatus from his presidency at Columbia in the early 1970s) who also produced albums, and during this period, he would use his position to make further investments in Broadway shows, ranging from *Camelot* to *Lolita, My Love*, and to wax albums for smash hits and important but less successful productions. It's thanks to Lieberson, for instance, that the original cast recording of Stephen Sondheim's *Anyone Can Whistle* was made. Lieberson also mentored Thomas Z. Shepard, who would go on to produce many of the most important cast recordings from the last three decades of the twentieth century.

Lieberson's final two records for Columbia came just a year before his death and are emblematic of his eclectic tastes and astute ear. In 1976, he served as producer for both the original cast recording of *A Chorus Line* and for the twentieth-anniversary revival of *My Fair Lady*.

ANDREW LLOYD WEBBER

(March 22, 1948–)
Composer

Lloyd Webber's work has captured audiences' imaginations for nearly a half-century, and he has written the music for four of the most enduring musicals of the last half-century, including The Phantom of the Opera, *which continues to have record-making runs in New York and London.*

In his autobiography, *Unmasked*, Lloyd Webber describes how, while he was still a 'tween, he developed an entire fantasy world: "[One] in which I could hide and where I was truly happy, a make-believe world with one common denominator, musical theatre." For it, he created his first songs.

It's not surprising that Lloyd Webber gravitated toward music and make-believe as a boy. His father was a composer and director at the London College of Music, and his mother played both violin and piano. Further, Lloyd Webber's parents began taking him to the theatre when he was five; there was an annual trip to holiday pantomimes for the family.

When he was seventeen, Lloyd Webber began working on a musical based on the life of Thomas John Barnardo, who, in the nineteenth century, established a number of orphanages in Britain. Concurrently, he received a letter from twenty-one-year-old lyricist Tim Rice suggesting that they might collaborate. There was immediate camaraderie, and together they finished the project.

The show, *The Likes of Us*, was not produced at the time, but the young men continued with their collaboration. They opted to create a pop cantata based on the biblical story of Joseph and his brothers, and in 1968, the result, *Joseph and the Amazing Technicolor Dreamcoat*, premiered in concert form at Westminster's Central Hall. Lloyd Webber's father provided accompaniment on the organ for this piece in which Lloyd Webber's music encompassed everything from Elvis Presley–like rock to gentle folk strains. The presentation did not lead to a full production at that time, but it would later go on to enjoy both Broadway and West End runs and become a favorite of both professional and amateur theatres around the world.

Lloyd Webber and Rice continued their exploration of biblical themes with *Jesus Christ Superstar*. They premiered this rock opera about Christ's final days on earth as a two-LP concept album. When a single from the recording was released in late 1969, the December 6 edition of *Billboard* labeled it as the "most controversial disk of the week," but buyers didn't care. The single—and the album—struck a chord, and the full recording ultimately reached number 1 on *Billboard*'s pop album charts.

Superstar, which once again demonstrated the composer's facility with a wide range of styles, arrived on Broadway in October 1971, dividing theatre critics. In his October 12 *Los Angeles Times* review, Dan Sullivan cited "Lloyd Webber's terrific tunes" as being among the show's strengths, but in the *New York Times* that same day, Clive Barnes wrote, "Most of the music is pleasant, although unmemorable." More troubling to the critics was Tom O'Horgan's direction. Nevertheless, the musical ran 711 performances and earned Lloyd Webber and Rice their first Tony nomination. In 1972, *Superstar*, in a different production, opened in the West End and ran for eight years.

After this Lloyd Webber turned to a new collaborator, playwright Alan Ayckbourn, and together they musicalized P. G. Wodehouse's "Jeeves" stories. The move, in some critics' opinions, was a heresy, but Lloyd Webber's melodies found supporters. In Kenneth Hurren's largely negative May 3, 1975, *New Leader* review, he described how the composer "catches the syncopation of the period quite expertly."

Working with Ayckbourn didn't mean that Lloyd Webber had abandoned Rice. Together they created the rock opera *Evita*, based on the life of Argentine first lady Eva Peron. Once again, a two-LP concept recording preceded the show's stage debut, which was directed with bold flair by Harold Prince. The musical was less rock-driven than many had expected. Still, the composer was expanding his musical palette, and George Oppenheimer remarked in his September 26, 1979, *Newsday* review, "The songs are generally prettier than those of the Webber–Rice 'Jesus Christ Superstar.'" *Evita* earned a Tony Award for best musical score.

Cats (1981) continued the composer's penchant for unlikely source material, using T. S. Eliot's whimsical poems to create a loosely structured theatrical fantasy.

Trevor Nunn's imaginative staging and Gillian Lynne's slinky choreography helped propel the show, which featured the breakout hit "Memory," to record-making runs on both sides of the Atlantic. *Starlight Express*, a family-friendly extravaganza about trains, followed, and though the pop music–fueled show failed to catch on in the United States, it ran 7,409 performances in London.

Classical sounds had always played a part in Lloyd Webber's musicals, and with *Song and Dance* (1982), Lloyd Webber delivered a score that was both pop-driven and composed of variations on Paganini's A Minor Caprice No. 24. And then, with *The Phantom of the Opera* (1986), he debuted one of his most lush and swirlingly romantic scores. Comparisons—some favorable, some not—to Puccini surfaced in reviews. Some critics praised Lloyd Webber's inventiveness in this regard. In his October 11, 1986, *Guardian* review, Michael Billington lauded the "comic jauntiness of 'Prima Donna' and the pavane-like stateliness of 'Masquerade.'" The musical, which reunited the composer with director Prince, opened in New York in 1988 and continues today, making it the longest-running show in Broadway history.

Following *Phantom*, Lloyd Webber's musicals continued to demonstrate his interest in bringing unusual stories to the stage. Not all of his ventures were successes. Such shows as *Whistle down the Wind* (1996) and *Stephen Ward* (2013) premiered and closed in relatively short order. Others during this period, though, *Aspects of Love* (1989) and *Sunset Boulevard* (1993), enjoyed healthy runs in both London and New York. Lloyd Webber also continued to write in a romantic, semi-classical vein with *Woman in White* (2003) and *Love Never Dies* (2010), his sequel to *Phantom*.

The composer returned to the rock 'n' roll roots that had characterized his first musicals with *School of Rock* (2015). For this show, about a would-be rocker who instills his iconoclastic ideals in some prep school students, Lloyd Webber garnered some of the best reviews of his career. Ben Brantley, in his December 6, 2015, *Times* review, called it the composer's "friskiest show in decades."

In 2018, Lloyd Webber celebrated his seventieth birthday, received a Tony for lifetime achievement, and became one of only a handful of artists to earn EGOT status when he won an Emmy for producing a television presentation of *Superstar*. As of this writing, he has announced his newest project, a modern take on the Cinderella story, and is also prepping a feature film version of *Cats*, slated to star, among others, Dame Judi Dench and Taylor Swift.

FRANK LOESSER

(June 29, 1910–July 28, 1969)
Composer / Lyricist / Librettist

Loesser's musicals set the stage for composers (such as Cy Coleman) who wanted to create musicals with varying sounds and tones, while as a mentor and music publisher he helped to launch the careers of many a budding musical songsmith.

In a July 29, 1969, *New York Times* obituary for this composer of such shows as *Guys and Dolls* and *How to Succeed in Business without Really Trying*, Albin Krebs described Loesser as the "musical black sheep of [his] family"; his father taught classical piano, and his brother was both a pianist and music critic. But Loesser, who refused his father's piano lessons and dropped out of City College, eventually succumbed to what Krebs described as "his gift for music and lyrics."

Loesser's songwriting career came after a series of jobs that included running errands for a jewelry business, reporting for *Women's Wear Daily*, checking food and service at a string of restaurants, and selling newspaper ad space. During this time, too, he was experimenting with songwriting. His daughter Susan relates in *A Most Remarkable Fella* that he and a group of friends "tossed around song ideas while they socialized" at a restaurant in upper Manhattan. Ultimately, Loesser and one friend, Carl Rice, took some of their work to a music publisher who put them on a retainer for a year. None of the work they submitted was published, and by 1930, Loesser moved on to other collaborators, including future Pulitzer Prize–winning composer William Schuman and Irving Actman.

It was Loesser's association with Actman that paved the way for the budding lyricist's Broadway debut. "[They] sang their own songs for their supper at the Back Drop, an East 52nd Street night spot," Krebs reported in Loesser's *Times* obituary, attracting attention and leading to an invitation to contribute to the 1935 Broadway revue *The Illustrator's Show*. The men contributed five numbers, and two were singled out in several reviews. John Mason Brown, in a January 23, 1936, *New York Post* review, remarked that Loesser and Actman's "Bang the Bell Rang" was the "only song that stands out at all."

The revue only lasted five performances, but the visibility they achieved led to a contract with Universal Studios, beginning a twelve-year journey through Hollywood and popular songwriting. During this time Loesser worked with a variety of partners, ranging from Burton Lane, Loesser's collaborator on "How'dja Like to Love Me?" and "The Lady's in Love with You," among others, to Hoagy Carmichael, with whom Loesser penned such hits as "Body and Soul" and "Two Sleepy People." A collaboration with Arthur Schwartz, "They're Either Too Young or Too Old," during this time resulted in one of three Oscar nominations for best song. Loesser ventured out on his own as composer-lyricist in 1942 with the wartime anthem "Praise the Lord and Pass the Ammunition."

Loesser returned to Broadway in 1948 with *Where's Charley?*, an adaptation of the popular late-nineteenth-century farce about a group of college men's romances and their efforts to pass one of their own off as a visiting aunt, a woman who could serve as their chaperone with their various dates. Loesser's score for the show is often both lush and romantic, keeping with the period, and yet thanks to his comic lyrics in such numbers as the rapturously overblown "My Darling, My Darling," also keep with the piece's farcical tone. Brooks Atkinson, in his October 12 *Times* review, praised Loesser for writing a "lively score in a number of entertaining styles." *Charley* went on to run 793 performances.

Loesser's remarkable versatility allowed him to move from this period confection to the more hardboiled *Guys and Dolls* (1950). For this musicalization of Damon Runyon's stories about gangsters in Times Square, Loesser created a dialect of sorts in his lyrics that aptly matched the tone and style of Abe Burrows and Jo

Swerling's book. Loesser's words are concurrently slangy and poetic. As for the music, Loesser once again demonstrated facility for writing in a wide number of styles, from gospel ("Sit Down You're Rockin' the Boat") to razzmatazz showbiz ("Take Back Your Mink"). More importantly, in these and others, such as two of the show's standards, "Luck Be a Lady" and "I've Never Been in Love Before," Loesser was writing for character and situation. The pinnacle of his achievement in this regard is "Adelaide's Lament," in which Nathan Detroit's long-suffering, long-term fiancée attempts to self-diagnose a cold that she just can't shake.

It took Loesser four years to complete *The Most Happy Fella* (1956), for which he provided music, lyrics, and libretto. The show, about an Italian winemaker living in Napa, California, and the much younger woman he marries, has been called an opera by some. Loesser often referred to it as an "extended musical comedy." Regardless of its categorization, the show, with forty numbers that range from aria-like solos to numbers such as "Standin' on the Corner" that became stand-alone pop hits, *Fella* was Loesser's most ambitious piece of writing. Atkinson, writing about it in a May 4 *Times* review, remarked, "In its most serious moments 'The Most Happy Fella' is a profoundly moving experience." The bold show, which anticipates epic, musically bountiful works such as *Sweeney Todd*, and has enjoyed revivals both on Broadway and in opera houses, ran for more than a year and a half.

Loesser's next two shows were as different from one another as they were from the ones that preceded them. In *Greenwillow* (1960) he evoked the sounds and speech patterns of rural America, and in *How to Succeed in Business without Really Trying* (1961), about a young man adroitly maneuvering his way up the ladder in a major company, Loesser brought corporate America to life through his winking lyrical cleverness and zesty, slightly edgy melodies. The show earned both a Tony and the Pulitzer and ran for three and a half years.

Loesser was unable to replicate this success before his death in 1969. He completed one musical, *Pleasures and Palaces*, which closed out of town before reaching Broadway, and left *Señor Discretion Himself* unfinished.

Loesser's Broadway career becomes all the more impressive when one factors in his work with his musical publishing company. It was through Frank Music that he helped to nurture new musical theatre writers, such as Meredith Willson and the team of Richard Adler and Jerry Ross. Loesser also encouraged Jerry Herman to continue his songwriting at a moment when the younger man was questioning his own abilities.

PATTI LuPONE

(April 21, 1949–)
Performer

Thanks to her vibrant, impassioned turns in a wide variety of tuners, LuPone has assumed the mantles of such stars as Merman and Channing, becoming, for her generation and the ones that have followed, a female personification of musical theatre.

At her audition for the Drama Division at the Juilliard School, LuPone performed Kate's epilogue from *The Taming of the Shrew*. In her eponymous memoir, she remembers John Houseman (a cofounder of the Mercury Theatre with Orson Welles, as well as one of the artistic directors of the dramatic arm at the school) saying, "I don't think that's what Shakespeare had in mind." The audition continued with an improvisation about receiving a rejection letter from the school (she nonchalantly threw it away) and a last-minute request to sing (she opted for "You Mustn't Be Discouraged," a song Jule Styne, Betty Comden, and Adolph Green had written for Carol Burnett). All were daring choices that got this Long Island–born actress admitted with a scholarship and are emblematic of the sort of work that has earned her a pair of Tony Awards.

After graduation she found she had both a diploma and employment security from the school for several years. Graduates were part of its ensemble that toured, offering a classical repertory, under the name the Acting Company. In 1973, the group played a limited Broadway run. LuPone had two principal roles and received raves. For her performance in Anton Chekhov's *The Three Sisters*, Allan Wallach, in his December 20 *Newsday* review, wrote, "[She] captures the radiance of a young girl that is transformed by boredom and fatigue," and in reviewing the troupe's *The Beggar's Opera* on December 24, the *New York Times*' Clive Barnes noted, "Miss LuPone, with her glittering presence, is one of the special favors of the company."

LuPone performed with the Acting Company for another two years, and when it returned to Broadway in 1975, she was playing another set of diverse roles, ranging from a young prince in Christopher Marlowe's *Edward II* to the prostitute Kitty in William Saroyan's *The Time of Your Life* to a vivacious Southern girl in Robert Waldman and Alfred Uhry's musical *The Robber Bridegroom*, which only ran fourteen performances, but LuPone earned her first Tony Award nomination for it.

After this season LuPone struck out on her own, performing in two plays by David Mamet and the 1978 musical *Working*. Then in February 1979, she snagged the title role in Andrew Lloyd Webber and Tim Rice's *Evita*. The show opened later that year, and in his September 26 *New York Times* review, Walter Kerr described her performance as having a "rattlesnake's vitality." That same day, Howard Kissel, in *Women's Wear Daily*, praised her "marvelous economy of gesture—with one cock of her elegant head, for example, she can convey the sultry arrogance of a low-class Spanish dancer as well as the hardness of an unyielding headmistress."

It was a star-making turn, and LuPone earned a Tony Award for it. She stayed with the show until early 1981, and after this she performed in a number of off-Broadway productions, including two other Mamet plays and a limited run of Marc Blitzstein's *The Cradle Will Rock*, again with the Acting Company. By 1984, LuPone was back on Broadway, first playing Nancy in a short-lived revival of Lionel Bart's *Oliver!* and then tackling a role in Dario Fo's surreal political satire *Accidental Death of an Anarchist*.

LuPone returned to *Cradle* when it played engagements around the country and then in London. After the show ended its engagement, she remained in the United Kingdom in order to start work on a new project. She was cast as Fantine in the

English-language premiere of *Les Misérables*. With these two performances in a single season, she garnered an Olivier for best actress in a musical.

Once back stateside LuPone accepted the role of Reno Sweeney (originally played by Ethel Merman in 1934) in a revival of *Anything Goes* at Lincoln Center Theater. LuPone made the role her own, prompting Frank Rich, in his October 20, 1987, *Times* review, to proclaim, "Patti LuPone is the top. . . . [She] has her own brash American style and, most of all, a blazing spontaneity: With this Reno, *everything* goes."

LuPone enjoyed a hit TV series *Life Goes On* for four seasons, then returned to the theatre to star as Norma Desmond in the world premiere of Lloyd Webber's *Sunset Boulevard* in the West End in 1993. After she and the composer had a very public falling out over the production, it didn't take long for her to return to Broadway. First came a highly acclaimed one-woman show in 1995; then, she took over from Zoe Caldwell to play Maria Callas in Terrence McNally's *Master Class* in 1996. Next, she acted in Mamet's *Old Neighborhood* in 1997.

Since that time LuPone has never been far from Broadway. In the course of twenty years, she's made appearances every two or three years. Unafraid of new material, she's originated roles in such musicals as *Women on the Verge of a Nervous Breakdown* (2010) and *War Paint* (2017), earning Tony nominations for each, and turned in highly praised performances in revivals of such classics as *Sweeney Todd* (2005) and *Gypsy* (2008), winning her second Tony for the latter.

Beyond all of this, LuPone has maintained a relationship with the Ravinia Festival in Chicago, where she has performed in concert versions of musicals ranging from *Anyone Can Whistle* to *A Little Night Music*, and she has also maintained an extensive career as a cabaret and recording artist. Among her other notable achievements beyond the realm of Broadway was a 2007 production of Bertolt Brecht and Kurt Weill's *Rise and Fall of the City of Mahagonny*, produced by the Los Angeles Opera and costarring Broadway's Audra McDonald. In a February 12 review for the *Toronto Star*, Richard Ouzounian informed readers that "LuPone is her usual brassy, take-charge self" playing the woman who runs an extravagant, dystopian American city. The portrayal, the critic wrote, was a "combination Condoleezza Rice and Simon Cowell." The staging was subsequently recorded and garnered a pair of Grammy nominations.

Her most recent outing has been a stint in a new production of the musical *Company* in London's West End. For her performance as Joanne in this 1970s classic, LuPone garnered a new set of critical bouquets. In his October 17, 2018, *Variety* review, Matt Trueman described her performance as "dazzling and awful at the same time—a martini mixed from measures of exuberance and scorn. She's joyfully joyless." In April 2019 Lupone won her second Olivier Award.

M

GALT MacDERMOT

(December 18, 1928–December 17, 2018)
Composer

MacDermot brought rock music center stage on Broadway, and in doing so, he helped to begin the transformation of the American musical theatre in the last half of the twentieth century.

Blaik Kirby opened his July 27, 1969, *Los Angeles Times* feature on this composer-lyricist by saying, "Galt MacDermot is the last person you'd expect to find involved with 'Hair.'" The reporter went on to describe MacDermot's home life (a wife and four children on Staten Island) and his background as a "former Baptist choirmaster." MacDermot, who, with his collaborators Gerome Ragni and James Rado, successfully brought rock music center stage in the theatre, was also the son of a Canadian diplomat and, unlike the dropouts portrayed in the "American tribal love rock musical," had a bachelor's degree from Cape Town University in South Africa.

His study of African music influenced his earliest composing, and he won two Grammys in 1961 for "African Waltz," an instrumental piece recorded by Cannonball Adderly. A March 13 *Billboard* review praised the blues-infused work for having a "flock of off-beat harmonies set against double-time rhythm."

MacDermot moved to New York three years later and split his time between composing and working in the recording studio, backing such artists as drummer Bernard Purdie and bassist Jimmy Lewis. During this same period, writers Ragni and Rado were starting work on the musical that would become known as *Hair*, and when they were looking for a composer, a friend suggested they contact MacDermot. They did, and the composer drafted some melodies. Ragni and Rado were enthused about what they heard, and the collaboration began in earnest. After others rejected it, New York Shakespeare Festival (NYSF) founder Joseph Papp agreed to mount the musical. In fact, he made it the inaugural production at the Public Theater in Lower Manhattan, where *A Chorus Line* and *Hamilton* would later premiere.

For the loosely structured musical about a group of hippies who are protesting the Vietnam War and embracing free love and all things antiestablishment, MacDermot wrote songs that encompassed not just rock and pop music but also jazz, African rhythms, and liturgical music. In the process such songs as "Aquarius" and "Let the Sun Shine In"—anthems for a generation—were created.

Hair officially opened at the Public on October 29, 1967, and the following morning, the *New York Times'* Clive Barnes cautiously endorsed the show. His highest praise was for the music, writing that it had a "rough, tough and lusty quality," and though Barnes was concerned about the piece's lack of structure, he also had to applaud its efforts "to jolt the American musical into the nineteen-sixties."

When the run at the Public Theater concluded, the show moved on to a nightclub for a brief run, and then a new producer brought it, with substantial revisions, to Broadway. *Hair* also had a new director, Tom O'Horgan, who had established himself staging freewheeling works off-off-Broadway. It was O'Horgan who inserted the infamous nude scene at the end of *Hair*'s first act, and when his staging opened in April 1968, critics were once again admiring, particularly of the music. Some, such as John J. O'Connor in a May 1 *Wall Street Journal* review, once again saw *Hair* turning the page on the form of musical theatre. He wrote that the show was as "significant in its way as 'Pal Joey,' 'Oklahoma!' and 'West Side Story.'"

Hair returned to Broadway in two incarnations after its premiere, most recently in an acclaimed Tony Award–winning revival in 2009, and Czech director Milos Forman brought the musical to the screen in 1979. Beyond the musical's theatrical legacy (such works as *Rent* and *Hamilton* are its direct descendants), it inspired a generation of musicians outside of the form. When MacDermot passed away in December 2018, musician Questlove tweeted, "King Galt. The broadway community is mourning his passing this morning (#Hair will love forever) but best believe he was the hip hop community's too . . . so many classics. . . . It fed 90s hip hop something crazy!"

Before *Hair* concluded its 1,750-performance run in 1972, MacDermot had brought another rock-driven show to the stage, a musical version of Shakespeare's *The Two Gentlemen of Verona*. With a book by John Guare and director Mel Shapiro and featuring lyrics by Guare, the piece merrily toyed with the original play about two best friends at cross-purposes in love and was presented by the NYSF as one of its Free Shakespeare in Central Park productions in 1971. MacDermot and Guare even outfitted it with an antiwar protest song, "Bring All the Boys Back Home."

Clive Barnes's assessment in his July 29 *Times* review was simply, "It takes off." In *Newsday* the same day, Leo Seligsohn enthused about MacDermot's music "exploding with some wild rock tunes." The critic added that the score "throbs with calypso rhythms and sighs with tear-drenched tones derivative of Victor Herbert." *Two Gentlemen* transferred to Broadway the following December, and when Tony Awards were handed out, the show beat *Grease* and *Follies* to snag the best musical prize.

MacDermot wrote another three musicals that played Broadway. Two of them, *Dude* and *Via Galactica*, opened within weeks of one another in late 1972 and folded quickly. His third, *The Human Comedy*, based on William Saroyan's novel of the same name, had book and lyrics by William Dumaresq and opened at the

Public in December 1983. Exploring the lives of people in a small California community during World War II, the show features a score that fuses period sounds and folk music with MacDermot's pop sensibility. Many applauded his breaking away from the sound of *Hair*, including Allan Wallach, who wrote in a January 22, 1984, *Newsday* review, "[His] music is warmer, sweeter. It flows through Saroyan's mythical America like a river carrying a gentle reminder of life's infinite possibilities." Audience interest and critical acclaim prompted a Broadway transfer, but sadly, the show—and its discrete charms—couldn't sustain itself commercially. It folded after only thirteen performances.

Until his death MacDermot continued composing and performing and in some instances developed scores for musicals, many of which were preserved on his Kilmarnock Records label. He also participated in the revival of *Hair* and two documentaries, including *Shapes of Rhythm: The Music of Galt MacDermot*, which was in the final stages of postproduction when he died. At that point, too, he was working with producers on revisions for a live presentation of *Hair* scheduled for NBC in the spring of 2019 that the network later abandoned.

CAMERON MACKINTOSH

(October 17, 1946–)
Producer

Mackintosh both produced four of the most successful and enduring musicals of the late twentieth century and turned musical theatre into a genuinely global commodity.

A trip to the theatre when he was eight years old seduced this future producing sensation. Specifically, it was the "magic piano" in Julian Slade's musical *Salad Days* that inspired the boy's wonder. In the show, a young couple finds that they have become guardians of an instrument that has the capability of sending anyone who hears it dancing into the streets. Mackintosh avers that he has never lost that sense of wonder, and on some levels, it is a childlike fascination with the theatre that has propelled him to being one of the most successful producers of the late-twentieth and early-twenty-first centuries. British theatre critic Michael Billington remarked in a May 30, 2014, feature for the *Guardian*, "I'm struck by how he has remained the same bubbly enthusiast I have known on and off for 40 years. . . . You go expecting to meet Citizen Kane: you get Peter Pan."

Mackintosh was raised in London, and while he was in his teens he worked as a stage manager at Theatre Royal Drury Lane. After his graduation from Prior Park College in Bath, he began to produce small touring productions in England. His life as a producer in the West End began in 1969 when he mounted a revival of *Anything Goes*, starring jazz singer Marion Montgomery. It lasted a mere twenty-seven performances.

Undaunted, Mackintosh pushed forward, mounting more shows. Some, such as a revival of *Salad Days* (1970), toured, and some played the West End, such as

The Card (1973), which starred Jim Dale. Mackintosh's breakthrough came in 1976 when he agreed to take a small revue that had been done regionally and produce it in London. The show, *Side by Side by Sondheim*, garnered some great reviews, and the visibility that Mackintosh had given it propelled it to a Broadway run a year later.

Even as he was enjoying the success of *Side by Side*, Mackintosh was developing a one-man show centered on music-hall star Harry Lauder. The producer wasn't eyeing this as a show for London but rather one that would enjoy an international run. After its premiere in Scotland, it toured England and then moved to South Africa and Australia.

Other productions, including revivals of *My Fair Lady* and *Oklahoma!* followed, and then in 1980, he brought *Cats*, with music by Andrew Lloyd Webber, to the stage. Although Lloyd Webber had written *Jesus Christ Superstar* and *Evita*, backers were difficult to come by. Mackintosh nevertheless persevered, not only securing the funding but also convincing Trevor Nunn, head of the Royal Shakespeare Company (RSC), to direct and signing Judi Dench for the role of Grizabella. (She had to leave the production after she tore a tendon in rehearsals.)

The musical, of course, proved to be an immediate success in the West End in 1981, and a Broadway incarnation opened the following year. At the same time, Mackintosh recognized that the unconventional, dance-driven piece had greater international potential than more-traditional, book-driven ones. It was, as John Gapper described it in a January 15, 2016, *Financial Times* story, a "show that translated everywhere."

Furthermore, the producer discovered that, when companies began to request rights to produce *Cats*, there was interest not only in the property itself but also in the production that had been created in London and later New York. It was because of this that Mackintosh began a new trend in producing, one in which he ensured that all future incarnations of a musical replicated what had been mounted originally. After *Cats*, Mackintosh continued this practice with three more 1980s megahits.

Before any of these, however, Mackintosh produced two shows that played on both sides of the Atlantic: a revival of *Oliver!* and then *Song and Dance* with music by Lloyd Webber. In London, other musicals that opened under his aegis included *Blondel*, a musical set in the Middle Ages with lyrics by Tim Rice, and *Abbacadabra*, a mash-up of fairy tales that had music by ABBA's Björn Ulvaeus and Benny Andersson.

One of the book writers for this latter show presented during the 1984 holiday season was Alain Boublil, and by the following year, Mackintosh was coproducing, with the RSC, another musical that Boublil had penned, this one with a score by Claude-Michel Schönberg: *Les Misérables*.

Like *Superstar* and *Evita*, this show had been introduced to the public as a concept recording in 1980. It was then produced at the four-thousand-seat Palais des Sports in a remote part of Paris. Mackintosh heard the recording a few years later and was immediately taken with it. He convinced Nunn about its possibilities, and in early fall 1985, the English-language version (by Herbert Kretzmer), codirected by Nunn and John Caird, premiered at the RSC's London home, the Barbican, and transferred to the West End by the end of the year.

As with *Cats*, the Broadway and subsequent international companies used the same design and staging that had premiered at the Barbican. Beyond this, and to an extent even greater than with *Cats*, the productions used the show's marketing imagery, specifically the iconic French waif logo, which was tweaked for both new incarnations and special events.

Mackintosh employed the same techniques for all of his subsequent productions, including *The Phantom of the Opera* (1986) and *Miss Saigon* (1989). With these four pieces, he began to successfully take his tuners into countries that had previously not been seen as markets for musical theatre, particularly the former Soviet bloc countries and later Asian markets.

A measure of the influence Mackintosh attained by the late 1980s can be seen with his production of Stephen Sondheim and James Goldman's *Follies* (1987). The producer not only assembled a glittering cast that included Daniel Massey, Julia McKenzie, and Diana Rigg but also convinced the writers to radically revise the property to make it more audience-friendly.

Mackintosh's most recent theatrical offerings have ranged from the stage version of *Mary Poppins* (2004) to *Betty Blue Eyes* (2011), the musical version of the film *A Private Function*, to entirely new productions of his greatest successes. In addition, he has brought American shows to the West End, including *Avenue Q* (2006); the popular revival of *Hair* (2009); and, most recently, *Hamilton* (2017).

HUGH MARTIN

(August 11, 1914–March 11, 2011)
Composer / Vocal Arranger

As a songwriter Hugh Martin's legacy will always be the bevy of American songbook tunes he penned for a movie, but the American musical will always be in his debt for having brought the art of vocal arrangement to Broadway.

This songwriter-performer who would grow up to have a profound effect on the way songs were delivered in Broadway musicals was raised in Birmingham, Alabama, and as a child he enjoyed something of an unusual home life, particularly for the period and region. His architect father—as well as his musically gifted mother, who frequently traveled to New York to satisfy her artistic yens—supported and encouraged their son's artistry. His mother went so far, in fact, as to steal a volume of Noël Coward's poetry from the library for her son.

Martin demonstrated his talents at the piano when he was just three years old, and by the time he was a teenager, he was trained as a classical pianist. But when, thanks to his progressive mother, he discovered George Gershwin's *Rhapsody in Blue*, he shifted away to jazz and later discovered a passion for theatre and movie musicals.

Eventually Martin came to form a jazz band that toured both nationally and internationally. He later settled in New York, where he continued to perform in niteries and audition for theatre work, landing a place in the chorus of the musical satire *Hooray for What!* The show was Martin's introduction to the professional theatre and to Ralph Blane, who was also in the chorus. The two men became fast friends and sang together as part of the quartet the Martins.

Martin landed a role in a play after *Hooray* had closed, and then, a letter that he wrote to Richard Rodgers forever changed the course of his career. In his autobiography this tunesmith recalls his 1938 missive to the composer: "Why is it I never hear anything resembling a vocal arrangement when I go to a Broadway musical?" Martin went on to praise the superiority of writing for the stage over that for most movies of the day and also explained, "I find I enjoy the surprises that musical movies give me when they elaborate on the simple verse and two chorus routines." Martin suggested that it might be a practice that Rodgers would want to employ.

Rodgers took the letter to heart and within a week had called Martin, requesting that the young man develop a vocal arrangement for a song in a show currently in rehearsal, *The Boys from Syracuse*. Martin complied, and in the process of arranging "Sing for Your Supper" for three female singers, he fundamentally altered the way that songs were delivered on Broadway. No longer would audiences hear straightforward deliveries of tunes, but rather songs would be split into sometimes-intricate harmonies or be delivered with musical variations.

Soon a new credit of "vocal arrangements by" began appearing in the playbills for Broadway shows, for both Martin and others. As the pioneer in the field, it was more frequently Martin, and in the space of just two years, he worked on Rodgers and Hart's *Too Many Girls* (1939), Cole Porter's *Du Barry Was a Lady* (1939), and Irving Berlin's *Louisiana Purchase* (1940). That same year, he also created arrangements for Vernon Duke and John Latouche's *Cabin in the Sky*, and in Martin's book he recalls Ethel Waters's reaction to his work on the show's title number: "You throw my voice around like toilet paper."

It wasn't long after *Cabin* that George Abbott, who had directed *Syracuse*, asked Martin about writing the songs for *Best Foot Forward*, a show Abbott was developing about a group of prep school boys and their efforts to impress a movie star. The director wanted to ensure that the show had a youthful sound given its subject matter. Martin wasn't entirely certain he could handle the task alone, so he asked Blane to join him. They wrote a handful of numbers as an "audition" and got the assignment. Their score eventually included such numbers as "Buckle Down Winsocki" and "The Three B's," and when *Best Foot* opened, Eugene Barr, in his October 10, 1941, *Billboard* review, called Martin and Blane a "force to be reckoned with."

Martin heeded the call of Hollywood after this, and there he served as vocal arranger on a variety of pictures, including *Girl Crazy* with songs by the Gershwins and starring Mickey Rooney and Judy Garland. He and Blane soon signed to write the songs for the Garland vehicle *Meet Me in St. Louis*, which contains such enduring numbers as "Have Yourself a Merry Little Christmas," "The Trolley Song," and "The Boy Next Door." For the movie, as well as *Best Foot*, Martin and Blane were co-billed as songwriters, but as Martin relates in his autobiography, they worked on numbers independently and simply put their names on one another's work. In the case of *St. Louis*, Martin penned all three of the hits.

He returned to Broadway as both composer and arranger in the late 1940s and early 1950s. In the former capacity, he was represented with, among others, *Gentlemen Prefer Blondes* (1949) and *Hazel Flagg* (1952). As a songwriter he provided the tunes for *Look Ma, I'm Dancin'* (1948) and *Make a Wish* (1954) and received some good notices for both. Brooks Atkinson, in a January 30 *Times* review of *Look Ma*, complimented the "cheerful" music and added that the songs were outfitted with the "most ingenious lyrics of the season." For *Wish*, Otis L. Guernsey Jr., in an April 19 review for the *New York Herald Tribune*, remarked, "The music swings along in step with a show that never pauses for breath."

As a composer Martin was represented on Broadway only two more times. In 1964, he wrote, with Timothy Gray, *High Spirits*, a musical version of Coward's *Blithe Spirit*, and in 1989, he composed new numbers for a stage version of *St. Louis*. But that didn't mean he had stopped working. He wrote songs for a half-dozen shows that went unproduced, and he continued to arrange for both stage and screen. At the time of his death, he was at work on a new score for a musical version of William Inge's *Picnic*.

MARY MARTIN

(December 1, 1913–November 3, 1990)
Performer

Mary Martin's winsomeness and warmth captured audiences' hearts around the world, as she both originated classic roles and lovingly brought her own grace to others on many a national tour.

When she was just five years old, this Texas native performed a song at a local fireman's ball. By all reports the crowd was enthusiastic, and as Ronald L. Davis reports in his biography of the Broadway star, she remembered, "I didn't fall in love with one face in the audience. I fell in love with all of them." She added, "It's been that way ever since."

Martin's affection for her audiences was matched by theirs for her throughout her five-decade career, which seemed to begin in just one electrifying night when she made her Broadway bow in *Leave It to Me!* in 1938. In the show, set in Russia and featuring a score by Cole Porter, Martin delivered "My Heart Belongs to Daddy," performed as faux striptease in a fur parka. Critics raved, and on November 20, less than two weeks after the show opened, John R. Franchey in the *Austin American-Statesman* reported on her breakthrough debut while also charting the circuitous route she had taken before attaining it: She had endured a disappointing stint in Hollywood, done some radio work, and also appeared in a musical that stalled en route to New York.

After *Leave It to Me!* Martin, signed to Paramount Pictures, returned to the West Coast and between 1939 and 1942 appeared in seven pictures, including the biopic *The Great Victor Herbert*, in which she was able to display her coloratura, and *Birth of the Blues*, where she had equal billing with Bing Crosby.

Broadway continued to call, and in 1943 she accepted the title role in S. J. Perelman, Ogden Nash, and Kurt Weill's *One Touch of Venus*. Martin claimed that she felt ill at ease playing such a great beauty (or at least a human version of a statue of the goddess), but her fears were misplaced. The morning after the show's October 7, 1943, opening, Lewis Nichols in the *New York Times* wrote, "She is graceful and alive as well as being beautiful and as well as giving the impression that she, herself, is having a wonderful time."

Martin, who had not been able to tour with *Leave It to Me!* did take *Venus* on the road and then segued into her next Broadway show, *Lute Song*, a musical adaptation of a classic Chinese piece. The show received mixed reviews, but Martin triumphed again. "Miss Martin has unofficially been designated a pillar of the theater," wrote Howard Barnes in his February 7, 1946, *New York Herald Tribune* review.

At the end of 1946, Martin made her West End debut in Noël Coward's *Pacific 1860*. The show, set on a fictional Pacific Island during Queen Victoria's reign and written for her by Coward, proved to be an unhappy experience for them both, and though she was offered the opportunity to stay in London to play the title role in *Annie Get Your Gun*, she turned it down. Instead, she asked to play the role in America on tour. She opened it to acclaim in her beloved Texas, and as she played around the country, theatregoers fell in love with her portrayal of the fabled sharpshooter.

Martin's next Broadway outing came in 1949, when she originated the role of Nellie Forbush in Rodgers and Hammerstein's *South Pacific* starring opposite Ezio Pinza. As she had with her two previous shows, she had qualms about this one; she was concerned about her voice being able to compete with that of her leading man, who was a bona fide opera star. Again, she had no reason to worry and crested to a new high professionally as she played a navy nurse struggling with her love for a widower who has children from an interracial marriage. Brooks Atkinson, in his April 8, 1949, *New York Times* review, wrote, "Miss Martin is a girl who can make her captivating without deluging her in charm." Martin earned a Tony Award for her performance and reprised it when the show debuted in London.

As the 1950s dawned, Martin was frequently seen in homes throughout the country as she made repeated appearances on television specials, notably the *Ford 50th Anniversary Television Show*, where she performed an extended and acclaimed medley duet with Ethel Merman. Thanks to these—as well as numerous recordings and her tours—her popularity only increased. It's little surprise, then, that expectations from both theatre fans and home audiences were high when she announced she would be playing *Peter Pan* in a production directed and choreographed by Jerome Robbins. After she captured Broadway's heart in the role, she did the same for the nation when the production aired on live TV.

Martin's next big Broadway outing came at the end of the decade, as Maria in Rodgers and Hammerstein's *The Sound of Music*. In reviewing her performance, the *Times'* Atkinson wrote on November 17, 1959, "She still has the same common touch that wins friends and influences people." He added that, at this point, Martin also retained the "same plain voice that makes music sound intimate and familiar."

Martin's next musical, *Jennie* (1963), earned her warm personal notices but eked out only a two-month run. But then she took on the title role in Jerry Herman's *Hello, Dolly!* and found yet another part in which to excel. She started in what producer David Merrick billed as the show's "international tour" in Minneapolis, and "Rees.," in the April 24, 1965, edition of *Variety*, called her performance there a "knockout . . . a rousing delineation of the role." Martin took the show to other US venues, and then it was off to Japan and Vietnam (where she played for American servicemen just outside of Saigon) in early fall 1965 before opening in London in December.

Martin's last musical outing came in 1966, Tom Jones and Harvey Schmidt's *I Do! I Do!*, a two-hander that also starred Robert Preston. The musical about a couple's life from their just-married youthful selves to their golden years earned them both raves. In a review filled with superlatives about their work, Atkinson, in the December 6 edition of the *Times*, summed it all up with "They're great."

As the 1970s dawned, Martin shifted her priorities toward her personal life and ultimately made only a handful of stage appearances, including a historic one-night-only benefit concert at the Broadway Theatre in 1977 that reteamed her with Merman.

AUDRA McDONALD

(July 3, 1970–)
Performer

McDonald has established herself as one of Broadway's foremost actress-singers, a performer deeply committed to stage work and to championing new voices for the musical theatre.

Recalling her childhood for the *Independent*'s Robert Butler for an August 15, 1999, feature, this six-time Tony Award winner and native of Fresno, California, said, "I remember being more on-stage than off-stage." Indeed, her early years included attending a performing arts high school and being part of a youth group that entertained at a dinner theatre before the main show. She even sang for the governor of California when she was fourteen.

After her graduation from high school, McDonald moved to New York to attend Juilliard to study voice. Not long after her graduation, she got her first Broadway gig, replacing in *The Secret Garden*. She took the show on tour in 1992, and then she snagged the role of Carrie, Julie Jordan's best friend, in a revival of Rodgers and Hammerstein's *Carousel*. Director Nicholas Hytner's thoughtful, innovative staging gave critics plenty to write about when the show opened on March 24, 1994, but even as they attempted to explain and extol how the director had reinvigorated a musical that was just a year shy of turning fifty, they found ways to toast McDonald. David Richards, in his March 25, 1994, *New York Times* review, wrote that she was the "real find of this production," adding, "[She] has a welcomingly open manner as Carrie, a vigorous voice, and a ready sense of comedy." It was a performance that earned her her first Tony Award.

McDonald segued into Terrence McNally's *Master Class,* in which she played a soprano who has the chance to learn from opera great Maria Callas. Initially nervous, McDonald's character overcomes her fears to finally lash back at the imposing diva. Her performance, which included delivering Lady Macbeth's "Vieni! t'affretta" aria from Verdi's *Macbeth,* garnered McDonald a second Tony Award, this time for best featured actress in a play.

Her third Broadway role—Sarah, a black woman who gives up her baby in turn-of-the-century New York in *Ragtime*—prompted Ben Brantley to enthuse in his January 19, 1998, *Times* review about the "humanity" that she brought to the part. He also added, "As always, she sings gloriously." Later that year, McDonald had her third Tony win.

At this point in her career, the actress-singer went into the recording studio for her first solo album, and she used it as an opportunity to showcase a new generation of songwriters, such as Jason Robert Brown, Michael John LaChiusa, and Adam Guettel. In discussing the album with Trey Graham for a February 2, 1998, *USA Today* feature, the difference between classical versus Broadway music arose, and McDonald observed about herself and the material she had selected, "[Their work] sort of touches both worlds, and mainly lands in the middle, which is where I think I lie. Not really on either side." When writing about the disc in the December 14 edition of the *Philadelphia Inquirer* that year, Clifford A. Ridley described the selections as "nothing less than the art songs of our time" and said that they were "delivered with riveting honesty and power by a once-in-a-lifetime voice."

LaChiusa penned McDonald's next musical, *Marie Christine,* a reworking of the Medea myth set in 1899 New Orleans. Critics were divided about the show but unanimous in their praise of her performance: "McDonald's voice wraps itself around the angular notes of LaChiusa's score with such mastery that her songs seem as direct and natural as speech" was Fintan O'Toole's assessment in his December 3, 1999, *Daily News* review.

McDonald shifted away from musicals for her next two Broadway outings: Shakespeare's *Henry IV* (2003) and Lorraine Hansberry's *A Raisin in the Sun* (2004). The latter high-profile revival also starred Sean Combs, in his Broadway debut, and Phylicia Rashad. McDonald's performance stood out, and she earned Tony Award number four.

Musical theatre returned to McDonald's life in 2007 with a revival of Tom Jones and Harvey Schmidt's *110 in the Shade.* Playing a spinster who thinks she might have found love in a huckster who arrives in her drought-stricken town, McDonald dazzled most critics. The morning after the production's May 9 opening, Brantley wrote in the *Times,* "She so blurs the lines between spoken and musical expression that one seems like a natural extension of the other," and the *Daily News'* Joe Dziemianowicz said her renditions of two of the show's biggest numbers were "exactly why you go to the theater."

After completing the limited-run engagement of this Roundabout Theatre Company show, McDonald dedicated herself primarily to television work, specifically the series *Private Practice,* and it wasn't until 2012 that she returned to Broadway.

And when she did, it was in a landmark piece of American musical theatre: *Porgy and Bess*. Directed by Diane Paulus using a revision from Suzan-Lori Parks and Diedre Murray, the production attracted divergent opinions, but McDonald's craft was beautifully showcased. Linda Winer, in a January 13 *Newsday* review, wrote that the actress had an "undercurrent of gravity" in her performance and delivered with a "voice that's luminous on the top, burnished in the middle and an astonishing technique that channels clear emotional truth." With *Porgy*, McDonald won her fifth Tony, her first in the leading actress in a musical category.

She followed this in 2014 with a bio-drama with music, *Lady Day at Emerson's Bar and Grill*, playing singing legend Billie Holiday. In an April 22 *Variety* review, critic Marilyn Stasio recognized McDonald's gifts as a vocalist but said, "It's her extraordinary sensitivity as an actor that makes McDonald's interpretations memorable." McDonald earned her sixth Tony for her performance.

Since that time McDonald has appeared in one more musical, George C. Wolfe's *Shuffle Along, or, The Making of the Musical Sensation of 1921 and All That Followed* (2016); released a new album, *Sing Happy*, a live recording of a performance she gave with the New York Philharmonic; and embarked on a national concert tour.

ALAN MENKEN

(July 22, 1949–)
Composer

This composer's knack for writing immediately catchy melodies in a wide variety of styles has captured audience's ears, oftentimes young ones, for nearly forty years.

Despite his family's fondness for both theatre and music, and regardless of the talent he had displayed as a child for writing songs, Menken's parents wanted him to pursue a career outside of the arts. "I come from a long line of dentists," he told Rod Currie for a July 18, 1995, feature in London's the *Spectator*. Eventually, though, Menken, who never really liked practicing Beethoven but enjoyed parodying him, studied musicology at New York University.

Just before finishing college, he joined the BMI Workshop, which had been founded by Broadway musical director Lehman Engel. "At the time I was more into being a rock musician than a theater composer," he told Lee Alan Morrow for a March 30, 1984, feature in *Back Stage*. It was a crucial juncture for Menken, and indeed, he began writing songs that eschewed the rock format. In the workshop he completed the Engel-designed assignments to help musical theatre writers during his first year, moving on in his second and third years to writing music for projects he initiated, including one based on Hermann Hesse's "For Madmen Only," a portion of the novel *Steppenwolf*.

To make ends meet during the 1970s, Menken was variously employed. He accompanied ballet classes, composed jingles, and wrote some music for *Sesame Street*. He also created material for revues and cabaret performers. Some of his earliest and best notices came in 1977 when David Summers appeared at the SoHo nightclub known as the Ballroom. Menken was Summers's musical director and accompanist and wrote some of the songs that the performer delivered. Howard Kissel reviewed the show for *Women's Wear Daily*, and in the June 27 edition of the paper he wrote that some of Menken's songs "have the feeling, the musical savvy, and the emotional resonance of 'standards.'"

During this period Menken met lyricist Howard Ashman and brought him into the BMI Workshop as they developed *God Bless You, Mr. Rosewater*. Based on Kurt Vonnegut's novel about a wealthy man who develops a social conscience and attempts to do good works with his family's fortune, the show eventually had an off-Broadway run in 1979, and though this first Menken–Ashman collaboration didn't succeed, critics, such as the *New York Times'* Walter Kerr, saw merit: "There's not only ambition but talent behind [the show]," he wrote in an October 15 review.

Three years and one revue later, Menken and Ashman had another book musical premiere, *Little Shop of Horrors*. Based on the Roger Corman B-movie about a man-eating plant from outer space and the nebbish florist's assistant who unwittingly abets in the alien's scheme, this off-Broadway tuner clicked immediately with audiences and critics. "The evening is as entertaining as it is exotic," wrote the *Times'* Mel Gussow on May 30. Part of the show's success lay in Menken's exceptionally tuneful score, which was influenced by doo-wop, rock, Latin, and country-western sounds. After premiering at the nonprofit WPA Theatre, *Little Shop* transferred to a commercial run at the Orpheum Theatre in the East Village, where it ran for five years. Before it closed, the musical was made into a major motion picture.

During this time Menken contributed toward a pair of off-Broadway revues and also came to have a fascination with classic Walt Disney animated feature films, thanks to the videos that he bought to watch with his first daughter. He described his reaction to the work to the *Spectator's* Currie in 1995: "It transcended era, it transcended style, it transcended age. I was just . . . inspired." Just as this was happening, Ashman received a phone call from Disney; the studio wanted to talk to them about an animated musical based on Hans Christian Andersen's *The Little Mermaid*. Menken and Ashman accepted the assignment, and using many of the principles about writing musical theatre that Engel espoused, they created the score for the movie that is generally credited with launching the renaissance of the animated feature film. Their work on *Mermaid* also resulted in an Academy Award for best song for "Under the Sea," and Menken won for best original score.

They were already at work on their next project when these awards were presented, writing songs for *Beauty and the Beast*, which was to be their greatest movie triumph. *Beast* eventually became a stage musical and gave Menken his Broadway debut but not until after Ashman's death from AIDS in 1991. For the theatre, additional songs were needed, and Menken turned to lyricist Tim Rice to supply them. When reviewing the production in the *New York Times* on April 19, 1994, David Richards compared Menken and Ashman's work on such songs as "Be Our Guest" and "Gaston" to that of Alan Jay Lerner and Frederick Loewe, and of the title song he wrote, "[It] speaks stirringly of love, as few Broadway ballads do

Victor Herbert (circa 1915–1920).
Library of Congress

George M. Cohan in 1935.
Library of Congress

Noble Sissle and Eubie Blake.
Bridgeman Images

Ethel Waters (circa 1943). *MGM / Photofest © MGM*

Bert Williams in 1922. *Library of Congress*

Joseph Urban (circa 1915–1920).
Library of Congress

John Murray Anderson (circa 1914–1916). *Library of Congress*

Ira Gershwin, George Gershwin, Morrie Ryskind, and George S. Kaufman in 1931. *Photofest © Photofest*

George Balanchine (circa 1930s).
Photofest © Photofest

Richard Rodgers and Lorenz Hart in 1936. *Library of Congress*

Cole Porter (circa 1938). *Photofest © Photofest*

Hugh Martin (circa 1942). *Photofest ©
Photofest*

Robert Russell Bennett in 1958.
Photofest © *Photofest*

E. Y. "Yip" Harburg in 1947. *Photofest* © *Photofest*

Ed Sullivan in 1955. *Library of Congress*

Carolyn Leigh (circa 1958). *Author's collection*

Boris Aronson (circa 1965). *Photofest © Photofest*

Jerry Herman (circa 1965). *Photofest © Photofest*

Lehman Engel (circa 1970). *Photofest © Photofest*

Michael Kidd (circa 1975). *United Artists / Photofest © United Artists*

Robin Wagner (circa 1980s).
Photofest © Photofest

Michael Bennett in 1969. *Photofest © Photofest*

Tim Rice (circa 1982). *Photofest ©
Photofest*

Jonathan Larson (circa 1994). *Photofest © Photofest*

Jack Donahue, George Gershwin, Sigmund Romberg, Marilyn Miller, and Florenz Ziegfeld, backstage at *Rosalie* in 1928. *Photofest © Photofest*

Oscar Hammerstein II and Jerome Kern during rehearsals for *Music in the Air* in 1935. *Photofest © Photofest*

Jo Mielziner with his set model for *Jubilee* in 1935. *Photofest © Photofest*

Maurice Abravanel, Kurt Weill, and Ira Gershwin at rehearsals for *Lady in the Dark* in 1941. *Photofest © Photofest*

Alfred Drake in *Oklahoma!* (circa 1943). *Photofest © Photofest*

Marc Blitzstein (standing) and Leonard Bernstein (circa 1945). *Photofest © Photofest*

Richard Rodgers, Irving Berlin, and Oscar Hammerstein II attend rehearsals in 1948. *Library of Congress*

Gertrude Lawrence in *The King and I* **in 1951.** *Photofest © Photofest*

Frank Loesser at the recording of the original cast recording of *The Most Happy Fella*. *Photofest* © *Photofest*

Adolph Green, Betty Comden, Judy Holliday, and Jule Styne rehearse *Bells Are Ringing* in 1956. *Photofest* © *Photofest*

Bob Fosse and Gwen Verdon (and Harvey Hohnecker [later Harvey Evans] in background) rehearse *New Girl in Town* in 1957. *Photofest © Photofest*

Mary Martin and Ethel Merman perform on the *Ford 50th Anniversary Television Show* in 1953. *Photofest © Photofest*

Stephen Sondheim, Arthur Laurents, Harold Prince, Robert E. Griffith, Leonard Bernstein, and Jerome Robbins rehearse *West Side Story* in 1957. *Photofest © Photofest*

Chita Rivera in *West Side Story* in 1957. *Photofest © Photofest*

Lee Adams, Gower Champion, Michael Stewart, Edward Padula, and Charles Strouse backstage at *Bye Bye Birdie* in 1961. *Photofest © Photofest*

Zero Mostel in *A Funny Thing Happened on the Way to the Forum* in 1962. *Photofest © Photofest*

Harold Prince, George Abbott, Liza Minnelli, Bob Dishy, John Kander, and Fred Ebb rehearse *Flora, the Red Menace* in 1965. *Photofest © Photofest*

Sheldon Harnick, Joseph Stein, Jerome Robbins, and Jerry Bock (seated) prepare for the London premiere of *Fiddler on the Roof* in 1967. *Photofest © Photofest*

Alan Jay Lerner, Moss Hart, and Frederick Loewe (circa 1960). *Photofest © Photofest*

Gwen Verdon, Goddard Lieberson, Cy Coleman, and Dorothy Fields at the recording session for the *Sweet Charity* cast album in 1966. *Photofest © Photofest*

Galt MacDermot at a recording session in 1969. *RCA / Photofest © RCA*

Stephen Schwartz and John-Michael Tebelak (circa 1973). *Photofest © Photofest*

Stephen Sondheim, Harold Prince, and Hugh Wheeler at rehearsals for *A Little Night Music* in 1973. *Photofest © Photofest*

Joseph Papp backstage at *The Pirates of Penzance* in 1983. *Photofest © Photofest*

Oliver Smith and Agnes de Mille
attend an opening in 1952.
Photofest © Photofest

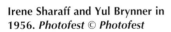

Irene Sharaff and Yul Brynner in
1956. *Photofest © Photofest*

Playwright Thornton Wilder with Carol Channing and David Merrick backstage at *Hello, Dolly!* in 1965. *Photofest © Photofest*

William Finn celebrates his Tony Award wins in 1992. *Photofest © Photofest*

Alan Menken in 2018 as the New York Pops celebrate his music. *Courtesy of Joseph Marzullo*

Michael John LaChiusa at the Tony Awards in 2018. *Courtesy of Joseph Marzullo*

Harold Prince. *Courtesy of Joseph Marzullo*

Nathan Lane celebrates his 2018 Tony Award win. *Courtesy of Joseph Marzullo*

Harvey Fierstein in 2018. *Courtesy of Joseph Marzullo*

Audra McDonald in 2017. *Courtesy of Joseph Marzullo*

Harvey Schmidt and Tom Jones celebrate receiving the 2017 Oscar Hammerstein Award for lifetime achievement from the York Theatre Company. *Courtesy of Joseph Marzullo*

Lin-Manuel Miranda in 2018. *Courtesy of Joseph Marzullo*

Patti LuPone celebrates her *War Paint* opening night in 2017. *Courtesy of Joseph Marzullo*

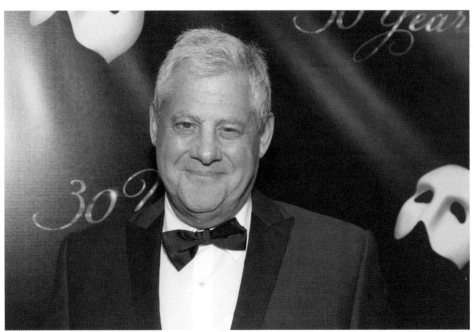

Cameron Mackintosh celebrates the thirtieth anniversary of *The Phantom of the Opera* on Broadway. *Courtesy of Joseph Marzullo*

Tommy Tune celebrates his caricature at Sardi's in 2017. *Courtesy of Joseph Marzullo*

Andrew Lloyd Webber celebrates the opening of the 2017 revival of *Sunset Boulevard. Courtesy of Joseph Marzullo*

these days." The production ran for more than thirteen years and also established the Disney studio as a producing power on the Main Stem.

For the remainder of the 1990s and the beginnings of the 2000s, Menken primarily concentrated on film work. He wrote the scores for *Aladdin* (1992), with lyrics by Ashman and Rice; *Pocahontas* (1995) and *The Hunchback of Notre Dame* (1996), with lyrics by Stephen Schwartz; and *Hercules* (1997), with lyrics by David Zippel, and his contributions on these animated features propelled him to an astonishing eight Academy Award wins. During this time Menken didn't entirely abandon the stage. In 1997, he and Tim Rice wrote *King David*, which reopened the New Amsterdam Theatre on 42nd Street, and he and Lynn Ahrens created a musical version of *A Christmas Carol* that was a holiday-time offering at the Theatre at Madison Square Garden for twelve years.

Since 2008, Menken has been a continuing presence on New York's stages, both with shows based on movies he has written (*The Little Mermaid, Newsies, Aladdin*) and ones written specifically for the stage, including *Sister Act* (2011); *Leap of Faith* (2012); and, more recently, *A Bronx Tale* (2016), which was based on Chazz Palmintieri's autobiographical work about hardscrabble youth in the titular borough and ran for nearly two years. Additionally, a stage adaptation of *Hunchback*, with new material, had its US premiere in 2014 and has gone on to enjoy numerous productions nationwide. During this time Menken received four Tony nominations and won one for his score for *Newsies*.

ETHEL MERMAN

(January 16, 1908–February 15, 1984)
Performer

This iron-lunged performer epitomized the brashness of the American musical as it came of age during the middle of the twentieth century. To many fans she was "musical theatre."

On October 15, 1930, a new star, seemingly born overnight, was championed as reviews of the musical *Girl Crazy*, which had a score by George and Ira Gershwin, ran. The show starred Ginger Rogers (still a few years away from her screen partnership with Fred Astaire), but an eighteen-year-old (at least that's what she claimed at the time) in a supporting role was the person critics were cheering. It was Ethel Merman, who, by all reports, stopped the show with "I Got Rhythm."

Merman, born Ethel Agnes Zimmerman in Astoria, Queens, had not simply sprung to life on the stage of the Alvin Theatre where *Girl Crazy* premiered. She had been working steadily and persistently toward her goal of establishing a career as a singer for several years. Her first appearances had been at lodges and clubs that her father habituated.

After high school she worked as a stenographer and quit one job to take another because she heard that her new boss worked with show business movers and shakers. She got an introduction to—and an offer from—a Broadway producer but turned it down because it was only a chorus role. Merman ultimately turned to singing in nightclubs and in such legendary vaudeville houses as the Palace in Manhattan and the Brooklyn Paramount. It was in this latter theatre that she was spotted by Vinton Freedley, who convinced Gershwin to hear her audition for *Girl Crazy*.

Merman followed *Girl Crazy* with appearances in *George White's Scandals* (1931), in which she introduced "Life Is Just a Bowl of Cherries," and the musical *Take a Chance* (1932), where one of her numbers was "Eadie Was a Lady." Her first genuine starring role came in Cole Porter's *Anything Goes* in 1934. Playing Reno Sweeney, a nightclub singer with an evangelical bent aboard a cruise ship, Merman originated the now-classics "I Get a Kick out of You," "Blow, Gabriel, Blow," and the musical's title song. In his November 22, 1934, *New York Herald Tribune* review, Percy Hammond described her as a "rough and subtle scarlet warbler" and noted that she "sings and acts a Broadway-show prima donna laughably and sincerely."

After *Anything Goes* Merman became Porter's de facto leading lady, and over the course of nearly ten years she appeared in four more Porter musicals: *Red, Hot and Blue* (1936), costarring Bob Hope; *Du Barry Was a Lady* (1939), costarring Bert Lahr; *Panama Hattie* (1940); and *Something for the Boys* (1943). Among the songs she introduced in these productions were "It's De-Lovely," "Make It Another Old-Fashioned Please," and "The Leader of a Big-Time Band."

In 1946, Merman became a performer-muse for another musical theatre great, Irving Berlin, when she played real-life sharpshooter Annie Oakley in *Annie Get Your Gun*. While Merman's direct performance style had meant that she could deliver Porter's intricate lyrics with precision, it was even more suited toward Berlin's no-nonsense songwriting style. Similarly, Berlin's work fit Merman perfectly, and two numbers from *Annie Get Your Gun* ("They Say It's Wonderful" and "Anything You Can Do") became Merman signatures for the remainder of her life.

The next Berlin-written show for Merman was *Call Me Madam* in 1950. Inspired by the flamboyant life of American socialite-ambassador Perle Mesta, this tuner about a straight-talking American diplomat in the tiny, fictional country of Lichtenburg suited Merman to a tee. In his October 13, 1950, *New York Times* review, Brooks Atkinson described her performance: "She is still lighting up like a pinball machine, and still blowing the music lustily throughout the theatre."

There was a misstep for Merman (and for everyone concerned) with *Happy Hunting* in 1956, but this was followed by her greatest triumph, *Gypsy*, in 1959. Based on burlesque performer Gypsy Rose Lee's memoir and featuring a book by Arthur Laurents, music by Jule Styne, and lyrics by Stephen Sondheim, this musical found Merman playing the mother of all stage mothers, Rose, who would stop at nothing to see her daughters win fame in vaudeville. The show found Merman delivering such tunes as "Everything's Coming Up Roses" and "Rose's Turn," a harrowing eleven-o'clock number delivered as her character breaks down, having seen both of her daughters move out of her life. In his May 22, 1959, review in the *Times*, Atkinson wrote, "[Merman] struts and bawls her way through it triumphantly."

Rose was the last role that Merman originated on Broadway, and she would make only two other appearances on the Main Stem during the next two decades.

In 1966, she reprised her turn in *Annie Get Your Gun*, and in 1970, she stepped into the title role in *Hello, Dolly!* In this latter instance, she was able to offer up two songs ("World, Take Me Back" and "Love, Look in My Window") that composer Jerry Herman had written when he had envisioned the show as a vehicle for her. Writing about her performance in the *Times* on April 14, Walter Kerr reported that her voice is "exactly as trumpet-clean, exactly as pennywhistle-piercing, exactly as Wurlitzer-wonderful as it always was." He also noted that the audience was giving her cheering standing ovations for each number.

Although Broadway was always Merman's primary professional home, she did venture to Hollywood throughout her career. She had the opportunity to reprise two of her stage performances on screen. The first came in 1936, when Paramount Pictures produced a severely bowdlerized version of *Anything Goes*. Seventeen years later, she starred in the film version of *Call Me Madam* to much happier results. Among her other films were *Alexander's Ragtime Band* (1938) and the cult favorite *It's a Mad, Mad, Mad, Mad World* (1963). Merman's work on the small screen ranged from musical specials, such as the acclaimed *Ford 50th Anniversary Television Show* (which paired her with Mary Martin) to game shows, sitcoms, and other fare.

Merman's last significant appearance was in 1982 when she made her Carnegie Hall debut with a benefit concert that looked back over her career.

DAVID MERRICK

(November 27, 1911–April 25, 2000)
Producer

During the course of his career, Merrick was responsible for both assembling several touchstones of American musical theatre history and for exposing US audiences to adventuresome, cutting-edge musicals from across the Atlantic.

An attorney-turned-theatrical-producer, Merrick, sometimes referred to as the "abominable showman," was responsible for bringing some of the most acclaimed musicals of the late 1950s and early 1960s to Broadway. In addition, as he did with his productions of plays, Merrick also introduced New York theatregoers to international musicals, even works that might have been deemed too risky by other producers.

Merrick was educated and practiced as a lawyer in his native St. Louis during his twenties. In 1940, a year after moving to New York, he invested in a production of Thornton Wilder's *The Male Animal* and ultimately went to work for that play's producer, Herman Shumlin. Two years later, Merrick singly produced John Patrick's play *The Willow and I*.

During the 1940s, the producer was associated with a trio of other plays, and then, in 1954 he brought a musical version of Marcel Pagnol's *Marius* film trilogy, *Fanny*, to Broadway. It was a production that Merrick conceived, and for it he negotiated the rights and assembled the creative team, which included Josh

Logan as director and coproducer and Harold Rome as composer-lyricist. The story was bittersweet, and for a first-time effort by a still-emerging producer, it was an unconventional gamble. The risk paid off. In a November 24 story in the *New York Times*, Brooks Atkinson cited it as "further evidence of the maturity of the musical theatre."

The combination of artistry and risk that were part of *Fanny* became, on many levels, the hallmarks of Merrick's career for the next twenty-five years, as he segued between producing plays and musicals. In the former category were such international works as John Osborne's *Look Back in Anger* (1957), Jean Anouilh's *Becket* (1961), and Peter Weiss's *Marat/Sade* (1965), as well as American plays, from Woody Allen's early comedy *Don't Drink the Water* (1966) to Michael Weller's drama *Moonchildren* (1972).

Merrick's musicals were an equally diverse lot. The first that he brought to Broadway after *Fanny* was a seemingly more commercial property, *Jamaica* (1957). It boasted a score by Harold Arlen and E. Y. "Yip" Harburg and starred Lena Horne and Ricardo Montalbán, but while *Fanny* ran 888 performances, *Jamaica* only reached 555.

The following year, Merrick's musicals ranged from the operatic, Gian Carlo Menotti's *Maria Golovin*, to the frivolous, the Parisian import *La plume de ma tante*. It was during this time that he began to exercise his considerable influence in the shaping and developing of musical properties, including the musical adaptation of Gypsy Rose Lee's memoir. Merrick obtained the rights to it before its publication in 1957, and he ultimately brought together book writer Arthur Laurents, composer Stephen Sondheim, composer Jule Styne, and director-choreographer Jerome Robbins for the project. Together they created the classic *Gypsy*, which bowed on May 21, 1959. Walter Kerr's review in the *New York Herald Tribune* the next day proclaimed, "It's the best damn musical I've seen in years."

Merrick had another tuner on the boards by that fall, and it was one that took six years to assemble: a musical version of Eugene O'Neill's *Ah, Wilderness!* In this instance Merrick teamed book writers Joseph Stein and Robert Russell with songwriter Bob Merrill, and the result was *Take Me Along*, which had in its central role TV star Jackie Gleason.

In the 1960s, Merrick imported numerous musical hits from London, including Lionel Bart's popular adaptation of Charles Dickens, *Oliver!* (1963). In 1964, Merrick brought *Oh What a Lovely War!*, Joan Littlewood's antiwar revue filled with popular songs from World War I, to New York. He also produced two pieces of semiexperimental musical theatre for American audiences: Leslie Bricusse and Anthony Newley's existential *Stop the World—I Want to Get Off* (1962) and the team's exploration of class differences, *The Roar of the Greasepaint—The Smell of the Crowd* (1965). All but one of these (*Stop the World*) were nominated for best musical Tony Awards.

As for shows that he assembled during the course of the decade, the list of musicals that achieved hit status includes *Carnival!* (1961), *Hello, Dolly!* (1964), *I Do! I Do!* (1966), and *Promises, Promises* (1968). There were also notable artistic successes that simply failed to catch on. Among these were *I Can Get It for You Wholesale* (1962), *110 in the Shade* (1963), and *The Happy Time* (1968). Merrick also had his share of misses, such as *Foxy* (1964), *How Now, Dow Jones* (1967), *Mata Hari*

(1967), and *The Baker's Wife* (1976). Perhaps most famous is the musical version of Truman Capote's *Breakfast at Tiffany's* in 1966 that starred Richard Chamberlain and Mary Tyler Moore, which Merrick closed in previews on Broadway before it ever officially opened.

When faced with bad reviews, Merrick was a shrewd manipulator of the media, and in 1962, just after the opening of *Subways Are for Sleeping*, he pulled one of his most famous publicity stunts. He found people who bore the same names as New York's first-string critics, brought them to the show, and asked them for quotes about the musical's merits. He assembled these "raves" in a full-page print ad that ran in some newspapers before editors realized what he had done.

Merrick's work as a producer continued in the 1970s, mostly with plays, including a late work by Tennessee Williams and new work by Tom Stoppard and Weller. He also spent a brief period in Hollywood, where, with such films as *The Great Gatsby*, he was unable to replicate his Broadway success.

He had not, however, forsaken musicals and produced *Sugar* (1972) and *Mack & Mabel* (1974). He had one last major success in his career with the stage version of *42nd Street*, which debuted in 1980 and ran for the remainder of the decade. Merrick suffered a stroke in 1983 that left him partially paralyzed and impacted his ability to speak.

Nevertheless, he did bring two more tuners to Broadway before he died in 2000: an all-black revival of the 1920s musical *Oh, Kay!* (1990) and a stage adaptation of Rodgers and Hammerstein's one original film musical, *State Fair* (1996). The former was notable more for one final Merrick publicity stunt than for its artistry. In an ad in the *Times*, placed after an unfavorable review and less-than-flattering mentions in the paper's theatre column, Merrick placed an ad tweaking the romance between critic Frank Rich and columnist Alex Witchel.

JO MIELZINER
(March 19, 1901–March 15, 1976)
Designer

Mielziner's work, inspired by his painter's eye, could transport audiences anywhere with beauty and sometimes-unflinching realism, setting standards for audience expectations of what the traditional book musical could look like.

In a March 16, 1976, *New York Times* appreciation of this master artist, Clive Barnes wrote, "His finished stage settings often had the charm of a landscape to them." Mielziner's work was indeed painterly—fluid and impressionistic yet also familiar and realistic, sometimes even gritty. And in the course of a nearly five-decade career, his unique vision and craft helped to bring the worlds of some of the theatre's most classic musicals to vivid life for the first time.

Born in Paris to American parents who were living abroad, Mielziner showed an early interest in and talent for visual arts. Mielziner's father, a portrait painter, encouraged his son both before and after the family returned to the States in 1909. By the time he was fifteen, the younger Mielziner secured a scholarship to the Pennsylvania Academy of Fine Arts, and after serving in the marines during World War I, Mielziner received two scholarships to study in Europe. He used his second to immerse himself in theatre abroad.

His early Broadway work consisted of some acting and stage management at the Theatre Guild and serving as an assistant to designer Robert Edmond Jones. Mielziner's first design credits came thanks to the guild, where he applied his scenic vision to, among others, Ferenc Molnár's comedy *The Guardsman* (1924) and Eugene O'Neill's epic and experimental *Strange Interlude* (1928). Another of his early credits was Elmer Rice's searing portrait of life in a New York tenement, *Street Scene* (1929).

Three months after this show premiered, Mielziner designed his first piece of musical theatre, *The Little Show*. The production required more than twenty-five different sets, and Mielziner used drops to ensure that changes occurred rapidly. Robert Littell, writing for the *New York Evening Post*, praised the solution in a May 1, 1929, review. In his opinion Mielziner had proven that "imagination, plus simple paint and canvas, is a hundred times more good looking and effective than acres of the usual expensive textiles."

Mielziner designed another revue and a trio of plays before tackling his first book musical, the Pulitzer Prize–winning political satire *Of Thee I Sing*. For this show, which breezed from hotel rooms in which nominations were brokered to Madison Square Garden to the White House, Mielziner designed with sparseness and a candid, never-flattering eye. Brooks Atkinson, in his December 28, 1931, *New York Times* review, commended the designer, saying his settings "aptly convey the shoddiness of the political environment."

As the 1930s progressed, Mielziner shifted between plays and musicals with ease. One of his notable successes came in 1936 with Richard Rodgers and Lorenz Hart's *On Your Toes*. The designer's work for this balletic spoof prompted Arthur Pollock in his April 13 *Brooklyn Eagle* review to comment that the production boasted "as fine and airy group of witty settings as the musical comedy stage has yet seen in this country."

Two years and fifteen shows later, Mielziner designed another Rodgers and Hart musical, *I Married an Angel*. For this fantasy about a heavenly being who sheds her wings for love, Mielziner deployed a pair of newly developed traveling curtains that simultaneously exposed and concealed scenic changes, helping to speed the action and give the production an overall grace. It was a technique that he would employ repeatedly in the years to come.

As World War II ended, he reteamed with Rodgers—and the composer's new writing partner, Oscar Hammerstein II—for *Carousel*. It was the beginning of a collaboration that would continue for a decade and include, among others, *South Pacific*, *The King and I*, and *Pipe Dream*. With each, Mielziner's designs transported audiences to the varied locales the writers were depicting, and Howard Barnes, in his April 8, 1949, *New York Herald Tribune* review of *South Pacific*, wrote, "The scenery and lighting by Jo Mielziner are not the least virtues of the exhibit. He has conjured two island settings with a minimum of ornamental nonsense." The show, grouped with others he designed that year, won Mielziner his first of five Tony Awards.

Mielziner not only realized the visions of this team during this period, but he also designed other classics, including *Annie Get Your Gun*; the politically savvy fantasia *Finian's Rainbow*; and that fairy tale of Times Square, *Guys and Dolls*. John Beaufort's December 2, 1950, *Christian Science Monitor* review for this last show praised Mielziner's work, calling it "muted and at the same time garish—a clever combining of antithetical elements."

As the 1950s—filled with more than three dozen shows for him—wound down, Mielziner provided the scenic and lighting design for another classic, *Gypsy*. In this show, which chronicles stripper Gypsy Rose Lee's journey to stardom in adulthood from a childhood spent in vaudeville with a domineering mother, he created a "production of nostalgic humors," capturing, as Atkinson opined in the *Times* on May 31, 1959, the "garish stages of yesteryear, the slatternly dressing rooms and the gaudy stage spectaculars."

In the 1960s, Mielziner concentrated primarily on plays (one notable exception was *1776* in 1969) and also consulted with architect Eero Saarinen on the design of the two theatres at Lincoln Center, the Vivian Beaumont and the Forum (now known as the Mitzi E. Newhouse). In the process, Mielziner utilized his extensive theories about theatre construction. The result of his work was, as press materials said at the time, a space to "answer the requirements of the past, cater to the fashions of the present and be capable of meeting the unknown demands of the future."

Mielziner continued working as he reached his seventies, designing Broadway's *Georgy* and *Look to the Lilies*. He died while *The Baker's Wife*, produced by David Merrick and starring Patti LuPone, who stepped in to replace the production's original leading lady, had an extended and troubled out-of-town tryout period. The show never reached Broadway, but in a review of its final engagement, the *Washington Post*'s Richard L. Coe noted in his largely negative October 7, 1976, review that the settings came from the "late, truly great Jo Mielziner." Coe added that it was only "from Mielziner's evocative intimacy for a small French village that I got my clue about what this production aimed to do."

LIN-MANUEL MIRANDA

(January 16, 1980–)
Composer / Lyricist / Book Writer / Performer

Quadruple-threat artist Miranda, with his musically diverse Hamilton, *has made the American musical be, once again, a topic of national conversation and interest.*

"He deeply loves musical theater and Broadway, and has since he was a child, and he deeply loves hip-hop and pop music as a whole, and has since he was a child," Oskar Eustis told Michael Paulson for an August 12, 2015, *New York Times* feature. Eustis, artistic director of the Public Theater, which produced Miranda's phenomenally successful, groundbreaking *Hamilton*, added, "He's not a tourist when he visits one or the other."

Miranda grew up in the Washington Heights section of Upper Manhattan, son of Puerto Ricans who moved to New York and met studying clinical psychology at New York University. It was his family's collection of cast recordings that drew Miranda to theatre music, and as for other genres, he gravitated to it all. In a November 20, 2016, *Guardian* feature, Alexis Soloski wrote, "[He] listened to his sister's hip-hop albums, the gangster rap his bus driver preferred, Disney movie numbers. Salsa and merengue followed him down the sidewalk, so did 1980s pop."

He wasn't only listening to music as a child; he was also starting to perform and compose, and later, during his college years at Wesleyan University, he wrote musicals, including an early draft of the musical *In the Heights*, which was performed by a student group there.

After graduating in 2002, he worked as a substitute teacher and wrote music for television commercials for politicians, including Fernando Ferrer and Eliot Spitzer. He also kept working on *In the Heights*, and in 2005, the musical received a workshop presentation at the Eugene O'Neill Theater Center's National Musical Theater Conference, attracting the attention of producers, who slated it for an off-Broadway production.

Set in the neighborhood Miranda calls home, the show, with a book by future Pulitzer Prize–winner Quiara Alegría-Hudes, centers on several generations of Latinos. Miranda's score encompasses salsa, merengue, hip-hop, and traditional Broadway sounds. "I just wrote music for the kind of musical I always wanted to be in," Miranda told Robert Dominguez for a January 17, 2007, *Daily News* feature. When *Heights* opened several weeks later, Charles Isherwood called it an "amiable show, which boasts an infectious, bouncy Latin-pop score by a gifted young composer" in a February 9 *Times* review. Almost exactly one year later, twenty-eight-year-old Miranda, who also starred in the production, watched as *Heights* opened on Broadway. The show ultimately won four Tony Awards, including best score for Miranda.

After *Heights*, Miranda worked with Arthur Laurents and Stephen Sondheim on a new Broadway production of *West Side Story*, providing Spanish-language lyrics for some of this show's classic songs, including "I Feel Pretty" and "A Boy like That," as well as translations for portions of Laurents's book. Miranda's next Broadway offering came in 2012, when he, along with Tom Kitt and Amanda Green, wrote the songs for the musical *Bring It On*.

Miranda was at work on another show between these two productions, a hip-hop exploration of founding father Alexander Hamilton. The world got a first taste of the piece in May 2009 when he performed an early excerpt for President Obama and First Lady Michelle at the White House. Over the course of the next six years, Miranda, often working with his musical colleague Alex Lacamoire, director Thomas Kail, and choreographer Andy Blankenbuehler, developed the piece through workshops at New York Stage and Film's Powerhouse Theater at Vassar College in Poughkeepsie, New York, and at the Public Theater.

The off-Broadway institution later slated the show, which became known just as *Hamilton*, for its 2014–2015 season. Even before the musical had officially opened, word circulated through New York and beyond that there was a hit in the making in the same theatre where *A Chorus Line* had premiered forty years earlier. The morning after the official February 17, 2015, opening, the *Times'* Ben Brantley proclaimed, "[*Hamilton*] shot open like a streamlined cannon ball on Tuesday night. When one of the young rebels who populate this vibrant work says, 'History is happening in Manhattan,' you can only nod in happy agreement."

Three months after the conclusion of its sold-out and extended run downtown, the production transferred to the Great White Way, with both Miranda's vibrant performance in the title role and his remarkable retelling of American history using a score containing not just hip-hop, but also jazz, R&B, Brit pop, and traditional Broadway sounds.

"A show about young rebels grabbing and shaping the future of an unformed country, 'Hamilton' is making its own resonant history by changing the language of musicals," was one portion of the praise that Brantley offered in his August 7 *Times* review. That same day, Robert Kahn reported for NBC, "The pastiche of musicians to influence the score is blink-or-you'll-miss-it beguiling: Notorious B.I.G., Gilbert & Sullivan, even Jason Robert Brown." Kahn left out Miranda's nods to some of the greats from the Golden Age of musical theatre, including Rodgers and Hammerstein and Lerner and Loewe.

The work went on to win eleven Tony Awards, and Miranda also won the Pulitzer Prize for drama for his creation. In 2018, and breaking with tradition, Kennedy Center Honors were bestowed on not just Miranda but also his collaborators, Kail, Blankenbuehler, and Lacamoire, for being "trailblazing creators of a transformative work that defies category."

Beyond his theatre work, Miranda's boundless energy has propelled him to a host of other projects. He has continued with the hip-hop comedy troupe Freestyle Love Supreme, which he founded in college. During 2018, he also oversaw the release of twelve digital singles related to *Hamilton*, including one he coauthored with composer John Kander.

Further, in 2015, he and J. J. Abrams wrote "Dobra Doompa" for *Star Wars: The Force Awakens*, and the following year, the animated feature *Moana* boasted songs he had written, including "How Far I'll Go," which earned an Academy Award nomination for original song. He has also tirelessly raised money for many causes, including disaster relief for Puerto Rico after the island was devastated by Hurricane Maria. In December 2018, he made his motion picture feature debut in *Mary Poppins Returns*, earning glowing notices for his portrayal of a lamplighter named Jack. Miranda's work extended to the small screen in 2019 as he served as executive producer of a miniseries about Bob Fosse and Gwen Verdon, and for the big screen he began work on the movie version of *In the Heights*. In January 2019, Miranda demonstrated how deeply committed he was to New York's theatrical life when he joined with other *Hamilton* collaborators to help save a New York institution: the Drama Book Shop.

ZERO MOSTEL

(February 28, 1915–September 8, 1977)
Performer

Mostel's journey to the musical theatre was a long one, but before he arrived, he gained the experience that allowed him to become one of the form's most gifted actor-comedians with a talent for imbuing farce with a hint of tragedy and for bringing hilarity to musical drama.

This performer, who will perhaps best be remembered for his portrayals of Tevye in *Fiddler on the Roof* and Pseudolus in *A Funny Thing Happened on the Way to the Forum*, is said to have gotten the name Zero because of his poor academic performance as a child. Other tales relate that he was given the name in adulthood by a press agent who bristled at the actor's given name, Samuel Joel. Regardless of how he arrived at being known as Zero, the moniker was the antithesis of his fiercely committed, funny, oversized performances.

Mostel's career path until 1941 was aimed at the visual arts. He had shown promise in painting as a child and studied art at City College of New York where he received a bachelor's degree. He then enrolled at New York University to secure a master's degree, but he never completed the program. Instead, he turned to teaching and lecturing on art history. Mostel peppered his presentations with comedy and jokes, and in 1941, he auditioned for a spot at Café Society Downtown, Barney Josephson's club on Sheridan Square that had a knack for showcasing new, exceptional, and sometimes unusual talent.

Josephson didn't hire the aspiring comedian right away, but once he did Mostel's routines immediately clicked with audiences and critics. Mostel started at Josephson's Village club in the winter of 1942, and by the following April he was working at Café Society Uptown. Mostel's set included an imitation of Charles Boyer, and he also mocked Adolf Hitler in a speech delivered in ersatz German. An April 15 *Variety* review from "Abel." recognized Mostel's "unique" style as well as the "fast pyramiding progression" of his career.

Indeed, this former painter-lecturer was having a meteoric ascent as a performer. As he was appearing at Café Society, he also secured a number of prominent appearances on radio and was cast in his first two Broadway shows. He did a brief stint as a replacement in the play *Café Crown* and then appeared on a bill with Broadway vets William Gaxton and Victor Moore in a vaudeville revue on Broadway called *Keep 'Em Laughing*. In his April 25, 1942, *New York Times* review, Brooks Atkinson praised Mostel as a "roly-poly zany with a voice that rattles the cellar." Two months later, Mostel had an MGM contract for $1,750 per week for the movie version of Cole Porter's *Du Barry Was a Lady*.

Military service followed, and Mostel entertained troops. After his discharge he was back on Broadway in 1945, appearing in another revue, *Concert Varieties*, which happened to also include Jerome Robbins's ballet *Interplay*. A year later, Mostel got his first job in a book musical. He was cast as Peachum in John Latouche and Duke Ellington's *Beggar's Holiday* and had billing second only to the show's leading man, Alfred Drake. Mostel's performance, which carried some of the hallmarks of his nightclub antics, was roundly dismissed by most critics, but it did not hinder his ability to work. Between 1949 and 1950, he made a half-dozen movies, continued to work as a nightclub entertainer, and had a stint with a television show bearing his name.

Mostel's career had a setback in 1953 after Robbins appeared before the House Un-American Activities Committee and "named names," including Mostel, who was called before the committee in 1955. He invoked his Fifth-Amendment right when asked about any previous membership he might have had with the party or organizations affiliated with it. After this he was promptly blacklisted in Hollywood. Still, Mostel managed to secure work in a few Broadway plays, all of which had meager runs. He did score off-Broadway when he played Leopold Bloom in *Ulysses in Nighttown*, a stage adaptation of part of James Joyce's *Ulysses*. Atkinson's June 15, 1958, *Times* review characterized him as "ideal" for the role, and a year later, he was reprising the performance in London.

Mostel had to wait until 1961 for similar acclaim on Broadway. It came when he was cast as the lead in Eugene Ionesco's *Rhinoceros*. In it he played a man who, like almost everyone else in his town, transformed into one of the beasts of the play's title. The absurdist comedy earned Mostel raves and a Tony Award, and after he finished touring in the piece he segued into his first musical role in more than fifteen years: the slave Pseudolus in *A Funny Thing Happened*.

The Stephen Sondheim–Burt Shevelove–Larry Gelbart musical borrowed from the comedies of the Roman playwright Plautus, and Mostel was on hand to play the chief clown. "Mr. Mostel is, really, a whole road company all by himself," Walter Kerr wrote in his May 9, 1962, *New York Herald Tribune* review, "because he possesses so many talents." Shifting from dark comedy to fast-paced slapstick earned Mostel a second Tony and proved to be his entree back to Hollywood. Four years later, he re-created his performance in the film version of the musical.

Before that, however, Mostel played in one more Broadway musical. On September 22, 1964, he opened in *Fiddler on the Roof* playing Tevye, the beleaguered patriarch of a Russian family enduring life under the rule of the tsar. The show itself was a landmark event, and critics found Mostel's performance irresistible: "His Tevye is a unified, lyrical conception," Howard Taubman wrote in *Times* review the morning after *Fiddler* opened.

With his back-to-back Broadway successes, Mostel's currency in Hollywood was renewed, and he enjoyed an active career in moviemaking until his death in 1977. On the screen, one of his most notable performances was playing Max Bialystock in Mel Brooks's *The Producers*. Before his death Mostel made two more Broadway appearances, reprising his performances in *Ulysses* (1974) and *Fiddler* (1976). On December 30, 1976, Clive Barnes described Mostel's work in the revival as a "fascinating, daring spectacle." Robert D. McFadden echoed this and expanded on this thought a year later in a September 9, 1977, *Times* obituary for the performer: This "actor's actor," as the writer described Mostel, "could look like a pile of tires or an elephant tiptoeing across a stage with pants on." "Most important," McFadden added, Mostel was the "theatergoer's actor."

N

TREVOR NUNN

(January 14, 1940–)
Director

Nunn, responsible for bringing two of the biggest hits of the past half-century to the stage, set standards for new levels of spectacle in musical theatre in the 1980s and has been central in a trend of reinvestigating Golden Age musicals.

This director, who for more than fifty years has moved with ease between plays and musicals, has been responsible for staging some of the most popular tuners of the late twentieth century and for reimagining many classic ones from Broadway's Golden Age.

Nunn was born in Ipswich, England, and discovered a love of Shakespeare at an early age. He received a scholarship to attend Downing College at Cambridge, and there he directed, among others, a production of *Macbeth*. In 1964, he joined the Royal Shakespeare Company (RSC), staging with codirector John Barton an acclaimed *Henry V*. Nunn went on to stage other plays by the Bard, along with important new works, and in 1968 he succeeded Peter Hall as the head of the RSC. In writing about the appointment, Irving Wardle, in an April 12 *New York Times* story, called Nunn a "wunderkind." Over the next ten years, the company flourished, and by 1977 it had nineteen productions running concurrently, and Nunn was also readying it for a move into a new home in London, the Barbican.

As early as 1969, Nunn indicated that musical theatre could be part of the RSC's programming under his leadership, and in an August 7 feature for the *Guardian* Terry Coleman noted, "He might do a musical, certainly didn't think it was beneath the RSC." Throughout the first decade of his leadership, the company employed noted composers to score its productions, and then in 1976, the RSC produced a full-scale musical, an adaptation of *The Comedy of Errors*, with book and lyrics by Nunn and music by Guy Woolfenden. Originally seen at the company's home in Stratford-upon-Avon, the tuner, which featured Judi Dench and Roger Rees, transferred to the West End the same year and eventually snagged the 1977 Olivier Award for best musical.

With the dawn of the 1980s, Nunn took his work with the RSC to new heights with a stage adaptation of Charles Dickens's novel *Nicholas Nickleby*. The ambitious two-part, eight-hour production boasted original songs by Stephen Oliver, who two years later would collaborate with Tim Rice on the musical *Blondel*. Nunn's success with this epic piece of theatre led to his next production, a commercial venture: staging Andrew Lloyd Webber's *Cats* for producer Cameron Mackintosh.

Nunn's environmental staging—audiences felt as if they had been deposited in an oversized garbage dump—did not exactly employ the stylistic storytelling that he had used in *Nickleby*, but there was a grandeur to both productions. Further, the sense of spectacle that Nunn instilled in *Cats* set the stage for theatregoers' expectations in musicals for the coming decade. Nunn exceeded anything that they might have imagined with his next commercial outing, *Starlight Express*. With this second Lloyd Webber show, about a race between trains from various nations, Nunn, working with choreographer Arlene Phillips, took the action into the auditorium, having the company, wearing roller skates, race on tracks that swooped up to and down from the balcony.

Critics dismissed the show, but it proved to be an instant hit with audiences, running eighteen years in the West End, just three years shy of *Cats'* twenty-one-year run. In 1987, a production of *Starlight* opened on Broadway, but it failed to capture New York's imagination and closed before reaching its two-year anniversary.

Another Nunn-directed show, *Les Misérables*, which was a phenomenal hit on both sides of the Atlantic, tempered *Starlight*'s quick Broadway demise. *Les Miz*, as it's now familiarly known, debuted at the RSC in 1985, and in it Nunn fused some of the spare storytelling that he employed in *Nickleby* with the more lavish visuals of his two recent Lloyd Webber collaborations. Although critical reaction to the sung-through adaptation of Victor Hugo's sprawling novel was mixed, theatregoers turned it into a popular hit, and the show set records for longevity in London, where it continues to this day, while managing a nearly sixteen-year run in New York.

Between *Les Misérables* openings, Nunn directed *Chess* in the West End in 1986, stepping in as a last-minute replacement for an ailing Michael Bennett and using Robin Wagner's designs that Bennett had overseen. In 1988, Nunn shepherded the musical, revised and redesigned, to Broadway, where it folded quickly. He then turned his attention to two more intimate musicals in London, notably *Aspects of Love*, based on a 1955 novella. The piece, about a septet of lovers, spanned three generations and featured music by Lloyd Webber, drawing a mixed critical reaction. It nevertheless proved to be a modest success in London before coming to Broadway for a brief year's run in 1990.

After directing a heavily revised version of Stephen Schwartz and Joseph's Stein's *The Baker's Wife*, Nunn staged *Sunset Boulevard*, an adaptation of the Billy Wilder film with a score by Lloyd Webber and libretto by Don Black and Christopher Hampton. Centering on an aging silent film star, it debuted in London in 1993, and for his work on it Nunn received plaudits for creating (with scenic designer John Napier) a visually stunning show: "Nunn's production, with its deft use of filmic bridging scenes, is technically superb" was Michael Billington's assessment in a July 13 review in the *Guardian*. As with the other Nunn–Lloyd Webber collaborations, the show came to Broadway the following year.

For the past twenty-five years, Nunn has concentrated primarily on staging and reimagining American classics, although he also has directed several new musicals (*Acorn Antiques* in 2005 and *Gone with the Wind* in 2008, among others). His first revival came in 1998, and it was Rodgers and Hammerstein's landmark *Oklahoma!* Nunn had hoped to reexamine and reimagine the classic for modern audiences, and for some critics he succeeded. Benedict Nightingale in a July 17, 1998, review for the *London Times* called it a "robust yet subtle revival" in which an "unfinished, insecure feel to the place extends to the characters."

The director followed this with imaginative revivals of *South Pacific* and *My Fair Lady* in 2001, *Anything Goes* in 2002, and *A Little Night Music* in 2009. This last production and *Oklahoma!* transferred to New York. His most recent musical outing came in 2016 when he brought a revival of *Cats* to Broadway.

P

Papp set a standard for developing and championing, in the nonprofit realm, innovative musical theatre work that had an ability to challenge while also succeeding commercially.

Born in Brooklyn, the man who became known simply as Joe Papp in New York theatre circles for more than fifty years started life as Joseph Papirofsky, and as a child, he came to know the joys of Shakespeare and the theatre courtesy of his local library. Papp, while working for CBS television, began to think about how he came to know the Bard's works (for free and on the page) and ultimately conceived of a way that would allow new generations to experience these classics, also at no charge but onstage. He founded what he called a Shakespeare Workshop and started offering free performances of Shakespeare on New York's Lower East Side. The organization, which eventually was known as the New York Shakespeare Festival, came to have a permanent home for its free performances in Central Park at the Delacorte Theater in 1961. Among the many luminaries whose careers started with the Shakespeare Festival and these free performances are Colleen Dewhurst, Kevin Kline, George C. Scott, Meryl Streep, and Sam Waterston.

In 1967, the festival expanded to have a year-round home at the Public Theater in Lower Manhattan, where new works were to be the organization's primary purpose. Key to the festival's mission at the Public from its inception were musicals, and the facility, which came to house five theatres, opened with the rock musical *Hair*. The Galt MacDermot–Gerome Ragni–James Rado musical later transferred to Broadway, starting the rock invasion of the Great White Way. Four years later, for a Free Shakespeare in Central Park production, Papp put composer MacDermot together with playwright John Guare and director Mel Shapiro to create a contemporary staging of William Shakespeare's *The Two Gentlemen of Verona*. The original plan was to simply add some songs to the Bard's classic, but the artists, supported by Papp, reworked the play more heavily, and the result was the 1972 Tony Award winner for best musical, *Two Gentlemen of Verona*.

When Papp approached Michael Bennett about directing a production in the park, the director-choreographer demurred, saying he would rather work on an idea for a musical under the festival's auspices. The result became one of Broadway's biggest hits, *A Chorus Line*, which enjoyed a fifteen-year, 6,137-performance run and earned, among many honors, the Pulitzer Prize for drama. The process by which Papp and the festival developed the show set new standards for creating new musicals at nonprofit theatres, both in New York and beyond. It also compelled Actors' Equity, the performers' union, to establish a new class of rehearsal contracts to allow artists to collaborate in informal workshop settings.

The festival's operations grew during the 1970s to also include programming at the Vivian Beaumont Theater at Lincoln Center, and there, concurrent with the arrival of *A Chorus Line* on Broadway, Papp produced a highly acclaimed revival of Kurt Weill and Bertolt Brecht's *The Threepenny Opera*, starring Raul Julia as Macheath. Papp's vision for alternative musical fare at the Public resulted in another Broadway transfer in 1978: Elizabeth Swados's examination of young people's experiences on the streets of New York, *Runaways*. That same year, Gretchen Cryer and Nancy Ford's feminist *I'm Getting My Act Together and Taking It on the Road* premiered downtown. Although it never transferred uptown, the tuner did run an impressive three years and spawned a national tour and a British incarnation.

In the 1980s, two more productions from the Delacorte made their way to Broadway. In 1981, it was Wilford Leach's acclaimed rethinking of Gilbert and Sullivan's *The Pirates of Penzance*, which boasted a company that included Linda Ronstadt and Rex Smith as its romantic leads, along with Kline, George Rose, and Estelle Parsons. This Tony-winning revival was followed in 1985 by Rupert Holmes's *The Mystery of Edwin Drood*, which musicalized Charles Dickens's unfinished novel of the same name. Papp trusted a pop songwriter to supply music, lyrics, and book for this latter show, and the producer's gamble paid off. *Drood* went on to win the Tony for best musical.

Only one other Papp-produced musical from the Public transferred to Broadway during his lifetime: MacDermot and William Dumaresq's adaptation of William Saroyan's *The Human Comedy*. This did not mean, however, that the producer had foregone productions of musicals downtown. Among the musical offerings at the Public during the 1980s were numerous other tuners with music by Swados, including *Alice in Concert* (1980), an adaptation of Lewis Carroll's beloved story. It was eventually filmed, with a young Streep in the title role, under the title *Alice at the Palace*.

Two years later, Papp gave Des McAnuff, who would go on to win Tonys for *The Who's Tommy* and *Jersey Boys*, an early musical credit by producing *The Death of Von Richthofen as Witnessed from Earth*, and in 1986, George C. Wolfe's satiric play with music, *The Colored Museum*, bowed under Papp's guidance. As the 1980s drew to a close, the Public was home to such musicals as *The Knife* (1987), which examined the life of a man who was undergoing a sex-change operation; William Finn's experimental musical about the Depression, *Romance in Hard Times* (1989); ˙ and another rock-infused musical, *Up against It* (1989), that, inspired by an unfilmed screenplay by Joe Orton, had a score by pop singer-songwriter Todd Rundgren. Papp's commitment to breathing new life into classic works also continued during the 1980s, and notable among the theatre's offerings was a production of Puccini's *La Bohème* (1984) that starred Ronstadt.

Subsequent to his death in 1991, Papp's successors, Wolfe and Oskar Eustis, helped to continue his mission of nurturing and developing innovative musical theatre. Under the former man's guidance, the institution produced such musicals as *Bring in 'da Noise, Bring in 'da Funk* (1996), choreographed by and starring Savion Glover; Tony Kushner and Jeanine Tesori's *Caroline, or Change* (2004); and the 1998 revival of the classic Leonard Bernstein–Betty Comden–Adolph Green *On the Town*. Eustis's successes have included Stew and Heidi Rodewald's *Passing Strange*; Alex Timbers and Michael Friedman's *Bloody Bloody Andrew Jackson*; Tesori and Lisa Kron's *Fun Home*; and Lin-Manuel Miranda's groundbreaking *Hamilton*, which coincidentally premiered in the theatre at the Public where the institution's first blockbuster hit, *A Chorus Line*, bowed.

COLE PORTER

(June 9, 1891–October 15, 1964)
Composer / Lyricist

Porter brought unquestionable sophistication and wit to the musical theatre in addition to a unique sense of sly sexiness that permeated both melody and lyrics.

Shortly after Porter's death, Sidney Burton, who had been an undergraduate at Harvard while the composer studied law there, shared a memory of first hearing Porter play his own work. In a letter to *Variety*, published on October 28, 1964, Burton wrote, "[Porter] had an extraordinary sense of rhyme and rhythm, both sophisticated innovations in those days. . . . His was even then a refulgent, never to be forgotten talent."

This brightly shining talent, to paraphrase Burton, came to Harvard by way of Peru, Indiana, where his doting and demanding mother introduced him to music, and his wealthy grandfather planned a career in business or law for him. It was the elder man's plan that transported Porter first to prep school in Massachusetts, then to Yale for undergraduate work, and finally to Harvard for law. Porter, who began composing before was a teen, continued to write music during his school years. At Yale he penned two football songs for the school that are still played today and wrote songs for the Yale Dramatic Association's musicals. While at Harvard he both studied and set his sights on writing for the theatre, eventually changing his major to music.

Porter got his first Broadway credits in 1915 with the revue *Hands Up* and *Miss Information*, a play with songs, including several by Jerome Kern. The following year, Porter opened his first musical in New York, *See America First*, which satirized George M. Cohan's patriotic tuners. The production lasted a mere fifteen performances, and most critics found it to be amateurish. There was one exception; the reviewer for the *New York Press* noted in a March 29 write-up that "some of the songs are particularly catchy."

Porter, after two years in Europe, was back in New York and being heard in the theatre when *Hitchy-Koo of 1919* premiered. The third in a series of revues show-casing Raymond "Hitchie" Hitchcock, the show gave Porter his first breakout song, "An Old-Fashioned Garden," which was recorded by two popular artists of the time, Olive Kline and Sam Ash. Porter contributed to another revue, *As You Were*, in 1920 and wrote the majority of songs for the 1924 edition of John Murray Anderson's *Greenwich Village Follies*.

Between these and after, Porter split his time between Europe (primarily France) and America, enjoying a carefree existence with the elite (artistic and oth-erwise) of both continents. The sophistication and blitheness of his existence, as well as his general outlook on life, had always been inherent to his songwriting, but in 1928, with *Paris*, his exceptional wit; facility for crafting infectious melody; and a sense of the risqué, often used as a way of channeling his gayness, which he hid from the world, combined to create his first signature song, "Let's Do It (Let's Fall in Love)." It was one of three numbers that he contributed to the show, and Richard Watts Jr., in an October 8 *New York Herald Tribune* review, exclaimed, "[Porter] was the flaming star of the premiere."

With *Fifty Million Frenchman* (1929), Porter wrote his first full score for a book musical. In the show about a wealthy young American in Paris attempting to make do without his fortune, Porter paid tribute to his second home overseas with his achingly lush classic "You Don't Know Paree." Porter also continued to pen numbers that could amuse with sexual frankness and double entendres: "Find Me a Primitive Man" and "Where Would You Get Your Coat?" In a November 28 *New York Times* review, J. Brooks Atkinson remarked that the "brisk" show was also "modishly salacious."

Three more shows and even more standards ensued, including "What Is This Thing Called Love?" from *Wake Up and Dream* (1929); "Love for Sale" and "Take Me Back to Manhattan" from *The New Yorkers* (1930); and "After You, Who?" and "Night and Day" from *Gay Divorce* (1932). Then, in 1934, *Anything Goes* premiered. With Ethel Merman in her first starring role, the show about romance and intrigue on a luxury liner took critics and audiences by storm. Little wonder, as Merman belted out not only the title song but also "Blow, Gabriel, Blow," "I Get a Kick out of You," and "You're the Top." Percy Hammond, in his November 22 *Herald Tribune* review, labeled Porter a "pet son of the Orpheus family," saying that he had written a score that was both "sentimental and ribald."

Porter's ability to combine emotion with sexiness in both his melodies and his words continued to shine as the 1930s progressed, particularly when he penned numbers for Merman who appeared in another three of his musicals between 1936 and 1940. One Porter song—"My Heart Belongs to Daddy," which was performed as a faux striptease in *Leave It to Me!* (1938)—helped make a star of another leading lady: Mary Martin.

The year before this show premiered, Porter broke both of his legs in a riding accident, and for the remainder of his life he was never fully free from pain. After *Leave It to Me!* he wrote another seven musicals between 1939 and 1946, but some-thing had changed. Atkinson describes it in his book *Broadway*, "The songs Porter was writing during this period had lost dash and impudence." Still, there were such gems as "Friendship" (*Du Barry Was a Lady*, 1939), "Let's Not Talk about

Love" (*Let's Face It*, 1941), and "Ev'ry Time We Say Goodbye" (*Seven Lively Arts*, 1944), among others.

Porter, however, returned in all of his glory in 1949 with *Kiss Me, Kate*, which centers on backstage drama at a Broadway-bound production of Shakespeare's *The Taming of the Shrew*. Porter's first wholly successful score in a post-*Oklahoma!* world of integrated book musicals brims with romantic melody, remarkable urgency, and zinging humor. Among its songs are "So in Love," "Wunderbar," "Always True to You (In My Fashion)," and "Were Thine That Special Face." Howard Barnes, in a December 31 *Herald Tribune* review, called it a "prodigal and exultant musical," adding, "Porter has written the gayest music and lyrics he has in years." His work earned him a Tony Award for best composer and lyricist.

Porter wrote only three more Broadway shows after this: *Out of This World* (1951), *Can-Can* (1953), and *Silk Stockings* (1955). The first only lasted only a few months, and the third just passed its one-year anniversary, but the second enjoyed a healthy run of 892 performances and contained more Porter classics, including "C'est Magnifique" and "I Love Paris."

HAROLD PRINCE

(January 30, 1928–)
Producer / Director

Thanks to his shrewdness as both producer and director, the American musical theatre has been enriched with both enduring, landmark works and also with ones that have intriguingly and inexorably pushed the boundaries of the form.

In his book *Sense of Occasion*, Prince relates one of his greatest fears when he was just fourteen: "The desire to work in the theatre had become an obsession to the degree that I wondered—worried really: If I didn't find a life in the theatre, how the hell would I live?" The teenager's fears proved unfounded. Prince, in adulthood, became one of Broadway's most influential producers and directors, ultimately winning more Tony Awards than any other individual artist.

Born and raised in New York, Prince's infatuation with the stage began when he was a boy and attended Broadway shows with his mother. Theatregoing on his own followed, and after attending the University of Pennsylvania, Prince began working for veteran writer-director-producer George Abbott. Prince served in a variety of capacities on Abbott's productions and in his office and began to obtain valuable knowledge about the assembly and stagecraft of theatre. Following Prince's service in the army during the Korean War, he returned to working with Abbott, stage managing and understudying in *Wonderful Town* (1953).

During this show's run, Prince—with Robert E. Griffith, another member of Abbott's staff and inner circle—made plans to produce a musical, an adaptation of Richard Bissell's *7½ Cents*, which centers on a strike at a pajama-making factory. Abbott directed (and coauthored the book with Bissell), and the result was

The Pajama Game. In the era of the McCarthy hearings, when unions and strikes were considered risky topics, the musical was a daring choice for Prince's debut, but the chances he took—including one on songwriters Richard Adler and Jerry Ross, who were writing their first full score—paid off. The show was an instant success when it opened on May 13, 1954, and launched Prince, then the youngest producer on Broadway, into his six-decade career.

With *Damn Yankees* (1955), a Faustian musical set in the world of baseball, and *New Girl in Town* (1957), a tuner based on Eugene O'Neill's dark barroom play *Anna Christie*, Prince continued to bring unusual—yet appealing—shows to the stage, even as he continued his mentor's tradition of working with new talent. *New Girl* brought songwriter Bob Merrill, who would go on to write *Carnival!* and provide lyrics for *Funny Girl*, to the theatre.

A second production in 1957 proved that Prince's taste and vision as a producer were unlike those of any other at the time. He, still working with Griffith, brought the landmark *West Side Story* to Broadway, allowing Jerome Robbins, Arthur Laurents, Leonard Bernstein, and Stephen Sondheim to create a wholly new sort of musical in which ballet, narrative, and song cohered in previously untried ways. Brooks Atkinson, in an October 6 *New York Times* review, didn't mention the producers by name when he wrote, "The fundamental distinction of 'West Side Story' is the courage with which it adheres to its artistic convictions and its unwillingness to make concessions to popular taste," but none of the creators would have been able to achieve their goals had they not had Prince and Griffith's full backing.

Fiorello! (1959), about New York City's Mayor Fiorello La Guardia, continued Prince's string of successes, and for it, songwriters Jerry Bock and Sheldon Harnick, along with book writers Jerome Weidman and George Abbott, earned the Pulitzer Prize for drama. In 1963, Prince assumed the role of both director and producer for another show with a Bock–Harnick score, *She Loves Me*. A vest-pocket musical set in a Hungarian perfume shop, the musical didn't have big chorus numbers, just a handful of singer-actors who played the store's patrons.

Prince served solely as producer for the seminal *Fiddler on the Roof* (1964) and as director-producer for the groundbreaking *Cabaret* (1966), in which he used Brechtian techniques to take theatregoers on a simultaneously entertaining and troubling journey through 1930s Berlin during the Nazis' rise to power. Writing about the production in the *Times* on December 4, Walter Kerr remarked that *Cabaret* "opens the door—part way, at least—to a fresh notion of the bizarre, crackling and yet beguiling uses that can be made of song and dance."

As the 1970s dawned, Prince and Sondheim began a collaboration that extended for more than a decade, one that fundamentally changed theatregoers' impressions of musical theatre, both in substance and form. With *Company* (1970), a loosely constructed tale of a bachelor's impressions of married life, the concept musical came of age, and then *Follies* (1971), a reunion of former showgirls, blurred past and present to explore the truths and lies buried within two couples' relationships. *Sweeney Todd* (1978) was a particular triumph, and this Grand Guignol descent into a man's bloodlust for revenge demonstrated Prince's vision for theatre at its most epic in scale.

There were three other productions in the 1970s that showed Prince working on a large theatrical canvas. Two preceded *Sweeney*. The first was a revival of *Candide* (1974), which rescued the 1956 musical with music by Leonard Bernstein from relative obscurity and brought a new expansiveness to environmental staging on Broadway. In *On the Twentieth Century* (1978), Prince, aided by Robin Wagner's deco scenic design, brought the grandeur of the famed luxury train the 20th Century Limited to the stage, and theatregoers were transported to lavish interiors, the front of the locomotive as it whisked along the rails, and the countryside as the train sped through the night.

Prince also demonstrated his distinct ability for staging works on a major scale with *Evita* in 1979. Richard L. Coe wrote in the *Washington Post* on October 28 about it (and the concurrently running *Sweeney*), describing Prince as "our peerless stage director," adding, "[He] is the contemporary stage master of images, precise, crystalline, theatrical visions that illuminate the texts and music of his favored associates."

Prince reunited with *Evita* composer Andrew Lloyd Webber for *The Phantom of the Opera* in 1986, and Prince's staging of this musical adaptation of the classic novel about a mysterious figure haunting a Paris opera house prompted the *Guardian*'s Michael Billington to comment on October 11, "Prince has caught the feverish, nightmarish bustle of Leroux's Opera House without diminishing the [characters]." The original London production, as well as the one that opened on Broadway fourteen months later, continues to run, setting records in both cities.

For the past twenty years, this visionary director's commitment to exploring serious themes in musical form has resulted in such productions as *Kiss of the Spider Woman* (1993); *Parade* (1998), which brought composer Jason Robert Brown to Broadway; and *LoveMusik* (2007), a bracing bio-musical about composer Kurt Weill. Prince's astonishing career has resulted in a total of twenty-one Tony Award wins.

R

TIM RICE

(November 10, 1944–)
Lyricist / Librettist

Rice's lyrics—colloquial, distinctly modern, and sometimes gently sardonic—have captured the ears of three generations, and his work as librettist with Andrew Lloyd Webber resulted in three of the most enduring musicals of the last half of the twentieth century, solidifying the appeal of the through-sung, pop musical.

Although music had been a passion for this multi-award-winning lyricist and book writer, Rice studied French and history for his A levels at Lancing College before entering the workforce in his late teens. He attended the Sorbonne in Paris for a year and then moved into the music business, working for EMI Records and also penning pop music lyrics. While Rice was looking for a composer with whom he might collaborate on an ongoing basis, a friend suggested he introduce himself to Andrew Lloyd Webber. Rice sent a letter to the younger man who agreed to a meeting, and in relatively short order he convinced Rice to join him on a musical he had started working on, one about Thomas John Barnardo, who had founded orphanages in England in the nineteenth century. They completed the project, titled *The Likes of Us*, but never found a producer. Nevertheless, the partnership clicked, and they moved on to write another piece.

Rice's second outing with Lloyd Webber was a pop cantata, *Joseph and the Amazing Technicolor Dreamcoat*. This retelling of the biblical story received a concert presentation at Westminster's Central Hall in London in 1968. Four years later, it premiered at the Edinburgh Festival in Scotland in a production that later played at the Young Vic in London. *Joseph* has since gone on to enjoy an international reputation, performed both professionally and by school and community theatre groups.

Before *Joseph* had hit the stage, however, Rice's third outing with Lloyd Webber had proven itself to be a global sensation. The show was *Jesus Christ Superstar*, and for this rock opera they followed an example set by the Who, recording a two-LP set of the show as a concept album in early 1970. It proved to be phenomenally successful on both sides of the Atlantic, with young listeners gravitating toward both Lloyd Webber's rock-driven score and Rice's colloquial, mod lyrics. "What's the buzz?" the apostles ask Christ, while "Try not to turn onto problems that upset you" is Mary Magdalene's advice to him. Less than two years after its release, *Superstar* debuted on Broadway, and in his October 13, 1971, *Newsday* review, George Oppenheimer wrote that Rice's lyrics had "skill, grace and taste." *Superstar*, in a different staging, played London's West End the following year, running for eight years.

The men also premiered their next musical through the release of a concept album in 1976. The show, *Evita*, explores the life of Argentine first lady Eva Peron and includes the future breakout hit "Don't Cry for Me Argentina." For this piece Rice expanded his style of lyric writing in the through-sung piece to encompass both darker tones and metaphorical approaches. The album, for instance, contained "The Lady's Got Potential," which uses the concept of insecticide to foreshadow the corrosive leadership the Perons will bring to their country. The song was replaced at the request of director Harold Prince, who staged *Evita* both in London and New York, but it was reinserted for the 1996 film version of the musical.

Evita opened onstage in London just over a year after the release of the LP and debuted in New York in September 1979. The following spring, when the Tony Awards were presented, Rice shared one prize with Lloyd Webber for best score and also earned one singly for best book.

After *Evita*, Rice and Lloyd Webber parted company, but in the years that have ensued they have sporadically worked together. Most recently Rice revised lyrics for an Emmy-winning television presentation of *Superstar*.

Rice, like the composer, also turned to other partners, including Björn Ulvaeus and Benny Andersson from the Swedish pop group ABBA. Together the trio wrote *Chess*, which centers on Cold War intrigue and the rivalry between two chess champions from America and Russia. As with the musicals Rice wrote with Lloyd Webber, *Chess* premiered as a concept album in 1984; spawned fans on both sides of the Atlantic; and produced several breakout hits, including "One Night in Bangkok" and "I Know Him So Well," which received a cover version in 1986 by Whitney Houston and her mother, Cissy. Stage versions of *Chess*, which premiered in London in 1986 and in New York in 1988, have not matched the album's acclaim, but the enduring popularity of the songs has resulted in new productions around the globe, often with revisions to Rice's original book.

Starting in the early 1990s, Rice joined forces with two new partners. With Alan Menken he wrote songs for the animated feature *Aladdin* (1992) to augment a score that the composer had begun with his partner Howard Ashman, who died of AIDS in 1991. One of the Menken–Rice numbers, "A Whole New World," won an Academy Award. Two years later, Rice provided lyrics for new songs for the Broadway stage version of the animated feature *Beauty and the Beast*.

During this time, Rice also wrote songs with Elton John for the animated feature *The Lion King*, which premiered in June 1994. Among the John–Rice tunes in the movie are "Can You Feel the Love Tonight?" and "Circle of Life," and in these Rice demonstrates his ability to craft lyrics with deeply felt emotion. The team won the Academy Award for the former number, while the latter and "Hakuna Matata" were Oscar-nominated. Three years later, Julie Taymor's acclaimed stage version of the movie opened on Broadway, where it has played continually for more than twenty-one years.

John and Rice were Tony-nominated for *The Lion King* and then won the award in 2000 for their updated version of *Aida*. In her March 23 *Newsday* review, Linda Winer remarked, "Here Rice's lyrics have the satiric bite rooted in his early work, especially 'Jesus Christ Superstar.' This includes Amneris' outlandish fashion runway song, 'My Strongest Suit' . . . and the insinuating numbers for Radames' evil father Zoser."

Rice rejoined forces with Lloyd Webber for new songs for a stage version of *The Wizard of Oz* (2011) and collaborated with Stuart Brayson on *From Here to Eternity* (2013), both of which played in London's West End. He and Menken also penned three new songs for a live-action movie version of *Beauty and the Beast* that opened in 2017.

CHITA RIVERA

(January 23, 1933–)
Performer

In a career that has spanned more than sixty-five years, Rivera has played musical comedy and drama, dancing up a storm all the while working with choreographers as diverse as Champion, Fosse, and Robbins.

"A Dancer Who Made No Effort to Achieve Broadway Fame" was the pullout quote for a May 29, 1960, *New York Times* feature on Rivera just after she had opened in *Bye Bye Birdie*. John S. Wilson's story illuminated how she had come to Broadway after spending six years studying at the School of American Ballet: by accompanying a friend to an audition for *Call Me Madam*. "I didn't care what happened, so I stood in the front line and was completely relaxed," she told Wilson. She ultimately got the job her friend had wanted.

Rivera, born Dolores Conchita Figueroa del Rivero, came to New York from her native Washington, DC, to study. With *Madam*, Rivera began her life as one of Broadway's "gypsies," chorus performers who move from musical to musical. For Rivera this meant stints in the Broadway companies of *Guys and Dolls* and *Can-Can* (dancing in both under the name Conchita Del Rivera). For a brief period, she adopted the stage name "Chita O'Hara," using it as she began work on *Shoestring Revue* off-Broadway in 1955. By the time the show opened, though, she was using Chita Rivera, and in a March 2 *Variety* review, critic "Geor." praised her work in portraying Marilyn Monroe in one sketch, saying, "[She] is a neat trick who dances nicely and scores as a well-known Hollywood blonde turned highbrow."

Only two months after *Shoestring* opened, Rivera was back on Broadway in *Seventh Heaven*. It marked the first time she was originating a role on the Main Stem, and she played Fifi, one of a trio of cocottes in this Paris-set tuner. The show received a cool reception, leading to a brief run, but Rivera walked away with some glowing reviews. "Chita Rivera is wonderfully explosive in a series of much too similar high-kicking routines," wrote Walter F. Kerr in his May 27 *New York Herald Tribune* review.

Her next show, *Mr. Wonderful*, starred Sammy Davis Jr., and the reviews for this musical about a man hoping to make a name for himself as a nightclub performer were not much better than those for *Seventh Heaven*. Still, Rivera got raves for her dancing, such as Thomas R. Dash's in a March 26, 1956, *Women's Wear Daily* review: "[She] sprinkles some much needed spice through her dancing."

After one more short run (*Shinbone Alley* in early 1957), Rivera got her breakthrough on Broadway. In September of that year, she created the role of Anita in *West Side Story*. The sizzle that critics had praised in her previous performances was fully showcased in this Jerome Robbins–staged show, and in his October 4 *Newsday* review, George Oppenheimer suggested, "[She] deserves to have a hurricane named after her for her tempestuousness," adding, "She has fire and grace and a real comic sense."

After *West Side*, Rivera starred in Michael Stewart, Lee Adams, and Charles Strouse's merry *Bye Bye Birdie*. In this she played Rose Grant, the long-suffering girlfriend of a man who manages the career of rock idol Conrad Birdie. Director-choreographer Gower Champion utilized Rivera's myriad talents to their fullest, crafting ballet sequences for her in both acts of the show. John Chapman, in his April 24, 1960, *Daily News* review, remarked that "Miss Rivera can dance—not hoof—but dance" and that one of Champion's "best numbers" was the one in which "she breaks loose on a solemn meeting of fez-wearing Shriners and starts to unwind." Rivera ultimately earned her first Tony nomination for her performance and had the opportunity to re-create it when the show premiered in London in June 1961.

Following *Birdie*, Rivera starred in two artistically intriguing tuners. First came a musical version of Dumas's *The Prisoner of Zenda* in 1963, which closed before reaching Broadway, and then a musical about a swindle perpetrated by a group of gypsies, *Bajour* (1964). During this time and immediately after, Rivera stepped up her work in nightclubs and on television, and for a brief period in 1966, rumors suggested she would return to London to play the title role in *Sweet Charity*. The part ultimately went to Juliet Prowse; Rivera did, however, get to play it on the national tour and later assumed the role of Nickie, Charity's best pal, in the film version of the musical.

Rivera didn't return to Broadway until 1975, and when she did, she reunited with *Charity*'s director-choreographer, Bob Fosse. The show was *Chicago*, and while its dark, sardonic edge might have been ahead of its time (compare its original run of 936 performances to the 8,900 and counting of the revival), Rivera's performance earned plaudits and a second Tony nomination.

The 1980s saw Rivera in a quartet of Broadway tuners, ranging from *Bring Back Birdie* (the ill-conceived sequel to *Bye Bye Birdie* that lasted only four performances) to the magic-driven *Merlin* (notable for its oft-delayed opening) to the revue *Jerry's Girls*. Between the second and last, though, came *The Rink*, which reunited her with the *Chicago* songwriting team of John Kander and Fred Ebb and costarred her with Liza Minnelli. The tale of a woman reuniting with her estranged mother garnered mixed critical reaction. Rivera's performance, however, was lauded, inspiring Frank Rich to comment, in a February 10, 1984, *Times* review, "[She] is a performer you could watch forever." *The Rink* brought Rivera her first Tony Award.

She has originated two more roles in Kander and Ebb shows, starting in 1993 with the title character in *Kiss of the Spider Woman*. Her portrayal of a glamorous screen siren conjured by one of two inmates in a South American prison won her a second Tony Award. Her work on the third Kander and Ebb show, *The Visit*, demonstrated her commitment to a new way of bringing a musical to Broadway; she played the role in a trio of regional productions leading toward its Main Stem premiere in 2015.

In the new millennium, she has also performed in revivals—*Nine* (2003) and *The Mystery of Edwin Drood* (2012)—and a biographical show on Broadway. In addition, she received a Kennedy Center Honor in 2002 and a special Tony for lifetime achievement in 2018.

JEROME ROBBINS

(October 11, 1918–July 29, 1998)
Director / Choreographer

In the course of the 1940s to 1960s, Robbins built on the balletic traditions in musicals begun by de Mille and Balanchine and expanded them to create dance narratives that encompassed entire shows.

In January 1945, just days after the opening of *On the Town*, the first Broadway show featuring his choreography, Robbins talked with the *New York Herald Tribune*'s Lucius Beebe about the show's success as well as his career: "Heaven knows, I'm full of ideas and ambition. All I need is for the ideas to be valid and the ambition to continue." For the next fifty years, he demonstrated repeatedly that he was lacking in neither and became—as Anna Kisselgoff labeled him in a July 30, 1998, *New York Times* obituary—"one of the 20th-century ballet's greatest choreographers and a towering innovator in Broadway musicals."

Robbins's professional career began on Broadway when he danced in such shows as *Great Lady* (1938) and *Stars in Your Eyes* (1939). He went on to perform with Ballet Theater (later American Ballet Theatre) as the 1940s dawned, and in April 1944 he made his debut as choreographer for the company with the ballet *Fancy Free*. The piece, with music by Leonard Bernstein, was an instant hit, and almost immediately after its premiere Robbins and Bernstein began to consider using it as a springboard for a musical comedy.

The men joined forces with book writer–lyricists Betty Comden and Adolph Green and director George Abbott, and the result of their work, *On the Town*, debuted on December 28, 1944. The musical focused on three sailors with a twenty-four-hour leave in Manhattan, and the creators, who had hoped to set new benchmarks for integrating the various components of musical theatre, succeeded. As

Edwin Denby wrote in a review in the January 21, 1945, edition of the *Herald Tribune*, "[The dances] generally emerge from the rest of the action and melt into it again so as to give value to a scene."

The choreographer reunited with Comden, Green, and Abbott for his next Broadway outing, which came just one year later: *Billion Dollar Baby*. For this satire about the Roaring Twenties, Robbins extensively researched dances of the era and melded them into extended dance sequences. His work added period authenticity to the show, and in a *Herald Tribune* review on January 20, 1946, dance critic Walter Terry wrote, "[He] has captured the tempo, the 'hotcha' attitude and the movement styles of the 20s."

Humor, which had always been a part of Robbins's style as a performer and had surfaced in some of the dances for his first two Broadway shows, came to the fore in his next two Broadway outings, *High Button Shoes* (1947) and a satire about classical ballet pretentiousness, *Look Ma, I'm Dancin'!* (1949). In both he created a number of rollicking dances, and in the former, there was notably one set at the Jersey Shore inspired by Mack Sennett's silent film comedies. Brooks Atkinson, in his October 10 *Times* review, described it as "hilarious . . . a combination of old burlesque routines and modern ballet techniques. Swift and insane, like a jiggly old film." *Shoes* earned Robbins his first Tony Award for best choreography.

During this period George Balanchine asked Robbins to join City Ballet, and in 1949, Robbins became associate artistic director. The new position did not, however, diminish his output on Broadway. Between 1949 and 1964, he would be responsible for another twelve shows and consult on a half-dozen more.

His most significant dances from this time came in 1951 with Rodgers and Hammerstein's *The King and I*, where his "The Small House of Uncle Thomas" put Harriet Beecher Stowe's novel through an Asian prism. This achievement prompted the *Herald Tribune*'s Terry to write in a May 20 review, "[He] has turned out a theater dance which is a joy to behold."

Three years later in 1954, Robbins had his first taste of staging a book musical when he codirected *The Pajama Game* with Abbott. Later that year, Broadway saw the first show that Robbins both directed and choreographed by himself: *Peter Pan*, starring Mary Martin. (He also was uncredited for penning the script.) He followed this children's fairy tale with a more adult one about romance in then-present-day Manhattan, *Bells Are Ringing*.

Robbins took on heavier fare with his next two pieces, both of which have become classics of the musical theatre. In 1957, he helmed *West Side Story*, and in this modern version of *Romeo and Juliet*, "everything contributes to the total impression of wildness, ecstasy and anguish," as Brooks Atkinson wrote in a September 27 *Times* review. Another glowing notice came from Walter Kerr in the October 6 edition of the *Herald Tribune*. The critic labeled Robbins the "Superman" of the show, marveling at his ability to maintain a "sense of seething pressure and detonating release" throughout the production, always finding "new and astonishingly fresh statement for it." The work earned Robbins his second Tony Award.

He followed *West Side* with the more comedic but still dramatic *Gypsy*, a journey from vaudeville to burlesque. According to John Chapman in his May 31, 1959, *Daily News* review, Robbins did a "wizard's job of directing . . . [and] made it look effortless and charming."

Robbins served as production supervisor (Garson Kanin was credited with direction) of another backstage tale, *Funny Girl*, which opened in March 1964, and then that September his production of *Fiddler on the Roof* bowed. Howard Taubman, reviewing this now-classic musical in the *Times* on September 23, marveled at the show and how, thanks to Robbins's guidance, it was an "integrated achievement of uncommon quality." Writing specifically about the choreography, Taubman added, "[Robbins] weaves dance into the action with subtlety and flaring theatricalism."

With the exception of one play, *The Office* (1966), which closed in previews, the artistic pinnacle of *Fiddler* marked the end of Robbins's association with Broadway for twenty-five years. During this time, he dedicated himself to the world of ballet. His return to the Main Stem came in 1989 with a compendium of dances from his musicals, *Jerome Robbins' Broadway*. In reviewing it Frank Rich reminded readers of Robbins's contribution to musical theatre: "Robbins musicals were steamrollers in which script, movement, scenery, song and dance all surged forward at once to create a seamless dramatic adventure."

Robbins, who died in 1998, may have eventually left Broadway, but his dances have never been far from the stage since his departure, as productions of his masterpieces continue to use in toto or in part his original choreography.

RICHARD RODGERS

(June 28, 1902–December 30, 1979)
Composer / Lyricist / Producer

Rodgers both composed some of the landmarks of American musical theatre and set standards for the integrated book musical, all the while delivering melodies that have enchanted generations.

"Richard Rodgers had ability as well as genius," wrote Brooks Atkinson in a January 1, 1980, *New York Times* tribute to the composer. Indeed, a man who both advanced musical theatre craftsmanship over the course of three decades and wrote songs that are known the world over had to have both.

Rodgers's musicality became evident at an early age, and his music-loving parents encouraged his playing piano and attendance of musicals, which led Rodgers to have an early appreciation of both classical and theatre music. He was not yet twenty and still writing the varsity shows for Columbia University when his first songs premiered on Broadway, all set with lyrics by Lorenz Hart, a former Columbia student. *A Lonely Romeo* (1919) had one Rodgers–Hart song, and *Poor Little Ritz Girl* a year later boasted seven Rodgers-composed numbers, complementing the work of veteran Sigmund Romberg.

Rodgers eventually transferred from Columbia to Juilliard, and he returned to Broadway in 1925, when he and Hart contributed roughly half the score to that year's *Garrick Gaieties*, notably the classic "Manhattan." Produced by the Theatre

Guild, these revues often took a satirical look at the industry, and Rodgers and Hart, in both this edition and the one that followed, took aim at standard-issue musical theatre formulas, notably those found in operetta. They were young writers who wanted to see musical theatre change.

Over the next twenty-five years, Rodgers's infectious melodies graced a host of musicals that often subverted or expanded the form. For instance, *Peggy-Ann* (1926), with a book by Herbert Fields, audaciously offered a musical that opened with dialogue rather than a chorus number. During the 1930s, his musicals broke further ground. In *On Your Toes* in 1936, Rodgers composed a full ballet that was part of the show's narrative, and with *I Married an Angel*, Rodgers, Hart, director George Abbott, and designer Jo Mielziner created a musical comedy where the décor became part of the action. Rodgers and Hart's pinnacle of undermining musical theatre norms came in 1940 with *Pal Joey*, which had an utter cad as its hero.

Throughout these and some other seventeen shows, Rodgers wrote songs with melodies that were by turns sweepingly lush, merrily bouncy, or infectiously poignant, each outfitted with a graceful, often-barbed Hart lyric. Rodgers and Hart's hits range from "This Can't Be Love" from *The Boys from Syracuse* (1938) to "My Funny Valentine" from *Babes in Arms* (1937) to "Bewitched, Bothered and Bewildered" from *Pal Joey*. Rodgers also demonstrated his ability to craft exceptional extended compositions with "Slaughter on Tenth Avenue," the centerpiece ballet from *Toes*.

Impressively, Rodgers's melodies had lives outside of the musicals for which they were written, and they also were married to their respective shows books, illustrating a point he made when speaking with the *New York Herald Tribune*'s Lucius Beebe for an August 29, 1937, feature: "The conditions imposed by the book make a composition difficult, but without them, so far as we're concerned there could be no music and lyrics at all."

Hart died in 1943, a year after his last show with Rodgers, *By Jupiter*, had opened. During the final years of their collaboration, Hart had become distant and increasingly difficult to work with, and even before Hart's death, Rodgers began working with Oscar Hammerstein II on writing a musical based on Lynn Riggs's play *Green Grow the Lilacs*. The result was *Oklahoma!*, which opened the door to a new sort of book-driven musical when it premiered in 1943. The *Herald Tribune*'s Howard Barnes simply announced it in the opening of his April 1 review: "Songs, dances and a story have been triumphantly blended at the St. James."

It was a beginning of a partnership that lasted until Hammerstein's death. Of course, the team produced other great and enduring pieces that fuse drama, comedy, music, and dance seamlessly, principally *Carousel* (1945), *South Pacific* (1949), *The King and I* (1951), and *The Sound of Music* (1959). There were also bold experiments, perhaps most notably *Allegro* (1947). For this completely original musical, Rodgers and Hammerstein employed a commenting Greek chorus to explore the ways in which success and acclaim can corrupt a good and talented man's professional intentions.

With Hammerstein, Rodgers's melodies shifted in tone. While Hart's words had always had a crisp detachment to them, Hammerstein's lyrics were more poetic and heartfelt. As a result, Rodgers's musicality blossomed further, leading to another canon of standards that include "You'll Never Walk Alone" from

Carousel, the title number from *The Sound of Music*, and "Hello, Young Lovers" from *The King and I*. And unlike the Rodgers–Hart team, who had a brief and unremarkable Hollywood period, Rodgers and Hammerstein's work was embraced by moviegoers, and in 1946, they won an Academy Award for best song for "It Might as Well Be Spring" from *State Fair*, the one musical they wrote specifically for the screen. Similarly, their television treatment of the *Cinderella* fairy tale became a beloved favorite of audiences in 1958.

Hammerstein passed away in August 1960, and after this, Rodgers wrote *No Strings* (1962), a timely show about an interracial romance for which he served, for the first time, as his own lyricist. Rodgers worked with Stephen Sondheim, Hammerstein's protégé, on *Do I Hear a Waltz?* (1965), Arthur Laurents's adaptation of his play *The Time of the Cuckoo*, about a single woman searching for love in Italy. Interestingly, given that Sondheim's lyric sensibility often recalled Hart's, Rodgers's melodies had the stylistic flair that typified his work during the 1920s and 1930s. However, the bittersweet piece failed to capture audiences' imaginations and folded after 220 performances.

Rodgers brought another three new musicals to Broadway: the biblical *Two by Two* (1970), the Henry VIII bio *Rex* (1976), and the sepia-toned *I Remember Mama* (1979), his lyricists being Martin Charnin on the first and third and Sheldon Harnick on the second, but none, despite his unflagging gift for melody, attained the sort of success he had enjoyed with Hart or Hammerstein. The trouble wasn't as much Rodgers's gift but rather changing tastes and styles.

Since his death in 1979, the musical has continued to evolve, and yet Rodgers's melodies and shows still inspire artists and transport audiences, notably with Bartlett Sher's revivals of *South Pacific* and *The King and I* for Lincoln Center Theater. Most recently, director Daniel Fish's drastically rethought revival of *Oklahoma!* at St. Anne's Warehouse in Brooklyn (which transferred to Broadway in March 2019) prompted Jesse Green, in an October 7, 2018, *Times* review, to admire "how beautifully Rodgers's music adapted itself to the country sound coming from [a seven-piece band]."

SIGMUND ROMBERG

(July 29, 1887–November 9, 1951)
Composer

Romberg's musical acumen allowed him to establish himself as one of the country's preeminent composers during the dawn of the twentieth century, and he wrote three of the most highly regarded American operettas, ones that are performed to this day.

Hungarian-born composer Romberg's earliest days in the United States were a model of a young man's tenacity. When he arrived in 1909 at the age of twenty-two, he had already been trained as a pianist and violinist, first in Vienna while he was a teenager and later at the University of Bucharest. And though he is reported to have had a letter of introduction to J. J. Shubert penned by Franz Lehár, Romberg spent five years toiling as an entertainer, slowly building a reputation as he moved from playing violin at restaurants to establishing his own ensemble and working as a bandleader. In 1913, he wrote a pair of dance pieces, "Leg of Mutton" and "Some Smoke," and by the end of the year, they had been recorded by several of the most popular dance bands of the day.

The two songs also prompted Shubert to engage Romberg as a staff writer for the shows he and his brother Lee produced. Romberg's first assignment was composing for the revue *Whirl of the World*. With it Romberg saw nearly two dozen of his songs, ranging from rags to ballads to sumptuous waltzes, come to life at Broadway's Winter Garden Theatre in a show that the critic in the January 11, 1914, *New York Herald* deemed the "best of the extravaganzas that Messrs. Shubert have presented there."

Whirl was the first of three shows at the venue that would feature Romberg's work that year. The third, *Dancing Around*, brought Al Jolson back to Broadway after an absence of nearly two years, and in it the comedian-singer scored with a quartet of Romberg tunes (with lyrics by Harold Atteridge), eventually taking them to the country at large when the show toured.

Between 1915 and 1916, another ten Broadway shows—including revues, musicals, and even a play with music—featured Romberg's melodies, and his versatility prompted one writer for the *New York Sun* to proclaim in the April 9, 1916, edition of the paper, "In the vernacular of Broadway there are two kinds of music writers. One is a song writer and the other is a composer. Romberg has very cleverly written himself into the latter category."

He finally had the chance to deliver a full score for a musical with *Maytime*, an Americanization of a German operetta. The varied critical reactions to this production demonstrate how difficult it was at the time for critics to categorize both the composer and the form, which was experiencing growing pains as a diversity of voices were coming to the fore. Some writers labeled it an operetta; others called it a play with music. As for Romberg's work, the *New York Times* noted on August 17, 1917, that it was "melodious, and never really objectionable," signaling that Romberg was not working in the jazz style that was growing in popularity. At the same time, the critic praised the diversity of the score, which included a raucous polka and Romberg's own take on an antebellum dance tune, "Jump Jim Crow."

As the 1910s wound down, Romberg wrote additional revue material for the Shuberts, as well as the songs for *Sinbad*, an extravaganza that starred Jolson. Romberg also turned to producing, bringing two pieces he scored, *The Magic Melody* (1919) and *Love Birds* (1921), and a nonmusical to the stage.

After these, Romberg returned to writing for the Shuberts, who used him for both their revues, including two editions of *The Passing Show* and other Americanized shows from Europe, including one by Franz Schubert that opened on Broadway in 1921 under the title of *Blossom Time*. The Viennese-set piece ran for 516 performances on Broadway and toured the United States for many years after.

In 1924, Romberg had the opportunity to write an original operetta score. He was paired with librettist Dorothy Donnelly, and together they adapted the German play *Alt Heidelberg* (*Old Heidelberg*) into *The Student Prince*. The Shuberts gave it an extravagant production—a male chorus of fifty, for instance—and on

December 25, the *New York Herald Tribune* music critic Charles Belmont Davis proclaimed it was "one of the best performances of opera comique we have ever seen."

The indefatigable Romberg followed this with three productions in 1925. He then joined forces with Oscar Hammerstein II, Otto Harbach, and Frank Mandel to write *The Desert Song*, which tells a romantic tale of a man's derring-do in Arab North Africa. It debuted November 30, 1926, and once again, Romberg's deftness with both classical sounds and more popular ones helped to ensure a hit. As Gordon M. Leland pointed out in the December 11 edition of *Billboard*, "[The music] should appease the fastidious without offending the plebian taste."

Romberg followed *Song* with a quintet of shows before premiering his next substantial operetta, *The New Moon*. Set in the late eighteenth century, the piece centers on a French nobleman who sympathized with the revolutionists who land in America and later on an island in the Caribbean. J. Brooks Atkinson's September 20 *Times* review called it a "strong and virtuoso score" that was "deep, rushing, [and] stirring."

During the 1930s and 1940s, new musical styles became the norm on Broadway, and though Romberg continued to write scores for new shows, none of his new works received the same sort of acclaim that he had enjoyed in the 1920s. At the same time, *Student Prince* and *New Moon* were frequently seen in revival, and he enjoyed some success in Hollywood during this time, most notably with *The Night Is Young* (1935), which contained the standard "When I Grow Too Old to Dream."

Ten years later, Romberg, working with the brother and sister team of Herbert and Dorothy Fields, broke through once again on Broadway with *Up in Central Park*, a look back at New York in the era of Boss Tweed that has overtones of and occasionally sounds like operetta but is, indeed, a musical comedy. Otis L. Guernsey Jr. labeled the show "charming" in his January 29 *Herald Tribune* review, adding that Romberg contributed a "lovely score." The production played a year and a half, holding its own alongside other musicals, such as *Oklahoma!* and *On the Town*.

Before Romberg's death six years later, he saw one more musical premiere, *My Romance*, and in 1954, *The Girl in Pink Tights*, which explored the creation of *The Black Crook*, was posthumously produced, giving the composer one last Broadway credit.

S

Schwartz's work has been seminal as young people's introduction to musical theatre. Pippin *and* Godspell *entranced one generation, while* Wicked *has spoken to another.*

In a September 18, 1971, *Washington Post* feature, Richard Coe reported how this composer-lyricist came to select his major at Carnegie Mellon University in Pennsylvania: "He thought of liberal arts until his father said: 'You've always liked theater in high school, why don't you look into that?'" It was a turning point for the young man because it was at this school that Schwartz met one of his earliest collaborators, laying the groundwork for what would become one of his breakthrough hits.

Schwartz enjoyed more than just theatre growing up on Long Island. While attending high school, he also studied piano and composition. After his graduation from Carnegie Mellon in 1968, he returned to New York, and by early 1971 he was invited to see a new musical based on the Gospel of Matthew that was playing a limited run off-off-Broadway at La MaMa ETC. The show, *Godspell*, had been written by another Carnegie Mellon student, John-Michael Tebelak, as a master's thesis project and used story theatre techniques, clowning, and song to bring the biblical tales to life.

Commercial producers who had heard some of what Schwartz had written in college hired him to write a new score for the piece, and in May, the show, with his contributions, transferred to off-Broadway's historic Cherry Lane Theatre in Greenwich Village. On May 18, the *New York Times'* Clive Barnes, though unable to endorse the show wholeheartedly, praised Schwartz's eclectic score. It was, he wrote, "enthusiastic and attractive" and varied from "operetta to salvation rock, from soft shoe shuffles to a kind of country and Eastern style."

Other critics were also mixed about the production, but audiences fell in love with the sweet-spirited piece, and it eventually made another transfer to the much larger Promenade Theatre off-Broadway, running there until 1976. In addition, the production picked up a quartet of Drama Desk Awards, including two for

Schwartz, and in 1972 the show's cast recording won a Grammy. In 1973, a movie version of the piece was released, and since that time, *Godspell* has become a staple for both amateur and professional theatres around the world.

Even before *Godspell* made its New York debut, Schwartz was at work on another religious work, Leonard Bernstein's *Mass*. Schwartz came to the project thanks to his agent, Shirley Bernstein, who introduced the young man to her conductor-composer brother. With the subtitle of *A Theatre Piece for Singers, Players, and Dancers*, the piece premiered at the Kennedy Center on September 8, 1971.

Schwartz's Broadway bow came just more than a year later, when *Pippin*, a musical he had begun working on at Carnegie Mellon, opened. Directed and choreographed by Bob Fosse, this musical, with a book by Roger O. Hirson, imagined Charlemagne's son on a search for identity in the shadow of his powerful father. Schwartz once again offered up an eclectic score for a tale ostensibly set in the eighth century. Reviews primarily concentrated on Fosse's stylish production, but still critics found room to praise (often in equal measure) the score. "Stephen Schwartz's trippingly bitter tunes . . . are perky, driving, and—fortunately— nearly omnipresent," was Walter Kerr's comment in his October 29, 1972, *Times* review. As with *Godspell*, *Pippin* has become a perennial favorite for theatre companies, enjoying an international reputation.

Schwartz's subsequent musical *The Magic Show* (1974), starring illusionist Doug Henning, was part book musical and part variety show. It proved immensely popular with audiences, running for four and a half years, and one of Schwartz's songs from it, "The Lion Tamer," has become popular in cabarets. In his next work, *The Baker's Wife* (1976), Schwartz stretched musically as he wrote songs about a French baker whose craft suffers after his younger wife runs away with her lover. This musical folded during an extended tryout period and never reached Broadway, although it has since gained a following of devotees, particularly because of Schwartz's richly melodic score, which contains another standard, "Meadowlark."

With *Working*, which was based on Studs Terkel's book of the same name, Schwartz turned his hand to directing as well as songwriting. The show took a look at ordinary Americans and their thoughts about their jobs and also featured numbers written by other writers, including Craig Carnelia, Micki Grant, Mary Rodgers, Susan Birkenhead, and James Taylor. The show drew—at best—mixed reviews, but Douglas Watt, in his May 15, 1978, *Daily News* review, was able to parse his dual reaction to the show, which he called "much too long." And yet he praised "Schwartz's sharp direction" and concluded with, "at its best it is exciting and you can hear America singing."

Working lasted only twenty-four performances, and as a result, Schwartz broke with the theatre for almost eight years. When he returned, he served as lyricist only, teaming with composer Charles Strouse and book writer Joseph Stein to write *Rags*, a sweeping look at the immigrant experience at the dawn of the twentieth century. The production lasted a mere four performances, but the songwriting team had stretched themselves as artists. "At those times when Strouse and Schwartz aspire to operatic passion, they come close to realizing their ambition," Allan Wallach commented in his August 22, 1986, *Newsday* review.

Schwartz, whose first success had explored biblical themes, returned to them for his next show, *Children of Eden*, a musical version of many stories from the book of Genesis that premiered in London in 1991. This show also fared badly with the critics and had just a brief run. As the 1990s continued, Schwartz, once again eschewing Broadway, turned to Hollywood, teaming with composer Alan Menken for *Pocahontas* (1995) and *The Hunchback of Notre Dame* (1996) and writing the songs for *Prince of Egypt* (1998). Schwartz earned three Academy Awards for this work, sharing two with Menken for the first and receiving one singly for "When You Believe" from *Prince*. Schwartz and Menken later adapted *Hunchback* for the stage, augmenting the score considerably, and since its American premiere at New Jersey's Paper Mill Playhouse, *Hunchback* has enjoyed numerous productions. Similarly, in October 2017, a stage version of *Prince of Egypt* debuted at TheatreWorks in Palo Alto, California, and has gone on to enjoy productions in the United States and abroad.

Schwartz, of course, has been represented on Broadway since 2003 with the immensely popular hit *Wicked*. Much like the songwriter's first shows, this look at the Land of Oz before Dorothy's arrival has clicked particularly with younger audiences, spawning legions of dedicated fans. And even as this production has played to consistently capacity audiences, both *Godspell* and *Pippin* have returned to Broadway, the latter becoming a Tony-winning revival.

IRENE SHARAFF

(January 23, 1910–August 10, 1993)
Costume Designer

Over her nearly five-decade career, Sharaff set benchmarks for bringing fashion acumen to musicals while also ensuring that costumes (whether opulent or ordinary) helped to define character and a show's milieu.

For a November 20, 1970, *Christian Science Monitor* feature, Sharaff, who had already spent forty years designing for stage and screen and who held an impressive five Academy Awards for her work, told Marilyn Hoffman, "The theater continues to fascinate me because it is so moving, growing, and fluid." Indeed, despite her illustrious reputation in Hollywood, Sharaff never abandoned creating clothes for the stage.

Fashion had always inspired this Boston-bred designer who studied art in both New York and Paris in her early twenties. When she settled in New York, she earned a living creating illustrations for such magazines as *Vogue* and *Harper's Bazaar*. At the same time, she served as an assistant to costume designer Aline Bernstein, working on Eva Le Gallienne's 1928 Broadway productions of *Hedda Gabler* and *Peter Pan*, among others.

Four years later, Le Gallienne engaged Sharaff to design both scenery and costumes for a new production of *Alice in Wonderland*. Her visuals were based on

John Tenniel's classic drawings for Lewis Carroll's book, but as Brooks Atkinson pointed out in his December 12 *New York Times* review, "[She] has reverenced the illustrations, adding to them colors that give the production a disarmingly lovely appearance."

Her work on *Alice* so impressed composer Irving Berlin that he asked her to contribute to his and Moss Hart's topical revue *As Thousands Cheer* the following year. For this Sharaff designed, among others, the costumes for "Easter Parade," in which she re-created a variety of styles and fashions from the late nineteenth century in shades of browns, beiges, and tans to replicate the look of rotogravures, the sepia-toned photographs found in that period's magazines. A report on the show's designs in the October 3 edition of *Women's Wear Daily* noted that it was the "one costume scene [that] especially stands out for its beauty and is quite worthy of a thousand cheers."

As the 1930s progressed, Sharaff repeatedly demonstrated her versatility and creativity, lending her talents to revues, such as *Life Begins at 8:40* (1934); spectacles, such as *The Great Waltz* (1934); and musicals, such as Cole Porter and Hart's *Jubilee* (1935). During this decade, too, she began working on musicals by Rodgers and Hart, providing contemporary clothes as well as fanciful period attire embellished with modern flourishes for their *The Boys from Syracuse*, set in ancient Greece. In a November 25, 1938, *New York Sun* review of *Boys*, Richard Lockridge commented, "[Sharaff] has seldom done a brisker, more engaging job."

Sharaff had the chance to demonstrate her couture acumen as well as her more fanciful side in 1941 with *Lady in the Dark*, which centers on a fashion magazine editor's psychoanalysis. "Irene Sharaff does some of her most exciting costumes in the realm of fantasy," was the assessment of a writer in *Women's Wear Daily* on January 24. "Practically everything possible emerges made of water-clear plastics . . . [including] many of the shoes."

It was during this decade that Sharaff began her long career working both in Hollywood and on Broadway. Her first assignment for the screen was *Meet Me in St. Louis* in 1944. As with her work on Broadway, Sharaff moved easily among periods, opulence, and simplicity, and this is perhaps best exemplified by her having won Oscars for both the spectacle *Cleopatra* and the film adaptation of Edward Albee's searing four-character drama *Who's Afraid of Virginia Woolf?*

One of Sharaff's most memorable creations came at the dawn of the 1950s: the flared crinoline dress worn by Gertrude Lawrence in Rodgers and Hammerstein's *The King and I*. The garment, with an exaggeratedly large hoop skirt, demonstrated Sharaff's sense of theatricality. Because of both its size and the weight she built into it, the champagne satin dress moved dramatically as Lawrence and Yul Brynner performed "Shall We Dance?" As a result, David Shipman reminded readers in Sharaff's August 25 obituary in London's the *Independent* that the "sequence had a panache rare in even the best musicals." After Lawrence's untimely death during the show's run, the actress was buried in the costume.

It was for this musical that Sharaff won her first and only Tony Award, although she was nominated another eight times. Among her Tony nominations were ones for the sprawling adaptation of Voltaire's *Candide* (1956), with Leonard Bernstein's classic score; Rodgers and Hammerstein's portrait of life among Asian

Americans in San Francisco, *Flower Drum Song* (1958); and the European bonbon *The Girl Who Came to Supper* (1963), which featured songs by Noël Coward.

Another of her nominations came for *West Side Story* (1957), where she notably demonstrated her meticulous attention to detail in what might be considered off-the-rack clothing. Harold Prince, in his book *Sense of Occasion*, recalls, "I didn't have much patience for the blue jeans Irene Sharaff 'designed' for *West Side Story*." They cost $75 each (over $650 in 2018), and to curtail expenses, Prince instructed the show's wardrobe mistress to replace them with store-bought denim. He returned to find the show not looking "as beautiful as it used to" and discovered the reason. The jeans didn't look right. Sharaff's jeans were of a special fabric and had been carefully dyed, aged, and redyed. "Our blue jeans were in forty subtly different shades of blue, vibrating, energetic, creating the *effect* of realism," Prince writes.

In the 1960s, her work on Broadway ranged, as always, from period to contemporary dress, and in the process, she styled some of Broadway's most prominent leading ladies, including Barbra Streisand in *Funny Girl* (1964); Gwen Verdon in *Sweet Charity* (1966); and Leslie Uggams in *Hallelujah, Baby!* (1967).

Sharaff's last original design came in 1973 when she created the costumes for a revival of *Irene*, starring Debbie Reynolds, but even after this, theatregoers would be reminded of Sharaff's exquisite eye and taste as revivals of such musicals as *The King and I* and *West Side Story* drew upon her designs. In 1989, her designs were also represented in the compendium *Jerome Robbins' Broadway*, where her work for these musicals, including the 1920s-set *Billion Dollar Baby*, was re-created.

HASSARD SHORT

(October 15, 1877–October 7, 1956)
Director / Designer / Producer

Short helped such artists as Irving Berlin, Moss Hart, and Kurt Weill realize ambitious and audacious scenarios and also innovated both scenic and lighting design in musical theatre.

For a March 27, 1932, *New York Herald Tribune* feature by Henry Albert Phillips, this director-designer shared an anecdote about his then-current hit *Face the Music*, telling the reporter, "In one instance Irving Berlin had made the simple notation in the scenario: 'Soft lights and sweet music! I'll put in the sweet music and it's up to you, Hassard, to give 'em the soft lights.'" The songwriter's note could sound flippant or even be interpreted as a kind of joke. It was, however, meant in earnest. By this point, Short, who had been working on Broadway for thirty years, had become known for his innovations in staging and lighting design, so much so that the General Electric Co. awarded him a medal for "revolutionizing stage lighting" in 1930.

Short was born in the British midlands, and by most reports he left school at fifteen to become an actor. His London bow came in 1895, and he worked continually in England in both musicals and plays until the turn of the twentieth century. Then, in 1901, American producer Charles Frohman put him under contract, and Short made his Broadway debut at the end of the year in *The Second in Command*, which boasted Lionel Barrymore as one of its leads.

Short's acting career in the States continued uninterrupted until 1919 when it was paused by an actors' strike. The hiatus spurred him to try his hand at directing and designing. He first put together a sequence for a benefit for out-of-work performers and then staged a full evening to raise funds. Both of these events led to Short's directing and providing scenic design for the musical *Honeydew* in 1920. Although it was just his first outing on Broadway, Short couldn't resist his impulses to try new things onstage, and the production marked the first time that performers on Broadway were lit from above. He achieved this effect, according to a *New York Times* obituary by putting an electrician "in a bosun's chair over the stage."

Short's career as a director had begun in earnest, and he staged three more productions in the ensuing twelve months, culminating with the inaugural offering at Irving Berlin's newly built Music Box Theatre on Forty-Fifth Street. Short not only staged the first edition of Berlin's *Music Box Revue* series, but he also figured prominently in suggesting design features unique to the new venue, notably the installation of the first permanent bridge behind the proscenium arch, where both lighting instruments and technicians could be placed out of theatregoers' view. Additionally, the theatre boasted a system of stage elevators that he designed. His use of these prompted Robert C. Benchley to quip in the October 13, 1921, edition of *Life* magazine that "in spite of his passion for freight-elevator effects . . . [Short] has made the whole revue a beautiful thing to watch."

Short staged the next three editions of the Berlin revues and then branched out to other projects and collaborators. In 1924, he was responsible for a musical version of the hit play *Peg o' My Heart*, and the following year, he directed *Sunny* by Jerome Kern, Oscar Hammerstein II, and Otto Harbach. For this show Short was working at the New Amsterdam Theatre, which is vastly larger than the intimate Music Box, and with one of the biggest musical theatre stars of the day, Marilyn Miller. His showcasing of the star proved ideal; critics raved about her work and the way in which it was supported by Short's staging.

As the 1920s wound down, Short directed a series of short-lived musicals, and then as the 1930s dawned, he returned to revues, starting with two featuring songs by Howard Dietz and Arthur Schwartz. First came *Three's a Crowd* (1930) and then *The Band Wagon* (1931), in which Short used revolving stages as never before: setting one inside another and having them turn in opposite directions. Brooks Atkinson in the June 14 edition of the *New York Times* applauded his work, saying that it made the show a "modern American revue closely related to the spirit of the age we live in."

Short reunited with Irving Berlin for his next two productions, starting with the loosely constructed musical satire *Face the Music* in 1932 and then the revue *As Thousands Cheer* in 1933. For this show, where songs and sketches were meant to feel as if they came from a specific section of a newspaper, Short achieved something of a *coup d'théâtre* for the first-act finale, Berlin's enduring "Easter Parade." With sets and costumes designed only in shades of brown and extensive use of cross-lighting, he created the illusion of an antique photo album coming to life.

Among Short's other varied projects during the 1930s were spectaculars (the operetta *The Great Waltz* in 1934 and the patriotic *The American Way* in 1939), a satiric book musical (*Jubilee* in 1935), and a revision of a classic (*The Hot Mikado* in 1939).

In the early 1940s, Short used his unique theatrical style and innovative techniques, abetted by scenic designer Harry Horner, to shift from reality to fantasy seamlessly in *Lady in the Dark*. Short's imaginative production design for the heroine's dreamscapes were, as Richard Watts Jr. put it in a January 24, 1941, *Herald Tribune* review, a "feat of showmanship" and "unquestionably brilliant."

Three years later, Short took a different tack and supervised Oscar Hammerstein II's English-language adaptation of Bizet, *Carmen Jones*. For this production Short opted to have his designers work in a single primary color for each act: yellow for the first, mauve for the second, blue in the third, and red in the final.

By the time *Carmen Jones* premiered, Short had been working on Broadway for more than forty years and would continue to do so for almost ten more, helming such productions as a revival of *Show Boat* (1947); the revue *Make Mine Manhattan* (1948); and another adapted opera, *My Darlin' Aida* (1952).

Short passed away four years later. In a *Times* obituary on October 10, 1956, his many innovations were recounted, including his having been the first director to remove footlights from a theatre, and he was lauded as an artist with a "special genius for stagecraft."

NOBLE SISSLE AND EUBIE BLAKE

(July 10, 1889–December 17, 1975) / (February 7, 1887–February 12, 1983)
Songwriters

Sissle and Blake smashed through racial barriers on Broadway in the 1920s, and with Shuffle Along, *they set a standard by which all African American shows would be judged for two decades.*

The subheading for an April 9, 1921, *Billboard* review of Sissle and Blake's *Shuffle Along* read, "At Last a Real Colored Show Is Offered—The Presentation of Negro Mirth and Melody Accomplished," and on May 23, 1921, the morning after the musical opened at Broadway's Sixty-Third Street Theatre, an unnamed critic for the *New York Times* praised it, citing particularly "its swinging and infectious score." Sissle and Blake, along with book writers Flournoy Miller and Aubrey Lyles (all African Americans), had created, along with the all-black cast, a hit that was being embraced by white audiences.

Blake, whose given name was James Hubert, reportedly demonstrated an early gift for music, and by the time he was twelve he had formed a band that would play for spare change on the streets of his native Baltimore. By the time he was sixteen, he had published a ragtime composition, "Charleston Rag," and from this point and through the early 1910s he worked as both a composer and performer. He eventually settled in New York and began performing at the Clef Club in Harlem. It was there that he met bandleader James Reese Europe and composer Will Marion Cook, who had written one of the earliest shows on Broadway to feature an all–African American cast, *Clorindy* (1898).

Sissle, who hailed from Indiana and was raised in Ohio, also showed facility for music and performance when he was young. He sang with his high school's glee club and after graduation joined a singing group that toured the United States. He eventually returned to Indiana for college, starting at Depauw University in Greencastle and later transferring to Butler University in Indianapolis. While he was in school, he earned money as a bandleader at the Severin Hotel there.

Sissle and Blake met not long after Sissle's time at Butler. They were both hired to perform at Riverview Park in Baltimore in 1915. There was an instant chemistry between them, not just as performers but also as writers, and they wrote their first song, "It's All Your Fault," not long after their meeting. In short order Sophie Tucker was performing it, and by August that year, an ad in the *Baltimore Sun* for an appearance she was making showcased the tune, touting it as a "triumph of the country in Songland, an unprecedented success, such as never has been."

Until 1917, Sissle and Blake performed together with various groups, including ones assembled by bandleader Europe. Their partnership was interrupted by America's entry into World War I when Sissle was drafted. He served with the 369th Infantry Regiment, a company comprised of African Americans in which Europe was also serving. Europe came to be the leader of the troop's band, which played to boost morale and during battle after the company had been deployed overseas. During the war, the 369th's band played in England and France, introducing audiences there to jazz.

While Sissle served, Blake, still in America, enjoyed a burgeoning career as a performer and recording artist, producing both piano rolls and records. The latter were for the Pathé label and featured the Eubie Blake Trio. In an April 1918 ad from the company, the group was touted as being "exponents of real 'jazz' and 'ragtime' piano work."

Sissle and his fellow soldiers returned after the armistice and were welcomed as heroes with a parade up Fifth Avenue. Not long after, Jim Europe and his Hell Fighters, as the band became known, began to tour, and among their ranks was Blake. By early 1919, the group was recording, and many of the songs they waxed were ones that Sissle, Blake, and Europe penned, including "Mirandy." A story in *Billboard* on April 26 reported that this number was being heralded across the country as the "piece de resistance" of the group's act. The report also mentioned that "one paper states that this song swayed the audience with a 'jazz' delirium when Europe's band let go with it."

Two months later, Sissle and Blake launched an act of their own in Harlem and soon began to tour on the Proctor's vaudeville circuit. When they appeared at Shea's in Buffalo, New York, late that summer, the critic for the city's *Evening News* wrote in a September 14 review, "This pair have a clever singing and pianologue act which brought forth a demand for an encore which had to be granted." Other praise during this engagement came from a writer in North Tonawanda's paper of the same name. This writer, on September 12, described Sissle as a "golden-voiced tenor" and Blake as "unquestionably the greatest pianist of his race."

Meeting another pair of performers and writers, Miller and Lyles, while performing at an NAACP benefit in Philadelphia a short time later brought Sissle and Blake to Broadway. As Richard Carlin and Ken Bloom report in their Grammy Award–winning liner notes to the 2016 CD *Sissle and Blake Sing Shuffle Along*, Miller and Lyles suggested a collaboration, saying, "You fellas write what Broadway would want and we'd like to write a show with you. We'll write the book and you birds write the music and lyrics." The result was *Shuffle Along*, which revised a plot from *The Mayor of Dixie*, an earlier piece Miller and Lyles had written, telling the story of two men who decide to run against one another for mayor of Jimtown, USA. The winner, they agree, will appoint the other as chief of police.

Sissle and Blake outfitted the show with some seventeen songs, including the enduring "I'm Just Wild about Harry," as well as such numbers as "Bandana Days" and the show's title song, which enjoyed popularity outside of the show for many years after its premiere and 504-performance run. James Whittaker, in a May 26 *Daily News* review, was so taken with Sissle and Blake's work that he commented, "There is material for ten successes in 'Shuffle Along,'" adding, "You are in the grip of racial genius when the songs begin."

After this success Sissle and Blake, along with another songwriting team, provided songs for *Elsie* (1923), a show set on Long Island about a young man whose wealthy parents attempt to destroy his marriage to a musical comedy actress. They continued writing material for Caucasian performers a year later with the song "I Was Meant for You." The number premiered in *Andre Charlot's Revue of 1924*, the show that brought British performer Gertrude Lawrence to Broadway, and she, along with Jack Buchanan, debuted the tune, which, featuring "velvety" music, was an "engaging song and dance," according to Percy Hammond in his January 10 *New York Tribune* review.

Toward the end of 1924, Sissle and Blake returned with another show featuring an all–African American cast, *Chocolate Dandies*, which also happened to give Josephine Baker her Broadway debut. Unfortunately, and despite a September 2 *New York Herald Tribune* review bearing the headline "'Chocolate Dandies,' Colored Show, Better than 'Shuffle Along,'" the show eked out a mere ninety performances.

A return to performing followed for Sissle and Blake in 1925 when they traveled to England. There they were greeted with exceptional critical and popular acclaim. A December 12 *Pittsburgh Courier* story detailed their activities in London. It reported that they had been dubbed the "American Ambassadors of Syncopation" and were enjoying extended engagements in theatres and music halls, often premiering new songs they had just written.

As a team they only returned to Broadway twice after this excursion. In 1933 and in 1952, they provided new material for revised incarnations of *Shuffle Along*. Individually, Blake contributed to several shows, including *Lew Leslie's Blackbirds* (1930) and *Swing It* (1937), and Sissle brought *Harlem Cavalcade* to Broadway in 1942.

Both men continued performing for the remainder of their lives. Sissle, in particular, enjoyed popular success as a bandleader in England during the 1940s. The songs they wrote have had a place on Broadway in a number of shows, including *Bubblin' Brown Sugar* (1976) and Bob Fosse's musical *Big Deal* (1986). Between these two, Broadway also saw a revue dedicated to Blake's music, *Eubie!* (1978), which ran for more than a year. Most recently, their music and story came to Broadway in 2016's *Shuffle Along, or, The Making of the Musical Sensation of 1921 and All That Followed*, a musical developed by George C. Wolfe that showcased the fascinating backstory of the first Broadway musical written by an all–African American creative team.

OLIVER SMITH

(February 13, 1918–January 23, 1994)
Scenic Designer / Producer

Smith's craftsmanship and always-varied aesthetic allowed artists ranging from Gower Champion to Moss Hart to Jerome Robbins to achieve their visions for some of Broadway's most lauded musicals.

Smith, born in Wisconsin and raised primarily in Pennsylvania, had his artistic training not in theatre but in painting and architecture. In fact, after his graduation from Pennsylvania State University in 1939, he received a scholarship to study as a fine-arts major at Princeton University. He had thought that he might become a museum curator, but before he enrolled in the program he took a year off to live in New York. During this time, he met playwright-novelist William Saroyan, and it was through this friendship that Smith developed an interest in theatre. Once he settled into his career, he would prove to be himself something of a renaissance man for the stage.

One of Smith's first stage credits allowed him to work with Saroyan as Eddie Dowling directed a pair of the playwright's one-acts alongside one from Irish dramatist Sean O'Casey. Smith's designs were "all that could be desired," as *Variety* critic "Rosen." put it in a March 4, 1942, review. Just one year later, in the April 1 edition of the *New York Herald Tribune*, music critic Virgil Thomson, reviewing *The Wind Remains*, a zarzuela (a Spanish form of musical comedy) that composer Paul Bowles had written based on a Federico García Lorca poem, called Smith's two-story set for the show a "marvel of ingenuity."

Leonard Bernstein, still early in his career, conducted the presentation of *Wind*, and future choreographic great Merce Cunningham was a dancer in it. But these were not the only luminaries with whom Smith was working. He had also designed the settings for Agnes de Mille's *Rodeo* (1942) for the Ballet Theater, where he ultimately became a resident designer and codirector. Concurrent with his work on de Mille's dance, he designed a production of *Rosalinda* (an adaptation of Strauss's *Die Fledermaus*) for the New Opera Company that transferred to Broadway, giving him his Main Stem debut.

When Smith was once again represented on Broadway, it was as both designer and producer for *On the Town* (1944), which brought Bernstein, Betty Comden, Adolph Green, and Jerome Robbins to Broadway. The show established that quartet in the theatrical world and proved Smith to be a producer of exceptional daring. His work in this capacity continued for another twenty-five years, and among the shows that came to Broadway under his auspices were the musicals *Gentlemen Prefer Blondes* (1949) and *Juno* (1959), as well as such plays as *No Exit, In the Summer House,* and Arthur Kopit's *Indians*. However, despite his successes and shrewdness in backing shows, which he turned to only to ensure he had work in his early days, it is as a designer that Smith will be remembered.

As the 1940s continued, Smith's design credits grew to include such musicals as *Billion Dollar Baby*, by Comden and Green and composer Morton Gould, and *Beggar's Holiday*. For his work on Duke Ellington and John Latouche's interracial reimagining of John Gay's *The Beggar's Opera*, Smith garnered some of his first out-and-out raves, particularly from "Kahn.," who, in a January 1, 1947, *Variety* review, noted, "[He] has designed some of the most exquisite settings of the season."

In the decades that followed, Smith was responsible for creating the visuals for such diverse (and landmark) productions as *My Fair Lady* (1956); *West Side Story* (1957); *The Sound of Music* (1959); *Camelot* (1960); and *Hello, Dolly!* (1964). In 1971, Smith attempted to explain his ability to segue between such varied work when he told Geri Trotta for a feature in the September edition of *Harper's Bazaar*, "I actually work in about three or four different styles," which he described as ranging from "romantic realism" to "realistic and sculptural." As a result, his designs simultaneously supported the musical itself and a director's vision. In his January 17, 1964, *Newsday* review of *Hello, Dolly!*, George Oppenheimer pointed out that, before Gower Champion's staging of the song "Dancing" had ended, "even Oliver Smith's graceful scenery is dancing."

Similarly, in a piece on *My Fair Lady* in the March 25, 1956, edition of the *New York Herald Tribune*, Walter Kerr praised Smith's choice to keep some designs "simple enough in outline to allow Cecil Beaton's brilliantly devised costumes undisputed rule of the stage." Kerr also recognized, on November 6, 1957, Smith's contributions to *West Side Story*. The critic described how Smith showcased the lovers Tony and Maria: "By lowering an enormously evocative cloudbank of floating fire escapes designer Oliver Smith lifts them into a precarious breathless isolation."

Not all of Smith's designs were for shows that attained the status of being legendary or broke ground with form, and yet they all presented their distinct challenges. For instance, there was *Baker Street*, a 1965 musical based on the Sherlock Holmes mysteries. In this Smith had to re-create Queen Victoria's Diamond Jubilee in miniature. Critic Louis Chapin deemed his work for this sequence "ingenious" in a February 20 review for the *Christian Science Monitor*, and his designs won him one of his ten Tony Awards.

At the other end of the spectrum was Tom Jones and Harvey Schmidt's *I Do! I Do!*, a two-character musical that examines a couple's marriage over the course of decades. Writing about this show in a December 6, 1966, *Newsday* review, Oppenheimer commented on the lack of chorus and scenery, remarking that the designer's spare work was "so attractive and inventive that it doesn't have to be lavish."

Smith's last new musical design credit on Broadway was Alan Jay Lerner and Burton Lane's *Carmelina* in 1979, although he continued to design for plays on Broadway and in regional theatres through the mid-1980s. In Smith's January 25, 1994, *Times* obituary, David Merrick, the prickliest of New York's producers, praised him, saying, "Most designers are masters of a single color. So if the basic color of a show is red, you get so-and-so; if it's green you get somebody else. You can get Oliver Smith for anything."

STEPHEN SONDHEIM

(March 22, 1930–)
Composer / Lyricist

Sondheim's songwriting has set new standards for both the style and substance of musical theatre work during the last half of the twentieth century.

In an April 22, 1984, *Newsday* story, Allan Wallach wrote that this composer-lyricist "may be our most sophisticated man of the musical theater, but his work is by no means limited as that term can suggest." And, in fact, Sondheim's musicals, many of which tackle difficult and serious subjects, have become as enduring as many of the ones that come from what some call the Golden Age of the Broadway musical.

Sondheim was born in New York to parents who were both part of the fashion industry. His father had established a successful business making women's dresses, and his mother created designs for her husband's company. The couple eventually divorced, and afterward, young Sondheim found a mentor in Oscar Hammerstein II, who had a country home in Bucks County, Pennsylvania, where Sondheim's mother would also sojourn. Sondheim frequently tells the story about sharing a musical he wrote as a teenager with Hammerstein and the insightful critique the book writer–lyricist provided as if it had been written by an adult.

Sondheim attended Williams College in Massachusetts where he studied composition and theory. During this period, too, he studied with Milton Babbitt, then teaching at Princeton, to discuss specifically composing for musical theatre. At Williams, Sondheim had two shows produced.

His Broadway debut came in 1956 when he supplied a title song for the play *Girls of Summer*. Before this he had written the scripts for several episodes of the television series *Topper* and the score for *Saturday Night,* a musical centering on a group of young friends in Brooklyn at the end of the 1920s that went unproduced until 1998.

The work Sondheim had done on this show, however, attracted the attention of others in the theatre community and led to him joining Leonard Bernstein, Arthur Laurents, and Jerome Robbins on *West Side Story* as the show's lyricist.

For this landmark retelling of Shakespeare's *Romeo and Juliet*, Sondheim penned the words for such classics as "I Feel Pretty," "Maria," and "Tonight," which John Chapman, in his September 27, 1957, *Daily News* review, described as having a "simple grace."

Although Sondheim was reticent to serve only as lyricist on another show, Hammerstein convinced him to accept the assignment of joining Jule Styne in writing songs for Ethel Merman and the musical *Gypsy* (1959). Once again Sondheim served up lyrics with gentle ease and poignancy ("Everything's Coming Up Roses"), unexpected double meanings ("Let Me Entertain You"), ribald humor ("You Gotta Get a Gimmick"), and psychological complexity ("Rose's Turn").

Sondheim's debut as composer-lyricist came in 1962 with *A Funny Thing Happened on the Way to the Forum*, a revisitation to Plautus's Roman farces with book by Burt Shevelove and Larry Gelbart. Sondheim's songs for the musical include "Comedy Tonight" and "Everybody Ought to Have a Maid." In his May 9 *New York Times* review, Howard Taubman noted that, with the latter number, Sondheim had helped the production's stars, including Zero Mostel, return to the "days when farceurs like the Marx Brothers could devastate a number."

Two years later, Sondheim reteamed with Laurents for a loopy piece of absurdist musical theatre writing, *Anyone Can Whistle*, about a bankrupt town, its corrupt leadership, and the inmates at a local asylum. The piece divided critics and lasted a mere nine performances. Sondheim returned to writing only lyrics for one more musical, *Do I Hear a Waltz?* (1965), which featured music by Richard Rodgers.

In 1970, Sondheim, working with director Harold Prince and book writer George Furth, brought *Company*, an examination of modern urban marriage, to Broadway. In it Sondheim's talent revealed itself in exciting, emotionally devastating new ways. In his April 27 *Times* review, Clive Barnes found the lyrics to have "suppleness [and] sparse, elegant wit" but complained that the music was "slick, clever and eclectic rather than exciting." Nevertheless, Barnes also admitted, "[He] must be one of the most sophisticated composers ever to write Broadway musicals." Tony voters had no reservations, and Sondheim won his first Tony.

Company set in motion a decade-long partnership between Sondheim and Prince that included *Follies* (1971), where Sondheim evoked sounds of a bygone era while never sacrificing his own musical voice; *A Little Night Music* (1973), which contains the songwriter's most famous song, "Send in the Clowns"; *Pacific Overtures* (1976), an exploration of the West's arrival in Japan in the nineteenth century that allowed Sondheim to explore Eastern melodic structures; and ultimately the pinnacle of their collaboration, *Sweeney Todd* (1979). Richard Eder, in his March 2 *Times* review, wrote, "[Sondheim] has composed an endlessly inventive, highly expressive score that works indivisibly from his brilliant and abrasive lyrics." Sondheim won his fourth Tony for the score, and *Sweeney* has gone on to several Broadway revivals, become part of the international opera repertoire, and been re-created as a major motion picture.

After the quick Broadway failure of *Merrily We Roll Along* (1981), which marked the end of his collaboration with Prince, Sondheim began working with playwright-director James Lapine and started to develop his musicals through workshop processes at nonprofit theatres. The first of these, *Sunday in the Park with George*, was developed at Playwrights Horizons off-Broadway in 1983 and arrived on Broadway the following year. The musical explores the life and work of impressionist painter Georges Seurat and imagines one of his descendants' artistic struggles. For it Sondheim created a pointillist score. Both intellectual and deeply felt, *Sunday* earned Sondheim and Lapine the Pulitzer Prize.

Into the Woods, their exploration of fairy tales and "happily ever after" that has become a staple for theatres around the world, bowed on Broadway in 1987 after a production at the La Jolla Playhouse in California, and in 1993, they brought *Passion*, their exploration of obsessive love, to the Main Stem.

Between these last two, Sondheim wrote *Assassins*. With a book by John Weidman, the piece explores the motivations of individuals who killed or attempted to kill presidents, and it premiered off-Broadway in 1990, debuting on Broadway fourteen years later. During the late 1990s and early 2000s, Sondheim dedicated himself to a musical exploring the lives of the Mizner brothers, which arrived in New York at the Public Theater in 2008 as *Road Show* after a regional production under the title *Bounce*. In 2004, he also augmented his score for an adaptation of Aristophanes's *The Frogs* (originally written in 1973) for a Lincoln Center Theater production. For many years, too, he has participated in revivals of his works on both sides of the Atlantic, most recently a gender-reversed *Company* that premiered in London in 2018, and he has been working with playwright David Ives on a musical based on two movies by Luis Buñuel.

Beyond his work in the theatre, Sondheim has had a sporadic career in Hollywood, writing the music and lyrics for the TV musical *Evening Primrose* (1967); scoring such movies as *Stavisky* (1974) and *Reds* (1981); and providing the songs for *Dick Tracy* (1990), for which he won the Academy Award for best song for "Sooner or Later." In 1993, he was awarded the Kennedy Center Honor, and beyond his eight Tonys, he has also earned eight Grammy Awards.

MICHAEL STEWART

(August 1, 1924–September 20, 1987)
Book Writer / Lyricist

In a career that spanned more than thirty years, Stewart wrote the books for two of musical theatre's perennial favorites and one of the 1980s' box-office bonanzas.

Stewart once "half-jokingly" complained to Bernard Carragher for a September 30, 1979, *New York Times* feature, "I don't know why any bright person would want to be a musical book writer. You're scorned by the critics, you get no recognition from the public." And yet, in a career that spanned more than thirty years, this writer penned the books for such classic musicals as *Bye Bye Birdie* and *Hello, Dolly!*, often earning plaudits from reviewers and theatregoers alike.

Stewart, by all reports, decided that he wanted to write for the theatre at the age of ten after seeing the original production of *Anything Goes*, starring Ethel Merman. He attended Queens College and earned a master's degree from Yale in 1953, by which point he had already contributed sketches to a Broadway revue, *Alive and Kicking* (1950).

After earning his Yale degree, Stewart, like so many other book writers of his generation, got early experience scripting for television and contributing sketches and lyrics to revues. He was a staff writer, along with Mel Brooks, for Sid Caesar's TV programs, and he contributed to Ben Bagley's off-Broadway *Shoestring Revue* (1955) and *Shoestring '57*, as well as Bagley's *The Littlest Revue* on Broadway (1956).

A friendship with composer Charles Strouse and lyricist Lee Adams that began at the summer resort Green Mansions, where the three collaborated on weekly revues, led to Stewart's first assignment as a Broadway book writer. In 1959, he was brought in to script a show that Strouse and Adams had been developing, *Let's Go Steady*, about an Elvis Presley–like rock star who's drafted. It eventually became *Bye Bye Birdie*, and according to John Chapman in his April 15, 1960, *Daily News* review, Stewart, along with director-choreographer Gower Champion, had "jampacked it with humor and lighthearted imagination." Not all critics were as enthused, particularly the *New York Times*' Brooks Atkinson, which set off a maelstrom of letters to the editor. Stewart and his collaborators, nevertheless, shared a Tony for best musical for their freshman effort.

Stewart also worked with Champion for his next two musicals. First came *Carnival!* in 1961 and then *Hello, Dolly!* with a score by Jerry Herman and starring Carol Channing in early 1964. The latter show and star were glowingly welcomed, and Stewart earned his first Tony for book writing, but as he noted fifteen years later, he could often be a critic's whipping boy. In a January 26 story for the *New York Times*, Atkinson lamented the flaws he perceived in the musical, which he had positively reviewed: "It makes do with a facile gag when it needn't. It tolerates vulgarities it can dispense with."

In 1966, Stewart branched out to playwriting, discovering critics could be even less forgiving for nonmusicals. *Those That Play the Crowns* imagined the world of the company of traveling actors from *Hamlet*, even as Tom Stoppard's similarly inspired *Rosencrantz and Guildenstern Are Dead* was premiering in England. *Crowns* lasted only four performances.

When Stewart, working with his sister and her husband, returned to musicals two years later, it was for *George M!*, a musical biography of George M. Cohan, starring Joel Grey as the early-twentieth-century entertainer. It was Stewart's first attempt at what has become known as a jukebox musical and used a host of tunes from Cohan's songbook to tell his life story. Complaints arose about the way in which the show shoehorned in Cohan's classic (and lesser-known) songs when the production bowed, but Stewart would put the lessons he learned on crafting this show to good use twelve years later.

The next Stewart book to reach Broadway was similarly nostalgic and reunited him with songwriter Herman and director Champion. *Mack & Mabel* focused on the tempestuous relationship between silent film pioneer Mack Sennett and his leading lady Mabel Normand, and while *George M!* had enjoyed a year's stay on Broadway, this new show lasted a mere sixty-six performances.

Stewart had written a show before this one, a modern love story, *Seesaw*, but withdrew his name from it after it had been heavily revised out of town. The show featured songs by Cy Coleman and Dorothy Fields, and in 1976, Stewart and Coleman rejoined forces for *I Love My Wife*, a look at two couples' awkward attempts at wife swapping. Stewart crafted a book that was unlike any that had preceded it. *Wife* had only four actors, who were supplemented by four band members onstage who played ancillary roles. In addition, he penned lyrics for Coleman's melodies. Their work earned a Tony nomination for best score, and a few years later, the team was again nominated for the sprightly Americana-infused tuner *Barnum*.

Later that year Stewart, working with Mark Bramble, who had penned the book to *Barnum*, crafted "lead ins and crossovers" (as the credit in the opening-night playbill put it and which Stewart later had producer David Merrick change to "book by") for the hit stage version of the movie *42nd Street*. The morning after the show opened, papers carried the news that director-choreographer Champion had died just before the curtain went up and also included respectful remarks for Stewart and Bramble's efforts in weaving a host of Al Dubin and Harry Warren's songs into the story line of the iconic Busby Berkeley picture.

Two days after the opening, Stewart was quoted in Toronto's *Globe and Mail* as saying he might be giving up writing musical comedies: "I don't love it any more. I loved it for 20 years. I like it, I respect it, but my heart does not quicken when I hear an overture any more."

And yet Stewart didn't turn his back on the form. He had two shows hit Broadway and one bow off-Broadway in the space of five years. And although one of those ran only four performances, *Harrigan 'n Hart*, it earned him one last Tony nomination for book writing.

Stewart passed away in 1987, and at the time of his death he was at work on a new musical with Coleman. It was a return to the sort of period lightheartedness that had inspired his greatest successes, and even after Stewart's death, Coleman attempted unsuccessfully to bring the work to the stage.

CHARLES STROUSE

(June 7, 1928–)
Composer / Lyricist

Strouse has made a twofold contribution to the American musical theatre, first bringing genuine rock 'n' roll to Broadway and then writing two works that have been many young people's introduction to performing musical comedy.

Native New Yorker Strouse developed a fondness for popular music at home, where his mother could often be found playing the latest hits on the family's piano. Fondness deepened when, at the age of fifteen, he enrolled at the Eastman

School of Music in Rochester, New York. "I became passionate when I got there," he told writers Al Kasha and Joel Hirschhorn for their book *Notes on Broadway*.

After graduation, and having studied composition, Strouse continued his education, studying privately with, among others, Aaron Copland and Nadia Boulanger. Strouse supported himself during this period by playing for dance classes, and it was through this work that he met dancer-choreographer Ray Harrison, whose credits included performing in the original cast of *On the Town* and assisting Hanya Holm on *Kiss Me, Kate*. Harrison suggested that Strouse join him at Green Mansions, an adult summer camp in upstate New York that provided original entertainment for its clientele. It was there that Strouse and a friend, Lee Adams (they met at a party given by a mutual friend), started collaborating in 1952, writing songs for the revues that were presented each weekend.

Strouse and Adams continued working together and separately for the next three years. Strouse, singly, contributed melodies to a minimusical that played at the Versailles nightclub in Manhattan and to *Shoestring Revue* (1955), which boasted an opening number that he penned with Michael Stewart and featured two future luminaries: Beatrice Arthur and Chita Rivera.

Strouse and Adams continued to get exposure through revues in 1956. First, they had songs featured in the West End revue *Fresh Airs*, which placed their work alongside the estimable British songwriting team of Flanders and Swann. Then, in May of that year, the team got its Broadway debut with *The Littlest Revue*. The show featured one song they penned, "Spring Doth Let Her Colours Fly," and in his May 5 *New York Times* review, Brooks Atkinson labeled it the "best staged sketch of the lot," praising Charlotte Rae, one of many future stars in the show: "[She] burlesques the condescensions of a Wagnerian opera singer with hilarious aplomb."

The pair did not return to Broadway for five years, but when they did, it was with a musical that both entertained and helped push the Broadway musical toward a new sound. It was *Bye Bye Birdie*. Strouse, who had enjoyed having one pop song—"Born Too Late" for the Pony-Tails—hit the charts in 1958, was the ideal composer for this musical about an Elvis Presley–like rocker who's drafted. The score fused Broadway styles with the sounds of early rock 'n' roll, and Walter Kerr, in an April 15, 1960, *New York Herald Tribune* review, called it a "frisky new musical." Not long after, it also became a Tony Award–winning best musical.

Strouse and Adams's follow-up was another youthful show, *All American* (1962), which centers on what happens when science is applied to strategizing football at a small college. With a book by Mel Brooks, it ran only eighty-six performances but did boast one song that became a standard, "Once upon a Time."

Sports were at the center of Strouse and Adams's next project, a musical version of Clifford Odets's drama about a boxer, *Golden Boy*, which starred Sammy Davis Jr. Strouse's score displayed a knack for combining melodiousness with drama. Howard Taubman, in his October 21, 1964, *Times* review, singled out Strouse's "sizzling tune" for "Don't Forget 127th Street," writing, "No one you can be sure, can fail to pay attention to this number."

Lighter fare lay ahead with the team's next two projects. In *It's a Bird, It's a Plane . . . It's Superman* (1966), Strouse wrote music that brimmed with fizziness appropriate for its comic-book roots, and his score for *Applause* (1970), a then-contemporary revision to the classic movie *All about Eve*, contained late-1960s pop sounds and even some early disco.

It took seven years for Strouse to have a new musical on Broadway, although his experimental musical *Six*, for which he wrote both music and lyrics, played off-Broadway in 1971, and a musical with a Strouse–Adams score, *I and Albert*, about Queen Victoria and Prince Albert, bowed in the West End the following year. The composer's return to the Main Stem was a triumphant one: He provided the music for *Annie*, which featured a book by Thomas Meehan and lyrics by Martin Charnin. For the show's score, Strouse incorporated sounds of the 1930s into his music, though its biggest hit, the now-classic "Tomorrow," was not period pastiche but influenced instead by 1970s pop, something that worried the composer at the time.

Sadly, *Annie* has been Strouse's last major hit, but it's far from his last musical. Since its debut, he has composed the scores for seven Broadway shows. Two of them, *A Broadway Musical* (1978) and *Dance a Little Closer* (1983), closed on their respective opening nights, and neither 1980's *Bring Back Birdie* (four performances) nor 1981's *Charlie and Algernon* (seventeen performances) fared much better.

Mayor—which had both music and lyrics by Strouse and a book by Warren Leight and examined Edward Koch and his administration—got enough positive reviews off-Broadway that it moved to Broadway for two months in late 1985. The following year, Strouse, lyricist Stephen Schwartz, and book writer Joseph Stein brought *Rags*, about the immigrant experience in 1910 New York, to the stage. This show contains the composer's most ambitious musical score. Frank Rich, in an August 22 *Times* review, remarked, "Strouse has really stretched himself here. . . . He uses his music to dramatize the evolution of American pop music." *Rags* only ran for four performances, but the creators continued to revisit it, most recently in 2017 when a heavily reworked version debuted at Goodspeed Musicals in Connecticut. David Thomson's revisions to the book and new contributions from Strouse and Schwartz prompted the *Hartford Courant*'s Christopher Arnott to write, "'Rags' is fully dressed, not a stitched-together attempt to salvage a few good songs from a forgotten show. Not ragged at all." There remains hope that this version might make its way to New York.

Strouse's last Broadway outing was in 1991 with *Nick & Nora*. Again, it was a short-lived show, but his work garnered praise. Clifford A. Ridley, in a December 9 *Philadelphia Inquirer* review, noted, "It's true to the period and always melodically interesting."

JULE STYNE

(December 31, 1905–September 20, 1994)
Composer / Producer

Styne took both the concept of a showstopper and a theatrical song hit to new levels.

Born in England and raised primarily in the United States, Styne, born Julius Kerwyn Stein, demonstrated gifts as an entertainer when he was just three years old; he performed an impromptu song when he and his parents visited a family friend, Scottish entertainer Harry Lauder, who spotted an innate talent in the boy. Piano lessons quickly followed, and after his parents immigrated to the United States and settled in Chicago, Styne began studying at the College of Music there. He won a contest with the Chicago Symphony before he was a teenager, and although classical music might have been in his future, he turned to dance music and playing in a burlesque house.

Styne toured with a number of jazz bands during the 1920s and also performed in nightclubs. In his September 21, 1994, *New York Times* obituary, Eleanor Blau quotes him as admitting, "I must have worked a couple of dozen mob joints." Styne composed his first song, "Sunday," while touring with one band in the mid-1920s, and not long after, he began working in Hollywood as a vocal coach, and composing became his focus. From 1938 to 1948, more than one hundred movies featured a song or score by the always-energetic Styne. Five of them, including "It Seems I've Heard That Song Before" and "I Fall in Love Too Easily," were Oscar-nominated. He, and frequent lyricist partner Sammy Cahn, eventually won in 1955 for "Three Coins in the Fountain." Styne and Cahn also wrote such tunes as the World War II hit "It's Been a Long, Long Time"; the holiday classic "Let It Snow! Let It Snow! Let It Snow!"; and one of Frank Sinatra's signature numbers, "Saturday Night (Is the Loneliest Night of the Week)" for the popular song market.

Styne and Cahn arrived on Broadway in 1947 with *High Button Shoes*. In a compliment to the composer's ability to evoke the era and the musical's milieu, Brooks Atkinson, in an October 10 *Times* review, wrote that the music was "simple in style and very pleasant to hear, like a well-oiled hurdy-gurdy." Two years later, Styne, working with lyricist Leo Robin, wrote the songs for *Gentlemen Prefer Blondes*, filling the show about a loveable 1920s gold digger with melodic flash and simplicity. In the former category were songs such as "Diamonds Are a Girl's Best Friend" and "A Little Girl from Little Rock," which helped make a star of Carol Channing. In the latter were "Bye Bye Baby" and "Just a Kiss Apart," which were receiving airplay before the show opened and firmly established Styne's reputation as a Broadway tunesmith.

Two years later, Styne had a pair of musicals open on Broadway. The first, *Make a Wish*, marked the beginning of his career as Broadway producer. The second, the revue *Two on the Aisle*, paired him with two new lyric-writing partners, Betty Comden and Adolph Green. The collaboration proved to be a perfect fit, as they shared an innate love of show business and a gift for erudition. T. A. Wise, in a July 24, 1951, *Wall Street Journal* review, called Styne's contribution "lively and sweet on the ears." As for the Comden and Green work, the *Times'* Atkinson called it the "pithiest material any revue has had in these parts for a long time" in his July 20 review.

Styne, Comden, and Green collaborated for another twenty-plus years. Their first outing following *Aisle* was additional material for *Peter Pan*, where their tunes included the ethereal "Neverland" and the Gilbert and Sullivan pastiche "Hook's Waltz." After this their shows included such popular titles as *Bells Are Ringing* (1956) and *Do Re Mi* (1960), and such standards as "Just in Time," "The Party's Over," and "Make Someone Happy" emerged from them. Less successful for the Styne–Comden–Green team were *Subways Are for Sleeping* (1961), *Fade*

Out–Fade In (1964), and *Hallelujah, Baby!* (1967), but even in these, critics and audiences could generally be assured of the mastery the three would display. When reviewing a revised version of the last musical in 2004, *Variety* critic Robert L. Daniels remarked in his October 13 write-up: "The jaunty score remains a sunny souvenir of the '60s, when lyricists Betty Comden and Adolph Green designed crisply witty and fervently romantic lyrics for the infectious melodies of composer Jule Styne."

Styne, whom John S. Wilson characterized in a May 24, 1964, *Times* feature as an "unusually energetic composer," did not limit himself to writing with Comden and Green during this time. In 1957, he teamed with Stephen Sondheim to write the songs for *Gypsy*, resulting in such classics as "Everything's Coming Up Roses" and "Let Me Entertain You," and in 1964, just two months before the opening of *Fade Out–Fade In*, *Funny Girl* premiered. The *Times*' Howard Taubman dubbed it "one of his best scores," and indeed, Styne had written two breakout hits, "People" and "Don't Rain on My Parade," as well as such estimable songs as "Who Are You Now?" and "The Music That Makes Me Dance."

Styne's next four shows—*Darling of the Day* (1968), *Look to the Lilies* (1970), *Sugar* (1972), and *Lorelei* (1974)—all had moments that showcased his ability to craft catchy melodies. The score for *Darling*, according to John Chapman in the February 11 edition of the *Daily News*, was "tip-top," and he pointed to songs ranging from the simple ballad "That Something Extra Special" to the "uproarious music-hall turn" "Not on Your Nellie" as examples. After *Darling* and such revolutionary shows as *Hair* and *Company*, Styne's sound unfortunately started to seem old-fashioned to both critics and theatregoers.

Sadly, for an artist who had reached pinnacles of critical and popular acclaim with *Gypsy* and *Funny Girl*, Styne witnessed his last four shows fail. *Bar Mitzvah Boy* (1978) ran for just three months in London's West End. On Broadway, *One Night Stand* (1980) closed during previews, never officially opening, and *The Red Shoes* (1993) played only five performances. *Treasure Island* (1985) didn't make it out of Toronto. These four shows did not, however, stain Styne's reputation or legacy, and after he passed away in 1994, the *Times*' Frank Rich, in a September 25 editorial, reminded readers that Styne was the "last great American songwriter to come from an era when great American songwriters seemed to give unified voice to an entire nation" and that Styne's music "defined the Broadway musical in its final golden era."

ED SULLIVAN

(September 28, 1901–October 13, 1974)
Producer / Television Personality

Sullivan's nearly four-decade career in print and on television made Broadway both accessible to and palpably exciting for people in even the tiniest of communities in America.

Sullivan, of course, will always be remembered as the man who gave American television audiences a "really big show" once a week for more than thirty years. But as important as his impressive longevity on the small screen is the way in which he served as one of the Great White Way's most enthusiastic cheerleaders, both before and during his variety program's run.

His journey to the life of TV host and emcee came through the athleticism of his youth. While in high school in Port Chester, New York, he received a dozen varsity letters thanks to his sports prowess, and he also wrote about sports for the local paper. He continued there after his graduation and eventually moved to a paper in Hartford, Connecticut. After this Sullivan shifted from paper to paper, eventually landing at the *Evening Graphic* in 1927. He started as a sportswriter and eventually became the paper's sports editor, and when its star columnist, Walter Winchell, left, Sullivan assumed his duties covering Broadway.

The shift wasn't as big a leap as it might seem. Sullivan had long enjoyed being a denizen of Manhattan's nightclubs and speakeasies, and indeed, while he was still working the sports beat, he, along with singer Nora Bayes, songwriter Irving Berlin, arts writer Ward Morehouse, and mayor Jimmy Walker, were among the notables at the October 1927 opening of Casa Lopez, located in the Winter Garden Theatre.

Sullivan's column debuted July 1931, and the move into the realm of celebrity and entertainment reporting proved to be a remarkable stepping stone for him. He soon was also appearing on radio. When he moved to the *Daily News* a few years later, his column became syndicated, and he began to produce, assemble, and host highly publicized special events. His activity in this latter regard reached its height during World War II with a performance at Madison Square Garden that raised nearly $250,000 for army emergency relief. During the early 1940s, too, Sullivan turned Broadway producer with two revues, *Crazy with the Heat* (1941) and *Harlem Cavalcade* (1942).

Beyond his column Sullivan had another ongoing duty for the *Daily News*, emceeing and coordinating the talent for the annual Harvest Moon Ball, a dance competition where there was a cash prize and generally some sort of short-term professional contract for the winners. In 1947, Sullivan entered his twelfth year as the show's host, and "Jose.," in a September 10 *Variety* review of that year's program, noted that Sullivan "naturally goes with the package. . . . [He] virtually grew up as an emcee via this series."

A year after this, Sullivan—all "grown up"—was introducing acts on a new television series on CBS, *Toast of the Town*. Its debut episode came on June 20, 1948. Critics from both industry papers and general interest publications had reservations about Sullivan's demeanor. In the *New York Times* on July 4, Jack Gould, for instance, complained about Sullivan's "extreme matter-of-factness" and "predilection for introducing his friends in the audience." Viewers, however, didn't mind, and in an October 27 *Variety* column, a writer went so far as to say home audiences had become "addicted" to Sullivan's eclectic offerings.

Broadway figured prominently in the program from its first episode, in which Sullivan introduced composer Richard Rodgers and songwriter Irving Berlin before a finale featuring Berlin's music. Other theatre-related segments on the early shows included a ballet sequence from *Allegro*, Jane Watson performing numbers from *As the Girls Go* (just a week after it had opened), and Nanette Fabray delivering a song from the Alan Jay Lerner–Kurt Weill tuner *Love Life*.

During this time, too, Sullivan, in his own way, championed racial integration in the medium. Within the first month of being on the air, Sullivan presented Lena Horne, Bill Robinson, Ella Fitzgerald, Cab Calloway, and Raul and Eva Reyes, and as Billy Rowe pointed out in November 6 *Pittsburgh Courier* column about performers of color on TV, "Sullivan has been the most democratic in his presentations and has given the Negro a chance to be seen." Meanwhile, other shows, as Rowe put it, relegated non-Caucasian performers to a "poor back seat."

In the 1950s and 1960s, people across America tuned in to the show (later officially dubbed the *Ed Sullivan Show*) and could generally count on having one of Broadway's current shows brought straight into their homes. Beyond these spots, Sullivan would occasionally host special tributes to great Broadway tunesmiths, and with ones dedicated to Alan Jay Lerner, Cole Porter, and Rodgers and Hammerstein, the American populace got a tuneful history lesson about them and their work.

In a similar vein, Sullivan lent his name and unique style to a dozen LPs showcasing the songs from classic musicals. In addition to being emblazoned with his picture, each bargain-priced album—$1.68 as compared to the then–industry standard of $3.98—had notes from Sullivan. These included both a synopsis of the show as well as personal anecdotes from him. On the *Oklahoma!* LP, for instance, he describes how "Dick" (Rodgers) and "Oscar" (Hammerstein) had to audition the material frequently to raise money for the show, and the reaction of his seatmate—former New York governor Alfred E. Smith—on opening night: "[He] stood up in the aisle and cheered as the curtain descended." Sullivan also shared, "The late George M. Cohan, the last time I had dinner with him at the Hotel Astor, declared that 'Oklahoma!' was the greatest American play with music he'd ever seen."

The *Ed Sullivan Show* left the air on June 6, 1971, and the indefatigable emcee entered a semiretirement before his death in 1974. Before this, however, he gave the Great White Way one final salute, assembling numbers, featuring the likes of Jack Cassidy, Ethel Merman, and Gwen Verdon, and brief interview clips with producers Joseph Papp and Harold Prince for *Ed Sullivan's Broadway* in 1973.

T

JEANINE TESORI

(November 10, 1961–)
Composer / Orchestrator / Artistic Administrator

In her career Tesori has brought award-winning playwrights to the realm of musical the-atre and with them created audacious and unexpected works.

In May 1997, the New York Drama Critics Circle awarded *Violet*, with a score by Tesori and book and lyrics by Brian Crawley, its best musical prize. The piece, about a disfigured Southern woman's cross-country journey to see a preacher whom she hopes will heal her, joined a select few off-Broadway musicals that had been so honored by this group. For Tesori, who was making her debut as a the-atrical composer, it was the culmination of a journey that had begun in the early 1980s. It was also the start of her rise as a preeminent musical voice for the new millennium, a writer committed to exploring serious themes in her work, often with noted writers unfamiliar with the form.

Her first interest in theatre had come when she was in her early teens and saw the original production of *Godspell* off-Broadway. She later told *Playbill*'s Michelle Vellucci for a July 2013 feature, "I will never forget the energy of sitting in a small theatre, and the very first time that the band kicked in." It gave her, she remem-bered, the "sense that I'm someplace where there's something happening, and I don't want to be anywhere else."

Despite this unique feeling and an interest in music that she had always had, Tesori enrolled at Barnard College as a pre-med major. Later, though, she switched to music, inspired by two summers she spent teaching at Stage Door Manor.

Tesori first contemplated writing *Violet* in the early 1980s, but she only began working on it in earnest in the early 1990s. In the interim, as she told Blake Green for a March 10, 1997, *Newsday* feature, "Life just took over." Indeed, Tesori had been busy with stints of musical directing, conducting on Broadway, and penning dance music for such shows as *The Secret Garden*. During the first years of the decade, she had also written another musical, *Starcrossed*, about the life of Gali-leo, which received a developmental workshop production at Goodspeed Musi-cals. Her first credited Broadway outing came when she created the new dance arrangements for the 1995 Broadway revival of *How to Succeed in Business without Really Trying.*

Tesori arrived as a composer on Broadway in 1998 when she provided incidental music for a starry production of *Twelfth Night* at Lincoln Center Theater. Ben Brantley, in his July 17, 1998, *New York Times* review, called her scoring "fantastical and wonder-struck, a fitting accent to the exquisite pipe dreams conjured by [the show's physical design]."

One more stint as musical arranger for Broadway followed, a celebration of midcentury jazz, *Swing!* (1999), and then in 2002, she got her Broadway debut as a composer with *Thoroughly Modern Millie.* Tesori did not get the chance to write a complete score for the show, which was based on the movie that starred Julie Andrews and Carol Channing and was set in the 1920s. Instead, Tesori augmented a half-dozen songs used in the film—by such writers as Victor Herbert, Sir Arthur Sullivan, James Van Heusen, and Sammy Cahn—with her own period-sounding numbers, and she delivered one showstopper, "Gimme, Gimme," for the musical's star, Sutton Foster (in Andrews's role of a young girl newly arrived in New York).

Tesori's next project, *Caroline, or Change,* couldn't have been more different from the frothy *Millie.* Set in Louisiana during the early 1960s, *Caroline* paired the composer with Pulitzer Prize–winning dramatist Tony Kushner. Together they created a musical that examined racial issues and the cultural divide between Northerners and Southerners, even as it told an emotionally rich story about a boy's relationship with his family's maid. Tesori's score fused rhythm and blues, early rock, gospel, traditional Jewish music, and a musical theatre vernacular. Originally slated for a limited engagement at off-Broadway's Public Theater, the production eventually moved to Broadway for a brief run. In reviewing the transfer, the *Village Voice*'s Michael Feingold remarked on May 5, 2004, "George C. Wolfe's production is a summit of beauty, its every moment heightened by the loving, subtle architecture of Jeanine Tesori's score."

Tesori undertook a significantly lighter commercial task in 2008. Working with playwright David Lindsay-Abaire, she musicalized the popular animated movie *Shrek.* The show bowed on Broadway in December 2008 and has become a staple for theatres around the country. Even as *Shrek* started its run, Tesori was working with downtown playwright Lisa Kron on a musical based on Alison Bechdel's autobiographical graphic novel *Fun Home.* As with *Caroline,* this piece about Bechdel's childhood and young adulthood in a small Pennsylvania town, her coming out, and her father's gayness began its life at the Public Theater. The day after its October 22, 2013, opening, *Newsday*'s Linda Winer praised the composer's work, writing, "[She] finds just the right internal voices for conflicted moods, with unpredictable melodies." A Broadway transfer followed a year later, and for it Tesori won her first Tony Award after having been nominated for all of her previous work.

In the summer of 2013, even as Kron and she were preparing *Fun Home* for the stage, Tesori became artistic director of City Center's Off-Center program, which was designed to bring well-regarded, off-Broadway musicals back to life in short-run, summertime concert presentations. Under her guidance and because of the appreciation of smaller musicals she developed as a young person, the initiative flourished and produced everything from Randy Newman's relatively obscure *Faust* to Marc Blitzstein's landmark *The Cradle Will Rock* to Tesori's own *Violet*. This latter offering later transferred to a limited-engagement Broadway run. She stepped down from her position after three seasons and was replaced by Michael Friedman, and, after his untimely death, Tesori returned to the program to serve as creative consultant of the series, working with its artistic director, Anne Kauffman.

Tesori's most recent musical, *Soft Power*, premiered at the Ahmanson Theatre in Los Angeles in the spring of 2018, featuring a script and lyrics by playwright David Henry Hwang. The show, which marks a first-time credit for her as contributing "additional lyrics" and carries the tagline of "a play with a musical," explores cultural appropriation and the impact that fictions have on reality. In reviewing the premiere for EW.com on May 17, Maureen Lee Lenker wrote that *Soft Power* had a "heady concept unlike any musical in recent memory" and described Tesori as having filled it with "lush, complicated melodies." Tesori will explore another unlikely subject in song soon. In September 2018, the Metropolitan Opera commissioned her to write an opera based on George Brant's *Grounded*, about a female fighter pilot who can only operate drones during her pregnancy.

TOMMY TUNE

(February 28, 1939–)
Director / Choreographer

Tune's direction and choreography have both elevated the nature of the concept musical and brought an exceptional sensuousness to the Broadway stage.

When Tommy Tune accepted a Tony Award for lifetime achievement, he facetiously quipped, "My father's great dream for me was the same as every Texas father's dream for their firstborn son—they wanted us all to leave Texas, go to New York, and dance in the chorus of a Broadway show. And I did it." Tune also moved on to directing and choreographing and in the process pushed the boundaries of the "concept musical."

After a childhood filled with dance and dance lessons, Tune enrolled at the University of Texas, and once he received his fine arts degree he moved to New York. He frequently tells the story of how, on his first day in the city, a friend told him to pick up trade papers, such as *Back Stage*, to scout for auditions. He did and snagged his first job immediately: dancing in a summer stock production of *Irma la Douce*.

His Broadway debut came a couple of years later with the Sherlock Holmes musical *Baker Street* (1965). *A Joyful Noise* (1966), choreographed by Michael Bennett, and *How Now, Dow Jones* (1967) followed.

It would take a few years for Tune to return to Broadway. In the interim he choreographed and danced in summer stock. He also appeared—opposite Twiggy—in Ken Russell's 1971 movie version of Sandy Wilson's valentine to 1920s tuners,

The Boy Friend. The auteur's kaleidoscopically lavish cinematic treatment of the relatively modest stage show drew some sharp criticisms, but Tune's turn as the secondary male lead won raves. In a December 17 *Newsday* review, Joseph Gelmis said that the "six-foot-six hoofer . . . does things with his feet that no one has done quite that way on the screen since 'Singin' in the Rain.'"

One year after the movie premiered, Tune got a call from Bennett, who was in Detroit to take over directing and choreographing *Seesaw*. Bennett wanted Tune to work as an associate choreographer. During the process of revamping the musical, Bennett had Tune step into a featured role. When *Seesaw* debuted in New York, Tune's work in a second act number was a showstopper. Clive Barnes, in a March 19, 1973, *New York Times* review, labeled him a "lithe, eccentric dancer and a natural performer" and described "It's Not Where You Start" as a "flamboyant affair with high steps, balloons, confetti and spangles." Tune won his first of ten Tony Awards for his performance.

After touring with *Seesaw*, Tune returned to New York, and after offering an offbeat solo cabaret show, he turned to directing and choreographing. His first outing came off-Broadway, Eve Merriam's *The Club*, a piece that examined chauvinism running amok in an all-men's establishment at the turn of the last century. It used period songs to illustrate its feminist points, and Tune's staging on a runway flanked by two pianos wowed reviewers. The *Times*' Walter Kerr described one dance performed by the all-female ensemble in male drag as a "rag tune [delivered] with such abandon that it looks as though their legs were broken and they were throwing them away." Kerr went on to lament not having more room to praise Tune's staging: "[It] is remarkable and should not be scanted."

This production set Tune on a course for another sexually charged piece of theatre off-Broadway, *The Best Little Whorehouse in Texas*. The musical was inspired by stories of a real-life brothel in Texas that had operated with the implicit support of local government for four decades, and Tune codirected the production and created its dances. Two of them received almost unanimous praise: a testosterone-fueled number for some college football players and an exuberant dance for a sexy cheerleading squad. Strong notices and audience interest after the show's April 1978 bow propelled it to a Broadway run two months later.

As indicated by his off-Broadway work, Tune wasn't necessarily interested in conventional properties, and *A Day in Hollywood/A Night in the Ukraine* (1980) was no exception. Composed of two related minituners—one a revue of songs from movies and one imagining a movie musical of a Chekhov play as performed by the Marx Brothers—the production allowed Tune to show his understanding and love for classic musical dancing (tap in particular), as well as his offbeat sense of humor.

Tune synthesized the aesthetics of these three properties for his next Broadway venture. In the musical *Nine*, there is the glamour of *Hollywood/Ukraine*, the sizzling sexiness of *Whorehouse*, and the strong-willed femininity of *Club*. Based on Federico Fellini's film *8½*, the musical unfolds in a black-and-white landscape of an Italian spa, only to burst into color as its central character, a film director having a midlife crisis, breaks through a creative block to begin a new film.

Tune was to only have starred in and choreographed his next Broadway show, *My One and Only* (1981), but ultimately codirected the production after a difficult rehearsal and tryout period. The exuberantly handsome musical, which drew its score from the Gershwins' song catalog, earned him a pair of Tonys, one for acting and one for choreography.

Following this production Tune reached the pinnacle of his creative life with two musicals in consecutive seasons, starting with *Grand Hotel*, a musical version of the 1930s novel and movie of the same name. Tune's spare, abstract direction and choreography prompted Walter Kerr to write in the December 17, 1989, edition of the *Times*, "Mr. Tune has seized upon one aspect of musicals—their permissiveness—and taken it about as far as it can go." Tune picked up Tonys for both direction and choreography for his work.

He earned the same prizes one year later for *The Will Rogers Follies*, which took the bio-tuner to new heights of abstraction, telling the life story of its titular star as if it were a lavish Florenz Ziegfeld production. The metatheatrics of the piece confounded some critics, but others, such as the *Daily News*' Howard Kissel in a May 2, 1991, review, were unapologetically bowled over by the show and Tune's work: "Glitzmeister Tune has never been more imaginative."

In 1994, Tune brought a disastrously received sequel to *Whorehouse* to Broadway and since then has contented himself primarily with performing. There have been occasional rumors (as recently as 2016 he described having meetings about future productions) of him returning to directing and choreographing on Broadway, but nothing has reached fruition.

JONATHAN TUNICK

(April 19, 1938–)
Orchestrator / Musical Director / Composer

In a career that has spanned more than six decades, Tunick has created the orchestrations for many of the landmark musicals of the late-twentieth and early-twenty-first centuries, often fusing traditional orchestral sensibilities with modern and contemporary musical ones.

"The orchestra is one of the theatre's big secrets," Tunick told Mervyn Rothstein for a September 15, 2005, Playbill.com feature, adding, "It can express . . . ambivalence, irony and conflict; feelings that, though unspoken, can be suggested subliminally by the orchestra."

Born in Manhattan, Tunick began his fascination with music while he was still in grade school, when his teacher would play records for the class. Tunick turned to playing clarinet and then attended the High School of Music and Art. During his college years at Bard, he began writing musicals and individual songs, some of which became part of Julius Monk's famed revues at the Upstairs at the Downstairs club in Manhattan.

After his graduation Tunick enrolled at Juilliard to study composition and also in Lehman Engel's workshop at Broadcast Music, Inc. (BMI). For summer work he began playing in the orchestra at Tamiment, the Poconos resort where many new musicals were workshopped. While there he also began arranging and orchestrating music, including material that was part of the revue *From A to Z*, which had, among others, Fred Ebb, Jerry Herman, and Mary Rodgers as its contributors. The piece eventually bowed on Broadway in April 1960, introducing Tunick to the Main Stem.

For the next eight years, Tunick supported himself through a variety of musical theatre–related activities and continued composing, including orchestrating one tuner, *How Do You Do, I Love You*, with music by David Shire, which closed in 1967 before reaching Broadway.

The following year, Tunick was at work on another show and it was his breakthrough as an orchestrator. *Promises, Promises*, an adaptation of the film *The Apartment*, brought pop songwriters Burt Bacharach and Hal David to Broadway. "It is something new in a genre which has been way behind the times," Tunick told Peter Hellman for a December 8, 1968, *Los Angeles Times* feature, going on to explain the innovations he was bringing to the sound of musical theatre: "We've got two electric guitars, fender bass and piano used as a melody instrument instead of for the usual harmonic fill-in business."

Less than two years later, Tunick was back on Broadway, having orchestrated *Company* and beginning what has become one of his most significant artistic partnerships in his long career, working with composer-lyricist Stephen Sondheim. For this show Tunick used singers in the pit, which he had also employed in *Promises*, helping to give the show a "mod" sound, particularly in its dance centerpiece "Tick Tock." At the same time, he wittily embellished "You Could Drive a Person Crazy," making it simultaneously reminiscent of older girl trio groups and modern ones.

The relationship with Sondheim has come to encompass the original productions of such works as *Follies* (1971), *A Little Night Music* (1973), *Pacific Overtures* (1976), *Sweeney Todd* (1979), *Into the Woods* (1987), and *Passion* (1994). In addition, Tunick has supplied revised orchestrations for many of the revivals of this songwriter's works, and in 1977 he won an Oscar for his work on the film version of *Night Music*.

The *New York Times*' Frank Rich recognized the closeness of the partnership and artistry shared by Sondheim and Tunick in an April 22, 1982, story, writing, "'Merrily [We Roll Along]' allows its author and his orchestrator, Jonathan Tunick, to comment on other songwriters while traveling through Broadway history." In this one sentence, Rich gives equal weight to both composer and orchestrator for the music that theatregoers hear. Similarly, in a feature in the summer 2013 edition from *Sondheim Review*, writer Sean Patrick Flahaven describes how Sondheim's "favorite example" of Tunick's work is the "orchestral textures in 'Buddy's Eyes' from *Follies*." Sondheim also points to Tunick's now-classic clarinet introduction to "Send in the Clowns" from *Night Music*.

Tunick's relationship with Sondheim did not mean that he was not working on other Broadway shows. During the 1970s, their most productive decade together, Tunick also orchestrated *A Chorus Line* with Billy Byers and Hershy Kay and *Ballroom*, among others. For the latter show, about middle-aged couples escaping the troubles of their late lives and looking for romance while dancing at the Stardust

Ballroom, John Beaufort noted in his December 20, 1978, *Christian Science Monitor* review, how Billy Goldenberg's score was "enhanced by Jonathan Tunick's reed-and-brass enriched orchestrations."

In the 1980s and 1990s, Tunick's diverse credits included orchestrating Maury Yeston's music for *Nine* (1981), David Shire's pop-infused songs for *Baby* (1983), Charles Strouse's lushly romantic score for *Dance a Little Closer* (1983), and even classic Rodgers and Hammerstein tunes for the revue *A Grand Night for Singing* (1993).

In 1997, Tunick won the first Tony Award for best orchestration for his contributions to the musical *Titanic*, which Michael Feingold called "elegantly perfect" in a May 6, 1997, *Village Voice* review. Since that time, Tunick has received an additional ten nominations for productions ranging from Michael John LaChiusa's epic *Marie Christine* (1999) to *LoveMusik*, a bio-tuner about Kurt Weill, to the quirky *A Gentlemen's Guide to Love and Murder* (2014) to the 2018 revival of Rodgers and Hammerstein's *Carousel*.

Tunick's Broadway activity has not meant that he has given up composing or that he has worked exclusively in the theatre. In the latter regard, one of his pieces, an opera based on the teleplay *Days of Wine and Roses* and featuring a libretto by J. P. Miller, was workshopped at the Eugene O'Neill Theater Center's National Musical Theater Conference in 1985. As an arranger he has worked with such artists as Joshua Bell, Neil Diamond, Patti LuPone, Audra McDonald, and Cleo Laine. With this last artist, he won a Grammy in 1998 for his arrangement of Sondheim's "No One Is Alone," heard on her album *Cleo Sings Sondheim*.

Tunick's exceptional artistry might be best demonstrated by the fact that he is one of a select group of artists to be an EGOT winner. In 1982, he earned an Emmy for his work on the television special *A Night of a 100 Stars*.

U

JOSEPH URBAN

(May 26, 1872–July 10, 1933)
Designer

Urban established new standards of opulence for musicals while also repeatedly demonstrating that grandeur could be cohesive, paralleling the early advances made in writing book musicals.

When this Austrian scenic designer and architect settled in the United States in 1911 at the age of thirty-nine, he arrived with an impressive résumé. He had been responsible for a new wing on the Abdin Palace in Cairo, designed the Esterhazy Castle in Hungary, created sets for more than fifty theatrical productions in Europe, and decorated the pavilions at the St. Louis Exposition. In all of these, he demonstrated a sense of grandeur and tasteful opulence, and after settling in the United States, he elevated the look of Broadway's musicals and revues to new levels.

Urban immigrated to work with the Boston Opera Company. After the group had disbanded in 1914, he moved to New York, and his first outing on Broadway was with a production of a play called *The Garden of Paradise*, a retelling of *The Little Mermaid* as a spectacle. Urban's designs overwhelmed critics, who scrambled for hyperbole. In a November 30, 1914, *New York Times* review, readers learned they could expect visuals of "exquisite beauty and unrivaled magnificence."

Given such critical endorsements, Florenz Ziegfeld Jr. engaged Urban's services. His first assignment for the impresario was the 1915 edition of the intimate *Midnight Frolic* series in January, and then that summer, Urban designed his first of many editions of Ziegfeld's *Follies*. When this show opened, critics and audiences were once again astonished by Urban's creations, which took audiences under the sea, to "Radiumland," and to a silver forest. Urban's designs carried the lushness and grandeur of the art nouveau movement, leading a *Times* critic to write on June 22, "We were in an enchanted land whenever Mr. Urban chose to wave his wand."

Two months later, Urban's work was championed in *Current Opinion* in a piece bearing the headline "Popular Triumph of the New School of Scene Painting." In it an uncredited writer compared the unity of vision that Urban brought to his designs for the *Follies* with the creation of the "box set," the realistic representation of a room within the confines of a stage: "Mr. Urban's [designs] are destined to create a new era in the popular theater of America."

Beyond their artistic relationship, Urban and Ziegfeld went into business together, jointly establishing a scenic studio that bore the designer's name. The venture meant that Ziegfeld could continue relying on this artist who was taking New York by storm, while Urban could control how his work moved from conception to reality.

In 1916, Urban provided the designs for six separate productions. There was one revue (the year's *Follies*); several book shows; and one spectacle, *Caliban of the Yellow Sands*, which Urban codesigned with Robert Edmond Jones and codirected with Richard Orynski. This last show was produced at the City College's Lewisohn Stadium in Upper Manhattan and was the culmination of a yearlong nationwide celebration of Shakespeare and his work. Written by Percy MacKaye and drawn from plays as disparate as *As You Like It* and *Troilus and Cressida*, the modern masque awed one reviewer from the *Christian Science Monitor*, who opened a May 25 review with: "It can be summed up in one word, unity."

Urban's last show for 1916 was a similar team effort—not on his part, however, but on the parts of producers Ziegfeld and Charles Dillingham and composers Victor Herbert and Irving Berlin. The result of their joint effort was *The Century Girl*, and for this combination of spectacle and vaudeville, Urban created a celestial staircase for the opening number, a setting for a submarine spectacle, and a crystal palace—the scene of a wedding—for the finale.

As the 1920s dawned, New Yorkers, thanks to the smaller, more intimate Princess Theatre musicals (most frequently written by Guy Bolton and P. G. Wodehouse with composer Jerome Kern), began to expect cohesiveness in a musical's storytelling. Ziegfeld brought these writers and the designer together for *Sally*, a sort of modern take on the Cinderella story. The production lacked some of the modesty of the Princess shows, but it clicked with critics and audiences. Heywood Broun, in his December 20 *New York Tribune* review, called it "gay, spirited and unusually decorative." Urban could make intimate sparkle vividly.

His prodigious output continued unabated after this, and he kept on moving fluidly between revues and musicals, including an early work with a score by Richard Rodgers and Lorenz Hart, *Betsy*, in 1926. A year later, Urban was back at work on a show with music by Kern. This new project featured a book and lyrics by Oscar Hammerstein II, based on an Edna Ferber novel. The show was *Show Boat*, and while the writers' work was championed as groundbreaking, so, too, were Urban's designs—"eighteen descriptive settings," as the *Times'* Brooks Atkinson called them on January 8, 1928—that swept theatregoers through the varied locales of Ferber's epic tale.

The production played Ziegfeld's eponymous theatre, which Urban had also designed. The venue on Fifty-Fourth Street opened in early 1927 with *Rio Rita*, and Urban told a reporter from the *Tribune* for a February 2 story, "There is nothing like it in the world. I have put a lifetime of experience and the mistakes of others into this building." Urban designed it along the lines of an ancient temple, doing away with sharp lines and instead using curves and arches. In fact, the auditorium was an oval, with no boxes, and it was filled with murals meant to instill in theatregoers a sense of the festiveness of any Ziegfeld show. The result was, according to Gordon M. Leland in the February 12 edition of *Billboard*, the "most perfect legitimate theater in New York."

Over the course of the next six years until his death, Urban designed an additional nineteen shows, including such productions as Kern and Hammerstein's *Music in the Air* (1932) and Sigmund Romberg and Irving Caesar's *Melody* (1933); served as architect for an additional three buildings in New York, including the International Magazine Building (now the Hearst Building); and created the lighting and color effects for the 1933 Chicago Exposition.

V

Verdon used her lithe body and equally agile sense of humor to captivate audiences in a way unmatched in her lifetime or since.

While growing up in California, this powerhouse performer, born Gwyneth Evelyn, just assumed everyone danced. "My mother had been a dancer, she taught dancing and all the children I knew danced," she told Murray Schumach for a May 31, 1953, *New York Times* feature. In fact, she herself had been dancing since she was three, and according to Rex Reed in a February 6, 1966, *Times* feature, "At the age of three, [she] entertained at a big MGM party thrown by Marion Davies. At six, she was billed as the 'fastest little tapper in the world' at the Shrine Auditorium." Her accomplishments as a child performer belied one reality: When she wasn't dancing, Verdon was wearing corrective knee-high boots because of a spate of illnesses that had left her legs weakened and deformed.

As she moved into her teens, Verdon continued dancing, and by the time she graduated high school, a career onstage or in the movies seemed inevitable. Eloping and having a child sidelined her for a brief period, but as she and her husband were separating, she joined Jack Cole's nightclub dance troupe. It was Cole who labored to bring Verdon to Broadway. He cast her in the chorus of *Bonanza Bound*, a Betty Comden–Adolph Green–Saul Chaplin musical that closed out of town in 1947. Verdon served as his assistant on the short-lived *Magdalena* a year later, and as a performer, she finally debuted on Broadway in 1950 in the revue *Alive and Kicking*.

After this Verdon returned to the West Coast, dancing in several pictures. During this period she met choreographer Michael Kidd, who was creating dances for the film version of the musical *Where's Charley?* When Kidd returned to New York to begin work on the musical *Can-Can*, he encouraged Verdon to audition, and though she had to convince composer Cole Porter of her vocal abilities, she won her place in the show.

Her casting turned into the breakthrough opportunity that most performers only dream about. Kidd choreographed an Apache dance for her. On opening night Verdon's performance literally stopped the show, and she had to be called back from her dressing room, where she had gone for a costume change. She ended up taking bows in her bathrobe. The next morning, in the May 8, 1953, edition of the *New York Herald Tribune,* Walter Kerr lauded her as the "dance discovery of the season." For her work in *Can-Can,* Verdon won both a Tony Award and a Theatre World Award, recognizing an exceptional debut performance.

Two years later, Verdon was back on Broadway playing Lola, the devil's seductive henchwoman, in *Damn Yankees.* Her work in this show, directed by George Abbott, again earned raves. In his May 6, 1955, review for the *Times,* Brooks Atkinson called her the "most alluring she-witch ever bred in the nether regions," describing her as "sleek as a car on the showroom floor, and as nice to look at." Verdon brought, he also wrote, "brilliance and sparkle to the evening with her exuberant dancing," and she won a second Tony for the show.

Bob Fosse had created her dances, and *Damn Yankees* marked the beginning of their complex personal and artistic relationship. They married in 1960 and shared an intimate artistic partnership until his death in 1987.

Verdon earned Tonys three and four with her next two Broadway outings. First came *New Girl in Town,* a musicalization of Eugene O'Neill's Pulitzer Prize–winning drama *Anna Christie.* An unlikely source for a musical (the play centers on a prostitute reuniting with her estranged father and his disapproval of her newfound romance with a sailor), the musical reunited Verdon with Fosse and Abbott. And while critics were not entirely convinced by the production overall, Verdon again scored with them. Her performance, Atkinson wrote in the *Times* on May 15, 1957, "would be an affecting job on any stage."

Fosse both directed and choreographed the musical that followed, *Redhead,* a murder mystery set in a wax museum in England. For her work in it, Verdon received more critical love notes, including one from *Variety.* In the February 11, 1959, edition of the paper, reviewer "Hobe." enthused, "In the painstakingly tailored 'Redhead' she enters the tiny circle of 'greats,'" who included Ethel Merman and Gertrude Lawrence.

It took a while for Verdon to return to Broadway, but when she did, it was in a show that Fosse created just for her: *Sweet Charity.* Adapted from Federico Fellini's *The Nights of Cabiria,* the musical about a dance hall hostess's bittersweet romances had its Broadway bow on January 30, 1966, and the next day, *Newsday*'s George Oppenheimer wrote, "I now realize what has been wrong with the theater these past few years. Gwen Verdon has been away from it."

Verdon was already forty-one when *Charity* premiered and had faced some physical issues, leading her to announce that she would not undertake another musical after it. But in the early 1970s, Fosse secured the rights to a property he had long wanted to adapt for her: Maurine Dallas Watkins's exploration of a woman on trial for murder in the 1920s, *Chicago.* Working with composer John Kander and lyricist and co–book writer Fred Ebb, Fosse created another showcase for his spouse-muse, and on June 3, 1975, the musical version of the play bowed. For some critics the satiric treatment of the justice system and its relationship (and/or similarity) to show business was too heavy or dark, but they could all agree that Verdon, along with costars Chita Rivera and Jerry Orbach, was in top form.

After this Verdon collaborated with Fosse as he created *Dancin'* in 1978 and served as his assistant on the 1986 revival of *Sweet Charity*. In the 1980s and 1990s, too, she found a new array of roles available to her on television and film. One of her most notable performances during this period was in 1985's *Cocoon*, a light-hearted look at aging. Her last work on Broadway came in the late 1990s as she served as artistic advisor on *Fosse*, a compendium of his dances.

W

ROBIN WAGNER

(August 31, 1933–)
Scenic Designer

Wagner's fusion of opulence, sly humor, and minimalism with advances in technology have helped to create some of the most memorable settings and visual encounters audiences have experienced in the theatre in the past forty years.

Frank Rich, in his December 21, 1981, *New York Times* review of *Dreamgirls*, commended Wagner's work, saying, "Like the show's voices, the set pieces . . . keep coming together and falling apart to create explosive variations on a theme." In this Michael Bennett–staged piece, the designer deployed metallic towers and bridges to assist the director-choreographer in creating, as Rich described them, "his special brand of cinematic stage effects." Wagner's work on this production was emblematic of how his artistry always supports both writers' and directors' visions while also pushing technology to serve his and their needs. As Wagner himself commented about *Dreamgirls* in an October 14, 1983, *Back Stage* feature, "We had to do a lot of things that hadn't been done before, using existing technology but stretching it in different directions."

Technology for scenic design, at least in the way Wagner used the word in the early 1980s, was virtually nonexistent when he entered the field in the 1950s. He started his career in his native San Francisco, and by 1958 he was working in New York designing a highly praised revival of Samuel Beckett's *Waiting for Godot*.

For the next ten years, and much like his forebears Boris Aronson and Jo Mielziner, Wagner gained experience by both working with established designers, such as Oliver Smith, and by designing on his own. Between 1958 and 1966, he designed more than two dozen shows in New York and beyond. Some were experimental; others (an *Annie Get Your Gun* in Pittsburgh that starred Ginger Rogers) were high-profile, commercial ventures; and still others, including many at Arena Stage in Washington, DC, were bold takes on classic works.

Wagner got his first full design credit on Broadway in 1966 with Jean-Paul Sartre's *The Condemned of Altona*, one of the earliest offerings at the newly opened Lincoln Center Theater. Two more plays followed, and then in 1968, he designed his first musical on the Main Stem, *Hair*. Most reviews centered on Galt MacDermot's rock score and the full-frontal nude scene, but Wagner's aesthetic, which could be both downtown minimal and uptown chic, wasn't ignored. In his April 30 *New York Times* review, Clive Barnes commended Wagner on a "beautiful junk-art setting." Eight months later, a second tuner boasting Wagner's designs opened. *Promises, Promises* was another show with a pop score (from Burt Bacharach and Hal David), and Wagner's work on it got some equally enthusiastic notices. It also established his theatrical relationship with Bennett.

In the first years of the 1970s, Wagner jetted back and forth between two period pieces set in the 1920s, *Gantry* (1970) and *Sugar* (1972), and two more-contemporary shows with rock scores, including Andrew Lloyd Webber and Tim Rice's *Jesus Christ Superstar* in 1971. Directed by Tom O'Horgan, who had also staged *Hair*, *Superstar* allowed Wagner to deploy some dazzling scenic effects, notably a butterfly large enough to hold four backup singers in sequined dresses that floated above the action, as Ben Vereen delivered the musical's climactic title song. The production earned Wagner his first Tony Award nomination.

In 1973, he reunited with Ed Sherin, a director with whom he frequently collaborated at Arena, for *Seesaw*, a musical version of the two-character play *Two for the Seesaw*. For this piece set in then-present-day New York, Wagner deployed a series of scrims as surfaces for lighting and projection designer Jules Fisher's still imagery of the city. During troubled out-of-town tryouts, Bennett replaced Sherin, and together Bennett and Wagner reconceived the way the gauze strips and panels were used. They set them in motion with the action, and in his March 19 *New York Times* review, Barnes championed their use, noting that "American musical theater has long neglected projection techniques. . . . [Wagner] makes a determined effort to catch up."

The designer shifted once again to the past for Jerry Herman's *Mack & Mabel* (1974), set during the silent film era, and then to the present with spare settings for Bennett's *A Chorus Line* (1975). Three years later, Wagner won his first Tony Award for *On the Twentieth Century*, for which he re-created the art deco splendor of the luxury train that whisked riders between Chicago and New York in the first half of the last century. In this production, too, Wagner experimented with giving theatregoers a cinema-like experience, providing them with exterior "shots" of the train and long "pans" of it as it sped through the night.

With Bennett, Wagner achieved other feats of theatrical cinematography in *Ballroom* in 1978 and *Dreamgirls* in 1981. For the latter, Wagner's elegant minimalism combined with technology won him his second Tony. Between these two Bennett collaborations was another musical, *42nd Street*, which was anything but minimal. Based on the Busby Berkeley movie of the same name, it afforded Wagner the opportunity to re-create some of the fantastic images associated with that director's films.

By the end of the 1980s, new technologies allowed Wagner to stretch further than he had previously, and in *City of Angels*, he used them to replicate the alluring menace and filmic techniques of 1940s film noir. In his December 12, 1989, *New York Times* review, Rich described how the production provided audiences with the experience of "swirling flashbacks, portentous tracking shots, and swift dissolves of movies."

In 1992, Wagner established a relationship with choreographer Susan Stroman as she created the dances for *Crazy for You*, directed by Mike Ockrent (who became her husband in 1996). With this and two Mel Brooks tuners that Stroman both directed and choreographed, Wagner had the chance to display his flair for lightheartedness. In his *Daily News* review on April 20, 2001, Howard Kissel remarked on the designer's use of mirrors in *The Producers*, set in Nazi-era Germany. He used them, Kissel wrote, "partly to parody the original 'Cabaret,'" adding that the touch "is unusually brilliant."

Wagner's output has slowed as he has moved through his seventies and into his eighties, and yet he has continued to work sporadically. Among his most recent designs have been a revival of *Dreamgirls* in 2009, in which he dramatically reconceived his original vision, and *Leap of Faith* on Broadway in 2012.

ETHEL WATERS

(October 31, 1896–September 1, 1977)
Performer

A performer who could shift easily from musicals to plays, Waters both broke racial barriers in the theatre and established herself as a preeminent interpreter of songs, regardless of their style or subject matter.

In 1921, and well before her Broadway debut, this singer-actress who broke down racial barriers both on Broadway and in the music business was making a name for herself around the country, performing with the band the Black Swan Troubadours. She was also being promoted as the "world's greatest blues singer" in relation to a new set of recordings that she was releasing on a label that also bore the Black Swan name. And as she made an appearance at the Regent Theatre in Baltimore, an uncredited reviewer for the city's *Afro-American* wrote in the paper's December 2, 1921, edition, "Her voice is of mezzo quality with that mournful sweetness that is regarded as characteristic of the Southern Negro—although she is a native of Philadelphia." As for her delivery, the writer lauded her as a "fine actress" who "knows how much to put in and how much to leave out of her interpretations" of songs.

Waters grew up in a suburb of Philadelphia, raised by her grandmother, who was a cleaning woman and would leave her granddaughter to play in the kitchens of the homes where she was working. At fourteen Waters started work doing laundry and ironing and later became a chambermaid at a Philadelphia hotel. As for school, she told a *Philadelphia Inquirer* reporter for a January 10, 1933, feature, "I went through Swarthmore College—in two weeks, cleaning."

Waters's interest in and gift for performing became evident when she was a teenager. She would frequently attend movies and vaudeville shows and found she could imitate the performers she saw. After she sang in an amateur talent contest at a blacks-only club in Philadelphia, she got a job performing there, and it was from these beginnings that Waters began to establish both herself and the Black Swan name. As her recording career continued in the last years of the 1920s, she broke ground by becoming one of the first African American vocalists to be accompanied by an all-white band. Among her sidemen were the Dorsey Brothers, Benny Goodman, and Gene Krupa.

Broadway audiences eventually got the chance to see Waters in 1927 when the revue *Africana* arrived at Daly's Theater, where Eubie Blake and Noble Sissle's *Shuffle Along* had once played. Waters was the show's headliner, thanks to her success as a recording artist, and on July 12, New York critics were anxious to tout her talents. "She is expert in the effortless retailing of a slightly 'blue' song; she has personality and a natural comedy sense," was the assessment of an uncredited *New York Times* critic, who went on to compare her to Charlotte Greenwood. In the *Brooklyn Eagle*, critic Martin Dickstein compared Waters to Gertrude Lawrence.

Waters clearly was a Broadway star in the making, and after *Africana* she was a staple on the New York stage for ten years. Her next Broadway outing was *Lew Leslie's Blackbirds* in 1930, and in it she introduced Blake and Andy Razaf's "My Handy Man" and "You're Lucky to Me." The following year, in *Rhapsody in Black*, Waters's material included "Where's My Prince Charming?" and "Dance Hall Hostess." In each she received excellent notices for her renditions of both comic and more serious material, but critics were underwhelmed by the productions.

She found more success two years later with Irving Berlin and Moss Hart's innovative revue *As Thousands Cheer*. In the show, whose songs and sketches each correspond to a section of a newspaper, Waters, in her first foray into a production that did not feature an all-black cast, had the chance to display the full breadth of her talent from comedy to drama and beyond. Among her numbers were the sultry "Heat Wave" and the pungent "Supper Time," in which she played a woman lamenting her husband's lynching. Writing about the show on October 15, 1933, Brooks Atkinson remarked, "[Her] magnetism can charge a whole theater with excitement." Similar reactions came in 1935 when she appeared in the Arthur Schwartz and Howard Dietz revue *At Home Abroad*, where she received equal billing with Beatrice Lillie.

Waters shifted to nonmusical work for her next Broadway appearance, DuBose and Dorothy Heyward's *Mamba's Daughters* (1939), and then she tackled her first book musical, playing a pious woman attempting to save her husband's soul in *Cabin in the Sky*. Atkinson, in his November 3, 1940, *Times* review, wrote that Waters delivered "with force and frankness that are completely overwhelming," adding, "Miss Waters is a thorough actress."

She reprised her performance in the film version of the musical in 1943, but the movie did not mark her first foray on screen. She made several shorts in the 1930s and, just before filming *Cabin*, appeared in *Cairo* with Jeanette MacDonald and Robert Young.

In the mid-1940s, Waters graced a pair of short-lived revues, and then in 1950, with Carson McCullers's *The Member of the Wedding*, she reached new heights artistically, playing a Southern maid who acts as a sort of surrogate parent to a preteen girl whose mother died in childbirth. It was a performance, John Chapman wrote in the *Daily News* on January 7, 1950, "that is loving and lovable and profoundly expert." Waters was nominated for an Academy Award when she revisited the role in the 1952 movie.

For the remainder of the 1950s, her career consisted primarily of movie and television work, and she returned to Broadway only once after *Wedding*: for 1959's *An Evening with Ethel Waters*. During this same period, she began performing with Reverend Billy Graham's evangelistic meetings, and in the 1960s and 1970s her work with his ministry and "crusades" became the focus of her life.

Waters died in 1977, and Leonard Feather, in a *Los Angeles Times* September 3 tribute, noted that she was a woman "who broke down racial barriers and defied musical pigeonholing," adding, "She was a singer-actress in the best sense of the word."

KURT WEILL

(March 2, 1900–April 3, 1950)
Composer

Weill composed the experimental Threepenny Opera, *which has become a modern classic, and went on to demonstrate that musical theatre with classical underpinnings could have popular appeal both onstage and on record.*

This German-born composer was writing music at an early age thanks to the encouragement of his father, a cantor in Dessau, Germany, and by the time Weill was sixteen, he was in Berlin studying with composer Engelbert Humperdinck, best known for his opera *Hänsel und Gretel.*

With his classical training, Weill became conductor of the opera in Lüdenschied, a small city in the west of Germany, but eventually he returned to Berlin. There he began composing symphonies, chamber music, ballet, and operas that combined his classical training with then-contemporary jazz sensibilities. The libretti for his first works were by some of Germany's most prominent dramatists, including Georg Kaiser, Ivan Goll, and Bertolt Brecht. It was with this last writer that Weill penned the critically and popularly acclaimed *Die Dreigroschenoper* (*The Threepenny Opera*) in 1928. This updated revision to John Gay's *The Beggar's Opera* ran more than two thousand performances in Berlin and received its Broadway premiere in 1933. When it did, a *New York Times* critic—identified with the initials L. N.—commended its "splendid" score, calling it "interesting, pleasant and quite in the air of early day sinners of London."

That same year, Weill and his former wife, actress Lotte Lenya, separately fled Germany, reuniting in Paris and then moving to London. They came to the United States in 1935 and quietly remarried, and he began to work with director Max Reinhardt and designer Norman Bel Geddes on the musical spectacle *The Eternal Road*, which did not reach the stage until 1937. In the interim Weill crafted a score for the Group Theatre for *Johnny Johnson*. With a libretto by Paul Green, the musical took an unflinching look at a soldier's existence during World War I. And in a November 20 *New York Herald Tribune* review, Richard Watts Jr. described Weill as "that brilliant German exile" and praised the production as being a "disturbing and often hilarious medley" of styles. As for Weill's music, Stirling Bowen, in a November 23, 1936, *Wall Street Journal* review, wrote that it "entertains and elucidates" what the critic deemed to be a "stage work of affecting beauty."

Two years later, Weill and Maxwell Anderson's *Knickerbocker Holiday*, a satirical look at the Dutch government of old New York, debuted. With a richly diverse score that contained a number that would become part of the American songbook, "September Song," the show and Weill garnered admiring notices. In his October 20, 1938, *Times* review, Brooks Atkinson said, "There is no style that he cannot assimilate or compose," adding, "This is serious composing for the modern theatre, superior to Broadway songwriting without settling in the academic groove."

Lady in the Dark (1941) paired Weill with book writer Moss Hart and lyricist Ira Gershwin, and together they penned a piece that focused on a fashion magazine editor and psychoanalysis of her dreams. When the show opened, it garnered raves for its star, Gertrude Lawrence; its physical production (overseen by both Hart and Hassard Short); and for Weill, who also found another of his songs, "My Ship," becoming a hit outside of the show.

Weill's next Broadway outing, *One Touch of Venus* (1943), had a book by S. J. Perelman and lyrics by Ogden Nash, starred Mary Martin, and imagined the titular goddess coming to Earth and falling in love herself. Weill's assimilation as a Broadway theatre composer led to this being considered one of his most accessible scores. In an October 13, 1943, *Variety* review, critic "Abel." cataloged the score: "'Speak Low' is unquestionably the boff ballad and will be Weill's most durable ditty. But that sturdy songsmith has also produced 'That's Him' (Miss Martin's personal socko solo) . . . and 'Wooden Wedding.'" With this latter number, Abel. prophesied that it "will last long after Petrillo signs on the dotted jukebox for all the diskers."

Weill returned to a more classical tradition with his next outing, a wanly received operetta, *The Firebrand of Florence* (1945), and after penning incidental music for a play the following year, he brought another three distinct and ambitious works to the stage. The first was a musicalization of Elmer Rice's *Street Scene*. A portrait of life among a group of people living in a New York tenement over the course of less than twenty-four hours, the piece had lyrics by Langston Hughes, and Weill said, in a January 5, 1947, *Times* feature, that it contained the "music of a summer evening in New York." His score combined beautifully with Rice's book and Hughes's lyrics, and it was a "musical play of magnificence and glory," as Atkinson put it in his January 10 *Times* review.

The composer joined forces with a new collaborator, book writer and lyricist Alan Jay Lerner, for his next project, *Love Life*. In this the men conspired to create a "vaudeville" that, as they described it for an October 3, 1948, *New York Times* feature, "tells the saga of 150 years of American home life [and] also the love life of two people." In the process they created one of the earliest examples of what would be considered a "concept musical," and when the show (which foreshadows, on some levels, later groundbreaking musicals such as *Cabaret*, *Company*, and

Follies) opened, critics were mixed, some hailing it for its innovations and others finding its loose, fragmentary structure and dark tone unsatisfying.

The composer reteamed with Maxwell Anderson for the 1949 musical *Lost in the Stars*, an adaptation of Alan Paton's novel about life in South Africa. The book proved to be a stumbling block for this tuner, but critics generally agreed that Weill had triumphed. Atkinson said, "It is difficult to remember anything out of his portfolio as eloquent as this richly orchestrated singing music."

Weill passed away before *Lost in the Stars* had concluded its run on July 1, 1950, but it wasn't his last Broadway premiere. Of course, there was an acclaimed, long-running production of *The Threepenny Opera* off-Broadway that opened in the mid-1950s, and thanks to Marc Blitzstein's translation it paved the way for one more Weill song hit, "Mack the Knife." In 1977, however, after revivals of *Johnny Johnson* and *Lost in the Stars*, one of his earliest pieces—*Happy End*, written with Bertolt Brecht and Elisabeth Hauptmann in 1929—finally bowed on Broadway in a production directed by Robert Kalfin, choreographed by Patricia Birch, and starring a young Meryl Streep.

BERT WILLIAMS

(November 12, 1874–March 4, 1922)
Performer

A performer whose legacy is sometimes overshadowed by his use of blackface in his routines was a groundbreaking force in integrating musical theatre.

The January 1918 issue of *American Magazine* featured an article titled "The Comic Side of Trouble" that had been written by this African American performer, who was then at the height of his career. In it Williams mused, "Nearly all of my successful songs are based on the idea that I am getting the worst of it. I am the Jonah Man, the man who, even if it rained soup, would be found with a fork in his hand."

The idea of laughing at one's own misfortunes was not so much autobiographical as it was shrewd social commentary from this performer who was born William Egbert Austin in the Bahamas and raised in America, first in Florida and then in California. While he was still a teenager attending Riverside High School there, Williams began performing in a variety of local minstrel shows. In one he met another performer, George Walker.

The two men became a team and developed an act they offered in blackface, mimicking the Caucasian performers' practice in minstrel shows and making it palatable for white audiences to see African American men on stage. In their routines the duo played standard vaudeville archetypes. Williams was a slick, wily man, and Walker was his slower—or, to use the unfortunate phrase of the day, "dumb coon"—friend. When they reversed the roles for one performance, they found audiences responding more enthusiastically to their sketches and songs. Thus, the die was cast for Williams's stage persona. He would perpetually be something of a sad sack who had to face the woes of the world head on.

As the nineteenth century turned into the twentieth, the team appeared in a pair of all-black shows that played at major Manhattan venues. The first, which they penned themselves, was *The Policy Players* in 1899. For this Walker devised the loosest of plots, about a couple of black men who attempt to enter the upper reaches of society. Critics were mixed about the merits of the show, but all agreed Williams's work was its biggest asset and that its best song was "The Man in the Moon Might Tell," which one critic likened to a song from Victor Herbert's recent musical breakthrough, *The Wizard of the Nile*.

After touring with *Policy*, Williams and Walker returned to New York for *Sons of Ham* in 1900. This production featured their original songs but had a book by Jesse A. Shipp (who had directed *Policy* and was once again staging) and Stephen B. Cassin. Critics, overall, felt that *Sons* was the superior of the two shows, and after its limited engagement the company left to tour. An outbreak of smallpox in the company, however, forced the show's closing just a month after the tour had launched.

In 1903, Williams and Walker were working once again with Shipp, who had assembled an all-black book musical called *In Dahomey*. They played a couple of detectives, Shylock Holmes and Rareback Pinkerton, searching for a lost casket, and the investigation took them from Boston to Florida to Africa, where they were made governors who rule in a "most hilarious style," as press materials promised.

When critics reviewed the show on February 19, they didn't spend much time talking about the plot. Instead, they focused on Williams and Walker, who were often favorably compared to the beloved team of Weber and Fields. With Williams they focused on his delivery of one song in particular: "The Jonah Man," which "convulsed the audience with every repeated stanza," as the uncredited *New York Times* critic reported.

Williams and Walker took *In Dahomey* on a national tour and later to England. During the company's engagement there, they played Buckingham Palace in a command performance for King Edward VII. Afterward, Williams told a wire service reporter, "It was the proudest moment of my life, to appear before my sovereign, for I am British-born, hailing from the Bahamas."

After appearing in two more musicals together, *Abyssinia* in 1907 and *Bandanna Land* in 1909, the team split up, and Williams, after one foray in a musical on his own, landed a place in the 1910 edition of Florenz Ziegfeld Jr.'s popular *Follies*.

Ziegfeld putting Williams into his lineup of entertainers was a bold move. It marked a first step in the integration of Broadway productions, and when cast members balked at the idea of performing in the same show as a black man, Ziegfeld reportedly told them they could leave. They were all replaceable. Williams, however, was not.

Williams scored with audiences and critics. The *Times* review on June 21, 1910, informed readers that "there is no more clever low comedian on our stage to-day than Bert Williams, and few, indeed, who deserve to be considered in his class." In terms of his material, the uncredited critic singled out "Constantly," a number in which Williams sang about his perpetual bad luck.

Williams's finest review, however, might have come from Booker T. Washington, who wrote in that September's issue of *American Magazine* that the performer's work contained humor "that [indicates] that it is the natural expression of a thoughtful and observing mind." Further, Washington wrote, "[He] is a tremendous asset of the Negro race."

An unprecedented—for an African American—contract with Columbia Records ensued, and as Williams continued in the *Follies,* he also continued to make historic strides. In 1911, he began performing with a white actor, Leon Errol, and the following year he was onstage with the Caucasian Ziegfeld girls.

Williams's last performance in the *Follies* came in 1920. In late 1921, he accepted a role in the new musical *Under the Bamboo Tree.* During out-of-town tryouts in early 1922, Williams collapsed onstage, withdrew from the show, and returned to New York. He died on March 4, 1922, at his home. Two days later, an author identified as P. H. in the *Times* paid tribute to Williams's artistry, also noting, "There he was, unquestionably, once a comic artist of first rank, doomed for the rest of his career to the environment of jigs and jokes, with the doors of advancement closed against him."

Z

FLORENZ ZIEGFELD JR.

(March 21, 1867–July 22, 1932)
Producer

This producer introduced a new level of lavishness to musical production and in the process helped to foster the careers of a host of performers while also developing the integrated book musical.

It's been nearly one hundred years since one of this man's eponymous *Follies* revues were seen on Broadway, but even today mention the name Ziegfeld and images of wildly extravagant stage shows come to mind. Nevertheless, these productions were much more than just opulent song-and-dance celebrations. They were showcases for a generation of new musical theatre talent. Such songwriters as Irving Berlin, Jerome Kern, Richard Rodgers, and Lorenz Hart all had songs in the *Follies* early in their careers, and the shows set a generation of performers on the path to stardom, including Fanny Brice, Eddie Cantor, W. C. Fields, and Will Rogers. As if his accomplishments with the revue were not sufficient, Ziegfeld's producing practices also played a role in the development of the classic book musical.

Ziegfeld was born in Chicago to German immigrant parents. His father, Florenz Sr., had been trained in music and was the founder of several influential music conservatories in the rapidly growing midwestern city. Florenz Sr. wasn't just a teacher, he was also a raconteur of sorts and central in bringing influential European musicians to the United States. It was the elder man's teaching and work in this latter regard that inspired his son.

Ziegfeld Jr.'s first efforts in producing coincided with the World's Columbia Exposition in 1893. His primary offering was a presentation of a strongman, the Great Sandow. The neophyte impresario transformed him into a celebrity once he began inviting the city's elite backstage to touch the he-man's muscles.

Three years later, Ziegfeld was in New York and produced his first show, a revival of an entertainment with music called *A Parlor Match*. It wasn't the most auspicious of debuts for him on the East Coast, but over the course of the next four years, Ziegfeld, working with varying producing partners, brought another six productions—four plays and two musicals—to the stage.

As the twentieth century dawned, Ziegfeld turned exclusively to musicals, and in 1904 he scored one of his biggest early successes, joining forces with Joseph M. Weber (half of the vaudeville team Weber and Fields) on *Higgeldy-Piggeldy*, a revue that featured Weber along with Ziegfeld's actress-singer wife, Anna Held. The show was an instant hit, and the following year, a second edition of what was described as a "brilliant musical extravaganza" in the January 28, 1905, edition of *Billboard* opened.

Ziegfeld's penchant for beauty onstage made headlines with *A Parisian Model* (1906) because of the cost of star Held's gowns, and he glamorized not just one actress but a bevy of them in *The Follies of 1907*. The show had been scheduled as a summertime entertainment offered in a rooftop "garden," but it extended well into the fall after transferring to indoor quarters.

It was the first in what became an annual series, which he complemented with other lavish revues and also extravaganzas. The latter contained, ostensibly, more of a sense of narrative. An early example of this kind of show was *Over the River* in 1912. It was based on a popular farce, *The Man from Mexico*, about a man who tries to elude imprisonment just over the border. Eddie Foy starred, and while the plot remained, there were also specialty acts inserted throughout. An uncredited *New York Times* critic informed readers on January 1, 1912, that the "result is rather puzzling."

It wasn't long after this that more-integrated book musicals began appearing, principally at the Princess Theatre as written by Jerome Kern, Guy Bolton, and P. G. Wodehouse, and in 1920, Ziegfeld recruited these men to write one for him. The result was *Sally*, a show that had the cohesiveness of their other works and the grandeur of a Ziegfeld production. Alexander Woollcott reviewed *Sally* for the *Times*, and after praising all of the creators, he told readers, "As you rush to the subway at ten minutes to midnight[,] you think of Mr. Ziegfeld. He is that kind of producer. There are not many of them in the world." The show became one of Ziegfeld's biggest successes, running an exceptional (for the period) 561 performances.

Other musicals followed, including *Kid Boots* (1924), starring Cantor; *Louie the 14th* (1925), with music by Sigmund Romberg; and *Betsy* (1926), with music and lyrics by Rodgers and Hart. Then in 1927, he opened the brand-new Ziegfeld Theatre, which he had specially built for his epic productions, with *Rio Rita*, another musical set in Mexico. In his February 3 *New York Herald Tribune* review, Percy Hammond dutifully related the show's story line but only after noting, "Of course you are not interested in the plot of a musical comedy." More important were the visuals, and Hammond assured readers that Ziegfeld had pulled from "his magic looms and color-pots, all of the eye-thrills known to extravaganza."

Ziegfeld had to move this production to another theatre to make way for his next, and once again, it was a show that was "another of those big Ziegfeld successes," as a critic for the *New York Evening Post* observed. But *Show Boat* was also something more. In this musical play based on Edna Ferber's novel, Oscar Hammerstein II had written a cohesive musical book that did not shy away from seriousness, and in the sprawling tale, Ziegfeld had a piece onto which he could lavish his usual attention. The *Times'* critic reminded readers that the show had been heralded from its out-of-town tryouts as "Ziegfeld's superlative achievement," and then added, "It would be difficult to quarrel with such tidings."

The producer slowed his production of *Follies* offerings after this, presenting editions only in 1929 and 1931. At the same time, he increased his producing of book musicals, despite financial hardships brought on by both the Depression and his extravagance. Before his death in 1932, he brought to the stage, among others, such shows as *Rosalie* and *Whoopee!* in 1928 and George and Ira Gershwin's *Show Girl* and Noël Coward's *Bitter Sweet* in 1929.

After Ziegfeld's death, a July 24, 1932, *New York Times* tribute summed up his work and career: "The one quality which Mr. Ziegfeld had above all others was taste—instinctive and unfailing taste."

Bibliography

HISTORY AND GENERAL BACKGROUND

Atkinson, Brooks. *Broadway*. New York: Macmillan, 1970.

Bloom, Ken. *Show and Tell: A New Book of Broadway Anecdotes*. New York: Oxford University Press, 2016.

Bloom, Ken, and Frank Vlastnik. *Broadway Musicals: The 101 Greatest Shows of All Time*. New York: Black Dog and Leventhal, 2010.

Engel, Lehman. *The American Musical Theater: A Consideration*, rev. ed. New York: Macmillan, 1975.

Green, Stanley, revised and updated by Cary Ginell. *Broadway Musicals Show by Show*, 8th ed. New York: Applause Theatre and Cinema Books, 2014.

Guernsey, Otis L., Jr. *Broadway Song and Story: Playwrights, Lyricists, Composers Discuss Their Hits*. New York: Dodd, Mead, 1985.

Hischak, Thomas S. *Word Crazy: Broadway Lyricists from Cohan to Sondheim*. New York: Praeger, 1991.

Kantor, Michael, and Laurence Maslon. *Broadway: The American Musical*. New York: Bullfinch Press, 2004.

Kasha, Al, and Joel Hirschhorn. *Notes on Broadway: Conversations with the Great Songwriters*. Chicago: Contemporary Books, 1985.

Suskin, Steven. *Show Tunes: The Songs, Shows, and Careers of Broadway's Major Composers*, 3rd ed. New York: Oxford University Press, 2000.

Viagas, Robert. *The Alchemy of Theatre, the Divine Science: Essays on Theatre and the Art of Collaboration*. New York: Playbill Books, 2006.

———. *I'm the Greatest Star: Broadway's Top Musical Legends from 1900 to Today*. New York: Applause Theatre and Cinema Books, 2009.

Wilk, Max. *They're Playing Our Song*. New York: Atheneum, 1973.

BIOGRAPHIES AND MEMOIRS

Abbott, George. *"Mister Abbott."* New York: Random House, 1963.

Aldrich, Richard Stoddard. *Gertrude Lawrence as Mrs. A: An Intimate Biography of the Great Star by Her Husband*. New York: Greystone Press, 1954.

Bach, Steven. *Dazzler: The Life and Times of Moss Hart*. New York: Alfred A. Knopf, 2001.

Bergreen, Laurence. *As Thousands Cheer: The Life of Irving Berlin*. New York: Penguin Books, 1991.

Bordman, Gerald. *Jerome Kern: His Life and Music*. New York: Oxford University Press, 1986.

Brown, Jared. *Zero Mostel: A Biography*. New York: Atheneum, 1980.

Burton, Humphrey. *Leonard Bernstein*. New York: Anchor Books Doubleday, 1994.

Channing, Carol. *Just Lucky I Guess: A Memoir of Sorts*. New York: Simon & Schuster, 2002.

Davis, Lee. *Bolton and Wodehouse and Kern: The Men Who Made Musical Comedy*. New York: James H. Heineman, 1993.

Davis, Ronald L. *Mary Martin, Broadway Legend*. Norman: University of Oklahoma Press, 2008.

De Giere, Carol. *Defying Gravity: The Creative Career of Stephen Schwartz from* Godspell *to* Wicked. New York: Applause Theatre and Cinema Books, 2008.

De Mille, Agnes. *And Promenade Home*. London: Virgin, 1989.

———. *Dance to the Piper*. Boston: Little, Brown, 1952.

Dietz, Howard. *Dancing in the Dark: An Autobiography*. New York: Quandrangle/New York Times Book Co., 1974.

Engel, Lehman. *This Bright Day: An Autobiography*. New York: Macmillan, 1974.

Epstein, Helen. *Joe Papp: An American Life*. Boston: Little, Brown, 1994.

Everett, William A. *Sigmund Romberg*. New Haven, CT: Yale University Press, 2007.

Ferencz, George J. *"The Broadway Sound": The Autobiography and Selected Essays of Robert Russell Bennett*. Rochester, NY: University of Rochester Press, 2007.

Feuer, Cy, with Ken Gross. *I Got the Show Right Here: The Amazing True Story of How an Obscure Brooklyn Horn Player Became the Last Great Broadway Producer*. New York: Applause Theatre and Cinema Books, 2003.

Flinn, Caryl. *Brass Diva: The Life and Legends of Ethel Merman*. Berkeley: University of California Press, 2007.

Forbes, Camille F. *Introducing Bert Williams: Burnt Cork, Broadway and the Story of America's First Black Star*. New York: Basic Civitas, 2008.

Fordin, Hugh. *Getting to Know Him: A Biography of Oscar Hammerstein II*. New York: Ungar, 1977.

Furia, Philip. *Ira Gershwin: The Art of the Lyricist*. New York: Oxford University Press, 1996.

Gilvey, John Anthony. *Before the Parade Passes By: Gower Champion and the Glorious American Musical*. New York: St. Martin's Press, 2005.

Goldstein, Malcolm. *George S. Kaufman: His Life, His Theater*. New York: Oxford University Press, 1979.

Gould, Neil. *Victor Herbert: A Theatrical Life*. New York: Fordham University Press, 2008.

Greenspan, Charlotte. *Pick Yourself Up: Dorothy Fields and the American Musical*. New York: Oxford University Press, 2010.

Hammerstein, Oscar Andrew. *The Hammersteins: A Musical Theatre Family*. New York: Black Dog and Leventhal, 2010.

Harris, Andrew B. *The Performing Set: The Broadway Designs of William and Jean Eckart*. Denton: University of North Texas Press, 2006.

Hart, Moss. *Act One: An Autobiography*. New York: Random House, 1959.

Henderson, Mary C. *Mielziner: Master of Modern Stage Design*. New York: Backstage Books, 2001.

Hirsch, Foster. *Kurt Weill on Stage: From Berlin to Broadway*. New York: Alfred A. Knopf, 2002.

Kahn, E. J., Jr. *The Merry Partners: The Age and Stage of Harrigan and Hart*. New York: Random House, 1955.

Kander, John, and Fred Ebb, as told to Greg Lawrence. *Colored Lights: Forty Years of Words and Music, Show Biz, Collaboration, and All That Jazz*. New York: Faber & Faber, 2003.

Kelly, Kevin. *One Singular Sensation: The Michael Bennett Story*. New York: Zebra Books, 1991.

Kimball, Robert, and William Bolcom. *Reminiscing with Sissle and Blake*. New York: Viking Press, 1973.

Kissel, Howard. *David Merrick: The Abominable Showman*. New York: Applause Books, 1993.

Lambert, Philip. *To Broadway, to Life: The Musical Theater of Bock and Harnick*. New York: Oxford University Press, 2011.

Laurents, Arthur. *Mainly on Directing:* Gypsy, West Side Story, *and Other Musicals*. New York: Alfred A. Knopf, 2009.

———. *Original Story By: A Memoir of Broadway and Hollywood*. New York: Applause Books, 2000.

———. *The Rest of the Story: A Life Completed*. New York: Applause Theatre and Cinema Books, 2011.

Lawrence, Gertrude. *A Star Danced*. Garden City, NY: Doubleday, Doran, 1945.

Lerner, Alan Jay. *The Street Where I Live: A Memoir*. New York: W. W. Norton, 1978.

Lloyd Webber, Andrew. *Unmasked*. New York: Harper, 2018.

Loring, John. *Joseph Urban*. New York: Abrams, 2010.

LuPone, Patti, with Digby Diehl. *Patti LuPone, a Memoir*. New York: Crown, 2010.

Maguire, James. *Impresario: The Life and Times of Ed Sullivan*. New York: Billboard Books, 2006.

Mamorstein, Gary. *A Ship without a Sail: The Life of Lorenz Hart*. New York: Simon & Schuster, 2012.

Martin, Hugh. *Hugh Martin: The Boy Next Door*. Encinitas, CA: Trolley Press, 2010.

McBrien, William. *Cole Porter: A Biography*. New York: Vintage Books, 1998.

McCabe, John. *George M. Cohan: The Man Who Owned Broadway*. New York: Da Capo Press, 1980.

Meyerson, Harold, and Ernie Harburg. *Who Put the Rainbow in "The Wizard of Oz"? Yip Harburg, Lyricist*. Ann Arbor: University of Michigan Press, 1995.

Morley, Sheridan, and Ruth Leon. *Hey Mr. Producer! The Musical World of Cameron Mackintosh*. New York: Backstage Books, 1998.

Pearson, Hesketh. *Gilbert and Sullivan: A Unique Portrait of an Immortal Partnership*. Middlesex, UK: Penguin Books, 1985.

Pollack, Howard. *Marc Blitzstein: His Life, His Work, His World*. New York: Oxford University Press, 2012.

Prince, Harold. *Sense of Occasion*. New York: Applause Theatre and Cinema Books, 2017.

Propst, Andy. *They Made Us Happy: Betty Comden and Adolph Green's Musicals and Movies*. New York: Oxford University Press, 2019.

———. *You Fascinate Me So: The Life and Times of Cy Coleman*. New York: Applause Theatre and Cinema Books, 2015.

Purdum, Todd S. *Something Wonderful: Rodgers and Hammerstein's Broadway Revolution*. New York: Henry Holt, 2018.

Rice, Tim. *Oh, What a Circus: The Autobiography*. London: Coronet Books, 1999.

Rich, Frank. *The Theatre Art of Boris Aronson*. New York: Alfred A. Knopf, 1987.

Rodgers, Richard. *Musical Stages: An Autobiography*. New York: Da Capo Press, 1975.

Rosenberg, Deena. *Fascinating Rhythm: The Collaboration of George and Ira Gershwin*. New York: Dutton, 1991.

Secrest, Meryle. *Somewhere for Me: A Biography of Richard Rodgers*. New York: Alfred A. Knopf, 2001.

———. *Stephen Sondheim: A Life*. New York: Alfred A. Knopf, 1998.

Strouse, Charles. *Put on a Happy Face: A Broadway Memoir*. New York: Union Square Press, 2008.

Symonds, Dominic. *We'll Have Manhattan: The Early Work of Rodgers and Hart*. New York: Oxford University Press, 2015.

Taper, Bernard. *Balanchine: A Biography*. New York: Times Books, 1984.

Taylor, Theodore. *Jule: The Story of Composer Jule Styne*. New York: Random House, 1979.

Tune, Tommy. *Footnotes: A Memoir*. New York: Simon & Schuster, 1997.

Vaill, Amanda. *Somewhere: The Life of Jerome Robbins*. New York: Broadway Books, 2006.

Wasson, Sam. *Fosse*. Boston: Houghton Mifflin Harcourt, 2013.

Waters, Ethel, with Charles Samuels. *His Eye Is on the Sparrow: An Autobiography*. Garden City, NY: Doubleday, 1951.

Wodehouse, P. G., and Guy Bolton. *Bring on the Girls! The Improbable Story of Our Life in Musical Comedy, with Pictures to Prove It*. New York: Limelight Editions, 1984.

Ziegfeld, Richard, and Paulette Ziegfeld. *The Ziegfeld Touch: The Life and Times of Florenz Ziegfeld, Jr*. New York: Harry N. Abrams, 1993.

Index

About the Author

Andy Propst is an arts journalist and the author of *You Fascinate Me So: The Life and Times of Cy Coleman* and *They Made Us Happy: Betty Comden and Adolph Green's Musicals and Movies*. His career has encompassed work with New York Shakespeare Festival founder Joseph Papp and Tony Award–winning director George C. Wolfe, as well as five years on-air at XM Satellite Radio's XM 28 On Broadway channel. His writing has appeared in *The Village Voice*, *Time Out/NY*, *Backstage*, and *The Sondheim Review* and online at the site he founded, AmericanTheaterWeb.com, as well as TheaterMania.com and BroadwayDirect.com.

He served as a judge for the Obie Awards (three years) and as a member of the nominating committee for the Drama Desk Awards (four years). In addition, he has served as a mentor for both the National Critics Institute and the National Music Theater Conference at the Eugene O'Neill Theater Center. He also teaches criticism for the Institute for Theatre Journalism and Advocacy portion of the Kennedy Center American College Theatre Festival.